To the memories of
Alice Ramsbottom Piper
and Edmund Humphrey King

A MOTHER'S SACRIFICE

Catherine King

sphere

SPHERE

First published in Great Britain in 2009 by Sphere
This reissue published by Sphere in 2018

Copyright © Catherine King 2009

1 3 5 7 9 10 8 6 4 2

The moral right of the author has been asserted.

A CIP catalogue record for this book
is available from the British Library.

ISBN 978-0-7515-7355-8

Typeset in Bembo by Palimpsest Book Production Limited,
Falkirk, Stirlingshire
Printed and bound in Great Britain by Clays Ltd, St Ives plc

Papers used by Sphere are from well-managed
forests and other responsible sources.

Sphere
An imprint of
Little, Brown Book Group
Carmelite House
50 Victoria Embankment
London EC4Y 0DZ

An Hachette UK company
www.hachette.co.uk

www.littlebrown.co.uk

Acknowledgements

I should like to thank the staff and volunteers of Local History and Archives at Rotherham Library, especially Betty Davies, secretary of FoRA, for help with the research for this story. My thanks also to all my friends from Rotherham High School who are a constant lively source of tales and folklore from their parents and grandparents, especially Susan Sheehy, formerly Liggins, for telling me about Sun Dial Farm, my inspiration for the location of Top Field. Finally, special thanks to my agent Judith Murdoch, my editors Louise Davies, Caroline Hogg and Emma Stonex, my publicist Hannah Torjussen and the hard-working production and sales teams at Little, Brown for a beautifully finished book.

Chapter 1

1835

They were prettied and ready by mid-morning. Their cottage kitchen was clean and tidy and a cut-up fowl was simmering slowly with barley over the fire. Quinta finished slicing carrot and onion at the kitchen table and stood up to tip them into the blackened pot. Her best gown was covered by a large apron. She was worried about the bottom edge of the skirt getting dirty if she had to help Farmer Bilton with Darby but her mother had insisted she wore it.

'Come to the front window, Quinta,' Laura called. 'I can see him. He's got a new horse. A beauty he is, too. Just look at that beast.' She coughed, and then added, 'Spring's on its way now. A bit late this year but the trees are greening up nicely.'

Quinta frowned and handed her mother a horn beaker of warm water with a calming honey mixture in it. It was time she threw off that cough. But even when she was poorly Laura Haig managed to look beautiful. Her skin was lined but still smooth and flawless. Unconsciously, Quinta passed her fingers over her own cheeks.

'Did you put your salve on this morning?' her mother asked.

'Not yet.'

1

'Go upstairs and do it now, dear.'

Quinta sat down in front of her mother's looking glass and took the cork out of a squat stone jar. Mother made the precious salve herself, using wool fat and rose-petal water and used it every day without fail. Quinta spread it quickly over her face and neck, rubbing it in vigorously until the greasiness had gone. She stared at her image in the spotted glass. Folk said she looked like her mother, although she couldn't see it. She had the same hazel eyes, but Quinta's hair under her cotton cap was darker, a rich burnished brown, thick and glossy, which she plaited and wound around her head. She wondered if, now she was fifteen, she might coil it differently and curl the front.

'Hurry, dear. He's here,' her mother called.

A large black hunter carrying its smartly dressed rider ambled into their grassy yard. They stood outside the cottage door as he dismounted, tethered the animal at their lean-to woodshed and removed his saddlebag. Quinta watched seriously as he slid his shotgun out of its long holster. He wore a thick buttoned coat, breeches and leather gaiters, and nodded formally as he approached them. 'Good morning, Mrs Haig, Miss Quinta. Where is he?'

'Down by the stream,' Quinta replied. Darby had not moved all night and Quinta was relieved his pain would soon be over.

'Best get on with it then.'

'We are pleased to welcome you here, sir. Will you stay for your dinner?' Laura asked politely.

He sniffed the air, looked from one to the other, nodded slightly and answered, 'Don't mind if I do.'

Quinta noticed her mother brighten and smile. Even if she didn't like Farmer Bilton, she knew that, as their landlord, his good opinion of them could be their salvation. Mother had been right to make an effort for his visit.

'I'll take the lass with me, Mrs Haig,' he said, adding, 'I might need an extra pair of hands.'

'Very well. Take care with your gown, my dear.'

Quinta ran ahead towards the stream. As soon as she saw Darby, quite still beneath his canvas blanket, she forgot about her skirts and knelt beside him. She fondled his ears as she held back her tears. She had ridden on his back as a child, sometimes sitting precariously on top of bulging sacks going to market before Father had made the cart. Farmer Bilton loaded his gun. At least Darby's end would be painless and quick. Quinta pressed her lips together as he approached.

'Move away from him, Miss Quinta. There's bound to be mess.'

She got up and stood on the muddy bank, unable to watch. Five-acre Wood across the water was still and quiet apart from – from . . . She narrowed her eyes, detecting a movement in the shadowy trees. It was too big for a fox. A deer, perhaps, but she thought not.

'Oh!' The shotgun went off, making her jump. The trees came alive with flapping squawking birds. It was over. She turned round in time to see the splintered bone and flesh oozing with Darby's blood, and her face grimaced in grief. Farmer Bilton drew the canvas cover over his mutilated head. She told herself that Darby was only a donkey, but she had loved him nonetheless. She took a few deep breaths to calm her distress. 'Thank you, Mr Bilton. Will the Hall take him away?'

'Aye. The kennel-man will send a cart over.' He rested the butt of his shotgun on the ground and surveyed the scrubby pasture and remains of a copse, and their small stone cottage roofed with red tiles. 'I'll take a look at the cowshed while I'm out here.'

It had been built in a similar fashion to the cottage by her father and fitted with wooden stalls inside. Father had learned carpentry as a labourer on the Swinborough estate before he became a smallholder. Holding the Top Field tenancy had been a step up for him; he had been lucky to gain it and had worked hard to make it profitable. But he had passed on two years ago and it was a struggle for Quinta and her mother to work the land without him. Farmer Bilton said little as he inspected. His expression told Quinta all she needed to know. He did not approve of what he saw.

'Will you come inside now, sir?' Quinta suggested eventually.

'Aye. That dinner smells good.'

He looked around with interest as they stepped into the kitchen. Quinta drew out their largest chair, the one Father had used, and said, 'Please sit down, sir.'

He did and Quinta brought over plates of stewed fowl and vegetables from the fire. Mother placed warm oatcakes on the table and said grace. The food tasted as good as it smelled and Quinta ate hungrily for a few minutes.

Farmer Bilton broke the silence. 'I can see daylight through that cowshed roof.'

Her mother looked anxious and explained: 'I lost some tiles in the winter storms. My late husband would have mended it by now if he were still with us.'

'Aye. It's hard for a woman living on her own.'

'She's not on her own. She's got me,' Quinta said firmly.

'And a bright little lass you are, too,' he responded.

'If it were the cottage roof, you would send your man to fix it,' Laura added.

'I might. But Joseph Haig put up the cowshed himself so it was his job to mend it.'

Quinta and her mother did not argue. Farmer Bilton drained his metal tankard of ale and Quinta poured more from the jug.

'Will you want payment for killing our donkey, sir?' Laura asked.

'This dinner is payment enough. I've sold him for the dogs at the Hall. He's not worth much, but I'll credit your rent for what they give me.'

'Thank you, sir. I'm sorry there is no bread. We have no flour left and it is too dear to buy until the harvest is in.'

He picked up a corner of oat biscuit and bit into it. 'This

4

suits me well enough. I'm a plain-living man—' He stopped and added, 'That is, I mean – gentleman.'

So he was rising to his new wealth, Quinta thought. He had been working his farm for as long as Quinta could remember and was now reaping the benefits of his efforts. Mother had told her that gentleman farmers had always owned this part of the hillside. But Farmer Bilton was a distant cousin on the female side. It had taken the lawyers two years to find him when the old farmer died and he'd had to change his name to Bilton to inherit. It was said that before then he was only a farm labourer in the next county.

He sat back in his chair and looked around. 'You have a pretty little place here; a pretty kitchen for a pretty lady.'

'Thank you, sir,' Laura replied.

Quinta thought that the ale was having a good effect on him. He didn't usually say anything to them that approached social conversation. She got up quietly to refill the jug from the barrel in the scullery.

'It is small compared with your farmhouse, sir,' her mother added.

'Aye. I'm thinking of building on to this cottage.'

Quinta heard this and her eyes widened. Was that the real reason he was here? He could have sent his farmhand to see to Darby for them. 'But you'd put up the rent,' she protested as she returned to top up his tankard.

'Aye.'

Laura said, 'Well, an extra room is a kind thought, but I am a widow, sir, and hard pressed to pay the rent as it is.'

'I know that.'

'We can find it, Mother!' Quinta responded. 'I can do more. Perhaps Mr Bilton could let us have a nanny or two in exchange for our donkey?'

'Shush, dear,' Laura said as he shifted his eyes from mother to daughter.

He shook his head slowly. 'You were a respectable little family, madam, when your husband was alive. But you neglect your duty on the farm, and on the Sabbath.'

'Mother has been ill!' Quinta protested. Her winter cough had persisted this year and the climb back from church was too much for her. Laura glared crossly at her interruption.

'You are wasting good land,' Farmer Bilton went on. 'You need a man here.'

Quinta began to feel uneasy. This was not at all what either of them had expected and she didn't like Farmer Bilton's disapproving tone or the way he called her mother 'madam'.

Laura looked down at her plate in silence.

'I want a man here, too,' he went on. 'And a fitting rent for my property.'

The silence lengthened until Laura lifted her head and said quietly, 'I can't afford any more, sir.'

'I know folk who can, though. They can work the land and turn it back into profit. The town is spreading with newcomers, with labouring men and their families who need feeding.' He speared a chunk of fowl on his plate and chewed on it slowly. 'I'll not have you wasting another year.'

'You want us out.' It was a statement rather than a question from Laura.

'That's about it, madam.'

'But where would we go?' Quinta exclaimed.

Farmer Bilton looked sideways at her and, although he did not smile, she thought his features softened a little. He said, 'I'm not a harsh landlord. I've let you stay for two years, watching you struggle.' He shook his head and pursed his lips. 'No man to mow and turn grass for hay, or clear the stream. It goes to rack and ruin, you see.'

'We have done our best,' Laura explained. 'We till a large garden and sell eggs and – and make cheese, too, when we can get the milk.'

'But only one donkey on all that pasture. And now he's gone, you think only of a goat—'

'Or two,' Quinta interrupted.

'Be quiet, dear. It is all we can manage, sir.'

'Aye.'

He resumed his eating and appeared to be enjoying his dinner. After another gulp of ale he asked, 'Will you have my rent at Midsummer?'

'I shall have half of it, sir.'

'But will you get the rest?'

Without a donkey to take their produce to market Quinta knew it would be difficult. She heeded her mother's wishes and stayed silent.

Laura had hardly touched her stewed fowl but she remained composed and replied, 'I can work for you, sir, to make up the difference. I am clean and frugal in my ways. Look around you, sir. You can see that I am a good housekeeper.' She hesitated, took a deep breath and continued: 'You have good standing as a farmer in the Riding, if I may say so, sir. I wonder, does the vicar ever pay you the compliment of calling on you, with his sister?'

Quinta saw Farmer Bilton frown and begin to look uncomfortable and she knew they did not. He was a bachelor and his farmhouse was ill furnished and unkempt. The vicar's sister had caused a stir in the village when she had come to live there, for although she was a spinster lady of maturing years, she trimmed her bonnets lavishly and it was said she was seeking a husband.

Laura went on, 'How welcome they would feel if you had a parlour maid to offer them a glass of sherry wine in your drawing room. I was a servant at the Hall before I wed, sir. I know how to do things properly for you.'

Quinta looked closely at him as his face set in a grimace. He was about the same age as her father had been when he died two years ago. His face was weather-beaten and lined, to be sure, but his wrists looked sinewy and strong and his hands were straight. Not like the knobbly, gnarled fingers of his bent old farmhand.

'And would you leave here?' he asked.

'I should not wish to unless my daughter comes with me. I have taught her all I learned from my time at the Hall. She would not be a burden.'

Quinta watched his face as he considered Mother's offer. He pulled his mouth to one side and nodded slightly. Then he said, 'Can she graft?'

'Yes, sir,' Quinta answered swiftly. 'I can till a garden, milk a cow, churn butter and make cheese.'

He glanced at her. 'Aye. I believe you.'

'However, I should like to stay in my home, sir. The old Squire promised my husband—'

'He made promises to me, too. Nigh on sixteen year ago, when I first came here. Did your husband tell you that?'

Mother did not talk of the past much and the old Squire was dead and gone, but Quinta knew her father had done him a great service and in return he had persuaded young Farmer Bilton to grant him a tenancy for Top Field. Bilton Farm had been neglected before its new owner arrived and three years advanced rent from the old Squire was a welcome sum to get the farm going again.

Her mother became flustered. 'You were glad of the Squire's help at the time. As indeed were we. Quinta, would you pour me a little ale, dear?' When she had taken a drink, she added, 'I am a respectable widow, sir, and I should serve you well as housekeeper.'

Farmer Bilton seemed to recover from his former uneasiness and looked from mother to daughter and back to her mother. 'Aye, you might at that.'

'You – you will consider me, sir?'

Quinta gave him more ale. He drank again and leaned forward. 'Do you know how old I am, Mrs Haig?'

'No, sir.'

'Past five and forty, madam. The years have run away from me. Now I am reaping the fruits of my labour. I visit my

8

neighbours and the shopkeepers in the town, and I see how they all have ladies wearing pretty bonnets to walk out with them.'

'As I say, sir, I can keep as good a house as any from round here.'

'I want more than a housekeeper, Mrs Haig.'

'My daughter and I can tend your garden and orchard, as well as your dairy, sir,' she added.

'I am looking for more than a servant.'

Quinta stopped eating her dinner, a forkful of fowl halfway to her mouth. What more did he want? Surely — surely he could not mean a — a wife? This was not what Mother had expected at all and her normally serene features had frozen into a surprised query. 'Please speak plainly, sir.'

'Come now, Mrs Haig. You womenfolk know of these things before we menfolk have even thought of them. I am looking for a wife, madam. A wife.'

'And you have come to me?'

'I have.'

Quinta watched the look of disbelief on her mother's face, closely followed by a nervous smile. Neither she nor her mother had expected this and wariness came into her mother's eyes, but she remained calm. 'You honour and flatter me, sir. But I had not thought of you in such terms. If you will allow me time to consider—'

'Time? Forgive me, madam. That is something I have little of. I have learned that ladies do not discuss their ages. But I must. You are, I fear, older in years than I?'

Her mother's face stilled. 'I have a grown daughter, sir, a gift from God, born in my later years.'

'But can you bear more children?'

Quinta was astounded by his forwardness and watched an angry flush creep up her mother's neck, around her chin and over her face, making it blotchy and unattractive.

'Please do not speak so when my daughter is present,' Laura

said tightly. She looked away and then down at her hands. Finally, she returned her attention to him as he calmly soaked up the last of his gravy with an oat biscuit and said quietly, 'You are disrespectful, sir. Quinta, would you fetch me some water from the barrel?'

Quinta rose to her feet.

'Sit down, Miss Quinta. This concerns you as well as your mother.'

Laura Haig turned her serious face towards their visitor. 'I do not deny my age. I am sure I would suit you well as a housekeeper. But that is all.'

'You mistake my meaning, madam. Yes, I shall take you as my housekeeper and be pleased to do so. But my greater need is for a wife.

Quinta noticed that her mother seemed to relax at this remark. She did too. He must be thinking of marrying into gentry and his lady wife would expect a woman to run the household for her. They had both misunderstood his needs and mother rallied in her response. 'I shall of course be happy to housekeep for whomsoever you choose for your wife, sir.'

Quinta watched him nod his head slowly. 'Do you think I have the makings of a good husband, Mrs Haig?'

'I do not know, sir,' her mother replied shortly.

'I am accumulating wealth and I have no kin to benefit from my fortune. Toiling in my fields has given me little time for courting and my years seem to advance more quickly nowadays.'

'Please do not prolong this interview, sir. Either you wish me to work for you or you do not. If you have finished your dinner, I believe our business is at an end.'

He ignored her plea, apparently intent on finishing his speech. 'I need more than a wife. I must have offspring, madam. Fruit of my own loins.'

'Sir!' Laura Haig was affronted by this airing of his thoughts. 'Do not continue this conversation when my child is present.'

'Child? She is no child. She is rising sixteen, is she not?'

'You will be kind enough to guard your tongue. She is a maid, sir.' Quinta recognised a firmness in her mother's tone that told her she was angry.

'Quite so. Your daughter will suit me as a wife down to the ground.' He turned to Quinta and raised his eyebrows. 'What do you say, Miss Quinta?'

Chapter 2

He expected Quinta to respond. But how? She glanced across at her mother for help and caught the look of sheer horror spread across her features. 'I – I – Mother?' What should she say? What could she say? The silent rage that lingered in her mother's eyes alarmed her even further. Her breathing was laboured and she began to cough.

Quinta answered hastily, 'I do not understand what you want of me, sir.' She rose to fetch her mother's cough mixture from the dresser, spooning it directly into her mouth. Her wheezing subsided and an awkward silence settled around the table.

Farmer Bilton turned his conversation towards Quinta and explained as though he needed her to be clear: 'Your mother can't give me children, lass. You can.'

Embarrassed, Quinta looked down at her plate and the silence stretched between the three of them. When she raised her eyes, she was shocked by her mother's expression of revulsion.

'Mother?'

But Laura Haig was frozen to her chair with distaste etched into her normally serene face. Her voice came out hoarse and barely audible. 'You wish for my Quinta to be your wife.'

'Aye. That's about the size of it. But I'll not leave you here on your own, Mrs Haig. I'll take you on as housekeeper as you wish. With this cottage empty, I can have the masons in by Midsummer and a new tenant before Michaelmas. It is an arrangement that suits us all, is it not?'

Quinta could hardly believe her ears. He wanted them both to leave the only home she had ever known, and – she swallowed – for her to marry him. He had just told them he was thirty years her senior. He was an old man! Surely her mother was a much better choice as a wife for him?

'You are too hasty, sir,' Laura whispered.

'I have no more years to waste if I am to have children before my half-century. I must have a bride soon, so you will give me your answer within the week.'

'I can give you my answer now, sir.'

'And your face tells me what that will be. Do not say no to me, madam. You will not be able to pay your rent at Midsummer. You'll be homeless. I can keep the pair of you out of the workhouse, so think on my offer carefully.' He stood up to leave. 'I'll send Seth to collect your donkey for the dogs as I promised. While you make up your mind, you can have all the skim to make cheese that your lass can carry.'

'My mind is already set, sir. Quinta will not marry you.'

'Of course she will! The old Squire said as much when the tenancy was drawn up. He said she would do for me when she was grown.'

'What!' Quinta had never seen her mother so angry. 'He had no right!'

'He was your late husband's patron, was he not?'

'My Joseph did not agree to that, I am sure.'

'He signed for the tenancy and that was good enough for me. I had done the old Squire a service by leasing Top Field as he asked, and he owed me.'

'You got your rent money in advance, didn't you?'

13

Quinta knew very little about the old Squire's patronage that had set her father up as a small farmer. It had all happened years ago. She listened intently.

'She was just a babe in arms at the time,' Laura added.

'Aye. That's why what he said then never crossed my mind again until just lately. She's a fine-looking lass, though. She'll do for me, all right.'

'She will not!'

His face darkened at her mother's firm rejection of his offer and he clambered to his feet. 'She will, madam, and I shall have my property by Midsummer. Or all my rent, of course,' he added cruelly. 'It's for you to choose.'

'You know that is not a choice, sir,' her mother said quietly.

'I should talk it over with your daughter first. She seems a sensible lass to me. Knows which side her bread's buttered. Who will sympathise with you when you are homeless if they know I offered marriage?'

Laura stared at him stonily and Quinta returned her eyes to her plate. She could not get used to the idea that this red-faced old man really wanted her to wed him. She had seen older gentlemen celebrate marriage in the village church, but they generally married widows, perhaps not as old as they were but certainly not as young as she. She looked up as Farmer Bilton spoke again.

'Thank you kindly for my dinner, Mrs Haig. When you have calmed yourself you will see the sense of my offer and I should welcome you in my house. Good day to you both.' He drained his mug of ale and stood up to leave, casting a large shadow over their table.

Her mother did not move. She seemed unable to stir from her chair. Quinta jumped to her feet to hold open the door for him. He was a thick-set burly man and he stood too close to her, towering over her on their threshold. 'Fine-looking lass,' he murmured half to himself with a twisted expression on his face. Then he bent down and spoke quietly by her ear. 'You'd like to wear a pretty bonnet for church, wouldn't you? And go to town to shop in the market instead of to sell?'

His nearness made her nervous and she nodded wordlessly. It seemed best to agree with him as he was their landlord. She curtseyed falteringly. He gave her a sort of smile, like the one the vicar used after her father's burial in the churchyard, and walked out to mount his fine horse. He may not be proper gentry, she thought, but he was a well-off farmer now, with increasing influence in the Riding. He could make life very difficult for her and her mother.

'Did Father really promise me to Farmer Bilton?' Quinta asked as soon as he had left.

'He did not *promise* you to anyone,' her mother protested angrily. 'It was the old Squire's suggestion and he could be a meddling old tyrant when it suited him. He thought he could rule the whole valley as his father had done before him. But things were different after the war with France. Just because he made his son wed the girl he'd picked for him—'

'He chose a wife for his son?'

'Of course he did. Would such a handsome fellow as Sir William have married her otherwise? She's not at all pretty and a very thin little thing.'

'Well, I expect there were other things about her that he liked.'

'Yes, my dear. There was a large dowry from her father's glassworks. The Hall and estate needed her father's money to keep it going.'

'Wasn't the old Squire very rich then?'

'Oh yes. But in the days after the old Regent, all the gentry wanted to live as the Royals did, with their gluttony and – and, well, with their wicked ways.'

Quinta's eyes widened. 'What wicked ways?'

'Never you mind.' Laura looked pensive. 'There was a time when we all thought his son would turn out the same. He was a wild one in his youth, too wild, and – and, well, his father

15

sent him away to the University. He calmed down after that, thank God.'

'Well, Sir William is very handsome. I remember the celebrations in the village when he wed. The ladies in their pretty gowns and bonnets, flowers in the church and decorating the horse and carriage that took them away afterwards. And there was a barn dance for the villagers, just like the harvest supper.' Quinta would like such a wedding for herself but knew it was unlikely and sighed, 'What do I have as a dowry?' She didn't really expect an answer.

'You have a beautiful countenance, my love, and that is your good fortune. And you are as pure as the day you were born. You will have a sweetheart who will fall so helplessly in love with you that he will not seek for any other dowry to become your husband.'

Quinta wondered where she would find this sweetheart. 'Like Farmer Bilton?' she responded tartly.

'He does not love you. He wants a skivvy; that is all.'

No, he wants children, Quinta thought, and that seemed a reasonable wish to her, but not to her mother, so she said, 'And more rent for Top Field.'

'When he inherited Bilton Farm he wasn't accepted by the gentry at first and he was too anxious to please his betters. He was hard-working, though. He laboured all hours to get that farm to rights and we all wondered if he would choose a local girl for his wife.' Laura took a sip of ale. 'But he was too mean-spirited to court a woman and who would want a miser for a husband?'

'Is he that bad? He has offered to help us.'

'He wants to help himself. It suits him to have us out of here.'

'But we would have a proper home at Bilton Farm,' Quinta argued.

'He does not have to wed you to give us that. It would be perfectly respectable for the two of us to live there as his servants. He asks too much.'

16

'But we don't want to end up in the workhouse!' She thought for a moment. 'We could ask for parish relief to pay our rent.'

'Dear heaven, no! Think of the shame of it.' Her mother gazed out of the window and muttered, 'Something will turn up.'

Quinta thought that they had been waiting two years for 'something to turn up' and it never did. When Father had been alive they had relied on him. He had been strong and resourceful and always got them through, whether it was bad harvests, illness or sick cows. He had known what to do.

'What will turn up, Mother?' she asked anxiously.

'I don't know.'

Neither did Quinta. But she had to do something. Mother might want her to have a sweetheart, just as she had had when she was young, but where would she find one in the work-house? Someone had to be sensible about Farmer Bilton's offer. Quinta did not want to wed him any more than her mother wished it. But neither did she want to be destitute.

She said, 'You must accept Farmer Bilton's offer for me, Mother. You do not have to be anxious on my account for I should not mind becoming his wife.'

Laura stared at her. 'My darling child, you do not know what it means to be a wife. I shall not let you do it!'

'Why not? He is not young and handsome but he has wealth enough for both of us.'

Her mother stretched out a hand. 'Come and sit by me and I shall tell you why not.' When she was settled, Laura continued: 'He is not as old as I am, my dear, but it is not about his age, for if you truly loved him his years would make no difference. Tell me, before he called today, did you think of him at all?'

'Sometimes. He is our landlord.'

'When you did think of him did your heart beat faster in your breast?'

Quinta let out a small guffaw. 'No.'

'Did you yearn for him to take you in his arms and kiss you?'

Quinta grimaced. 'Never.'

'That is because you do not love him as you should love a husband. You cannot marry him.'

'But why do I have to love him, Mother, if he gives us a home?'

Quinta saw a spark of irritation in her mother's eyes and realised she had annoyed her.

'There are things in marriage that need love,' she answered shortly.

'What things?'

'Married things. If you do not love him, how are you to share his bed? How are you to lie with him and have his children? You do not want to be doing married things with a man you do not love.'

'But we would be living in his farmhouse instead of the workhouse!' Quinta persisted.

'Did you hear what I said?' Laura's cough erupted noisily but she struggled on. 'Marriage is for ever and I shall not let you tie yourself to him for the rest of your life.' She breathed in hoarsely. 'I have said no. Now that is enough!'

Quinta knew when Mother was angry and that was now. She didn't like them to quarrel because it made her mother's chestiness worse. 'I'm sorry, Mother,' she said. 'I'll mix some honey and warm water for you.' When she brought the drink she added, 'If he had offered marriage to you instead of me, would you have wanted that?'

'No! But if he had asked me I would have wed him instead of you. I would have put up with him.'

Quinta frowned. 'Would it be so awful?'

'Yes, it would, more especially for you because, to you, he *is* an old man. You – you are a lovely girl and you will grow into a beautiful woman and have a handsome young gentleman to court and wed you.'

Quinta wasn't so sure. Where would she find a 'handsome young gentleman'? There were two ladies in the village whose sweethearts had taken the King's shilling and not come back, and those ladies were still spinsters. Their lads had been killed in Spain or on the battlefield at Waterloo, or taken their bounty and a dark-haired maiden to settle in foreign parts. Most of the men who stayed behind had gone down to the navigation in the valley to mine coal or make iron or glass. There were plenty of young girls in the town for them to wed.

The only handsome gentleman she knew was Sir William, and he was no longer young. His father had lost two boys before him to the war and would not let his third son fight, insisting he managed the estate and made a good match. And he did. With his wife's dowry he built furnaces for iron-smelting, using coal he found beneath his feet. She had seen him in church sitting beside his pallid wife dressed in her silken gowns and bows, and had wondered what it felt like to wear such finery. Sir William's older sister had worn French bonnets, before she had married her Scottish laird and left the village.

'But Farmer Bilton will look after us and buy me a new bonnet.'

'And you will have to share his bed to pay for it!' Laura snapped.

'Well, how else are we to pay for our keep?' she answered petulantly.

It was then that her mother struck her. With the flat of her hand across her face. Sharply, and it stung. Her mother had never hit her before in her life. Not ever. Quinta was so surprised she stood there, speechless, rubbing her hand on her reddening cheek.

'Do you know what that will make you? You must never think like that again. Never! Do you hear me?'

Bewildered, Quinta simply nodded. But she didn't understand. She went to church and read the Bible. She knew right from wrong and it's not as though she wouldn't be married to Farmer Bilton. Annoyed, she asked, 'Then why would it be right for you to marry him?'

'Because it would! Because I am older and I have had a husband before. You – you are young and pretty and untouched and he's not having you. He's not! Tell me, would you have *ever* looked on him as a husband if he had not suggested it?'

Quinta had to admit to herself that she would not. When the hunt came through Five-acre Wood she thought that some of the Squire's friends were dashing and handsome as they chased the hounds and she had had a fancy that, one day, she might be a lady to one of them. But a fancy was all it was. Or ever could be. She shook her head.

'He does not love you, my child. Nor demand that you love him. All he wants is the use of your young body to bear his children.'

'Yes, I see that now,' Quinta answered. Now she understood why Mother had hit her. 'But what'll we do? We'll never get the rent we owe him and he'll turn us out. Where shall we go?'

'I don't know.'

Quinta did. The workhouse. She had walked past it once, in the town, when the gates were open, and glimpsed the wretched folk inside. That's where they sent you if you had no work and nowhere to live. There was a family living in a makeshift hut on the moor beyond Five-acre Wood that was better off than the desperate souls in the workhouse. Is that where she and mother would end up? Living rough and scavenging off the land? Quinta couldn't let that happen. Mother would never survive the cold nights, not with her cough.

'But if he makes us homeless, why should we not live in his house?'

'I cannot live under his roof knowing you had to share his bed to pay for it.'

'But I want to look after you properly and have that cough seen to. I could try and love him, Mother.'

'You don't know what you are saying, child.'

'Stop calling me child,' Quinta said irritably. Farmer Bilton did not think of her as a child. 'I am of an age to be wed.'

'Yes, and I won't see you as a wife to an old man,' her mother retaliated sharply. Then her face softened a little and she added, 'Oh Quinta, my darling, you are beautiful and I want better for you. A handsome young man who will adore you and court you as your father did me.' She started to wheeze again.

'It's time that chestiness went, you know. You have had it for months now. Go upstairs and rest. You don't cough as much when you lie down.'

'Who will see to the pots and the tea?'

'I shall, and the hens and the garden. And I'll do a bit of gleaning in the fields before the daylight goes.'

'The wheat's nowhere near ready for harvesting yet.'

'Oats might be ready and they are better than nothing.'

'You're a good girl, my little Quinta. I'm sorry I slapped you.'

'Yes, I am, too.'

'But you mustn't ever think like that again. Noah Bilton is a wicked man for even suggesting it and I am very angry with him.'

Quinta heaved a sigh. It was all very well her mother having dreams and fancies for her, but they could not survive at Top Field without Father. They would be homeless and destitute by Midsummer.

Chapter 3

'Farmer Bilton's here again, Mother.'

'Come away from the window.'

'I wish he wouldn't ride along the brow every day like this, reminding us he's there,' Quinta commented. 'He never used to.'

'He never wanted us out before,' Laura answered. 'He'll go when he knows we've seen him.'

'In that case I shall show myself now.' Quinta took a tin bowl from the table and went out of the front door before her mother could stop her.

'Good morning, sir,' she called. She was too far away to see his response and she did not wait for it. She straightened her spine and whisked around the side of their cottage and out of his sight.

The sun was up but the air was fresh. Top Field was the highest point hereabouts and it caught the breeze winter and summer alike. She was not used to the pasture without Darby yet, and habit caused her to look for him as she walked across to the wooden henhouse. He had taken them backwards and forwards to market as long as she could remember. But he couldn't pull the donkey cart to market anyway as one of the shafts had broken and she didn't know how to mend it.

Beyond the pasture was Five-acre Wood which belonged to the Hall. A fast-flowing stream marked the boundary. It was a crisp morning for late May and, where the sun's rays lit up the flowing water, a gentle mist rose from the scrubby ground. May was always a lean month, when their winter vegetables were over and new crops were too young to pull. Still, they had the hens to keep them going. As she shooed them out of their coop, she was glad of her woollen shawl knotted firmly across her chest. She found three small eggs and knew there would be more as the days grew longer.

Her attention was diverted, quite suddenly, by a sharp crack splitting the quiet air. Birds cawed raucously and scattered upwards from their roosts. Who was out shooting? It was a similar noise to the shot that had made old Darby start and slip in the mud a few days ago. Once down he had been unable to get up again; she remembered his pain.

She thought it was too early for hunting unless a rogue fox had got into the breeding pheasants and the gamekeeper was seeing him off. She scanned the woodland for signs of a gun but thought the shot must have come from the moorland beyond the woods. She hoped it wasn't poachers or travellers. They were all to be feared. At Easter she had heard tales of vagrants about and her anxiety mounted. She took the eggs indoors, relieved to note that Farmer Bilton had ridden out of view.

Laura Haig was dressed and downstairs, stirring porridge in a blackened iron pot suspended over the kitchen fire. She wore a clean apron over her neat gown and a pretty lace cap on her head. Even in their straitened circumstances, Quinta thought, she did not let her standards slip.

'Only three today,' Quinta said.

'Enough for a Yorkshire pudding,' her mother replied.

'If we had any flour.' When Father was alive he had made sure the pantry was always well stocked and since he'd passed

23

on Quinta had taken over many of his tasks. 'I could ask the miller for credit until we have vegetables to sell.'

'Your father never had to do that. Not even in our early years up here.'

If her mother had not sounded so wistful, Quinta would have been irritated by this response. She missed her father as much as her mother did but they needed to look to their future now. It was a bleak prospect but she said brightly, 'I'll make some more oatcakes when the fire's hot enough.'

After breakfast Quinta went outside for more wood. They had a few trees on the edge of their land and one of them, not far from the house, had obligingly died and fallen in a winter storm. She hacked away at the smaller branches with her father's small axe and wondered if she would ever be strong enough to tackle the trunk.

Her cheeks were glowing when she stacked the wood in her arms. She jumped as another shot disturbed the woodland peace again and nearly dropped her logs. She'd rather there were several volleys as that would indicate a shooting party, not a lone hunter. They were a long way from the village and even further from the Hall.

'What was that shooting?' her mother asked as soon as Quinta stepped inside the kitchen. It was the only room they had downstairs, but it was large and well furnished with a strongly made table and dresser, a couch and a matching fireside chair showing signs of wear. They had striped curtains at the back and front windows, too. Laura had sewed them herself. But that was years ago and the colours were fading now.

Quinta moved to the fireplace and tipped the logs on to the hearth to dry out. 'I don't know. It came from the moor, I think.'

'We'd best stay indoors today. What about the hens?'

'I'll keep an eye on them. If it was a fox, it might have got away.'

'Well, the second shot probably got him even if the first

didn't.' Laura Haig chewed on her lip. 'I hope it's not poachers. They must be desperate to be out in daylight, but it has been a long cold winter for everybody this year.' She pushed a stoneware mug in Quinta's hand. 'I've warmed some ale for you.'

'Thanks.'

'I'll make tea this afternoon.'

'That'll be nice.' Her mother liked to make tea to drink in the afternoon. She had a proper caddy with a lock and key, just as her ladyship at the Hall did, that she was proud of, and she laid out her best china cups and saucers as she had done in her days in service there. 'We have honey for the oatcakes too,' Quinta added cheerily. 'Are you feeling better now?'

This last winter had gone on for too long. Storms had lifted the tiles off the cowshed and their food stores were right down. The ground was too frozen to sow beans early on and spring had been late coming so their hens had only just started to lay.

'We could ask the Hall for a nanny for milking,' Quinta suggested.

Laura stared out of the window dreamily. 'When I was working at the Hall, the old Squire used to give his tenants a young goat at Christmastide. It was tradition; a goat one year and a pair of trousers the next.'

'It's different now. The old Squire passed on years ago and his son's in charge.' Quinta liked the young Squire. Well, he wasn't young. But he was forward thinking, energetic and interested in new ideas about everything.

'He's not our landlord, anyway,' her mother responded wistfully. 'I wish he was. Farmer Bilton isn't real gentry.' Mentioning his name seemed to annoy her. 'He doesn't know what's right.'

'They say he's a good farmer.'

'Yes, I'll give him that. His stock has breeding even if he doesn't.'

'Well, times change, Mother.'

'That's true enough. Menfolk don't want to work on the

land any more when they can get better wages in the mines and forges by the navigation. I don't know what the Riding is coming to with all the smoke and smells down there. I shan't mind if we never go to market again.'

Quinta minded. She looked forward to travelling into town for the market. It was an up-and-down road and a tiring walk but she enjoyed the hustle and bustle when she arrived. 'We have to,' she responded briskly. 'Otherwise we'll have no money for rent or food.'

'We need flour and candles, too.'

'It'll soon be summer, Mother, when the days are longer. We can do without candles until the end of the harvest.'

'Oh, I must have one by my looking glass. The ladies at the Hall always had two, one at each side.'

We're not at the Hall, Quinta thought, but said, 'We'll go to market when our carrots and beet are big enough to sell. They won't be long now.' But even as she said it, she wondered how she would get her garden produce there without a cart or a donkey. 'Will you walk down to the village for church tomorrow, Mother?'

'It's the climb back that tires me, dear.'

'You can take your time. The sun is quite warm now.'

'Perhaps I shall try. It will be good for both of us to get out for a while. We shall both look our very best. Stoke the fire to heat water, dear, and I'll get the curling tongs and flat iron from the cupboard. I was a parlour maid before I married your father, and when they had house parties I helped out the ladies' maids. Good, I was, they all said so. I shall show the village what a beautiful child I have raised.'

Quinta watched her mother's eyes sparkle at this thought. She lifted the tin bath from its hook in the scullery and placed it on the stone flags in front of the fire. She needed more wood to keep it burning. And water from the stream. It was teatime before the bath was ready.

They sat facing each other by the firelight in the soft warm water, their knees drawn high. Mother unfolded a small brown paper package of soft soap for their hair.

'I was saving it for Midsummer.' She scooped a little of the slimy jelly in her fingers. 'Here. Rub it in well.'

Quinta washed her long brown hair and watched her mother do the same. She leaned over the side of the bath to reach for a pitcher of clean lavender-scented water to rinse away the soap, noticing the grey that streaked her mother's waves. They splashed around in the precious warmth until it began to cool, then stood up to wipe each other down and apply salve to their hands and feet.

Quinta pulled the bath aside and put the rug back, then drew chairs near the fire to comb and dry their hair. 'That was nice, Mother.'

'Yes. It makes me feel like a lady again.'

'You'll look like one tomorrow in your Sunday gown.'

'You too, love. You've grown well lately and have a good shape on you.'

'I take after you.'

Laura gave a gentle laugh. 'I'm saggy now. I have been for a few years, so I'll need you to pull the laces tight in my corset.' She reached for the hot tongs from the kettle hob. 'Can you curl the front for me? I'll have my lace cap over the rest.'

'Shall I cut the front of mine like yours?'

'No, dear. Just draw yours up and wind it in a knot at the back of your head. That shows off your features better. You have a lovelier face than mine.'

Mother had never said that to her before and Quinta was startled into silence.

'There is a sweetheart out there for you somewhere, my dear,' Laura said dreamily. 'He might not be a wealthy gentleman, although that would be very nice if you loved him.' She stared at the fire. 'A tradesman would suit, with a regular wage, who can read and write like your father.'

Quinta liked the idea of a sweetheart, especially if he was as

27

clever as her father had been, but she wondered yet again where she would find him in Swinborough village. However, she enjoyed trimming her Sunday gown with freshly laundered ribbon and adding the same touch to her bonnet. Her mother, too, became quite excited at the prospect of dressing for church. She slept badly though, coughing for most of the night, and nothing seemed to ease it. The next morning she was too exhausted to get up for breakfast and their walk to church was out of the question.

Quinta worried that her mother was not getting enough nourishment. They had oat biscuits and pease pudding made with eggs from the hens, but if she had some milk she could curdle it for cheese. Farmer Bilton had offered them his left-over from the dairy and he would only feed it to his pigs if she didn't have it.

When she collected Laura's breakfast tray she said, 'I think I'll walk over for some skim today.'

'Not from Farmer Bilton, you won't.' Clearly, her mother was still angry with him.

'Home Farm might have some to spare.' It was down the valley, near to the Hall it served, and further to carry, but worth the climb back, for them to have fresh milk.

'It's Sunday. They'll be in church.'

'There'll be a maid in the dairy. Cows are milked every day.'

'Very well, dear. Take one of my embroidered handkerchiefs for the dairymaid.'

Quinta set off down the track with her yoked pails. She had no intention of going all the way to Home Farm and carrying two buckets of milk back up Bilton Hill. Farmer Bilton was only halfway down. He had said she could have all the skim she could carry and Mother needed the nourishment. She dawdled down the track until she was sure he would be in church. He always sat alone, in the pew behind the Swin-boroughs, as his distant cousins had done before him, and bowed his head to his betters when they swept past him.

When she arrived, Seth, his farmhand, was nowhere to be seen. Farmer Bilton trusted him enough to cook and clean in the farmhouse as well. It was said in the village that you never knew whether the smell from the kitchen was their dinner or the pig swill he was boiling up. But Quinta could not detect any cooking and he was the only other person who went into the house. She dreaded to think what it was like inside.

'Seth!' she called. He didn't appear and she guessed he was in church with his master. Well, she would just have to help herself. Farmer Bilton had said she could, hadn't he?

There was no skim in the dairy. The morning's milking was still cooling in the pans. She helped herself to a ladleful from a small churn. Oh, it was so rich and creamy and still warm from the cow! A pailful of that was worth three of skim for her mother. She hesitated, wondering whether she dare take it without permission, and while she dithered, heard horse's hooves outside. It must be later than she realised. Best show myself and leave quickly, she thought. She hurried through the open door.

'Well, if it's not the maid from Top Field skulking in my dairy!' Farmer Bilton was standing outside holding the reins of his horse. His tweed jacket and moleskin breeches looked new, as did his polished leather gaiters. They creaked when he moved.

She was not in her Sunday gown with its new ribbons. She pushed a few straying strands of hair back under her soft calico bonnet. 'I – I – you said I could have the skim, sir.'

His large black horse was restless, but he was a big strong man and he held the bridle firmly as walked slowly towards her. 'Has your mother decided to accept my offer for you, then?'

'No, sir. She doesn't know I'm here.' Quinta felt quite ill at the thought that she had deceived her about coming here, especially when Farmer Bilton stood so close to her that his height and breadth overwhelmed her.

'You've deceived your own ma?' he said.

She felt small beside him and moved backwards towards the open dairy door. 'I – I wanted to make cheese for her.'

'And you were you hoping to be gone before I got back, eh?' He didn't take his eyes off her as he tied the reins to a nearby cart.

She nodded and looked down at her muddied boots.

'Then you're not the honest little lass your ma would have me think?'

Exposed as having betrayed her mother, she felt even worse about her deception. Anxious to get away, she glanced over her shoulder. 'I'll just get my pails and be on my way, sir.'

'No you won't. 'Tis God's will the vicar gave a short sermon today, and that my black stallion needed a gallop home.' He stepped forward so that she was obliged to move backwards into the dairy. 'He has sent you to me.'

Faced with denying the Lord's work, Quinta could only mutter, 'If you say so, sir.' Once inside the dairy he kicked the wooden door behind him shutting out the light, and in spite of the cool stone interior she felt hot and flustered. 'B-but we ought not to be alone, sir. What if Seth found us?' Seth drank at the alehouse in the village and she knew Farmer Bilton was mindful of his reputation with the local gentry.

He hesitated, then muttered, 'He has to walk up the hill,' and advanced towards her, adding, 'Besides, we are to be wed. Your ma will have to come round to my way of thinking. She'll not see you in the workhouse.'

Quinta noticed beads of sweat erupting on his brow and realised it had been a mistake to come here. Her mind raced for a way out. He was a God-fearing man and wanted to impress his betters in this respect. Perhaps she could appeal to his religious ways? She crossed her hands over her chest, closed her eyes and bowed her head piously. 'But, sir, it is the Sabbath.'

It seemed to work. At least something happened for she heard him make a groaning, gurgling sound in his throat. When she opened her eyes he had half turned away from her and was leaning on the wall. And – oh dear – one of his hands was over his breeches where – where his private parts were! Mortified, she stood stock still and said, 'I – I think I hear Seth coming back.'

His voice was thick. 'You – you get your ma to take my offer, do you hear me?'

Quinta knew there was no chance of that and replied quietly, 'May I go now, sir?'

He waved his arm at the milk pans. 'Take what you need.' He pushed himself away from the wall and lumbered outside. She heard him lead his horse away.

Shaken, she considered leaving the milk. Mother would not change her mind about Farmer Bilton and it felt like stealing. But she had said she was fetching it from Home Farm so she could not return empty-handed. Miserably, she tipped the creamy, cooling froth into her pails and hoisted the wooden yoke across her shoulders.

She had racked her brain to find a way out of their situation. If she sold all their hens and vegetables at the market, Mother could pay the rent. But how could she take them to market without a cart or a donkey? And what would they eat next winter? Assuming, of course, that they had a roof over their heads after Michaelmas, for the Lord only knew where that quarter's rent would come from. If he turned them out as he threatened they would have to go to the workhouse. Or starve and die on the moor.

Laura felt better later on and enjoyed her egg custard when it was ready.

'Will you get up today?' Quinta asked.

'It's no good, love. I haven't the strength any more. We can't stay here. It's been such a struggle since your father passed on.'

'We could ask Farmer Bilton to lower the rent for us.'

'He won't do that. I've never known any landlord do that.

Besides, we have decent land here. He can get what he asks from a younger family or one with a strong lad about the place.'

'I'm strong, Mother.'

'Yes, you are. And if I were like you we might manage. But I can't work the hours in the garden as I used to.'

'Then what'll we do?'

'I don't know.'

'I could go into service at the Hall, as you did at my age.'

'If you want a proper position you have to go to that girls' school first and it costs money.'

'You could teach me, Mother.'

'I've already taught you what I know. Anyway, the young Squire's wife only wants girls from the school for her maids.'

'Her cook might take me on in the kitchen. She told me she would; last summer when I took over our lettuce glut.'

'Without any learning you'd have to do all the pot-washing and scrubbing.'

'I can scrub.'

'Not all day and every day, you can't. I'll not let you. Besides, your father wanted better for you, and so do I.'

Quinta tried to smile. She didn't mind doing the scrubbing at the Hall. She would have liked a chance to work there, where there were lots of people coming and going all the time. Nobody ever came to this corner of Top Field because it wasn't on the way to anywhere and you had to climb a steep hill to get here. She supposed that's why it was leased out. Even Seth used a horse and cart to check the boundary walls.

Bilton Farm had tradesmen calling from time to time. But strangers wouldn't scale the hill track without good reason. Well, it was their loss, she thought, gazing out of the window, for Top Field had one of the most beautiful views hereabouts. Nonetheless, Quinta missed the company of other folk when they didn't go down to the village.

If she worked in the Hall kitchens she would have money to help Mother. Laura was ailing and wanted more than cheese and eggs to regain her energy and bloom. She needed the apothecary and he cost money. Unless . . . unless you could get to the Dispensary in town. The Dispensary treated men from the mines and manufactories, and anyone could go there. Well-off folk paid for it. They weren't all like Farmer Bilton, she thought. But if she toiled at the Hall from dawn until dusk, how could she care for her mother?

There did not seem to be an answer.

Chapter 4

Later that afternoon, Quinta added some honey to a mug of heated milk and steadied it carefully as she carried it on a tray up the narrow stairs. She jumped as she heard a gun go off outside and spilled the milk over her fingers. 'Bother!' she exclaimed under her breath. She was more concerned about losing the precious milk than scalding her hand.

'What was that?' her mother called from the bedchamber.

'It sounded like that gun again.' Again, and on a Sunday, when everyone was home with their families? 'I hope it's not poachers.'

'Do you think it might be?' her mother said anxiously.

Quinta plumped the pillows to help Laura sit up and look out of the window. 'Those folk on the moor, I expect.'

'They wouldn't have a gun, not unless they stole it.'

Quinta agreed and changed the subject. 'You're getting really thin, Mother,' she said. 'You need more dinners inside you. Shall I kill another of the hens?'

'No, love. They've plenty of grass to eat now and they're laying well. Wait until the winter when they go off lay.' Mother paused and looked sad. 'If I last that long.'

'Don't be silly,' Quinta said quickly. 'You're much better now.' She gave her the milk and honey. 'Will you take some of your cough mixture?'

'There isn't much left. I'll save it for night-time.'

'The sun gets warmer every day. Why don't you put on your best lace cap and sit outside for a while?'

'I will. I do feel a little stronger now.'

Quinta was pleased to hear this. She glanced out of the window and thought she saw a movement in the trees beyond the stream. 'I think there's a young deer in the woods. I hope it doesn't come into our garden and eat all my young shoots. The hunt won't be coming through for weeks yet.' She hurried down the stairs with thoughts of scaring away any creature who dared to invade her precious crops and darted out of the back door.

She froze. There was a man limping across the pasture. He was a large man, with grey shaggy hair and bushy beard, leaning heavily on a crutch and carrying a . . . a shotgun? Well, she thought it was a shotgun because it was long-barrelled, but it was narrow, not like the scatterguns she recognised.

Guns cost money and this man looked like a vagrant. Was he a footpad? Had he stolen it and was about to rob them in their home? Terrified, she turned hastily and rushed back indoors, locking and bolting the door behind her. No sound came from her mother. She hoped she had not seen the man. Quinta crouched at the bottom of the stairs and held her breath, hoping he would pass by.

'Is anyone at home?' The voice was accompanied by a rapping on the door. Quinta stayed as quiet as a mouse, but she heard the bed creak above her head.

A minute later the kitchen darkened as a bulky shape blocked the light from the front window. He saw her and tapped on the glass with his fingers. *It wasn't the same man.* This one was younger, with a shorter beard and not grey at all. *There were two of them.*

'I mean you no harm, miss,' he called. 'I have rabbit.' He held up a brace to show her. 'You can have them in exchange for a bed for the night in your cattle stalls.'

He had seen inside the cowshed! Well, the door was no longer secure and the roof leaked so badly that they couldn't even use it to store food. Their winter supplies of oats and beans were kept in the tiny upstairs chamber where Quinta used to sleep. She shared the big bed with her mother now.

But he had rabbit. Mother liked a rabbit stew and she was much in need of meat to help her get well. 'Who are you?' she answered.

'My name is Patrick Ross, miss.'

'Where are you from?'

'We're passing through.'

'We?'

'My father is with me. I am looking for work, if you have any to offer, miss.'

Slowly, Quinta stood up and went to the window. He stepped back so that she could see the rabbits properly. They were a decent size and just killed because she could see fresh blood on the fur. But he was not the cripple with the shotgun. He was young, not much older than she was, and tall with straight limbs. She peered round him, looking for the other man.

'Where is he?' she demanded. 'Where's the one with the gun?'

'He's in your cowshed. His leg is bad and he needs to rest up.' Patrick Ross stepped forward and his wide shoulders filled the window space. He pushed his offering against the case-ment, leaving a smear of blood on the glass. 'Do you want these or not?'

He had a handsome face, this fellow, she thought, with strong cheekbones tanned by the weather. A battered hat pulled down as far as his black eyebrows hid most of his long black hair. His eyes were deep set, light, she thought, and thickly fringed with lashes. Perhaps he was one of the itinerant labourers from

Bilton Farm: he had on the same kind of thick country clothes and heavy boots that they wore.

The rabbits were too tempting to ignore but she hesitated and asked, 'Why does he need a gun?'

He shook them in her face and answered shortly: 'For these.'

So it was a hunting weapon of sorts, Quinta thought. The rabbits were a good size though, and fresh. Stewed with dried beans, they were enough for her and her mother to feast on for a week.

'Open the window and look,' he went on. He sounded impatient.

She was torn between her caution where strangers were concerned and wanting his kill. The window was small, perhaps too small for him to climb inside for he was a large man. She fiddled with the rusty catch until the hinges creaked open. He slung the rabbits across the ledge. 'There's more where they came from.'

'Where's that then?'

'Out on the moor. The woods give us shelter, but the nights are cold up here and my father needs more comfort.'

The nights were even colder out on the moor where the biting winds whipped across your face summer and winter alike. She took the rabbits from him before he changed his mind, automatically testing the weight in her hand.

'Well? Can we stay?'

She dreaded to think what Mother would say but if she kept the door locked and barred all night they would be safe. 'Where are you heading?' she hedged.

'South Riding.'

'Well, you've reached it.'

'I know. We've been following drovers' trails for weeks.'

She pursed her lips. 'With a shotgun?'

'It's a rifle.'

'A what? Oh, never mind. It scared me half to death when it went off earlier and I spilled hot milk on my hand,' she complained. She was still cross with herself because she felt guilty that she had deceived her mother about where the milk had come from. She thrust her reddened hand at his face.

He didn't flinch. 'My father has an ointment to soothe that.'

'I have my own.'

'I'll work as well to make up for your injury.'

'What do you mean?'

'You have chores need doing.' There was a hint of derision in his voice.

For a cupful of spilled milk? She bit back the reason their farm was run down. It might not be wise to tell him there was no man living here. He was a ruffian, she decided, intent on stealing from them. But what was there to steal from Top Field nowadays? And she'd already taken the rabbits from him. She dropped them to the floor out of his reach in case he wanted them back. 'The cowshed roof leaks. If you mend it you can stay the night.' She dreaded to think what her mother would say.

'Two nights.'

'I don't know.'

He stared at her and challenged, 'It's sixpence for the rabbits.'

Her mother liked a rabbit stew and Quinta had dried apples and her own cider in the pantry to cook with it. She couldn't give them back. She hoped her mother would understand. 'Very well. Two nights, if you'll saw up that fallen tree over there, too.'

He looked at the gnarled old trunk with raised eyebrows. 'You drive a hard bargain, miss. But it's a deal.' He spit on his palm and held out his hand through the open window.

Quinta blinked. She'd seen traders in the market do that. Only men, though. She was wary of him; he was a stranger and not to be trusted. There was a tightness in her chest that made her hold her breath. His eyes swung back to her face but he did not smile and the intensity of his gaze sent a shiver of fear down her back.

She hesitated and looked down at her small, work-roughened

hand. His was a large hand, tanned like his face from the outdoors and its fingers were long and straight with blackened nails. It was the first time she had faced a stranger and struck a deal in this way. She straightened her spine, spit on her own palm and slapped it against his. 'Deal, Mr Ross.'

His size and obvious strength were threatening to her but she refused to be frightened by him. She was aware of her heart beating faster than normal and breathed deeply to calm herself.

He, also, appeared to relax. He removed his hat in a surprisingly deferential manner. 'I'm obliged to you, Miss . . . ?' When he raised his eyebrows she noticed his eyes were blue, a dark stormy hue that moved quickly now and took in all around him.

'Qui—' She stopped. 'Haig. Miss Haig.'

He gave her a bow of his head and turned to walk away. A big man, she noticed, with a hefty pair of shoulders and long straight legs. He was handsome, all right. As he retreated to the cowshed she noticed his boots. They were worn and dusty but resembled those worn by Sir William, black with tanned leather cuffs. She wondered what Mother would say when she told her that strangers were staying in the cowshed for two nights. But she had struck a good bargain, she thought, and Mother ought to be pleased.

'Who is it, Quinta? Who are you talking to?' Mother's voice carried well down the stairs.

What should she say without alarming her? Quinta closed the window, picked up the rabbits and slung them on the stone slab by the sink in the scullery. She heard floorboards creaking as Mother moved around to dress. Quinta went to the fire to stir a thickening milk and barley porridge for tea. She ladled it into a deep bowl and scraped a spoon round the honey jar for a trace of sweetness. There wouldn't be any more until later in the year.

'You look well, Mother,' she said brightly when Laura appeared.

'Who was that? I saw him go into our cowshed. Has Farmer Bilton sent him?'

'He's a . . .' Better to tell the truth, she decided. 'He's a traveller.'

'Not a gypsy!' Her mother was alarmed.

'I suppose he could be.' As she thought about this Quinta's anxiety mounted again. 'He's looking for work.'

'Well, there's none here that we can pay for. You should have sent him on his way. What is he doing in our cowshed?'

'He's going to mend the roof,' Quinta answered quickly. She told her mother about the earlier exchange and the bargain. 'And we'll have all the logs we need and dinners for a week,' she finished.

'What else will they want for all that work?' Mother exclaimed.

'Don't fret yourself. They'll be gone in two days.'

'After they've stolen everything we have!'

Quinta chewed on her lip. Their cart was in the cowshed along with wood that father had stored to season and make furniture from. 'Don't fret so, Mother, it makes you cough.' She peered out of the window. 'He's started work already.' She stood for a few minutes watching him as he dragged her father's ladder out of the cowshed and leaned it against the stone wall. He checked all the joints before he climbed, steadily, testing each rung with his foot until he reached the top and surveyed the broken, gaping roof tiles. 'Sit down and try and eat some of this porridge, Mother. You need to get well.'

Quinta gutted and skinned both rabbits and was soaking them in a bowl of brine when her mother came into the scullery with her empty bowl and said, 'There are two of them. The other one is a cripple.'

'It's his father.'

'Well, I don't like the look of him.'

'He's resting his leg. That's why he wants to stay in our shed.'

'He's a vagrant. I'll tell him to leave now.'

Quinta put a hand on her arm. 'Don't go out there. His father has a gun. I saw him crossing the pasture earlier.'

'A gun? And you said they could stay? Oh my heaven, what were you thinking of?'

You, she thought, but kept quiet as her mother continued: 'We'll be murdered in our beds!'

Anxious herself, Quinta tried to calm her. 'The gentry have guns. They are not murderers.'

'These men are not gentry. Look at them. They're vagabonds.'

Quinta had to agree and a locked and barred door was no defence against a gun. She said, 'The son was civil to me when we talked.'

'I'll speak to him this time and tell them to leave.' Laura went across to the front window and opened it. 'Mr Ross. A word with you, if you please.'

He looked around from the cowshed roof. His father had disappeared again. He climbed carefully down the ladder and came over to the cottage. 'Good morning, ma'am. You must be Mrs Haig?'

'That's right. What's this I hear about a gun?'

'It's my father's, ma'am. He uses it for hunting.'

'Where is it?'

'Inside there.' He gestured towards the cowshed.

'It's in my cowshed?'

'You are quite safe, ma'am. We are honest travellers seeking honest work.'

Quinta had followed her mother from the scullery with blood on her hands. She stood behind her and listened.

'I want to talk to your father,' Laura said. 'Bring out the gun first and put it by the fallen tree where I can see it. Then ask him to step outside.'

Mr Ross did as her mother asked and his father limped towards them leaning heavily on his crutch. Quinta held her breath and hoped they would not turn nasty towards them.

'That's far enough,' Mother said. 'Who are you and where are you from?'

'George Ross, ma'am. I hail from the South Riding.'

'You have kin in these parts?'

'Orphaned as a child, ma'am, and sent out as a gamekeeper's lad when I was ten.'

The mention of a respectable trade impressed Quinta. Her mother, too, she guessed, for Laura did not reply immediately. A gamekeeper was trusted; unless he turned poacher, of course.

'That's not a gamekeeper's gun.'

'No, ma'am. I was a rifleman in the Duke of Wellington's army.'

'A soldier?'

'A sergeant, ma'am. I fought at Waterloo.' He put a hand on his thigh. 'Where I got this.'

Quinta saw her mother's eyes widen. A sergeant! And a war hero! It was before Quinta was born but folk still talked of England's victory over Old Boney in France.

'Will your son mend our roof?'

'He will, ma'am. And fill your woodshed and be pleased to.'

Quinta saw Patrick Ross frown and guessed he wasn't exactly 'pleased' about their arrangement. She began to feel proud of her side of the bargain. 'There are tiles in the cowshed,' she said.

'Yes, I found them,' he replied briefly.

'Two nights?' Laura asked.

'If you please, ma'am,' the sergeant replied. 'I should be much obliged to you.'

'Have you food?' Quinta blinked in surprise at her mother's change of tone.

'A brace of partridge, ma'am.'

Partridge! Quinta hadn't tasted that since her father had died.

'Where did they come from?'

'The moor. But I see one or two have a taste for your garden greens,' Sergeant Ross answered.

'Yes, they do.'

'May I ask who owns the woodland?'

'Belongs to the Hall on the other side of the stream. I hope our rabbit isn't from there. I want nothing to do with any poaching.'

'We took it from the moorland.'

'Well, that's allowed. Anything this side of the stream is ours.'

His son, who had been standing quietly by his side until now, said, 'You have snares in your cowshed. Why do you not set them?'

'Father used to do that for us.' As she spoke, Quinta remembered how he put them down to keep rabbits off their garden as much as to give them dinners. But she didn't know how to snare a rabbit, only how to how to skin and gut them on the kitchen slab. She looked at the blood drying on her fingers and added impulsively, 'I'm sure I could do that, Mother, if someone showed me how.'

Mother cast an impatient glance in her direction. 'You may take wood for a fire,' she said shortly.

'Thank you, ma'am.' Sergeant Ross passed a gnarled hand over his unkempt beard. 'I am in need of hot water.'

'Two nights,' Laura repeated. 'Good evening to you.'

'Good evening, ma'am. Miss.' He bowed his head, turned and limped back into the cowshed. His son followed silently, and was soon at work again on the cowshed roof.

'Make sure you keep the door barred, Quinta. And don't let either of them inside for anything. Do you hear me?'

Chapter 5

The following morning Quinta went out at daybreak to fetch water from the stream. She hoped to be safely back indoors before Sergeant Ross and his son stirred from their sleep.

'Good morning, Miss Haig.'

'Oh!' Quinta thought she was early enough to avoid the travellers, but Mr Ross was already by the water with an old bucket from the cowshed.

'This rock is the best spot,' she advised, stepping on to the flat boulder. She dipped an empty bucket into the fast-flowing water. When she straightened he had straddled the gap between bank and stones and was stretching out his hand for her bucket.

'Give it here,' he said.

She hesitated at first then handed it over. He did not seem so threatening in the morning sun. She dipped another bucket into the water and handed it up to him. 'Pass me yours and I'll fill it for you while I'm here.'

'Thank you. My father likes a dish of tea in the mornings.'

Quinta had watched him light a fire and set up a wooden trivet at the side of the cowshed last evening. He had mended the roof until nightfall the previous day and his father never came out to lend a hand; neither did he tend to the fire, or the partridge as it roasted on its makeshift wooden spit.

'Is your father's leg improved this morning?' she asked.

Mr Ross frowned and nodded. 'He should rest it more.'

'Did he really fight at Waterloo?'

'He nearly died there.'

'Were you with him?'

He half laughed; scornfully, she thought. 'I wasn't born then. How old do you think I am?'

She shrugged and didn't answer. It was hard to tell, but apparently he was younger than she'd realised. Waterloo was twenty years ago.

He turned and stared at their cowshed and his face darkened as he said, 'I didn't even know I had a father until he came to find me afterwards.' He sounded angry, almost bitter.

'Has his leg troubled him ever since?'

He lifted two of the heavy buckets, leaving her with one. 'He should have a surgeon to look at it.'

'There isn't one here. He has to come out from town for folk who can pay him. There's a Dispensary in town, though, for the labourers in the manufactories. Your father would be better off in the town. You can take a carrier cart from the village in the valley.'

'I see.'

Good, thought Quinta. Mother would be pleased to hear they would be moving on soon.

They walked slowly to the cottage, carrying the buckets of water.

'When did you last use that donkey cart in your shed?' he asked.

'One of the shafts is broken.'

'I can see that. I could mend it for you.'

'We haven't got a donkey any more.'

'You could push it yourself. You look strong enough.'

45

Maybe I could, she thought. I could push it to market and sell our vegetables. 'Mother says it needs a new piece of wood.'

'There's some across the rafters in there.' He tossed his head to indicate the cowshed. 'Have you got any nails?'

They had some upstairs in her father's tool box. 'We can't pay you,' she said.

'I'll fix it if your mother will let us stay a few more nights.'

She didn't think it was a good idea to encourage strangers. But they needed the cart fixing. 'I'll ask her,' she said.

They parted at the cowshed door and Mr Ross went inside to his father.

Quinta placed the heavy buckets of water outside the scullery door and straightened her back, taking a few minutes to enjoy the clean fresh air. She felt his presence before she saw him, astride his horse beyond their cottage on the track up to the moor. What was Farmer Bilton doing there at this hour of the morning? Angrily, she marched towards him.

'You have no right to spy on us like this!'

'I'm looking out for my property. I've heard there are vagrants about.'

She wondered if he had seen the sergeant and his son. 'Well, this is our land, not yours!'

'Only while you pay me rent.'

'We'll get your money.'

He sneered and swung down off his horse, leaving the reins trailing. 'Why hasn't your ma been to see me about you yet?'

'She – she's poorly.'

'She's stubborn, you mean!' He grabbed her arm roughly and yanked her towards him. 'My patience is running out.'

'Let go! You're hurting me!'

He ignored her plea and shook her as if to emphasise his strength. 'I will have my way. If you don't want to end up with no home you'll make that clear to her.'

'You can't make us do what you want!'

'Can't I? I have the vicar on my side.' His fingers bit painfully into her flesh.

'He won't be if I tell him about this!'

He relaxed his hold on her and replied, 'You would try the patience of a saint.'

She broke free, rubbing her bruised arm vigorously. 'And you can get off our farm!'

His mouth turned down in a grimace, but he gathered the reins and remounted. Quinta watched him ride away, taking the time to calm down. They were well away from the cottage but she hoped Mother hadn't heard any of this conversation; they needed their cart mended more than ever now and she went indoors to tell her about Mr Ross's offer.

Laura was suspicious. 'Why does he want to help us?'

'He's asked to stay a few more days in our cowshed,' Quinta explained. If he doesn't go off with the cart when he's fixed it, she thought suddenly. 'He said his father had to see a surgeon.' She realised that was why he had offered to mend the cart. Not for them but to take his father to town. She had thought it was a good idea at first, but now she wasn't sure and added, 'You are right, Mother, he wants the cart for himself and not for us.'

'I knew it! They'll steal everything from us and you as well!'

'Do be calm, Mother. Who would want to steal me?'

'Farmer Bilton wanted to take you from me, my love.'

He still does, she thought, but said, 'The garden is growing well now. If we took a cartload of crops to market we might manage the rest of the rent at Midsummer.'

'What? Sell all our young vegetables?'

'They'll fetch a good price this year and we can buy flour and sugar.'

'And scented soap and beeswax candles,' her mother breathed.

'Well, don't forget we'll have to save some seed for me to plant as well,' Quinta countered. 'Oh Mother, do let Mr Ross mend our cart. We haven't been to town for ages.'

'It's a long way, my love. And a cartload of vegetables will be heavy to push.'

'Seth might help, Mother. It's mostly downhill until we get to the Hall. And it won't have as much in it on the way back.'

'Well, I'm not much use these days.'

'Nonsense! I'll go to the Dispensary for more of your cough mixture.' Quinta felt excited by their plans. 'Oh, Mother, you were right. Something has turned up for us.'

But her mother was still dreaming. 'We'll buy meat pies for our dinner and – and – and an orange, an orange each. We must go to the draper too, and buy ribbons.'

'And pay Farmer Bilton his rent?' They both went quiet as they pondered on this. Then Quinta added, 'Even if we do, Mother, he doesn't want us here any more. What if he turns us out?'

'Your father was a legal tenant. Besides, the Squire will have something to say if he does.'

'What's he got to do with it?'

'He – he – his father arranged the tenancy in the first place.'

'You've never told me why, Mother. What did my father do for him?'

'He was a good servant,' Laura said in a rush.

'Why did the old Squire let him go, then?'

'Do stop quizzing me! It's all in the past now.'

'Quite so, and the new Squire is all for changing things. He'll side with Farmer Bilton and say I should wed him.'

Her mother looked away and did not answer, which made Quinta think that she was right about this. 'We ought to find somewhere else to live,' she suggested gently.

'Aye, we might do that. I don't want to live in the town, though. It makes me cough so much.'

Quinta privately thought that anything and everything made her mother cough these days. Perhaps when she was at the Dispensary she could ask for some stronger medicine than her usual mixture.

'Maybe there'll be a gentleman in town looking for a house-keeper?' Quinta added brightly. She actually thought that even if there were, he'd have plenty to choose from in town and not be interested in a poorly widow, but she added with a smile, 'The cook at the Hall will vouch for you.'

A week later, Patrick Ross and his father were still living in the cowshed. The roof was sound and their stock of wood for the fire was rising every day. Quinta did not meet him at the stream again; he went earlier and she did not see him. Only when she worked in the garden and he was sawing or chopping wood did he acknowledge her, with a formal bow of his head. She hardly knew he was there until he wheeled the mended cart out one sunny morning.

'He's finished it, Mother.'

'What's that, dear?'

'Our cart. It's mended. Come and see.'

The two women stood side by side at the window. 'Shall we go outside?' Laura suggested.

'Where's the sergeant? I can't see him anywhere.'

'He rests inside the cowshed for most of his time. I think we can trust them now.'

'I'm not so sure, Mother,' Quinta cautioned.

'Well, they would have been off by now if they were going to steal from us.'

Quinta lifted the wooden bar from across their front door and turned the heavy key in its lock. She took her mother's hand and together they stepped outside. Patrick Ross was wheeling the cart around and checking its wheels.

'Good morning, ma'am. Miss.' He nodded briefly in their direction. 'Your cart is as good as new. It was well made in the first place.'

'Indeed it was,' Laura replied. 'My late husband learned his carpentry from a master.'

He swivelled the shafts around. 'Miss Haig? Can you push it?'

Quinta took hold of the shafts. It was heavy and unwieldy but she soon got used to it. However, she wondered how much extra weight she could manage.

'How is your father?' Laura asked.

'He is much improved, thank you, ma'am. The rest has helped him.'

'Will he take refreshment with us?'

'Mother, no!' Quinta tugged at her mother's hand.

'Fetch a jug of ale and mugs from the scullery, dear.'

When Sergeant Ross came out of the cowshed, they saw he had shaved and his boots and coat were brushed so that he looked clean and tidy, though Quinta was surprised at how pale he was. His face showed the strain of continuous pain and he kept closing his eyes as he moved carefully with the aid of his crutch.

'Sit down, Father.' Mr Ross moved the wooden tray from where Quinta had placed it on a mounting stone outside the cowshed.

'Over here.' Quinta pointed to an upturned half-barrel that served as a table. She was aware that Mr Ross was watching her as she poured the ale and handed him the largest of their stoneware mugs. He nodded his thanks wordlessly and his serious features sent a shiver of uneasiness down her spine. He had not shaved and his dark growth of beard gave him an unkempt, hostile appearance. She was not as sure as her mother that either of them could be trusted. He carried the ale to his father who swallowed it easily and with relish.

'I should like to stay longer, Mrs Haig,' his father said. 'Until my leg has recovered enough to make the journey into town. My son can work on your farm to pay rent for your cowshed. If I may say so, ma'am, there is much to be done here.'

'We do our best,' Quinta answered quickly.

'Indeed you do, miss. Forgive me, my comment is not meant as criticism to your good selves. I merely observe that this is fertile land that is underused.'

As though we do not know that, Quinta thought impatiently.

The sergeant continued, 'With my son's help you can grow more to fill your barrow for market, and for your own winter larder.'

'A full barrow is of little use without a donkey,' Quinta responded irritably. 'I shall not be able to push it.'

'I can.' It was the first words Patrick Ross had spoken about the venture.

'We have to sell as much as we can before quarter day,' Laura said thoughtfully.

Quinta noticed father and son exchange glances and realised that they had discussed her and Mother and made an accurate assessment of their circumstances. She felt humiliated that her mother had made it more obvious to these strangers that they were failing. 'I've told you, Mother, I can find work at the Hall,' she chided.

'There's a big market in town on Midsummer's Eve, dear,' Laura responded.

In time to pay our rent, Quinta thought.

'It is not many weeks until then, ma'am,' the sergeant added. 'Already my leg is less swollen and I should like to rest here longer, if I may.'

His son stood by silently, his face expressionless as though the decision did not involve him. Yet he would be doing the work. Quinta tugged at her mother's hand and said, 'They are strangers. I don't think we should.'

Then Mr Ross spoke again. 'I told you, Father, we are not wanted here.'

'But you are,' Laura responded hastily, 'if you can farm as well as you mend things.'

'My son was raised on a farm.'

The sergeant was a farmer then, Quinta thought, and said, 'You told us you were a soldier.'

'And that is true, miss. How do you think I got a French musket ball in my leg? They took it out on the battlefield and nearly killed me in the process.' He grimaced as he spoke and then added, 'But I lived, although this knee has not been right since. My son has farmed his way across England through all seasons as I hope you will discover. Now, can we stay or not, Mrs Haig?'

'Until Midsummer,' Laura answered.

Quinta marvelled at the improvement in her mother's appetite and strength. She tended the fire, cooked and baked more, leaving Quinta to work in the garden full time. Patrick Ross worked from early morning at the far side of their land near to the moorland, where the pasture was overgrown with bramble and scrub. He sharpened tools, cleared ditches and tamed hedges until dusk and she saw little of him. His father became more mobile and came out frequently with his rifle to shoot rabbit, partridge and wood pigeon that dared to approach their vegetables. Laura returned the sergeant's frequent gifts of meat with fresh oat biscuits and pots of nourishing broth that Quinta left on the mounting stone. Mr Ross seemed to avoid her, but one warm afternoon, his father came over to her garden and stood watching her at work.

'Are you walking out with anyone?' he asked.

Surprised, Quinta blinked and didn't reply straightaway.

He explained, as though she did not understand: 'You must have a sweetheart hidden away somewhere.'

'No, I haven't!' she replied indignantly. 'And why must I?'

'You are very pretty.'

'Oh!'

'Hasn't anyone offered for you yet?'

'As a matter of fact someone has,' she replied loftily. 'My mother said no to him.'

'Did she?' he replied. 'Have you said no to him as well?'

'I – I . . .' Quinta realised that she might have implied the opposite to Farmer Bilton when she had fetched milk for Mother. And he continued to ride their boundaries, keeping his eye on them. He must have seen Sergeant Ross and his son by now.

'Did you wish to wed him?'

'I don't think that is anything to do with you.'

'Indeed it is not. But I should like to know all the same. Here, I've made this for you.' He handed her a wooden dibber, fashioned from a solid piece of wood and perfect for sowing her beans and seed potatoes. It was smooth and comfortable to hold.

'Thank you. This must have taken you a long time to make.'

'I have little else to fill my days. Would your mother care for a wooden bowl to grace her table?'

'I'm sure she would.'

As she continued her weeding Quinta couldn't decide whether the sergeant wanted anything in return for his gifts. She wanted to think not but wasn't sure. By teatime she was thirsty and her mother brought out barley water to drink. The sergeant called loudly for his son to join them and he did, without pulling on his shirt, and his back and chest glistened with the sweat of his labour. He didn't sit on the grass with the rest of them but scanned the track down the valley as he drank and said, 'There's a rider coming up.'

They had few visitors to Top Field and Quinta stood up beside him to look until the thumping of hooves on sun-baked earth grew closer and she recognised the horse. 'It's Farmer Bilton,' she said.

'Who's he?' Mr Ross asked.

'Our landlord.'

The horse slowed in a cloud of dust, whinnied and snorted as Farmer Bilton pulled on his reins. 'What's going on here?' he demanded.

Quinta and her mother exchanged glances, but, surprisingly, Mr Ross spoke first. 'Farming, sir.'

'And who might you be?'

Quinta thought it was no business of his but she did not

want to anger him further. Neither did her mother, who replied, 'Visitors, sir.'

'More likely poachers, if you ask me.'

Patrick took a step nearer to the horse. 'We are not, sir. And we stay by invitation of Mrs Haig.'

Farmer Bilton ignored him and turned to Laura. 'Travellers, then, and vagrants, invited on to my land by you, madam. Folk in the village are talking already and when Sir William hears about this he'll back me to get you out.'

'But we are working the farm!' Quinta retaliated.

'That remains to be seen. A bit of hedging and ditching won't make any difference. I made you an offer and I advise you to take it. I want you out of here by quarter day. All of you.' He tugged at the reins, turned the horse around and dug his spurs into its flanks. The creature, already foaming at the mouth, flared its nostrils and galloped away.

No one said anything as they watched him leave in a dusty cloud. Quinta glanced at her mother and the sergeant who were both frowning. But it was the look on Mr Ross's face that startled her. He was furious. His eyes were stormy and his lips set in a contemptuous grimace.

Quinta, too, was angry at Farmer Bilton's boorish and bullying behaviour and, after he had disappeared down the track, she said, 'We'll get him his rent, Mother, even if I do have to scrub floors at the Hall.'

'It's not just the money, dear. He's right. I've looked at the agreement and it says I must practise good husbandry, as your father did.'

'You hold the tenancy, Mrs Haig?' the sergeant queried.

'It was transferred to me when my husband died.'

'Well, the land here is in good heart,' Mr Ross commented.

'My son knows more about farming than I do,' the sergeant explained.

'It will take a year or two to bring it back to profit,' his son added.

'We haven't got a year or two,' Quinta responded.

'Then I'd best get on,' Mr Ross said briskly and set off back to his work.

Farmer Bilton did not call again to speak to them but Quinta saw him frequently from her garden, riding his black hunter around the edge of their land. She knew he meant what he said about turning them out and he had influential people to support him. But they had a chance for reprieve with Mr Ross's help and as Midsummer approached she became excited by the prospect of going to town. Her young crops had thrived and she worked from dawn until dusk harvesting and preparing them for market.

They set off shortly after daybreak. Laura inhaled the morning air and said, 'Quinta, lock the door for me, dear, and take the key round to the woodshed. Mr Ross is ready to leave.'

'I see he has brushed his jacket and found a clean necker-chief for his throat,' Quinta observed as she obeyed.

'He's shaved his beard, too.' Laura put her head on one side. When Quinta came back she added, 'He has handsome features, don't you think? The same strong jaw as his father, but his lips are more defined.'

'Lower your voice, Mother. He will hear you.'

'Nonsense, dear, he is already moving away with the cart. His face is less rugged than the sergeant's and his skin has a finer texture.'

'From his mother, I expect. I wonder who she was.' Quinta was reminded how little she knew about Mr Ross and his father. 'Mother, do you think this is wise to leave the sergeant here alone?'

'You have secured the cottage, dear, and he cannot journey with us. What else can we do?'

Sergeant Ross was able to walk with them as far as the track to Bilton Farm, about halfway down the steep descent to the village. As they set off down the hill Mr Ross had to put all his weight in front of the cart to prevent it rolling away. Laura followed behind with the sergeant.

As they approached the track for Bilton Farm, Quinta saw a familiar rider approaching. She had been looking forward to a break from her labours in the garden, but now she groaned, 'Oh no.'

Farmer Bilton dismounted and walked his black hunter towards them. 'So, Mrs Haig, you've decided to leave after all?' His eyes strayed towards Quinta.

She answered, 'No sir. We are going to market.'

'What's in the cart?' he demanded.

'Our garden produce and kindling for market. You will have your rent on our return, sir.'

'We'll see about that. Bring it to me at the farmhouse.'

Quinta didn't want her mother to trudge all that way and intervened, 'Will you not meet us here? You can see our approach.'

'I said bring it to the house. And I want all of it before nightfall.'

'Of course, sir.'

Farmer Bilton led his horse away.

'He's a harsh landlord,' Mr Ross commented. 'I remember his sort from when I was a boy.'

Quinta waited for him to say more, but he didn't, so she simply said, 'He wants us out.'

Laura, who had caught up with them, added sourly, 'He wants more than that.'

They said goodbye to the sergeant and he sat on a dry-stone wall in the rays of a rising sun until they had disappeared from view. As they trudged through Swinborough, they passed a few villagers who were gathering early, waiting for kin to walk to market, or for the morning carrier to take them into town. One or two nodded in their direction and Quinta was aware of whispering as they moved on. It reminded her that Patrick Ross was a stranger and she knew very little about him or his father. As she walked beside him she experienced, again, a fearfulness that sent a shiver down her back.

After the village, the road climbed Potters Hill past the Hall. The cart was heavy, filled with baskets and sacks, some hanging over the side, held on with every last rusting nail and piece of twine they could find.

'I'll help you push, Mr Ross,' Quinta volunteered.

'There is no need. But if you wish . . .' He handed one of the shafts to her.

She bent her back into the task and pushed. 'It would not be such a burden if you had not chopped so much wood. Who will pay you money for all this?'

'Innkeepers. Housekeepers in merchants' houses. Towns are full of people who have to eat. How are they to cook their food?'

'They have coal, of course.'

'So they need wood to light it.'

'But surely they can chop kindling for themselves? Even I can manage that!'

'I do not doubt that. Many town folk are not as resourceful as you, Miss Quinta.'

She was silenced. He had proved her wrong and flattered her at the same time. Her breathing became laboured as they approached the summit.

'I'll take over now,' he said. 'Your mother needs your arm.'

They stopped for rest at the top. The town sprawled below them: smoking chimneys and furnaces, a glint of water from the navigation and brick terraces of labourers' cottages snaking through the bustle. Already carriers and merchants were gathering to water their horses at the spring by the crossroads.

'Not far now,' Quinta observed.

Mr Ross narrowed his eyes and nodded. He said very little. He didn't smile much either. She wondered what sort of life he had led up until now and the kind of man he really was. Normally so withdrawn, she noticed that he seemed to cheer as they drew near to town. While Quinta and her mother were displaying their produce in the marketplace he said, 'I'll take the cart and make haste to sell the wood. I must visit the Dispensary for my father.'

'My mother has need of a stronger medicine to ease her chest,' Quinta said. 'Will you get some for her?'

'Does she not wish to talk to the apothecary herself?'

'She is tired from this walk and will have to rest. You know how her cough sounds.'

'Very well.' He disappeared with their cart into the market crowds.

Chapter 6

'There are so many people! Where do they come from?' Quinta stood at the corner of the market square and gazed in wonder at the throng.

'All the manufactories you can see down by the canal, and from the pit villages round and about. Look at those beasts over there! The butchers'll be busy tomorrow.'

'Do you think we'll be able to buy a bit of butcher's meat tonight, Mother?'

'We'll see. You hold on tight to the purse for me and watch your back. Midsummer Eve attracts all sorts.'

They had a pitch by a corner and next to an alley that led away from the square. Quinta and her mother were kept busy all morning selling their produce while Patrick took his kindling wood off in the cart, heading up the hill to where fine houses had been built for the owners of the new manufactories. These newcomers were not gentry, but they had servants and carriages that were paid for by their profits.

It was a fine day, warm and sunny, and they sold everything before noon. They had enough for the rent and to buy flour.

Quinta stowed her takings safely in a drawstring pouch under her skirts, then stacked her baskets and empty sacks by the wall behind them. Laura coughed as she helped and Quinta wondered when Patrick would be back with the medicine.

'You look pale, Mother,' Quinta said. 'Rest a while. I'll fetch dinner from a pie-seller.'

When she returned with hot meat pies, Laura was asleep on the sacking in front of their baskets and she hadn't the heart to waken her. She left her pies behind the baskets and joined a crowd to watch a juggler throwing lighted flares in the air. Then she sat on a low stone wall in the shade, near to where her mother was still sleeping, to eat her dinner.

She had noticed a group of three people arrive in the square and walk backwards and forwards without any obvious interest in buying. The gentleman, who wore a smart coat and a tall hat over very straggly hair, and the younger of the two women eventually departed in the direction of the inn and the older woman picked her way across the market debris to where Quinta was sitting. She was dressed in a very fancy gown embellished with pleats and bows and had on a bonnet trimmed with matching ribbons. Quinta thought she was gentry and stopped chewing as the woman approached her.

'On yer own, are yer?' She didn't speak like a lady.

'No.'

'Looking fer work, eh?'

'No.' Not now, she thought, aware of her full purse safely hidden away.

'I know where a lass like you can earn a sovereign a week. Think of that. A whole sovereign. It's enough fer yer ter buy a new gown and bonnet whenever yer want.'

Quinta didn't believe her, but she wondered what she was talking about. 'Where's that then?' she asked.

The woman stretched out her hand. 'Come wi' me and I'll show yer.'

Quinta recoiled, staring at her hand. It was gnarled and

knobbly but adorned with several glittery rings. 'No, thank you. Go away,' she said firmly.

The woman persisted. 'Look at all these gent'men around yer. All wi' money in their pockets. Where do they come from?'

'They live here, don't they?'

'Aye, lass, they do. They work in the mines and manufactories or fer the railway company. Some are proper gentry, spending their pa's riches. Plenty ter go round, yer see.'

Quinta didn't see and went back to eating her pie.

The woman looked impatient and then curiously intent. She took a step closer and asked, ''Ave you never 'ad a sweetheart?'

She shook her head as she chewed and remembered the sergeant asking her the same question.

'Never? You still a maid, then?'

'Of course I am!' Quinta replied indignantly.

The woman's bony fingers enclosed her wrist. 'Come wi' me, ducks.'

Quinta tugged at her hand but the woman would not release her. She dropped her pie in the struggle and muttered, 'Let me go, I don't like you.'

And then the woman whistled. *She put her finger and thumb between her lips and whistled like a man!* Quinta's eyes widened as the younger woman she had noticed earlier loomed close, apparently from nowhere. She was very pretty and had rouge on her cheeks and lips and – and, oh, Quinta realised she had rouged her bosoms where they thrust out of her gown without any muslin to cover them. She wore coloured feathers in her tangled hair and reminded Quinta of the travelling players that visited from time to time.

The girl took hold of her other wrist with fingers that felt like iron bands and jerked her forward. Quinta half fell off the wall.

'Leave me alone. I'm not coming with you!'

'Get her down the alley quick,' the older woman said. Her tone had changed from wheedling to anger and she began to haul Quinta after her. When Quinta resisted, the woman seethed at her companion, 'Put yer back into it, girl.'

'No!' Quinta pulled against both of them as they dragged her away. She turned her head and yelled, 'Mother! Wake up, Mother! Help me!'

'What's going on?' Mrs Haig roused from her slumber and rolled to her knees. 'You leave my Quinta alone,' she called. Then she stood up and raised her voice and, between coughs, wheezed, 'They're taking my Quinta. Stop them! Somebody help her!'

A small crowd gathered to stare and the older woman turned a bright smile on them and said, 'Don't listen ter 'er. This girl is my daughter and that drunk over there was trying ter steal 'er from me.'

'That's not true!' Quinta protested loudly. 'She isn't a drunk, she's my mother!'

'Yes, I am!' Laura echoed. 'I was asleep, that's all, and this – this *madam* is stealing my Quinta.' By now Mother was on her feet and lunging at the older woman, prising her fingers from Quinta's wrist. At the same time Quinta kicked at the younger one and bit her arm. The girl yelped and let go. With her free hand, Quinta curled her fingers into a ball and punched at the woman, catching her on the side of her nose.

The woman gave an anguished cry and put both her hands over her face. 'You little witch. I'll 'ave yer fer that! You see if I don't.' She turned quickly and disappeared down the alley, closely followed by her rouged companion.

Quinta turned anxiously to her mother. 'Mother, are you all right?'

'Are you?' Mother held on to her tightly and buried her face in her shoulder so her voice was muffled. 'They were going to take you away from me. Oh, Quinta my love, I don't like being in the town. Let's go home now.'

'Mr Ross hasn't come back with our cart yet,' Quinta protested.

'He'll catch us up, I'm sure.'

'I'd rather wait. Look, this place is full of butchers, so why don't I buy some meat trimmings while we wait? We have enough money and it'll make us a nice pudding tomorrow.'

'We-e-ll, I suppose you could. But be quick, dear, and leave the purse with me, just to be on the safe side. I've got a pocket in my drawers.'

Quinta glanced around before hitching up her skirt to untie the leather thong securing her purse on her underskirt tapes. Then she handed it to her mother who bunched up her own skirts and hid the purse from view.

'I won't be long.' Quinta smiled, picking up a basket. She hurried away, lifting the edges of her gown clear of the rotting vegetables and animal droppings that littered the cobbled square. The taverns were already noisy with farmers and traders celebrating their successful trading.

She found a row of small stone houses just off the High Street. A large red-faced buxom woman stood outside one of them in front of a slate-topped table. She caught Quinta's attention with her bloody fingers and raucous voice. 'Ox skirt and meat trimmings,' she yelled. 'Gotta clear this lot afore nightfall, me ducks.' She laughed, hacking away with a large knife. 'Got a fine forequarter hanging in the back yard ready for my slab and another ox beast standing.'

'Have you baked any pies today?' Quinta asked. Mother's dinner had been crushed in her scramble to help, and Quinta had only eaten half of her own.

'Have I baked? Nonstop night and day! But they've all gone by now. Sold the last one hours ago.'

Quinta bought a chunk of ox kidney and suet which the butcher's wife wrapped up in a generous piece of beef skirt and tied it round with twine. She was pleased with her bargain and cheered by the prospect of meat pudding tomorrow. She placed her precious purchase in the bottom of her basket and slung it over her arm.

* * *

Laura sat on the empty sacks as she waited and felt uneasy when she glanced down the alley. A man was looming out of the shadows. She had noticed him earlier in the square with the women who had tried to steal her daughter. He was young and brawny-looking and his presence made her nervous. Oh Lord, he was walking towards her! Where was Quinta?

'Good evening, missus. A very pleasant one it is, too. 'Ave you 'ad a good day at the market?'

'Who are you?' she asked. As she did her hand went automatically to confirm her purse was still there under her skirts in the pocket of her drawers. He smiled at her with fleshy lips and she took an instant dislike to him. He was a thick-set and burly, an ox of a man with a dark swarthy skin and black eyes. But he was well shod and wore a fancy waistcoat with an elaborate necktie. It was the showy kind of dress favoured by the new manufacturing gentry in town. He didn't sound like them, though. He spoke roughly like one of Farmer Bilton's itinerant labourers.

'What do you want?' she demanded.

'Nothing, excepting a bit o' conversation.'

Laura sat stiffly in silence.

''Ave you far ter get 'ome?' he asked.

'No. Have you? I've not seen you in the marketplace before.'

He smiled at her with his fat lips but not with his glittery dark eyes. They stared at her piercingly and she wished that he'd move on. She wondered why Quinta was taking so long to fetch the meat. His manner was shifty and he had a crooked nose, one that had been broken at some time. In a fight, she didn't doubt. She had a close view of his boots and saw they were the kind favoured by Sir William himself, black with a natural tanned cuff and dear to buy. Very smart, too, she thought, but the hair escaping from his tall hat was tangled and greasy.

'I'm new ter town,' he volunteered. 'I'm still finding my way around. I saw you selling yer vegetables in the marketplace earlier, with a girl.'

'Not me,' she answered shortly.

His eyelids narrowed and his fleshy lips pressed together. 'Well now, I am sure I did, missus.'

'What is it you want?' she demanded shortly. She was beginning to feel uneasy about this fellow and wondered whether to call out for someone. She decided not. He might turn nasty.

'I know 'ow 'ard it is ter get by these days, what wi' rents and the price of flour going up all the time. I got work in the town fer yer lass, you know, wi' proper wages and a decent 'ouse ter live in.'

'Decent house?' That's not what Laura Haig had seen. Ordinary working folk lived squashed together in rows of damp hovels no better than their cowshed.

'Aye,' he went on. 'A big 'ouse 'as ter 'ave a lot o' lasses to keep it straight fer the folk that live there.'

'Servants, you mean?' Like the Hall. Laura Haig only knew of the Hall at Swinborough, which had a lot of maids.

'That girl of yours would do well fer 'erself, I can tell yer.'

'Oh yes? How do you know that, then?'

'Because I do,' he snapped harshly. He seemed to think better of this reaction and added, 'I saw 'er with you.'

Laura was glad that Quinta was not present. She didn't like this man at all. 'Well, she's gone. She went off home an hour ago.'

He looked around. 'Is that 'er over there wi' the basket?'

'No. Besides, I know for a fact she's already suited for work.'

Suddenly he bent over her menacingly and breathed, 'You're a liar, old woman.' He grasped the coils of hair at the back of her head and yanked her head upwards, making her call out in pain. 'If I can't 'ave the lass, I'll 'ave that purse off yer.'

'I haven't got a purse,' she denied. 'She's taken it with her!'

'We'll see about that, you stubborn old crone,' he growled and reached under her skirt to the exact spot in her drawers.

'No,' she squealed, struggling to throw him off. 'Help! Help!'

But he pushed her down easily, throwing her sideways and

flinging back her skirts, exposing the side of her drawers. He tore at the sagging pocket and grasped the leather pouch of coins. 'This'll do fer now. But I'll be back fer the girl. I know she's from round these parts somewhere.'

'No! You can't take that! It's for my rent. Give it back to me. Oh! Help me, somebody!' She raised her voice to a shout. 'Quinta! Quinta! Help me!'

Quinta was enjoying looking at the shop fronts on the other side of the square. The market stalls had been taken down and the crowds had thinned, but she heard a high-pitched call that she recognised as her mother and turned with a startled cry. She saw the man in his tall hat bending over Laura with her skirts all over the place and shouted, 'Stop it! Stop it! I'm coming, Mother!'

Hoisting her own skirt clear of the ground, she ran for all she was worth, crying, 'Get away from her!' As she approached, the man straightened. He had their purse in his hand but he didn't run off. He turned towards her and she saw his face, his dark and threatening features, break into a sneering smile. She slowed and looked around for a weapon, picking up a heavy stone and holding it behind her back. He noticed and sniggered. 'Come on then, lass.'

'Are you hurt, Mother?'

'Stay away from him, Quinta. He's a wrong 'un.'

'But he's got our purse,' she answered and shouted at the man, 'Give it back!'

He held it in his outstretched hand. 'Here. Take it.'

'No, Quinta, don't!' her mother yelled. 'He can keep it!'

But Quinta was not going to let all their hard-earned rent money disappear without a fight and she walked towards him cautiously, testing the weight of the stone in the hand behind her back.

He gestured with his arm. 'Do you want it or not?'

She stopped well away from him and stretched out her hand.

Her fingers closed over the pouch. Before she knew what was happening, his other hand had come round, cuffing her soundly on the side of her head, dazing her and knocking her off balance. She fell to the ground, losing her grip on the stone and within seconds he had scooped her up and hoisted her over one shoulder like a slaughtered pig. She screamed and began pummelling his back with her fists as he broke into a run down the shadowy alley. He held on to her tightly and panted, 'Shut up and keep still or I'll cut you. I mean it. I've got a knife here.'

She quietened immediately. Where was he taking her? He'd stolen their money so why did he want her as well? For her virtue, as Mother has said? His arms were like metal bands around her legs as he jolted her along. She raised her head and was alarmed to see another man running after him. Dear heaven, were they in this together? Were they were going to take her away, defile her and then leave her to die in a field?

Ignoring the danger she began to scream. 'Mother! Stop them! Somebody help me!' Her head, already muzzy from the blow, began to spin. She felt the acid from her stomach working toward her throat, burning her. Saliva ran copiously into her mouth and, her head bouncing upside down, she tried to swallow. Bright lights flashed behind her eyes. She squeezed her lids tight shut to stop them but it made no difference.

The other man was catching up and a moment later she was being pulled about by him. He dragged her from her captor's shoulder, scuffling and shouting, 'Give it here, you ruffian!' Dazed, she heard yelps and the sound of coins scattering to the ground. They were fighting over her money – her rent money! She needed every last farthing of it!

Suddenly, it was over. She was free and her attacker was melting into the darkness of the alley. Her rescuer was joined by a plainly dressed lady and her mother, who was taking back her purse. Quinta scrambled to her feet and, as she did, a thin vomit rose in her mouth mixed with her saliva and she was sick on the ground. She retched and retched; her knees buckled and she fell to the ground in a daze until, oh Lord, Mother was there, lifting her head and cradling it in her lap.

'All right, my love, he's gone now. You're safe.'

There was a frightened expression on her mother's face. She was rubbing the hair on the side of Quinta's head.

'Ow! That hurts, Mother. It's where he hit me.'

'You'll have a bruise there tomorrow. But that's all, thank the Lord. This gentleman saw off that awful man off. He dragged you off him and even saved most of our money. He got away with some of it, though.'

'He is a very slippery character, madam, if I may say so,' the gentleman commented. 'I've seen him before, waiting around for young girls and persuading them into all sorts of wicked ways. There are evil folk about these days.'

'I am much obliged to you for your intervention,' Laura said.

'Yes. Thank you, sir,' Quinta echoed.

The stranger nodded his acknowledgement. 'You have a lovely daughter, madam. I should get her away from here as soon as you can. Trade has been good today and the ale is already flowing copiously.' When he was satisfied no lasting harm had been done, the gentleman and his lady took their leave.

Laura feverishly counted the coins in her purse. 'We can't afford any flour now. What are we going to do?'

'Make do with oats as we've always done. Have we got enough for the rent?'

'Not quite.' Laura started to cough.

'If this is town you can keep it,' Quinta observed miserably.

'It never used to be like this. Let's get back to Top Field as fast as we can.'

Still raw from her tussle, Quinta agreed. 'I'm as anxious as you to go home. If only Mr Ross would return with our cart we could leave now! Where is he?' She scanned the marketplace but there was no sign of him. 'We don't know anything about him or his father. They could have told us a pack of lies! A sergeant indeed!'

Laura looked sad and replied, 'Do you think he has gone off with our cart?'

Quinta nodded. 'And he has our share of the money from the kindling. We shouldn't have trusted him in the first place. I don't think his father has a bad leg at all. It was just a ruse to get our sympathy.'

'Oh no!' Laura groaned. 'And we've left him at home.'

'His son is probably with him now, and filling the cart with Father's tools and furniture.'

'You locked the cottage door,' Laura pointed out.

'And I left the key in the woodshed.'

'Oh Quinta, what shall we do? I thought they were decent folk.'

'What else can you expect from travellers, Mother? They get by on their wits. They took us in right and proper, they did. We'd better get back. Come on, Farmer Bilton wants his rent before nightfall.'

They trudged on, leaving the smoke and the grime behind, sometimes overtaken by others hurrying home with their gains or purchases from the market. Quinta was relieved when she saw the crossroads ahead and a rider refreshing his animal at the horse trough.

'Oh thank the Lord,' Laura sighed. 'I must take the weight off my feet. I'm feeling quite weak.'

'Here, sit on this bank and I'll fetch you over some water.'

'Have you anything to carry it in?'

'I'll find something. Lie back and rest, Mother. The miller's cart has gone already. He must have sold all his flour for today. Are you hungry?'

Laura nodded.

'Me too. A drink will keep us going and it's not far now.'

Laura sighed again. 'It's a pity about Sergeant Ross. I thought he was an honest man. I'm not usually wrong.'

'He was charming enough but I didn't trust his son. He was too aloof for my liking. Well, he's gone now and I'm not sorry.'

'We couldn't have got to market without him, dear.'

'He's got our cart out of the bargain! Anyway, Farmer Bilton might let us stay now and if I plant more seeds quickly I can earn the rent by next quarter day.'

'Given a good growing season,' Laura cautioned. 'It's at times like this that I really miss your father.'

Quinta gave her a hug. 'You've got me.'

'I nearly lost you today, though. If my Joseph had been with us that man would never have dared to drag you off.'

The incident in town had been very frightening for Quinta but she tried to reassure her mother. 'I got away, didn't I? I can't think why he was interested in me in the first place.'

'I can. You are young and very pretty.'

'Well, I wouldn't have been much use, I'm sure, because I would have run away from him as soon as I could!'

'No, you wouldn't. He would have locked you up.'

'But why?'

'It's time you knew about these things, my love. Evil men like that keep pretty young girls as prisoners in – in – wicked houses, and – and – and then sell their virtue time after time to any man who pays them for it.'

'What!'

'It's true and I don't want us going into town again. Not on our own. Not ever.'

'Not ever? How else are we to sell our vegetables?'

'I don't know. But I do know that I don't want to lose you.'

'We have to get our rent, Mother,' Quinta argued. It was all very well her mother saying these things but she wasn't being practical. She would never get enough money by Michaelmas if she didn't sell what they grew at the market.

She wondered whom she could ask for help. Not Farmer Bilton, that's for sure! But who else was there?

Chapter 7

'*There you are! Why didn't you wait for me?*'

Laura sat on the edge of the horse trough while Quinta bathed her bruised head in the icy water. She was tired and hungry and her head hurt. The movement of water as it trickled gently from the spring was mesmerising and she had closed her eyes, dreaming longingly of the oat biscuit waiting for her at Top Field.

'It's Mr Ross!' her mother exclaimed.

Startled, Quinta turned sharply. 'It is you! I thought you had gone for good.'

'But I had your cart with me.'

Mother and daughter exchanged glances silently.

'You thought I had stolen it?' he added tightly.

Quinta faced him defiantly and said, 'Yes, we did. You didn't come back to the marketplace for any dinner.'

He looked hot, as though he had been rushing to catch up with them, and his tone was resentful. 'It took a long time to sell the kindling. I wanted the best price. Then I went to the Dispensary for medicine. That was crowded with folk and I had to wait my turn.'

'Well, don't sound so offended! What else would we believe? If you knew what a day we have had in town, you would think the same!'

'Quinta, do calm down. We have our cart.'

She quietened and asked, 'Did you get something for Mother?'

'Yes. I had a consultation with the apothecary.'

A frown creased her brow. He would have had to pay extra for that. 'How much do I owe you?'

'Nothing. I had money from the kindling and we agreed to split it.'

'Is there any left?' Quinta asked anxiously.

'Yes. I bought flour from the miller half an hour ago.'

Quinta looked in the cart and, sure enough, there was a sack of flour among other supplies that he had purchased in town.

He lifted both shafts and began to push it. 'Can we get going? I want to get back to my father. I have medicine for him, too.'

'I'll take one side,' Quinta volunteered, stacking their baskets and sacks on top of the flour.

'Look to your mother, Miss Quinta. She is weary.' He set off purposefully towards Swinborough village.

The two women linked arms again and Laura whispered, 'Oh, I am so very pleased to see him, aren't you?'

'No.' Quinta wasn't at all sure about Patrick Ross. There was something dark and unknown about him and it vexed her. The sergeant was more forthcoming and Mother thought quite highly of him, too. That is, before they believed he was at home robbing them. And they had believed it. The travellers were, after all, strangers and only interested in Top Field because it had an empty cowshed for them.

Refreshed and more cheerful, they were soon over Swinborough hill and through the village. The sun was dipping when the hill track to home rose steeply in front of them. Mother slowed as they climbed and Quinta noticed beads of sweat on Patrick's brow. But his pace did not ease. He took off his jacket, flung it on the cart and bowed his head, leaning into the incline. On the more difficult parts of the slope, his boots slipped backwards over loose stones.

'Will you not take a rest, Mr Ross?' Quinta called.

He shook his head briefly and continued to push.

'Oh look!' Laura exclaimed. 'The sergeant is waiting for us!'

Mr Ross raised his head. His father had walked down as far as the track to Bilton Farm and was sitting on the low stone wall. He quickened his pace, causing him to puff and pant even more.

'Mother needs to rest now, even if you don't,' Quinta said to him as they approached the sergeant. Father and son were already deep in conversation.

'Sergeant Ross!' Laura said as she settled beside him on the wall. 'You won't believe what has happened to me in the market-place! I was set upon by a ruffian who stole my purse and tried to steal my daughter, too. A kind gentleman saw him off, thank goodness.'

'Where were you, Patrick?' his father asked.

'Mrs Haig and her daughter were ahead of me,' he explained. 'I didn't know – it was all over by the time I caught up with them.'

'Yes. We left town early after that,' Laura added.

'Did you get your purse back?' the sergeant asked.

'I did.'

'With all its contents?'

'We lost some of our takings, sir,' Quinta answered.

'Give Mrs Haig what's left from the kindling, son.'

'All of it?'

The sergeant nodded emphatically.

'But we agreed to split it, Father. You need—'

'Do as I say.'

Silently Mr Ross handed over the coins.

'Will you have enough now, ma'am?'

'Just about. Thank you, sir. I can only repay in kind, I'm afraid.'

'Eggs from your hens and vegetables from your garden will suffice.'

'We shall not be with you much longer, ma'am,' Mr Ross added firmly. 'Shall we, Father?'

The sergeant shrugged wordlessly.

Quinta was anxious to be rid of the responsibility of carrying the money and asked, 'Mother, shall you take the rent to Farmer Bilton now?'

'Yes, my dear, in a few minutes.'

'Your mother is tired, Miss Quinta,' the sergeant said. 'Can you not walk across the field for her?'

'Not on her own!' Laura protested. 'She's not going to Bilton Farm on her own!'

The sergeant responded, 'Of course not, ma'am. Patrick will go with her and we shall rest while they are gone.'

'Oh, would you, my dear? I am quite exhausted.'

Quinta took the pouch and set off briskly. She wanted to get this over quickly: to pay Farmer Bilton his rent and tell him not to bother her any more. Mr Ross soon caught up with her and fell silently into step.

The sergeant found a bank of dry grass that faced the setting sun and covered it with an empty sack. He leaned heavily on his crutch and held out his hand. 'Take a nap, if you wish, Mrs Haig.'

'Thank you, sir, but be assured I shall not sleep, not after the incident in town.' However, she took hold of his roughened hand and lowered herself awkwardly to the ground.

'You'll be quite safe. I shall look out for you.'

'You are a gentleman, Sergeant Ross. I have not been to market in a while and it has taken its toll on my strength.' She lay back and closed her eyes, grateful for the springy turf beneath her aching back.

'It has been a long day for us all,' the sergeant replied. 'But the sun's rays over the distant hills lift the spirits. It was the memory of evenings like this that kept me going through the worst of my injuries.'

'There were others as well as your leg?'

'Oh yes indeed. My scars are healed. But my leg is a constant reminder that I almost died. And there were times when I wished I had.'

'Oh, surely not?'

'I pulled through eventually, and the war was over and my – my sweetheart had been taken home along with her father's regiment. My battle injuries had been judged fatal and they had left me to die in a French monastery.'

'How dreadful for you.'

'I don't remember most of it. But when I did show signs of recovery, I was nursed like a newborn until my strength returned. And then I was angry.'

'Angry? But you had lived!'

'The army had been my life for so many years and I was too crippled to be a soldier.'

'Had you not had enough of fighting?'

'It had had enough of me. That was the hardest medicine to take. But I had time to think. It was a whole year before I was well enough to travel to England. I had two ambitions: to find my lost sweetheart and to marry her.'

'Did you succeed?'

'Not quite.'

She must have found another, Laura thought, believing him to be dead, and said sympathetically, wondering where Patrick's mother was, 'You have a son to be proud of, sir.'

'It took me years to find him and then it was not a happy reunion,' he said dourly. He gazed across the rolling hills at distant red rays lighting up the evening clouds and stayed silent for a long time. Finally he went on: 'Her father was an officer. She did not tell him that I wished to wed her, or that we had been lovers on the eve of the battle. As her parents danced at the Duchess of Richmond's ball she consented to become my wife and we could no longer resist the love we had for each other. Nor did we wish to. After the victory at Waterloo, he told her I was dead and took her back to Ireland to marry one of their own, one of their Irish gentry.'

'I'm so sorry.'

It was such an inadequate thing to say, but he seemed to appreciate it and answered, 'So am I. She was with child. My child. My son.'

'Your Patrick? Then you found her eventually?'

'It was eight years before I knew he existed and another two before I tracked him down in Ireland. When her parents discovered she was with child, they had her locked away in a convent. No one would tell me where she was, or even acknowledge the existence of a child. When I did find her, I could not get near to her. The local militia would have shot me. But my army pay served me well. It loosened a few tongues and I found out what had happened to my son.'

'And?'

'He had been farmed out to some poor Irish crofters who treated him like an animal. He was half starved and I was so horrified when I saw the squalor he was living in, I cried. He was ten years old! I told him I was his father and whether he believed it or not he came away with me without a backward glance.'

'Anyone can tell you are father and son just by looking at you.'

'Patrick did not know that. He had never seen himself in a glass. I got him out of there and across the Irish Sea as fast as I could and we have been together ever since. I had money and learning from my soldiering. I taught him all I knew as we travelled and he grew tall and strong. When my knee failed, Patrick supported me. He worked and he learned more from his masters. We were five years on a farm in the North Riding, but I always hankered to come back to the South Riding, to come home.'

'It is no longer the pleasant place of your childhood memories, sir. Smoke and dirt scar it. There is more sin. You heard what happened to me and there was an earlier incident with my Quinta in the marketplace today. I'm not letting her go there ever again,' she finished.

'These manufacturing towns grow more like London every year. The King and his followers set such a bad example. Do you know how many offspring he has sired? And not one of them with his lawful wife!'

'The rich must be the same all over. I know. I was a servant at the Hall before I married.'

Sergeant Ross ran his gnarled hands through his iron-grey hair. 'You know, Mrs Haig, she is a pretty one to be sure, that girl of yours. You should get her wed before any serious trouble befalls her. Has no one offered for her yet?'

'That's not your business, sir,' she answered sharply.

'Sorry, ma'am. I didn't mean to interfere. I was thinking of her safety, that's all. And yours. It's a tough life for any woman without a man to take care of her.'

'You don't have to tell me that.' Laura was angry because he was right. She did not want her child to lose her innocence yet, but Quinta was a grown woman now and Laura had noticed herself the glances she attracted from gentlemen. She was ready for marriage; if only there was a handsome young suitor to wed her instead of grimy old Farmer Bilton. The sergeant did not respond, so Laura added, 'You are right, sir. She has had an offer, but he is not suitable. He did not love her, neither did she love him.'

'The gentry have never let that get in the way of a good match. If there is respect and consideration, love will come later.'

'You did not choose that path, Sergeant Ross,' Laura pointed out.

'No, ma'am.'

'Me neither.'

'But my son suffered. So did I.'

'I didn't. I had a devoted husband and I wish my daughter to have the same.'

'I sincerely hope she does,' he replied before falling silent.

Chapter 8

'Who's there? Show yourselves. I have a shotgun and I'll use it if I have to.'

She heard the voice from the rear of the farmhouse. As she approached Bilton Farm, Quinta's stomach was already rumbling with hunger and the smell of roasting mutton in the air made her feel even weaker.

'It's me, Farmer Bilton. It's Quinta Haig with your rent.'

Mr Ross had walked in silence for most of the way. She rounded the corner of the building to where the kitchen sash window had been thrown wide open and a rickety wooden table stood on rough ground by the duck pond. The table was covered with the remains of what appeared to have been a substantial meal and Quinta eyed the leftovers enviously. Hens were pecking at the grass around the table legs and four geese began screaming and cackling at them as soon as they arrived. Mr Ross shooed them away. He did it so easily and naturally that Quinta thought he must have been brought up on a farm.

There were five around the table. Farmer Bilton, Seth his bent old farmhand and three ill-dressed dirty individuals that,

Quinta guessed, were farm labourers who slept in the barn. Three oil lamps lit up their faces in a ghoulish way. They were all the worse for ale or cider.

'I'll just take the money over to him,' she whispered, hitching up her skirt to reach her purse.

Mr Ross put a hand on her arm. 'Stay here. Give me the rent money and I'll put it on the table for you.'

'You don't have to.'

'I think I do. Look at them!'

Reluctantly, Quinta handed over her leather pouch.

'I have your rent, sir,' he said loudly, 'from Mrs Haig.'

Farmer Bilton put down his metal tankard. 'Who are you?'

'My name is Ross, sir.'

The farmer twisted in his carver chair and looked him over carefully. When he spoke his speech was slurred. 'Oh aye, I see you now, one of the travellers; you and the crippled old man. Poachers an' all, I'll wager. I've heard a gun go off on the moor. I'll have the constable on to you if I catch you on my land. Where's the maid, then? Where's the maid from Top Field?'

'Do you mean me, sir?' Quinta came forward.

'Stay where you are, miss.' Mr Ross placed himself squarely between her and Farmer Bilton.

'Get out of the way, you upstart!'

'No, sir, I shall not. You are in no fit state to greet a lady.'

'And who do you think you are to pass comment on me?' Farmer Bilton demanded.

'I have told you, sir.'

'A traveller? Ross, you say? Scots? Irish? A navvy, I'll be bound.'

'My father was soldier, sir.'

'Aye, an' we all know where they come from. Workhouses and prisons. Scum of the earth!'

'He was a gamekeeper's lad here in the Riding, sir.'

But Noah Bilton wasn't interested. He stretched awkwardly in his chair. 'Where's the maid, I said? Bring her round to where I can see her.' He held out a wavering arm in Quinta's direction.

'Stay where you are, miss,' Mr Ross urged. He dropped the pouch of coins on the table and added, 'You have your rent, sir. Good night.'

But as he walked away there was a crash and the rattling of knives and dishes as Farmer Bilton brought his tankard down heavily on to the wooden table.

'*You dare to defy me when you are on my land! I said bring the maid to me now!*' he yelled.

'Don't fret, Mr Ross,' Quinta said urgently. 'I'll just say good night to him and then we'll leave.' She nipped past him before he could stop her and stood in front of Farmer Bilton, wondering how she could have been so stupid as to think she might become his wife. He was a boorish, drunken oaf. Mother was right. Who would be desperate enough to wed him?

'You'll find it's all there, sir.'

He loosened the lacing and tipped the coins on to the table, counting them slowly before letting out a harsh grunt.

'And I shall find work during the harvest so you will have your Michaelmas rent, too, when it is due.'

'It's not right,' he growled. 'You working on other folks' land while mine lies fallow. I want a man at Top Field, tilling my land. I will have it back, I say. I will!'

'Please don't turn us out, sir.'

Farmer Bilton must have picked up her beseeching tone because he went quiet for a minute and looked steadily at her. 'Your mother knows what to do about that, my lass. And so do you.'

Quinta looked down at her feet. She hadn't totally understood what was going on when he offered for her. But she did now. Her mother had been so right about him. He did not care for her. He wished only to use her as he did his breeding stock. He was a horrible man.

'Are you hungry, lass?'

Quinta eyed the remnants of the meal: the leg of mutton, dish of peas and a crusty cottage loaf probably from the Hall kitchen, a bowl of stewed gooseberries and pitcher of cream from his dairy. It was so thick that the drips around the side were congealing before they could slide to the table. There was cheese, too, and flagons of ale and cider. She was unable to stop her mouth watering and she swallowed; twice. 'No, sir,' she lied, 'and I have to get home before nightfall.'

'You've plenty of time, then. It's Midsummer. Look at this.' He picked up a horn-handled carving knife with shreds of meat and juices smeared across its blade, leaned forward and hacked a chunk off the cooling joint. He speared the meat with the knife point and thrust it at her. 'Take it. Best in the Riding.' When she remained still he moved the morsel nearer to her face. '*Eat it,*' he ordered.

The juices ran down the blade and it smelled delicious. She was hungry but feared the way Farmer Bilton was brandishing his knife and her mouth became dry. She wished she had listened to Mr Ross and kept away from the table. The knife blade was very close to her chin and he kept moving it towards her in short jabs that were unfriendly and intimidating. He was a horrid man and she wanted to be as far away from him as she could. She put up both her hands as though to protect herself from the blade but did not know how to take the meat without cutting her fingers.

Her left hand grasped his knuckles to still his hand and it did. Quite suddenly. He leaned forward in the light and Quinta saw that his dark eyes were bloodshot. She had not seen him behave this way before. He was sober and deferential in church and always bowed his head to the ladies and his betters. Now he was drunk and demanding and he frightened her.

Hesitatingly, she wrestled the meat from the knife point with her other hand and bit off a small amount. She grimaced as she tried to chew it without saliva. But it was, as he said, juicy and tender. She swallowed hastily to push it down her throat as fast as she could and felt it move through every inch of her gullet until it sat like a lump of stone in her stomach.

He smiled at her, but to Quinta it was more of a sneer, a triumphant sneer. 'There's plenty more where that came from. Think on it, lass. Meat and drink on the table every day. You talk to that mother of yours about my offer.'

'She won't change her mind.'

'Won't she?' he scoffed. 'Well, you tell that high and mighty madam her rent goes up from Michaelmas.'

'You can't do that!'

'Can't? Who says I can't? It's my land and I can increase the rent when I like.' He slid the coins into his pocket and shoved the pouch towards her. 'Don't you forget that when you talk to her. I will have my way. You see if I don't.' He tipped back his head to swallow the last of his ale and then slumped forward on to the table. His silent companions stared at her. She shivered. To think she had seriously considered his offer. She felt a tug on her sleeve.

'Come along, miss. It's getting late.' Mr Ross was actually pulling her away.

'Good night, sir,' she said politely.

Farmer Bilton raised his head and lifted his tankard. 'More ale, Seth,' he growled.

'Hurry, miss.' Mr Ross was striding quickly and she stumbled to keep up. But he held her arm firmly, so she had to. 'He's drunk. Couldn't you see that?'

'Well, yes, but he is our landlord.'

'I don't care who he is. Didn't your mother teach you to keep away from drunken men?'

'Yes,' she muttered. 'Can you please slow down?'

'Not yet,' he snapped.

But he did, eventually, and Quinta was quite out of breath. 'Sit here a while.' He gestured to a dry-stone wall.

'Why are you so angry with me?'

'I'm not.'

'You're clenching your fists.'

He opened his fingers immediately. 'I'm angry with him.' He tossed his head in the direction of Bilton Farm. 'Did you see those poor wretches at his table?'

'You mean the ones sharing his mutton?' she challenged.

He laughed harshly. 'Well, they're grown men so he can't get away with starving them. If he beats them they could beat him back.'

'Why would he beat them?'

'His sort doesn't need a reason, but stealing food would be enough.'

'Stealing anything, I should think. Were you beaten as a child?'

He didn't answer at first, until she asked, 'Were you in the workhouse?'

He laughed again, without humour. 'That would have been preferable for me. Do you know what fresh baked bread smells like to a starving boy who had been up since dawn lifting well water and mucking out horses? I was only allowed leftover bread. If there were no stale crusts I starved, so I used to eat the horse's oat mash because if I took anything from the kitchen, I was whipped.'

Quinta frowned and her mouth turned down at the corners. 'You had to steal food?'

'I didn't think it was stealing. They were supposed to feed me.'

'Where was that?'

'A hovel in Ireland where I was farmed out when I was born. The English bastard, they called me; fit only for the stables. I slept there, too, in the hayloft. And in winter I had to risk spending the night among the hooves and droppings in the stalls to stop myself freezing to death.'

'How cruel! And how awful for you! Were you there for long?'

'Ten years; I only remember about half of them. I remember

the guv'nor, though. He was like your Farmer Bilton, coarse, selfish and surly. He always carried a horsewhip and I'd get it across my back or legs for no reason except to remind me what it felt like in case I forgot. I was no better then a slave!' He stopped suddenly and his voice was quieter when he said, 'Come on, we'd better get moving.'

Quinta jumped down from the wall. 'I'm sorry. It must have been dreadful, growing up like that.'

He shrugged. 'I knew no other life. But I had a strong instinct for survival and grew cunning. I planned from an early age to run away. I might have become a genuine vagabond if my father hadn't found me and put me straight. I try to forget it these days, but the way Farmer Bilton behaved just now brought it all back to me.'

'I haven't seen him drunk before. He likes his own way but I never thought he'd increase our rent like that. He might change his mind in the morning. I hope so, because Mother can't afford it as it is.'

'That won't stop him. No one can deny that your land is worth a good rent and with the price of food rising, he has a point. He's not a gentleman, though, even if he is your land-lord. And he seemed to have more than a passing interest in you. Does he have a wife?'

'Mother thinks that nobody will have him in spite of his wealth. Leastways, none of the women around here would live in his squalid farmhouse.'

'He talked of an offer he'd made to your mother.'

Quinta hesitated, wondering how much more to tell him and eventually added, 'Mother thought she might housekeep for him at one time.'

'Seems like a good idea. He might attract a wife then. What happened?'

'She didn't like his terms. She's a proud woman, my mother.'

'I see.' He frowned. At least he thought he did and guessed that a brutish man like Farmer Bilton might not bother with a wife and expect more than housekeeping duties from an attractive widow like Mrs Haig. 'I'm sure that was for the best. She probably knows him better than you do. He's coarse and selfish. Not gentry either. How did he get the farm in the first place?'

'It was entailed and the only direct heir was killed in one of the battles in Spain before Waterloo. So it came to him. We're told he's a distant cousin through the female line. She married beneath herself and had a son, so he inherited. He comes from Derbyshire, I think. He's a good farmer though. Everybody says so.'

'Well, your holding is small in comparison to his. But if it was worked well it would support a decent rent.' He hesitated. 'I'm sorry. I didn't mean to be rude. The two of you do your best.'

'When Father was alive we kept a milking cow and made hay for her winter feed. I remember a bullock once and sheep on the pasture. Father's beasts always fetched a good price at the market.' She sighed. 'I'll have to find work. There'll be a hiring fair on Lammas Day when the harvest starts.'

'And leave your mother here alone?'

'They'll have to take both of us. What else can I do? If we don't give Farmer Bilton his dues, he'll turn us out.'

'Your mother isn't well.'

'I know. She's never had a cough that lingered so. If only she could throw it off.'

'I talked to the apothecary about her. My father asked me to. He learned much about ailments during his soldiering. I have a strong mixture that will help her.'

'Thank you, Mr Ross. I am grateful to you.' She meant it. It was the longest conversation she had had with him and she realised that he was articulate and educated, as well as being a good farmer. But he had had a difficult childhood which, by his own admission, had set him on the road to becoming a vagabond and she wondered how much of that cunning remained. She fell silent again until they approached their parents.

'Please do not speak of Farmer Bilton's behaviour. Mother worries so,' Quinta whispered.

'Very well,' he replied. 'You must tell her of the rent increase, though.'

'Tomorrow, when she is rested.'

'Will you walk and talk with me, miss? It will make the last stretch home bearable,' the sergeant asked as he struggled to his feet. 'If your mother has no objection?'

'Of course, sir.' Quinta would rather have stayed by her mother's side, but as Laura seemed to approve of the arrangement, she felt obliged to agree. They moved slowly as Laura was weary and the sergeant's leg pained him.

'It was generous of you to give us all the kindling money, sir,' she said.

'Not at all. It is your wood.'

'And your son's labour.'

'Which pays for our rent of your cowshed.'

Quinta did not argue. She understood only too well the value of such a bargain. And she had learned today that town-folk were ready to pay well for all their produce. This had surprised her at first as they could just as easily grow vegetables for themselves, and many did so in their long narrow gardens. But there were lodging houses and inns to supply as well, and she reflected that life in the town was very different from Top Field. She wasn't sure she agreed with her mother about not going to market any more.

'Can you read and write, miss?' the sergeant asked.

'Oh yes. My father learned how from the vicar when he was a lad. He taught my mother and me. We have a Bible indoors and story books, too. We read them to each other on summer evenings. Then in the winter, when it's dark, we try and remember the stories and talk about them after the candles have burned down. Father had books on animal husbandry, too, but Mother isn't interested in that.'

'Are you?'

'Yes, I am. I do what I can on the farm. But there is the indoor work as well and Mother can't do so much these days. When Father was alive, we kept a cow, you know, and made cheese from the milk and grew turnips and barley to feed her.'

'You have no hankering to live in town?'

'Not really. Though I did envy one or two of the young ladies I saw there. They wore such pretty bonnets. Like the ladies at the Hall wear to church. I do so like a trimmed bonnet for Sundays.'

Progress was slow. Even Mr Ross slowed down before they reached Top Field. It was dark when they arrived but the night air cooled their tired, heated heads. He helped Quinta to unload their supplies and carry them to the cottage. Mrs Haig picked up a basket and sagged against the cart to gather her strength.

'I'll check the hens,' Quinta yawned.

'No, I'll do that tonight,' Mr Ross volunteered. 'And see to them in the morning for you. Take your mother indoors, miss.'

'Thank you kindly, sir.' Laura turned to his father. 'You have a fine son there, Sergeant Ross.'

'Aye, I do that. Good night, ma'am. Miss Quinta.' He limped towards the cowshed.

In the kitchen, Laura flopped on a chair. 'Oh, my feet! Light a candle, dear, while I take off my boots. Is there any water?'

'Plenty. We'll wash off the dust before bed. Bring the candle to the scullery when you're ready.'

Quinta poured some cold water into a bowl in the stone sink and splashed it over her hands and face, enjoying the refreshing cold. She dried herself with a square of old bed-linen. 'Shall I bring the bowl through for you, Mother?' she called.

'Oh, would you? I don't think I can get out of this chair for a minute or two.'

Quinta took some clean linen and held the bowl while her mother washed her hands and face. Then she placed it on the floor and said, 'Put your feet in there. It'll cool them off.'

Laura leaned back in her chair and sighed. 'What a gentleman that Sergeant Ross has turned out to be. We were indeed lucky when he happened by our little farm and wanted to stay in the cowshed.'

'His son is anxious to move on.'

'He told me they were trying to reach town, but his father's leg was too swollen. The sergeant has to see the surgeon himself. I believe his knee is very painful now. Too painful.'

'What do you mean?'

'His son has bought him laudanum from the Dispensary.'

'He got medicine for your cough too, Mother.'

'Yes, he explained about it as we walked. There is plenty of work Mr Ross can do round here to pay for their lodging while his father gets well. I might ask him to do more for us. What do you think?'

'We agreed only until Midsummer to pay our rent. Farmer Bilton does not approve of them. He thinks they're poachers, or worse.'

'Well, we've paid our dues to him so I don't care what he thinks,' Laura responded crossly.

'Of course you do, Mother! He's our landlord.' Quinta washed and dried her mother's aching feet, massaged her legs and eased on her felt slippers. 'The sergeant is very charming, I grant you, but he is a stranger and we don't know anything about him apart from what he has told us. As for his son, well, he – he barely says a word. I don't think we can trust him.'

'He suffered hardship as a child.' Laura told her what the sergeant had said. 'I believe him, dear. If he was lying he wouldn't have admitted that his own son was a – a – well, you know.'

'A bastard?'

'Quinta! Where on earth did you hear that word?'

'He – Mr Ross – told me a little about his childhood.'

'The sergeant said his mother was gentry.'

'I don't believe him. They're travellers, Mother. We shouldn't let them stay any longer.'

She thought her mother would agree and was surprised when she defended them. 'But they aren't gypsies, dear.'

'They could be footpads or anything.'

'They would have stolen from us by now if they were.'

'Well, there's nothing to steal here and the sergeant is weak. He's just resting up to gather his strength to move on. Tell them to leave, Mother. I'll feel safer when they've gone.'

'I feel safer with them here.'

'Mother?'

'That ruffian in town was dressed up like a gentleman, but he was a real bad lot, Quinta. If the furnaces and manufactories in town are attracting that sort we need some protection. What if he had followed us home? There's no constable out here.'

Quinta agreed. 'I wish Father were here,' she said.

Laura reached out for her hand. 'But he isn't, dear. The sergeant is no deterrent to any roving vagrants, but the sight of Mr Ross about the place might be.'

They stared at each other in silence until Laura said, 'Was Farmer Bilton pleased to get his rent?'

Quinta was relieved to be talking of something else, but it was not cheering news for her mother. 'Not really. He says he's putting it up next quarter day. I think he means it. I'll have to find work, or he'll turn us out.'

Her mother heaved a sigh.

'He said I should talk to you about his offer.'

'For you? Never!'

Quinta now agreed wholeheartedly with her mother about this and shivered. She could no more wed that dreadful old man than she could paint her face like a young woman she saw in the marketplace.

'Don't fret, Mother. The Hall will take me on for the harvest.'

I might even find a sweetheart, she thought. How wonderful, if she were courted by a respectable young man from the village! If Mother approved she could meet his family at church and walk out with him on Sunday afternoon. Mother would make tea and scones for when he visited . . .

She stopped dreaming. The men who came to work on the harvest were itinerant labourers like those at Farmer Bilton's table earlier that evening. She took her mother's hands and pulled her to her feet. 'Come on. It's time for bed. Will you take a little of your new medicine tonight?'

Refreshed and clean, they went upstairs. Although Quinta was tired out, she lay awake thinking of the future. Going out to work might be an answer. But she would not be able to keep the garden going, and the farm would deteriorate further. Even if she could pay him at Michaelmas, Farmer Bilton would have a sound reason to evict them and any countryman would agree. With the price of food rising, it was their duty to get the best out of their land.

Quinta was sure her mother was right to refuse Farmer Bilton's offer. She was not so sure as her mother about their lodgers in the cowshed. The sergeant was affable enough but his son, by his own admission, was cunning and this made her wary. He was withdrawn and aloof, communicated only when asked and gave the minimum of information.

It was as though he had no feelings. The only time she had seen a spark of real anger was when faced with Farmer Bilton's uncouth behaviour. Now she knew about his birthright and his childhood she wondered if that was the reason. She did not know what it was like to be treated so cruelly. If he were to be believed, the poor orphans in the workhouse had a better life than the one endured by Mr Ross when he was a child. There was something unknown about him that, Quinta acknowledged to herself again, made her cautious; something dark and dangerous that frightened her.

However, there was no doubt that he could farm and he had some education . . . She stared at the blackness, irritated by the way he intruded into her thoughts.

Chapter 9

When Patrick joined his father in the cowshed, he was sitting on the ground, leaning against a wooden stall. A candle stuck on a log was burning low.

'Not asleep yet?'

His father held a spirit flask in his hand. 'I need this to dull the pain first. Come and sit awhile. I want to talk to you.'

Patrick sat on the log and unlaced his boots. 'One of your serious talks, is this?'

'It is. Did you sell the pearls?'

He reached under his jacket for a leather pouch of coins. 'Feel the weight of this. Jewels were easier to carry around.'

'Aye, that's why I bought them in the first place.'

'Well, this amount of gold is heavy.'

'I'm going to need it, son. This leg of mine is bad. What did they say at the Dispensary?'

'The town is well provided with medical men. It has a physician and a surgeon. The surgeon will be able to help you. He was an officer in one of the King's regiments.'

'Oh? Which one?'

'The apothecary told me he was with the Sixty-fifth. He

saw service in India and Arabia. But his wife died and he came home. He resigned his commission and settled in the Riding to continue his calling.'

'This is good news. He will know what to do.'

'The apothecary expected me to bring him to see you.'

'Not here. I'll go into town as I planned.'

'It's a long way but there's a carrier cart from the village.'

'I'll keep the laudanum for that journey.'

Patrick frowned. 'He said you shouldn't delay. You haven't been honest with me about how bad it is. Is that why you were so keen to rest here?'

'I'd like to have reached town.'

'I'll get you there, Father, even if I have to carry you on my back.'

'It won't come to that. And Top Field has much to offer.'

'They're decent folk, I grant you. But this place is slowly dying.'

'You can turn it round for them, son.'

'There's no future for them in that. They won't be able to keep it going when we move on.'

'Well, I won't be moving on from the South Riding. That's what I want to talk to you about. This travelling life is too much for me now.'

'The surgeon said he could help you! It'll take time to heal but—'

'Listen to me, son. We've had the best of times together since I found you and I am proud of the man you have become. But I have to stop now. You can go on, though, if you want to.'

'I'm not leaving you. If your roots are in the South Riding then mine are, too. I'll find work in these parts.'

'You could stay here.'

'They can't afford a hired man. Anyway, the landlord wants them out.'

'Aye. Mrs Haig was telling me. I can see why. They're not making the best of it.'

94

'Well, be fair, Father. The girl is strong enough but the widow is too old to work the land.'

'I reckon her bloom had already gone when she bore the child.'

'She carries herself well, though.'

'Aye, she does.'

Patrick wondered just how interested his father was in Mrs Haig. 'She's sick, Father. That cough of hers . . .'

'Aye, I know, and she only has the one daughter to care for her. A pretty young thing, though, don't you think?'

Patrick glanced at his father. He agreed but didn't say so. The short time he'd been in the Riding had shown him that many country girls of her age had a freshness and vitality that attracted him. Not so in the town, he thought. They were worn down by the smoke and the dirt and disease that were prevalent there.

'Isn't she?' his father pressed.

Patrick made a positive sound in his throat and nodded.

'I – I've seen the way you look at her, son.'

He detected a questioning tone in his father's voice that he took to be a warning. His father always behaved respectfully towards any woman they met on the road, and he expected his son to do the same. 'She's safe with me,' he responded quickly. 'Miss Quinta is still a maid and a decent, hard-working lass. She's not like Mary-Ann was when we were on the canals, flaunting herself before me all the time.'

'Aye, well, Mary-Ann did all the chasing for you. And she should have told you she was already wed.'

'Yes, she should,' Patrick muttered bitterly. He had had a narrow escape. Her husband would have killed him when he got back from the coast. 'I won't touch Miss Quinta, I promise you.'

'She has that same look about her as Mary-Ann. Dark hair and fresh-faced. Pretty, too and, well, very womanly for a young lass.'

Patrick gave a low laugh. 'You don't have to tell me that. I have eyes.'

'And a lust for her, I'll wager.'

'I've told you. I shall not approach her.'

'But do you want to? The blood in your veins is as red as mine was at your age.'

Patrick considered how well his father knew him and replied, 'We're leaving soon. There'll be distractions enough for me in town.' But as he said it, he realised he didn't want to go anywhere near the girls in town, with their rouged cheeks and matted hair.

'That's not what I'm thinking of, son.'

'Well, what are you getting at?'

'Do you think that you could wed her?'

'What?' he spluttered. 'Me? Wed Miss Quinta? How much of that spirit have you drunk?'

'You could work this farm and hire yourself out as a game-keeper's lad as well. You'd have a home for when I'm finished.'

'What do you mean, "when you're finished"?' His father did not reply and he added, 'What are you not telling me about your leg?'

'My knee won't mend now. It's the end of the road for me.'

'We'll settle here, then, in the South Riding, where you were born. It's as good as anywhere to put down roots.'

'Top Field would suit you well, son.'

'Suit me? This is about you, not me, and we are far from town.'

'It would be a decent home for both of us.'

'So you want me to wed to give us a home? Getting wed is more than just settling somewhere,' Patrick retaliated sharply.

'Aye, it is, and I wouldn't want you to wed if you don't want to.'

'Well, I don't want to. Not yet awhile anyway.'

'Then we'll move on into the town and find lodgings there.'

But Patrick knew his father felt the same about town-living as he did. 'You'd prefer to stay out here though, wouldn't you?'

'Aye, I would. A bracing wind and a snug byre beat the smoke and smells of manufactories any day.'

Patrick agreed. Although, even if they stayed, they would be out by Michaelmas. The rent would be too much for the widow unless she put the land to better use. He wondered where they would go. Perhaps they had kin to take them in. Winter months were always hard for them, too, especially his father. That's when his leg troubled him most. And it was getting worse, so they'd better move nearer to town while the roads were easy to travel. He said, 'The surgeon advised you not to delay in going to see him.'

'This rest is taking down the swelling. It's only five or six weeks to the harvesting and you'll easily get work then. There's bound to be a Lammas Day hiring fair somewhere.'

'You really want to stay?'

'If the widow has no objection.'

'But why?'

'I've told you. The maid.'

'Oh no, Father.' He shook his head wearily.

'You're not understanding me, son. I know what's wrong with my knee. There's poison in it. My only chance will be for the surgeon to cut it open and take out the pus.'

Patrick's face contorted in despair and he groaned.

'At least the pain will be easier afterwards. But it'll take most of our gold, especially with the looking-after that I'll need.'

'Well, it's a good use of our money, I'd say.'

'There won't be much left for you.'

'I don't need it, I can work. Anyway, I'll take care of you.'

His father shook his head. 'You've got to think about your own future now. I don't want you staying on the road.'

'I like this life.'

'With the two of us, aye. But you won't like it when you're on your own.'

It was not something Patrick wanted to think about. But when he recalled the labourers he'd seen at Farmer Bilton's table he wondered if he might end up like those wretches: worked like animals and treated worse by their masters. The memories of his ill treatment as a child had not faded and he knew how cruel both men and women could be to those they despised.

'There are coal mines and ironworks round here if you've a fancy for them,' his father suggested.

'They're not for me. I need the open sky and the wind in my face.'

'You're my lad, all right. Not that I ever doubted it as soon as I saw you. But what you need to look to now, son, is respectability. If you're to settle in the Riding, you must be accepted and trusted by folk that live here. You don't want to be an outsider.'

'I can deal with it.'

'But I don't want that for you, not for the rest of your life. You'll soon be one and twenty, my lad, and able to control your own life. I want to see you set up for the future and you could do it here. You could have this farm in healthy profit within a five-year, if you're blessed by the seasons.'

'I know that.' He covered his eyes with the heels of his hands.

'Do you know, also, how hard it is to get your name on a tenancy like this one? It's the chance of a lifetime and it's fallen into your lap.'

'Not quite. You can't be certain the landlord will approve of me.'

'Or that the widow would either, unless . . .'

'. . . the daughter will wed me. You really want that, don't you?'

His father took a swig from his spirit flask. 'She's a bonny lass. I thought you might have welcomed such an attachment.'

'Any red-blooded man would. But to wed her, Father, on such a brief acquaintance? A wife is for life. You taught me that yourself. You're asking too much of me.'

'Aye, maybe I am. I am thinking of myself, and of ending my days here.'

Patrick gazed at his father. 'You've come to the South Riding to – to *die*?'

He half laughed. 'Not yet awhile, son.' Then he became serious. 'I dreamed of these gentle hills, you know. In the war, in the mountains of Portugal and Spain when the sun baked the rocks hot enough to fry eggs, I dreamed of the soft rain on my face in summer and the wind whipping across the moor in winter.' He took another swig of his spirit.

After a pensive silence, Patrick ventured: 'How can you be so sure that Miss Quinta will want to wed me, anyway?'

'I can't, and neither can you. But a faint heart never did win a fair maiden.'

This made Patrick smile. 'Why don't you ask the widow to wed you instead?'

'Wed me? A cripple? And have the prospect of you bringing another wife into their home? I should not let you do that to them. If we stay it's the daughter or no one for you.'

'Perhaps no one is better than a tie without affection.'

'Well, I should not want you to wed her without having affection for her. Although the gentry marry their offspring for gain all the time and make many a happy match.'

'And many an unhappy one, too.'

'Aye, I know, but this one is your sort of lass.'

'What's my sort of lass, then?'

'Miss Quinta. Dark-haired, fair-skinned and comely.'

Patrick had to agree and kept silent.

'Sharp-witted, too; more so than her mother. Why don't you sleep on the notion, son? This is good land and you could do a lot worse than Miss Quinta for a bride.'

Patrick lay awake thinking about her for most of the night. Since Mary-Ann he had been more careful where he cast his eye. Indeed he had not searched for female companionship of late. His concerns had been with finding food and shelter for his father as they made their way to this part of the Riding.

But he admitted to himself he had noticed Miss Quinta from the shelter of the woods before he saw the cowshed. He had lingered, covertly, and watched her fetch water, hack away at the fallen tree and labour in her garden. He thought she had noticed him in the woods when the donkey was despatched.

His father was perceptive. Were she older and not a maid he would have considered a dalliance with her. But Miss Quinta was innocent in the ways of men and, yes, his father was accurate in his assessment that she would make him, indeed any man, a good wife. It's just that he was not ready to wed. Not yet. His father would understand that when he told him in the morning.

The following dawn was bright and sunny. Quinta and her mother were exhausted from their journey to town; neither stirred to see it. Clouds were gathering, blotting out a sun already high when Quinta rose, feeling refreshed but achy from the long walk. She dressed quickly and went downstairs to get the fire going. Within an hour the rain began to fall. Relentlessly. She wrapped a shawl around her head to fetch water from the stream and opened the scullery door to see two pailfuls, already waiting for her. Between them nestled a clutch of hen's eggs wrapped in a piece of old sacking.

A smile of gratitude lit her features, quickly followed by a suspicious frown. She glanced towards the cowshed, but it was closed up and the fire outside long extinguished by the downpour.

'You will ask them to leave today, won't you, Mother?' she urged as she began stripping the fat off the skirt of beef to render in a tin dish by the fire.

Her mother was taking the meat that was left and cutting it into pieces. She had already sliced up the ox kidney and put it in vinegar to sweeten. 'The ground will be nice and soft after this downpour. I think I'll ask Mr Ross to turn over some of the pasture for garden. It's not too late to put in more roots for the winter.'

'They'll be lodging with us until August for doing that!' Quinta exclaimed.

'A boiled pudding and a wheaten loaf should take care of the payment. Then they can go as soon as he's done.'

Quinta chewed on her lip. It was a sensible suggestion, but her mother was too well disposed to the travellers for her comfort. She wanted to see them on their way today. However, she put her misgivings aside to enjoy their day together, kneading and baking bread dough, rendering dripping, stewing beef with kidney and boiling puddings for their pantry.

Her day was marred only by the sight of Farmer Bilton riding into their yard on his big black hunter. She heard the horse whinny and watched him through the front window. His broad-brimmed hat was pulled well down over his eyes and he wore a large waxed coat to protect him from the rain. It spread out over the horse's rump as he walked it around their yard looking into every corner. But he didn't dismount, or even call them to come out. Eventually, he turned the horse's ahead away and left.

'Just inspecting his property,' Laura commented. 'He should be pleased we have some help at last.'

Quinta didn't think he looked pleased. Perhaps he was frowning against the weather. It was certainly bad today. Good for the potatoes and turnips in their garden, but not so good for his fields of wheat.

By evening the first crusty loaves of bread were cooling on the hearth and two puddings for tea, wrapped in greased calico, hissed as they simmered in boiling water over the fire. The rain eased to a steady, soaking drizzle. Quinta's face was red and shiny from the kitchen fire. 'I'll have to fetch in more wood or we'll have none dry for the morning.'

Laura picked up her shawl. 'I'll go out at the same time to the cowshed and ask about the digging.'

'Wait for me to come with you,' Quinta cautioned.

After a whole day toiling in the heat, the rain felt soft and refreshing on her rosy cheeks and Quinta lifted her chin and opened her mouth to drink in the moisture. Such bliss! She stopped in her tracks to inhale the damp air. Her shawl dropped away from her head as she licked the drops from her lips and closed her eyes. When she opened them, Mr Ross was standing quite still in front of her with his arms full of logs. He had come round the side of the cottage from the lean-to where they stored their wood.

'Oh! I didn't expect to see you!'

He was staring at her seriously and silently and his brow furrowed slightly as he said, 'These are for you. I'll put them by the front door.'

Quinta stared back at him. He was bare-headed and very wet. His thick black hair was flattened on his skull and curled round his cheeks and neck. His tanned wet face had a glow about it that suggested recent toil. He must have been out there, chopping wood in the rain. The damp flush on his cheeks contrasted startlingly with his fiery blue eyes making them intense and jewel-like between the long black lashes. His straight black eyebrows drew closer together.

Her open mouth smiled falteringly. 'Thank you. Mother would like a word with your father. Will you ask him to step outside?'

'Why don't you go inside? Out of the rain.'

'Very well.' She turned. 'Mother?' But her mother was already knocking on the cowshed door. Quinta caught up with her as it opened.

'Mrs Haig! Come along in out of the wet!'

Quinta followed her mother into the dark dwelling. When her eyes had adjusted to the darkness she was surprised at how spruced and clean it was. And tidy. The dust and cobwebs from the rafters and wooden stalls had gone, and the stone walls, where there was no wooden cladding, were lime-washed. Freshly lime-washed! She could smell it still. 'You have done this today!' she exclaimed, looking down at an old pail streaked with lime and water, and an even older brush. Her father's, she guessed.

'But we had no lime to make the wash!' Laura protested.

'My son brought it from the town yesterday. It was in the cart. You have no objection, have you, ma'am?'

'I – I – Why, no. It's just that – well, I am in your debt, sir, and I am here to ask more of you. That is . . . I mean of your son.'

'You owe me nothing, ma'am. I should expect to do this if I paid you rent in the traditional way. What is it you want of my son?'

'Farmer Bilton is going to increase my rent from Michaelmas. I need more of my land turned for garden crops.'

Quinta noticed that this seemed to cheer Sergeant Ross. He didn't smile but his eyes brightened and it made her cross that their bad fortune seemed to play in his favour. He answered, 'My son will oblige you with pleasure, ma'am.'

'Shouldn't you ask him first?' Quinta enquired politely.

'Yes, shouldn't you ask me first, Father? We are planning to move on, are we not?'

Quinta blinked. Mr Ross's voice was by her ear. She hadn't realised he was standing so close behind her and she was aware of his words breezing fiercely across her damp hair. He sounded irritable.

Laura answered. 'Indeed I understand that, sir, which is why I offer victuals in return for your labour. Fresh baked wheaten loaves and meat puddings for you both.'

'Well, that would tempt the most footloose of travellers, ma'am, but this lodging is payment enough for my son's work. I am able to pay for our victuals, ma'am, and I shall.'

'And then you can leave as soon as you wish,' Quinta finished anxiously.

'Yes,' echoed Mr Ross.

'I should like the pasture to be double dug, sir, and ready for sowing.'

'That takes longer, Mother,' Quinta intervened, 'and we should not want the sergeant to delay his journey. I am sure I can rake soil and break down clods as well as any man.'

'Not as quickly though, if I may say so, miss,' Mr Ross commented. 'I'll prepare your ground, Mrs Haig.' He looked directly at his father and added firmly, 'Then we'll be on our way.'

His father waited until mother and daughter had left before responding: 'I am aware that my idea has angered you, but you will be civil to me in front of these ladies.'

'Sorry, Father. But Miss Quinta has made her views about us plain. I believe she wanted to hear what I said.'

'Then you must ease her mind. She will be working in her garden while you are digging and you will be courteous to her. Is that understood?'

'Of course. But there will be little time for social exchange.'

'Make time.'

When Patrick didn't reply, his father added, 'I should like you to think again about Miss Quinta.'

Surprised, Patrick said, 'My concern is for you.'

'Then you should know it is possible that the surgeon will not cut my leg open. He will cut my leg off.'

Patrick swallowed. He covered his eyes with his hand to shield a threatening tear. He was aware of this possibility, though neither had actually talked of it until now. Despair welled in his throat and he couldn't speak.

'Your concern must be for your own future. You have a whole life before you. Think on it, son.'

Chapter 10

The rain had stopped the previous evening and a brisk breeze coupled with the natural drainage of a hill farm enabled Patrick to start turning the pasture the following day. He had worked steadily across the marked-out plot, stopping at the end of the second row to stretch his back, remove his waistcoat and take a ladleful of water from the bucket.

As he walked back to his spade, he noticed Miss Quinta among her rows of vegetables, earthing up potato plants. He stopped to watch her for several minutes and acknowledged a desire rising in his groin. He turned away from his digging and walked towards her. She must have heard him approach yet she continued to concentrate on her task.

'Good morning, Miss Quinta.'

'Good morning, sir.'

Working Top Field reminded him of the happiest five years of his life. From the age of thirteen to eighteen he and his father had laboured together on a farm in the North Riding. They lodged in the farmhouse, ate with the elderly farmer and his wife, and learned animal husbandry and crop growing. They would still be there now if the farmer had not died, his wife taken into an almshouse and the farm sold.

'It's a fine day to be out of doors.'

'Yes, indeed.'

'. . . after yesterday's downpour.'

She carried on raking her soil.

He persevered. 'Your pasture is well drained.'

She glanced sideways at him. 'We are on a hill, Mr Ross.'

'If we are to work alongside each other, will you not call me Patrick?'

'No, sir!' she replied quickly. 'What if Mother heard me?' She carried on heaping the soil into mounds around the potato stems.

He suppressed a sigh. 'The rain will help your potato yield.'

'I hope so.'

He picked up a handful of dirt and tested the texture in his hand. 'The soil under your pasture is as fertile as this.'

'Mother will be pleased.'

'Yes,' he answered ineffectually, and wondered what to say next.

She stopped and straightened. There was a smudge of mud on her brow where she had pushed a straying strand of hair under her cap. 'Did you want anything else, Mr Ross?'

'Would you care to take a walk with me this evening? The sunsets are beautiful to behold.'

Her eyes widened and he thought he must have shocked her. 'No!' she exclaimed. 'I – I mean, thank you, Mr Ross, I cannot. I must help Mother with the chores.' She bent to carry on with her gardening.

Patrick shook his head in exasperation and turned away. Miss Quinta was a dutiful daughter and very close to her mother, who had no doubt warned her against him. But she knew her own mind and clearly it didn't include a friendship with him. Perhaps she thought as most others did, and viewed him as a vagrant or poacher. He was aware of a rising annoyance that this should be so, and returned to his digging to attack the soil with more vigour.

At the end of the day, after stripping to the waist and sluicing himself at the water butt, he shared one of Mrs Haig's meat puddings with his father by their camp fire outside the cowshed.

'You've made a good start on the new plot.'

'The soil is easy to dig. Fertile, too.'

'You can make a go of this farm, son. It's been well run until recent times and it is worth the extra rent. Show that brute of a farmer what you can do with his land.'

'And wed Miss Quinta,' Patrick commented.

'Is that such a hardship for you?'

Patrick recalled watching her at work in her garden with the gentle breeze riffling her skirts and thought that it would not be. He said, 'No. I think the burden would be with her.'

'I saw you talking together earlier today.'

'I opened a conversation with her. She closed it.'

'Try again. Give her time to get used to the idea.'

He shook his head emphatically. 'She is not interested in me, even as an acquaintance. I am a traveller not to be trusted and nothing will change that.'

'She is young, and a little frightened of you, I think.'

'Frightened of me? Surely not?'

'Have patience with her. She is not Mary-Ann.'

Patrick let out an impatient cry. 'How can you talk of the two in the same breath? She is nothing like that trollop. Quinta is – is – young but . . . Oh, I don't know, the responsibilities here make her seem older than her years.'

'Indeed. She can run this farm as well as her mother.'

'Yet she is innocent of – of so many things.' He lowered his voice. 'Her mother has guarded her virtue to the point of isolation. I am not sure she knows how to be courted, let alone be loved by a man, but—' He stopped suddenly.

'But what?'

He lowered his voice. 'I should dearly like to show her, Father.'

His father laughed gently. 'It is as I thought. Oh Patrick, were I your age again! She has the body of a woman and does think as one yet . . .'

'It is not something to jest about, Father. I think we should move on before this becomes too embarrassing for all of us.'

'You want to leave her for some country ruffian to woo and wed?'

'No! Of course I don't. But she has formed an unfavourable opinion of me and I fear I cannot persuade her otherwise.'

'You do not think she is worth fighting for?'

'Quite the opposite. But I cannot force myself on her if she will not have me. Accept it, Father. We do not suit each other and that is an end to the matter.'

'An end? You are giving up on her so soon?'

'She has made it clear that—'

'That she is a young girl and naturally wary of strangers.'

'She is wary of travelling people. I cannot change what I am.'

'You are not a gypsy.'

'I might as well be as far as Quinta is concerned,' Patrick responded irritably.

'You don't really believe that, do you?'

'Perhaps it is her mother who objects to me?'

'Aye, you may be right. I'll talk to her.' He took a sip of his laudanum mixture. 'Before this addles my brain completely.'

Patrick grimaced. The medicine was necessary but he had seen its debilitating effects on others. He said, 'You've meddled enough, Father. You have opened my eyes to a future here and I am persuaded. Now leave me to my task. If I am to court Miss Quinta, I'll speak to her mother myself.'

Quinta took off her dusty gown to wash in the scullery before tea. She had eaten only bread and soup for dinner and was hungry. Mother had a pudding with some vegetables boiling for tea and was resting upstairs until they were ready. She struggled into her bodice, leaving the buttons undone as she hurried to the fire to check on dinner. She wandered to the front window and saw Mr Ross at the water butt sluicing away the grime from his digging. Embarrassed, she shrank back, pulling together the front of her gown and hurriedly fastening the buttons.

He could not see her. Indeed he was too intent on his own task to even notice her, but she felt his presence in their yard. Cautiously she approached the glass and stared. His back was bare and his black hair was wet, slicked down and glossy. He was drying his chest with a towel and she could not take her eyes off him.

'Quinta?'

'Oh, I didn't hear you come downstairs.'

'What are you staring at?'

'Nothing.'

Her mother was standing beside her at the window. She took her arm. 'Come away, dear.'

Quinta was aware of a heat rising in her cheeks, heightened by the intensity of her mother's scrutiny. 'I – I – I know it's rude to stare. I didn't mean to. He didn't see me.'

'He is a very handsome man, my dear.'

'Mother, I – he – that is, Mr Ross asked me to walk with him after tea.'

'Did he? Well, a little company and conversation will do you no harm, as long as you stay in sight of the cottage. What did you say to him?'

'I said no, of course. He's a stranger, Mother!' she answered with surprise. 'We were both frightened of him when he arrived.'

'I did not know his father then. Sergeant Ross is honourable. He has a respectable manner and has brought his son up to behave the same.'

'Do you mean you approve of the way they live?'

109

'Well, no. Though Mr Ross seems to be a hard-working young man.'

'So you think I should walk with him?'

'I did not say that. Do you want to?'

'I don't know.'

'Then do not. If you wanted to, you would know.'

'How would I know?'

'You would look forward to being in his company.'

'Even though he is a traveller?'

Exasperated, her mother responded: 'He is not a vagrant! His father has means and they travel here for the Dispensary in town. Do you wish to spend an hour in his son's company?'

Quinta thought that she might and glanced sideways at her mother. When she saw her pained expression, she hurriedly changed her mind. 'No.'

Mrs Haig gave a small smile and nodded as though satisfied with this response. 'You are wise beyond your years and I am proud of you, my dear.'

The next day Quinta was up at dawn in her garden and after her breakfast of porridge and honey she slung a wooden yoke across her shoulders and tested its weight. She had two milk pails full of fresh vegetables for the Hall kitchen. The cook there always said she never had enough for the servants' hall and she would give her cheese to carry back in return.

Patrick watched her set off with her load across the fields and frowned. She was pretty enough. Healthy and strong, too, and he relished the prospect of bedding her. But that would come after he wed her and he still wasn't so sure about marriage. The kitchen door stood open and he rapped his knuckles on the bleached wood.

Mrs Haig dried her hands and stepped outside. 'What is it?'

'I wish to speak with you, ma'am.'

'What about?'

'Your daughter, ma'am.'

110

She gestured towards the old furniture nestling in the shade of the walnut tree and settled herself in a carver chair. 'Well, you are a man of few words so you'd better get on with it.'

Patrick remained standing. 'I should like your permission to walk out with her, ma'am.'

'Walk out with her? Do you mean you wish to court her?'

'Yes, ma'am.'

'Is my daughter aware of your wishes?'

'I have approached her but she has not responded to me.'

'Then perhaps she does not like you.'

'She does not know me, ma'am. And will not, unless you will allow me to court her.'

'And why should I? What have you got to offer her?'

He felt uncomfortable. He had no home, no prospects, no way of earning a living except by his wits and the sweat of his back. But since his austere childhood in Ireland he had known that he could think faster than most others, even the gentry who were supposed to be educated. He was confident that, given the chance, he could support Quinta and her mother. And his father would be content.

'I can provide a future here for your daughter and your good self, ma'am. Given your leave I can turn in a healthy profit from this land and you – both of you – will be secure in your home.'

Yes, Laura reflected. That is why I have not sent you on your way. She said, 'You are a handsome fellow, sir, tall and strong, and I believe you can restore my little farm. But you are not what I want for my Quinta. You must have caught the eye of many a young maid on your travels. What is special to you about her?'

'She is very pretty, ma'am.'

'Is that all?'

'If you give your blessing, ma'am, I should like to know her more.'

'Would you indeed? Then it is not the prospect of my tenancy after I am gone?'

He was taken aback by her frankness. Clearly she thought

111

as his father did, but Mrs Haig was not quite right about him and he answered honestly. 'I had not thought as far as that, ma'am. I considered only that with my knowledge and toil and the determination of your daughter, there is a living here, a living for all of us.' He was surprised himself with this response. But it was not a lie and the more he thought about it, the more he believed it. He scanned the land around him and added, 'It is perfect for a growing family.'

He didn't know why he said that, except that an image had flashed across his mind as he thought about this smallholding in the future. He saw it alive and thriving. In the picture was his wife churning butter under the shade of this very tree, with children playing around her skirts; his children. He blinked back the scene. He was not even sure that Quinta had been the wife in his vision and he wondered what had caused him to conjure up such an ideal. It was the addition of children, of course. If he did marry, children would follow. Children? The notion alarmed him. He was not ready for such responsibility yet. He was not ready for marriage and all that it entailed. What was he doing even thinking about it? This was an insane idea of his father's!

But as he regretted his impulsive words, Laura Haig's heart leaped. A family! Children! Yes, a whole brood of them. Babies! Top Field would have the babies that she had longed for herself as a young woman and never been blessed with. Her dreams took over her thoughts. Quinta would have those joys that she had been denied and, God willing, she would be spared for a few more years to share them, too.

If she could be sure that Mr Ross would be half the father to his children that the sergeant was to him she would look on him more kindly. But, in spite of his young years, he had seen much more of life than her daughter had and she wondered if he was a man who was easily distracted by pretty women, and whether his eye would wander when her darling Quinta was swollen with child.

112

To his credit, all his contacts with ladies that she had seen had been well mannered. She recalled that he was even respectful to the occasional street woman who had approached him on their way to market, fending off ribaldry with gentle wit rather than the bawdy jest and foul language of others.

'A growing family,' Mrs Haig repeated slowly. 'Do you love my daughter, sir?'

'Love her?' He was caught off balance again, not expecting such a direct question. But he answered honestly. 'I cannot say that I do, ma'am. Her countenance attracts me as no other has before, but I cannot know if I love her unless I court her. And without your leave I will not approach her. Neither would she let me, ma'am.'

'Quite so. She is young and rightly cautious of you. You are well versed in the ways of the world, more than your years would indicate, if I may be so bold, and you have more experience of life than she. I should not wish you to take advantage of that.'

'Indeed, ma'am, I should not. You may be assured that I would guard and protect her virtue.'

'I am not sure I believe you, sir. I have seen you stare at her as she works in our garden.'

'I do not deny her beauty. I am sure others have noticed it too.'

Laura was reminded of the unfortunate incidents on market day and of the sergeant's counsel regarding her daughter's future.

He went on, 'You have my word that I have not so much as touched her hand, ma'am, nor shall I without your permission.'

She was not reassured and replied, 'You are a travelling man, sir. How do I know that you will not tire of stability and resume your wanderings?'

'I have travelled only with my father. I have led this life because he is my father. He served his country well. He searched for me and found me, and now he has come home to the Riding, he wishes to stay here.'

'I do not doubt he is a hero. But he did not marry your mother.'

'It was not his fault, ma'am. He would have, after the victory at Waterloo, but her parents disapproved of him. They took her back to Ireland and told her he had perished on the battle-field. When he found her, he was too late. She was already a Bride of Christ.'

'Yes, he told me.'

'It was the greatest day of my life when he took me away from my foster parents and their cruelty and squalor. I have never, ever wanted to go back.'

'Well, you have shown yourself to be civil and hard-working, sir. But this counts for nothing if my Quinta does not like you. And I believe she does not.'

Patrick felt a coldness creep around his heart, and then a spark of anger. Mrs Haig was a good mother and her daughter obeyed her. But Patrick thought that sometimes this was against Miss Quinta's own wishes. He wondered if this might be the case now; if, given an opportunity, her daughter might enjoy a little freedom to express herself more openly towards him. He wanted that. He wanted to know more about Mrs Haig's bright and beautiful daughter.

'I believe she does not know me, ma'am,' he countered and thought, She cannot if you do not let me court her.

He hoped Mrs Haig did not realise how uncertain he felt about this conversation. But he could not ignore his father's deteriorating condition, or the fact that he had kept so quiet about it through the long cold winter. If he could do this one last thing for his father and bring him some contentment, then he would. But neither could he ignore a mounting excitement as he anticipated Miss Quinta as his sweetheart. He wanted to win her and to do that he needed to win her mother's approval first. He said lightly, 'Perhaps you will speak with your daughter on my behalf, ma'am.'

'Indeed I shall not. You must win her good opinion for

yourself, if you can.' Mrs Haig stood up to indicate the end of their interview. She sounded quite haughty to Patrick, as though he would be wasting his time. She went on, 'If you do you will have my blessing and, with Farmer Bilton's permission, this tenancy too. That would be good news for all of us, I'm sure.'

This mention of their landlord made Patrick hesitate. He'd noticed the way the old farmer looked at Quinta. He coveted her and if Patrick married her he was quite sure Farmer Bilton would make life difficult for him. This match-making of his father's might not be such a good idea after all.

Chapter 11

'Do you think you will be able to manage church tomorrow, Mother?'

Laura coughed and shook her head. 'The medicine helps but I have not the strength for the climb afterwards.'

'We haven't been for weeks! We must take fresh flowers to the grave.'

Her mother passed a hand over her eyes. 'I'm so sorry. I wish we still had Darby. He would carry me up the hill.'

'I could go without you,' Quinta suggested tentatively.

'No, dear. Farmer Bilton will be there.'

'But I'd give Mr Wilkins news of you. I am surprised neither he nor his sister has called to see you.'

'Farmer Bilton is doing that parish duty for him. You have seen him! Snooping around every day on that new horse of his. He's like a buzzard, hovering, waiting to swoop down on his prey.'

'Well, he'll have seen the improvements Mr Ross has made. My new garden is ready for seedlings. He has been advising me on the planting.'

'You have been speaking to him?'

'A little, as we worked. Please don't be alarmed. He has been very civil, always, and he knows a great deal about farming. He asked me about the village church in the valley.'

'I imagined he was of the Catholic persuasion.'

'He said he was as a child, but worships as his father does now, with the Church of England.'

'You have been conversing of things other than farming, then?'

'Not really. Well, he did ask if he might escort us both to church. And the grave will need tending. What would Father think?'

Laura groaned. 'It is so difficult for me to do these things now.'

'But not for me! Please say I can go.'

'Very well. I shall walk with you to the brow and meet you there on your return.'

'You may trust him if we are in church, Mother. Mr Ross is gracious towards me and very civil.'

The next morning, Quinta rushed through her early morning chores and then changed into her Sunday-best gown. It had been her mother's, fashioned from a Hall cast-off, and was of good quality blue-striped silk. The bottom edge was faded and worn, but it had ribbon and pleating on the bodice and full petticoats.

'Will you stand still for a minute while I brush down your skirt?' Laura complained good-humouredly.

'Ooh, you have laced my corset tight this morning.'

'No, 'tis just right. Tuck this muslin in your neckline at the front. I've brought down your Sunday bonnet.'

'Oh! You've trimmed it with a blue ribbon. How pretty!'

Her mother stepped back and smiled. 'You really are very lovely, my dear. Remember what I have told you. And don't forget to curtsey when spoken to by your betters or elders.'

'Even Farmer Bilton?'

'Especially him. But avoid him if you can.' Laura looked out of the front window. 'Mr Ross is waiting. He has made himself look smart.'

Quinta agreed. His jacket and trousers were spruce and his boots polished. He had shaved and – and – the sergeant must have cut his hair! It no longer curled around his collar. He wore a red necktie but no hat. She guessed he didn't have a proper one, only the cap he wore when digging. When she approached him, he did not offer his arm and they set off a yard apart. Her mother and the sergeant followed to the brow of the hill, sat on a bank and watched them until they were out of sight.

'You have such a fine view of the valley, Mrs Haig.'

'Yes indeed. This is when I forget the hardship of my life on this farm, and the cold of winter, and know why I never want to leave.'

'I'll walk a little further. Would you be so kind, ma'am?'

Laura heaved on the sergeant's arm as he struggled to his feet with the aid of his crutch. The effort made her cough. 'Excuse me.' Her words were lost in her handkerchief.

'Does the medicine not give you ease?'

'At night. I do not take it in the day as it makes me sleepy.'

'My son said there was a physician in town as well as the apothecary. You would benefit from his counsel.'

'It is too far for me to go there and back in one day.'

'He will visit you here.'

Laura did not respond.

'You are sick, Mrs Haig. You should see a medical man.'

'I cannot afford it!'

'I'm sorry. I did not mean to anger you.'

'I worry about my daughter, sir, if anything should happen to me.'

'Well, my son would take care of us all if you would allow him.'

'Yes. I believe that is why you stay. He covets my tenancy, sir.'

'It will not be yours for much longer, ma'am, if your land-lord has his way. Do you not think it would belong as well to him? He is a farmer.'

Laura saw the sense in that. 'But he must also win the affec-tions of my daughter, sir. She does not like him. And – and I shall not encourage her.'

'You do not approve of him?'

'No, sir. That is I – I . . .'

'You want better for her. He is the daughter of a gentle-woman, ma'am. Tell me, if Miss Quinta loved him would you give your permission to their union?'

Laura thought about this and replied, 'If he loved and wanted her, too. Yes I would.'

'Then I have a proposition for you, ma'am. I must visit the surgeon soon and I shall need lodgings in town and a – a companion.'

'I am aware that you and your son will be leaving us.'

'I'd like him to stay here and farm while you travel by carrier with me to town.'

'And lodge with you, sir?'

'Yes, but only as my lady companion as if you were in my employ. Nothing more, I assure you, ma'am, except perhaps for you to see the physician.'

'With my daughter?'

'Ah. No.'

'You cannot mean that I should leave her here with your son?'

'It will allow them to explore their feelings for each other.'

'And more besides!' Laura was astounded. 'Your son, no doubt, has experience in these matters,' she added shortly. 'I have told you, sir, my daughter does not like him.'

'Forgive me, Mrs Haig, your daughter does not know him. A proper arrangement would remedy that. I suggest a Lammas Day agreement.'

Laura's eyes widened. 'Certainly not, sir! They have fallen from fashion in the Riding.'

'I am sure that is because our young folk do not stay in the countryside as they used to. They journey to town for employment. Who knows how they behave when they lodge with strangers?'

'I know my Quinta.'

'A Lammas agreement is more than a betrothal, ma'am. In remote areas it was considered as binding as any church marriage.'

'But a marriage that lasted only through the harvest! They were free to separate by Michaelmas.'

'If they found they were not suited, yes,' the sergeant argued. 'That is precisely why I suggest it for our children.'

Laura shook her head and murmured, 'She is too young.'

'Do not be hasty, Mrs Haig. Reflect on the benefits for everyone of such a match. Times are hard and this is a way through for us all.' There was an awkward silence. He reached into his pocket for his flask. 'Will you take a little spirit?'

Laura took a sip of the brandy. She was shocked by the sergeant's suggestion. Lammas Day arrangements used to be popular when a whole village of men were supported by labouring on the farms. Now most of them had moved to the town for pit or furnace work, and to choose their brides. And she had heard tales of men and women there not even bothering with a church service to bless their union.

It was wrong. The gentry were to blame; the old Regent and the King had set such bad examples for their subjects. She had always seen the sense of Lammas Day matches, but not for her Quinta. Yet she could not ignore the fact that she was ailing and she wished to see her daughter safely wed.

'Thank you for the flowers. It was kind of you to pick them for me. How did you know I would be visiting my father's grave?'

'I didn't. But I guessed he was buried in this churchyard.'

'My sister, too.'

'You had a sister?'

'She was much older than me.'

'I'm sorry you lost her.'

He sounded as though he really meant it. She would have liked a sister or brother to alleviate the loneliness of Top Field. She quickened her step, looking forward to church, to the hymns and to the conversations afterwards. A path led off the track to the back of the church burial ground and Quinta led the way so she could tend the grave and lay her flowers.

Eliza Haig. Joseph Haig.

'Eliza was your sister?'

'Yes. She died the year I was born. I think that is why Mother is so protective towards me. I am all she has.'

'I assumed you were the fifth child as your name suggests.'

'Five-acre Wood,' she explained. 'I was born in Five-acre Wood.'

'I see.'

'Let us go in. Mother said to sit at the back.'

The small church was full and a whole family crowded in after them, squashing Quinta against the stone wall at the end of the pew. They knelt to say a prayer and found there was little room to sit when they got up.

'Excuse me,' he whispered as they were squashed together. Through her skirts she could feel the firmness of his thigh pushing against hers and his arm was pressing on her shoulder. He leaned forward to give her more room, and then lifted his arm over her head to rest it along the back of the pew. She could feel it across her back and his fingers curled gently round the curve of her shoulder to ease it away from the rough stone.

There was no room to move away from him and she did not wish to protest and cause a scene in the church. She turned to face him, frowned and raised her eyebrows. But he was smiling. His eyes crinkled at the corners and lit up his handsome features, giving them a warmth she had not seen before.

Surprised and totally disarmed of her objection, she resumed her concentration on the hymn book.

Quinta was disappointed that hardly anyone from the village noticed her. Two brief nods were all she received, from kitchen maids at the Hall whose gaze wandered when they became bored with the sermon. There was a baptism at the end of the service, which accounted for the full congregation. Mr Wilkins moved to the font and the parents carried their sleeping infant to join him. The family next to Mr Ross also crowded around the font and he moved nearer the aisle so they both had a view of the proceedings.

The cheerful family seemed to have so many children already, the older ones ushering the smallest and urging them to be quiet. The father was a labouring man, less smartly dressed than Mr Ross, she thought, and the mother looked almost as old as Laura. The young ones were as clean and neat as could be expected from one of the poorer families in the village. But they all smiled fondly at the babe and were obviously delighted by this new addition to their numbers.

When the cold water on the child's head woke her and she cried, there was a surge forward to comfort her and a murmur of sympathy rippled around the church. Quinta watched with interest and felt a tiny pang of envy. For the first time she understood her mother's sadness at not bearing more children. This family was poor but they had each other. She glanced sideways at Mr Ross. He, like her, had had a lonely childhood too and she wondered what he was thinking.

When the baptism was over, the congregation stood dutifully and waited for Sir William and his Lady to leave. Quinta thought she wasn't plain at all and looked very lovely in her gown and bonnet. Farmer Bilton followed them. He walked out stiffly looking straight ahead at the back of Sir William's neck and, thankfully, did not acknowledge her or Mr Ross.

Then she became aware of nudges and whispers from some

village folk as they filed out past her. She rehearsed her mother's instructions and stood quietly until everyone had left.

'Wait here, Mr Ross,' she whispered, 'until the vicar is free to meet you.'

Quinta emerged from the church porch into the sunlight.

'Mr Wilkins, sir.' She curtseyed. 'My mother sends her apologies for missing your services of late. She is not in the best of health. We had hoped for improvement with the coming of summer but sadly this has not been so.'

'I am sorry to hear that, Miss Haig. Your landlord has kept me informed, and I have to say that I am quite disturbed by what he tells me.'

'But we have help on the farm, sir. May I present Mr Ross?' She turned and stretched an arm into the darkness of the porch.

'You have brought the ruffian to my church?'

Quinta's eyes widened. He wasn't a ruffian! And even if he was, he was one of God's children, too. She saw Mr Ross's face darken with anger as he stepped into the light. He held his head high, stood squarely in front of the vicar and bowed stiffly. His annoyance seemed to have disappeared when he looked up. 'I am your servant, sir,' he said formally. 'And the Lord's servant, too.'

Mr Wilkins seemed lost for words for a moment and was rescued by his sister, who had detached herself from conversation with Lady Swinborough's personal maid.

'Mr Wilkins! I see you have a new addition to your flock!'

Quinta stared at her in awe. She had a sallow complexion and was past thirty years of age, but she wore a light summer gown of a delicate lilac colour, with a matching bonnet and parasol that made Quinta forget her mother's counsel not to covet what other ladies wore. She felt dull and dowdy in comparison and looked around for acquaintances of her own age, but, delayed by the baptism, they had gone speedily home to their dinners. She had waited inside for too long.

'Will you introduce me, brother dearest?' Miss Wilkins asked with her eyes on Mr Ross.

'No, I shall not. Go back to my parishioners.'

'But surely this gentleman is one of your parishioners?'

'Beatrice!' the vicar hissed. 'Do as I say.'

His sister took a lingering look at Mr Ross and turned away reluctantly. In contrast his eyes were stony. Blue flint, thought Quinta, and was glad that Mr Wilkins had sent his sister away.

The vicar nodded briefly to Mr Ross and then addressed her: 'Miss Haig, you are indeed lucky to have Mr Bilton to watch over you. He told me he has offered – he has offered help. Your mother should know better than to refuse him. You will ask her to reconsider and to – to refrain from encouraging gypsies to my parish.'

'I am not a gypsy, sir.'

'You are a vagrant who is taking advantage of a needy widow.'

'Oh no, sir, you are wrong. Mr Ross has—'

Before she could finish, Mr Ross had bid good day to the vicar and taken her arm. He urged her down the path that led to the back of church. 'I have had enough of your vicar for today,' he breathed in her ear.

She shook his hand free and responded swiftly, 'My mother suggested that I present you and I am sorry he was so rude. I did not expect that; nor did my mother or she would not have advised it.'

'Well, I am not surprised. His opinion of me was already poisoned by your landlord. Farmer Bilton has the ear of the gentry and he has used it.'

Quinta feared that Mr Ross was correct. 'Please do not tell Mother about this. In spite of your assistance, she is prone to much fretting these days.'

'The vicar said your landlord had offered help. Why did you not accept?'

'I might have, but Mother said no. She was very firm.'

'You might have? I don't understand.'

'I was concerned about Mother and our future. I – we – we were near destitute until you and your father happened by and I did not wish to see her in the workhouse. I told you Mother thought she might become his housekeeper. He said he would employ her. Only . . .' Quinta hesitated about telling him. 'Only I had to go, too.'

Mr Ross frowned. 'Well, your mother could not desert you for him.'

Quinta bowed her head, examined the dust on her boots and said quietly, 'As his wife.'

'*His wife?*' He took hold of her shoulders and turned her to face him. 'He wanted *you* as his wife, and not your mother?'

'He – he said Mother was too old because he wanted children but I would do for him instead.'

'How dare he treat you in such an unfeeling and cavalier fashion? I am not the one to take advantage of a needy widow. He is.'

'Mother was furious and I understand why. I have grown up a lot this spring.' Unaccountably she felt her tears welling. She had looked forward to church so much but the vicar had been unkind and Miss Wilkins had made her envious. She had missed talking to the maids from the Hall, too; they would have made her feel better about her situation.

He searched her eyes with his and his face held a softness she had not seen before. 'Your mother is wise.'

Her throat closed with emotion. She loved her mother so much and worried about her all the time.

'You look so unhappy,' Mr Ross added. 'The visit to your family grave has saddened you.'

Unable to speak, she shook her head wordlessly. After a pause she swallowed and replied, 'I take strength from the Lord. It's just that my mother's cough is not getting better and I don't know what to do.' A tear spilled out and she fell forward to bury her face in his jacket. She felt one of his arms around her

125

and a hand on the back of her bonnet, realised what she was doing and hastily turned away from him, searching for her gown pocket and her handkerchief. 'Oh, do forgive me, Mr Ross. What must you think?'

He took her handkerchief from her, gently wiped her eyes and brushed a straying strand of hair from her damp cheek. 'I think you are brave and kind and as honest and as wise as your mother. It pains me to see you in such distress.'

She inhaled deeply and composed herself. 'I am recovered now. See. I am smiling.'

'Yes, I do see,' he replied seriously.

'There.' She tucked her handkerchief away and braced her shoulders. 'I should like to go home now.'

He held out his arm for her. 'I should like to escort you.'

She hesitated, and then placed her hand on his. 'Thank you, sir.'

'Will you call me Patrick now, Miss Quinta?'

'I do not think so, not until you have asked my mother to address you so first, and she agrees.'

'Very well.'

They started their slow ascent of Bilton Hill. This visit to church had shown Quinta a different aspect to Mr Ross. She had felt as angry as he with the vicar's prejudice. He had shared her worries with sympathy and behaved kindly towards her distress. She had considered him dark and dangerous until now. But today he had shown her that his nature held a gentle compassion, too. She resolved not to follow the vicar's example and judge him hastily. There was more to know about Mr Ross; much more.

'I shall tell Mother that we exchanged a few words with Mr Wilkins, but not that he talked of Farmer Bilton. Will you support me in that?'

'If you wish.'

'Thank you. Oh, and please would you lower your arm before Mother sees us?'

He did and they returned as they had left, walking side by side, at least one yard apart.

After a good dinner of braised stuffed partridges that had been shot in their garden by the sergeant, Quinta wandered from the table and found a patch of grass to lie on her back and gaze at the sky. The weather was mild. A few clouds masked the sun from time to time; butterflies flitted among the meadow flowers and bees buzzed about the blossoms. Quinta imagined there would have been many such family Sabbaths if her sister had lived; at least until her father died, when that dream was lost for ever. The ale she had taken with dinner made her sleepy and she drifted into a doze.

She was roused by the sound of a lively conversation.

'They use them in Scotland.' It was the sergeant's voice.

'We are not in Scotland, Father.'

'I witnessed them with soldiers in Spain and France.'

'But they were meant for harvest-time,' Laura protested, 'for men and women who did not know each other well.'

Quinta stood up quickly and returned to the shade of the tree. 'What were?'

Patrick answered: 'Lammas Day arrangements.'

'What are they?' she asked.

He stood up and drew out a chair for her. 'Come and sit down, Quinta. Our parents talk about us more than we know.'

Her mother explained: 'They are binding agreements taken during the early part of the harvest between men and women of marriageable age. A couple made a promise to each other that if they were suited after living together as man and wife during the harvest, they would marry. If the match was not an agreeable one, they parted without ill feeling towards each other.'

'Well, I've never heard of them,' Quinta stated. She knew what might happen if a woman lived as wife to a man. 'What if there's a child?'

'Quinta! Do not be so outspoken.'

'Marriage follows, of course,' Patrick answered quickly.

'Even if they are not suited?' Quinta retaliated. 'It doesn't sound a very satisfactory arrangement to me.'

The sergeant intervened firmly: 'If they are not suited, they will not love each other and so there will be no possibility of a child.' He was looking at his son.

Quinta saw that her mother was embarrassed by the conversation, so she was surprised when Laura said to her, 'They were considered to be very sensible arrangements, my dear.'

'You're not thinking of one for me?' she asked incredulously. Suddenly the whole day fell into place. The sergeant providing meat for their table, Mr Ross – Patrick – taking her to church and now her mother's discomfort with her opinions. 'You are,' she stated flatly.

'Wait,' the Sergeant said. 'Before we discuss this matter further, there is something I wish to know and you will be kind enough to answer me honestly, Mrs Haig. This is no time to spare my feelings, or those of my son.' He emphasised the gravity of his question by rising awkwardly at the table. 'My son never knew me until he was a grown boy because my sweetheart's father disapproved of me. I will not have history repeat itself. Mrs Haig, do you approve of my son as a fitting suitor for your daughter?'

Quinta knew the answer was no.

'I do.'

Wide-eyed, Quinta stared at her. '*You do?*' She and Patrick spoke together.

'You would have me wed to a travelling man?' Quinta added.

'I should have you wed to a farmer, and a first-rate one at that, capable of taking on this tenancy and of prospering. I should have that for you, my love.'

'And you said I should never give myself to any man for gain,' she breathed angrily.

'Nor shall you!' Laura retaliated. 'That is why I agree with the sergeant on this matter!'

This made Quinta's fury worse. 'You agree that we should live as husband and wife outside of wedlock? Really, Mother! Have you gone quite mad?'

'No,' the sergeant responded quickly. 'Of course not; Patrick will continue to live in the cowshed and work on the farm as he does now.'

'And you will look after the garden, and tend to household matters as befits a farmer's wife,' Laura added hastily.

'Then how is it different from the way we live now?' Quinta asked irritably. No one answered at first until she prompted, 'Mother?'

'I – I shall accompany the sergeant to town and – and seek treatment for my cough.'

Quinta was overjoyed to hear this, and said, 'Then, of course, I shall come with you.'

'No, dear. You must look after the summer crops and the hens. I shall stay in town until the sergeant is well enough to return.'

'You will leave us here alone?' Patrick asked, staring at her.

Quinta felt as though she had been cornered and turned on him sharply. 'Are you a party in this conspiracy as well? Is that why you took me to church; to prepare me for this – this charade? She was satisfied that he looked taken aback by her accusation. How could he have behaved so kindly towards her after church whilst he schemed against her like this?

Laura looked hurt. 'Please do not be so angry, dear. I was opposed to the notion at first, but I am thinking of your future; of safeguarding the farm for you. I am not well. You are young and – and you need protection.'

'But I can look after myself and you as well, Mother! Why do I need *protection*?'

'Your landlord,' Patrick said quietly.

Quinta was silenced. The threat of Farmer Bilton's actions continued to hover over Top Field.

Laura stretched out her hand towards her daughter. 'The

sergeant has assured me that Patrick will take great care of you.'

Quinta clasped it gratefully. 'But why do we have to have this – this arrangement?'

'Think of it as a kind of betrothal, dear, that you may withdraw from without consequence.'

'I cannot believe you agree to this. You will not be here to be my chaperone.'

'That is true.' Her mother frowned at the sergeant. 'I am indeed concerned for my daughter's virtue, sir.'

The sergeant answered swiftly. 'They will not lie together, Mrs Haig.'

'Lie together?' Patrick looked angrily at his father. 'Dear God, Father, you make too many presumptions.'

'Do I?' The sergeant raised his eyebrows and Patrick fell silent.

'So nothing is lost if we find we are not suited!' Quinta observed, and then demanded, 'What will happen then?'

Eventually Patrick replied, 'Your mother will return here to you and I shall join my father in town. Your life will continue as if we had not been here.'

'Impossible!' she responded scornfully.

Whatever this Lammas Day arrangement brought, Quinta knew she would never be quite the same as before Patrick came into her life. She realised that she had felt more fondly towards him after their visit to church. But she did not love him and was not clear how she would know if she did.

She made another attempt to protest. 'Patrick, surely you wish to be with your father when he visits the surgeon?'

The look of pain that crossed his brow gave Quinta her answer. He no more wanted this arrangement than she did. It was their parents' doing and, much as she loved her mother and wished to obey her, there were occasions when she did not care to. This was one of them.

She wondered whether Patrick felt the same towards his

130

father. You could not tell with him. The flashes of emotion that he showed were quickly quashed. But she noticed them. And it was because of that that he intrigued her so. She wanted to get to know him better. She laughed silently to herself. That was what Lammas Day arrangements were about.

When he did not reply, she realised that she was outnumbered in this argument and pursed her lips defiantly. 'Shall I fetch more ale?' she suggested crossly, lifting the empty jug.

Patrick stood up. 'Father and I have things to discuss.'

'And I must prepare for my journey,' Laura added. 'Quinta, will you come inside and help me?'

When they had left the table, the sergeant said, 'Well, her mother has given you her blessing. You have to win her yourself now. If she falls in love with you, would you marry her?'

'Yes,' Patrick answered. He was a little surprised that he admitted it so readily. But, since he had considered Quinta in that light, his acknowledged lust for her had deepened into a stronger desire, one that only marriage could satisfy. He coveted her. He wanted to own her, all of her, to the exclusion of all others. Was this what love was?

'You will ask her to wed you before you bed her, son.'

'But you just made a promise on my behalf that I would not lie with her!'

'And I know it is one you will not keep if she falls in love with you. So, you will ask her to be your wife and you will wait for her answer.'

'And if she says no?'

'She won't.'

'You sound very sure of that.'

'You cannot mean this, Mother. I want to be with you,' Quinta insisted.

'I have to think about what will happen to you when I am gone,' Laura answered seriously.

131

'So you have agreed to this only to secure my future.'

'I could have secured your future as a wife to Farmer Bilton. Of course I have concerns about leaving you! I am your mother. You must tell me now if you are not willing to do this.'

'Well, he is handsome and strong. He has wisdom and manners.'

'Do you trust him?'

Quinta thought about this and was sure of her answer. 'Yes. He is a man of principle.'

'Then my mind is easier. If he is half the man his father is I shall be very happy for you. This way, you will know for sure whether you can love each other.'

'How shall I know that I love him, Mother?' she asked.

'You will want him, my love, you will want him to hold you and kiss you and possess you in a way that no other can. You will know. God willing, when the sergeant and I return, we shall announce the banns and have the ceremony before Michaelmas. There will be much to celebrate.'

Quinta knew better than to argue further and asked, 'How long will you be away?'

'No more than a fortnight.'

'Where will you stay in town, Mother?'

'We shall lodge at an inn near to the Dispensary.'

'You will need your best gown, then.'

'Yes. Fetch my box from the store room. Patrick will carry it to the village and we shall take the carrier into town.'

'I shall miss you.'

'And I you, my love. We have been happy here, but we cannot work this farm alone. If you can make a match with Patrick I shall no longer fret about your future.'

Quinta placed the travelling box on the bedchamber floorboards and laid out her mother's clothes on the bed.

That night, she lay awake feeling an uneasy excitement about her future. She no longer feared Patrick Ross. But could she love him? And surely he would have to love her, too? She doubted that he would. Farmer Bilton had not loved her, only desired the use of her body, so why should Patrick Ross be any different?

Chapter 12

Her mother hugged her tightly. 'My little girl, you are so grown up now.'

Quinta smiled falteringly. She thought she had grown up years ago, but she knew her mother meant more than running the farm. 'Two weeks only, Mother. Not a day longer.'

'Patrick will look after you, dear.' She turned to him. 'Your father has promised me that I can trust you with her. Do not let me down.'

'You can be sure of that, ma'am.'

Quinta glanced at him quickly. His face was serious and so dark that she would have thought him quite menacing if he were still a stranger to her. But she had revised her opinion of him and wondered if, perhaps, he had doubts about this agreement.

Patrick loaded the box on to the early-morning carrier and paid the carter as Mrs Haig squeezed her daughter's hands and said goodbye. Then he took his father's pack and crutch and helped him climb awkwardly into his seat.

'Remember what I told you, son,' Sergeant Ross whispered in his ear. 'If you do bed her—'

'I shall not.'

'Listen to me! I am your father and I have more knowledge of these affairs – and of you, Patrick. She has her mother's approval. If she takes a mind to tempt you—'

'Were I so lucky . . .' he retaliated swiftly.

'If you bed her you must wed her,' his father insisted softly.

Patrick blinked. 'You really believe I shall?'

'I do. So promise me that if you do you will make her your wife. Promise me.'

'I promise.' His father relaxed and nodded to him with satisfaction in his eyes.

Patrick added ruefully, 'But I should be better going with you to the surgeon.'

'Your future is here with Miss Quinta. Begin it now.'

Patrick handed him his crutch. 'I've put more sheep's wool in the padding.' He adjusted the strapping on his father's hunting bag slung across his chest. 'Send word if you need me.'

The sergeant smiled wryly but did not answer as he watched his son assist Mrs Haig into the cart and settle her beside him before jumping nimbly over the side. They jolted against each other as the horses began to move. He did not look back. He dared not. Mrs Haig was sure to return to her daughter within the fortnight. But his absence was likely to be prolonged. The laudanum helped with his pain, but he feared the worst for his leg. He hoped he would not be limping with a peg leg when he did come back to Top Field.

He hoped, also, that the young folk would make a go of it. It was a sensible arrangement for both of them. They needed each other in equal measures, and his instinct told him they were right for each other. Mrs Haig, too, had accepted the good sense of it. But she was a woman of romantic inclination and wanted a love match for her daughter, and Miss Quinta, God bless her innocence, didn't really know what she wanted except to please her mother.

His son had voiced reservations. But Sergeant Ross had none.

He knew he was right. He had seen many a young soldier in his life follow their lusts only to find their hearts ensnared. He knew his son's heart better than the lad did himself.

Patrick watched the carrier cart with his father's retreating figure for a long time.

'This is a difficult time for your father,' Quinta said quietly. 'I am sure you would prefer to be with him.' He didn't reply, but Quinta thought she was right. She added, 'Mother will send for you if – if he asks her. She will look out for him.'

'As I shall look out for you in return,' he replied briefly.

'I shall not be a burden to you, I assure you.'

He didn't respond and this irritated her. He did not deny it. Did his silence mean that he did not agree with her? He laboured hard but he said little, and how were you to know a person if he did not converse? At that moment, she felt lonely and trapped in this arrangement. Without her mother she had no one to turn to for counsel or assistance, not even a friendly neighbour.

Quinta waited until the slow-moving carrier had disappeared and then went on briskly, 'Well, I have much work to do in the house and garden.'

Patrick inhaled deeply. 'You go on ahead. I'll call at the farrier. You have a plough in your cowshed. If I can hire a beast, I'll turn the pasture ready to sow grain next spring.'

She climbed the hill alone, absorbing his words. Next spring? Had he already decided to stay? Had they all decided he would stay? She pondered this thought as she chased a rabbit out of her rows of peas and set to work in her garden.

She did not hear his approach and he must have stood watching her for several minutes before she straightened, stretched and saw him. 'Did you get a beast?' she asked.

He shook his head. 'None to be had. They are all taken by the harvest.' He was carrying a parcel wrapped in sacking and he held it high. 'Venison. There are too many young deer this season and they're eating crops so the Hall is culling them. The farrier's wife had set up a butcher's slab outside her home.'

'Venison? Oh, show me.' She hurried towards him.

It was part of the foreleg, fresh killed for the blood had soaked into its wrapping. 'This will feed us for days,' she marvelled. 'I'll take it indoors now.' He handed it over. 'Thank you. What will you do if you cannot plough?'

'I'll start clearing the sluices and drain that swampy patch.'

'The pond?' Quinta had forgotten about it. It was on the edge of their land, downhill from the cottage. Father had dug it out and diverted the stream to keep fish but it was full of reeds now and the surrounding ground was boggy so she never ventured near it.

'Yes. Before that, though, I'll show you how to lay rabbit snares to keep them off your greens.'

'Oh, there's no need.'

'But there is,' he argued. 'You will increase your yields. Look, I know you don't want this arrangement and you agreed only to please your mother, but we're stuck with each other for nigh on two weeks and we have to make the best of it.'

So that is what he thought! 'I – I – Yes, of course.' She retreated to the cottage with the venison.

He waited patiently with the snares for her return. He showed her where to place them in a brisk, matter-of-fact manner. When he had finished she said, 'Thank you. I'll check and reset them when they need it. Will you eat your dinner in the kitchen with me?'

'If you wish.'

'The hare that your father shot on the moor will be ready by noon.'

It felt awkward at first, having a hulking great man sitting at the dinner table instead of her mother. His hair was wet and slicked down where he had washed before coming indoors. He had kicked the caking mud from his boots and used the boot-scraper, too. He was hungry and her bread disappeared twice as fast as usual. She was aware that he watched her for much of the time, but, reassuringly, he smiled more.

Without the frown that frequently furrowed his brow, he was remarkably handsome. She realised how different it was to be living with a man in such proximity. Her mother knew that, of course, but she had to learn it. Quinta thought that even though she didn't approve of this arrangement she was finding it an intriguing experience.

As soon as he'd finished he stood up and thanked her. She had made oat biscuits with dripping and he pocketed some to take with him to the pond.

'I'll make venison pies tomorrow,' she said as he left, and went to look for herbs to season them.

The afternoon was hot and she walked upstream to collect water running directly off the moor. It was the coldest clearest nectar and worth the climb. She carried her bucket carefully, enjoying the warm summer sunshine. He came to meet her, scooping out a ladleful and swallowing thirstily.

'I thought I heard a rabbit in one of your snares. He may need finishing off.' He bent to pick up a large flat pebble. 'Shall I?'

'I can do it. The garden is my responsibility and I must learn how to protect it.' She left the bucket in the yard and took the stone from him. 'Where is he?'

'Follow the squeak. Best look sharp and put him out of his misery.'

She nodded and hurried away with her head bent.

She knelt beside the dying animal, distressed as he tried to jump away and then squealed at the pain. He was weakening. The wire had tightened on his hind leg. Already it had shaved bare his fur and blood was running. Her father had often despatched rabbits in his snares. It couldn't be so very difficult. You just hit the creature hard at the side of the head; very hard.

She raised her right arm and tested the weight of the stone. Good and heavy. She pressed her lips together, closed her eyes tightly and dropped her hand. The creature squealed and began to twitch. She brought the stone down again. Then again and again until she was sure it would not squeak or twitch any more. Then she dropped the bloodied stone as if were red hot and found she was breathing heavily.

'I think he's dead now.'

'Oh! You startled me.'

'I thought you said you could do this,' he said, picking up the stone. 'One hit should be enough.' He released the rabbit's leg and reset the snare. 'You haven't killed before, have you?'

She shook her head. 'My father used to do it.'

'You miss him, don't you?'

'Yes. Don't you miss your mother?'

'You don't miss what you've never had.'

'You had foster parents, though?'

'You mean the couple who took me in? They were a cussed old pair who were only interested in how hard I could work for them. They kept me alive as cheaply as they could and didn't care how harsh they made my existence. I was just another Englishman's bast—' He stopped and shrugged. 'Sorry, but I do feel bitter about the way they treated me.'

She knew what he had been going to say. It was a slur on his character and Quinta felt the injustice of it. 'It wasn't your fault.'

'No. But I suffered the disgrace.'

Perhaps that was why his father had searched so diligently to find him and then kept him moving about the country. She thought of the baptism in church. Even though the family was poor and ill shod, it was respectable.

He gazed past her at the pasture. 'Your father farmed Top Field well. How did he come by it in the first place?'

Quinta shrugged. 'I'm not sure. My mother said it was just after I was born. He did a favour for the old Squire at the Hall and in return he persuaded Farmer Bilton to issue the lease. The old Squire gave him three years' rent in advance.'

'He must have saved his life or something.'

'I guess so. He's dead now so I don't suppose anybody will ever know.'

'Not even your mother?'

'I think she does. But I've asked her and she won't tell me.'

'Well, it is in the past now, though if your father was a hero she would not want it forgotten.'

Quinta had not considered this before and wondered whether she should probe further.

'Are you angry with your mother?' she queried.

'She was a dutiful daughter, but I should have liked a different childhood.'

'Life must have been hard for you as a traveller without a home.'

'Quite the opposite. I'd rather be with my father on the road than treated as an animal by some rancid old farmer.'

Like Farmer Bilton's itinerant labourers, thought Quinta. Patrick sounded angry and she bit at her lower lip. She picked up the flaccid rabbit, still warm and soft. 'I should go back.'

'No, don't go. I didn't mean to upset you.'

'I'm not upset. You are.'

'Not really. I just wish my father had found me sooner.'

'I expect he does too.' She put out one hand to get up. 'I'll get this gutted and skinned.'

'Let me do that. Stay awhile.'

'Very well.' She sank back to her knees and the rabbit dropped from her hands.

He took a large huntsman's knife from a leather sheath attached to his belt and squatted down beside her to slit the rabbit's belly, tossing aside its steaming guts. Then he pushed his fingers between the fur and the flesh and began to prise away the pelt.

Quinta watched his strong deft fingers work. He was better

at it than she was. His hands were strong. Everything about him was strong. He finished by cutting off the head, then wiped his knife on the fur and laid the naked animal in its own skin as a wrapping.

'Thank you,' she said.

She'd cook it for their dinner tomorrow. He toiled hard in their fields and needed meat every day. He was probably used to eating it all the time with his father on the road. She wondered if they ever went poaching and decided that they probably did. You never knew with strangers. But he didn't seem a stranger to her any more. Now he was more like a friend, kneeling beside her and looking at her with his head on one side. She smiled at him.

The blue of his eyes darkened suddenly and his lips moved slightly. He ran his tongue over them briefly and she had a sudden desire to do the same with hers. She looked down, flustered and confused. She wanted to lean over and – and – and *kiss him*. She wondered if he wanted the same for he seemed to edge closer to her.

Then he carefully slid his knife back into its leather sheath and hitched it out of sight under his jacket. 'I'll get back to work. There's more than a fortnight's labour in clearing that pond.'

She carried the bloodied animal back to the stream, gave it a good wash in clean water then took it indoors to soak in brine ready to cook for the next day.

The balmy days gave way to chilling breezes racing up the valley. The winds took on a force that whipped her skirts about and took her cotton bonnet clean off her head. Quinta feared her winter cabbages would be rocked from their roots as they struggled to establish a firm footing. Patrick stopped burning the brambles and spent reeds from the pond as he could not control the smoke and flame.

Farmer Bilton rode by during the first week of her mother's

141

absence. Now that she was alone in the house Quinta felt more nervous of him. He rode right into their yard and walked his horse slowly around, looking at everything, hoping, no doubt, to find fault with their efforts to put their land to better use. She went outside and stood waiting patiently for him to leave.

'What's going on back there?' he barked.

'We are clearing the pond and sluices, sir.' She had to raise her voice as the wind took away her words. 'We can use that corner of the pasture if we drain the marsh.'

'It's too late to plant grain.'

'This year maybe, but, God willing, we'll have some next summer. And roots will see us through the winter. We'll have more than we need, sir. Perhaps you can take some for your stock, in lieu of the extra rent?'

'I thought the cripple and his lad were moving on.' When she didn't reply he added, 'Where is your mother?'

'Busy, sir. It's harvest-time.'

'Is she in the kitchen? I'll have a word.' He prepared to dismount.

Quinta darted forward. She had an uneasy feeling about Farmer Bilton and didn't want him in the house. He was a surly, ill-mannered brute. His only saving graces were that he was known to be a good farmer and wanted to please his betters. Perhaps he was having second thoughts about Mother being his housekeeper? 'She's not here, sir,' she said loudly. 'She's out visiting.'

'I don't believe you. In this gale without you?' He tugged at the bit, turned his horse and spurred him to a canter down the track.

Later, at dinner, she told Patrick about his call. 'He asked what you were doing.'

'Did he want anything else?'

'Only to speak with Mother. I said she was out.'

'Very wise. I don't trust that man.'

'Me neither.'

★　　★　　★

142

From that day Patrick kept his eyes and ears peeled for Farmer Bilton. The pond was out of sight of the track unless you were on horseback and Patrick frequently straightened to his full height to scan the hillside. He was not surprised to see the familiar black horse picking its way through the scrub.

'You! Get over here.'

Patrick put down his scythe and clambered clear of the brambles.

'A visit to church doesn't make you one of us, you know,' Farmer Bilton called.

'What do you want, sir?' he answered.

'I want you off my land. You and the cripple. I heard he took the widow to town on the carrier. Taking advantage, that's what he's doing, and turning her head with a bit of gold. Well, I'll not have him bed her on my property.'

Patrick clenched his fists. Big as he was, Bilton was old and he could have him off that horse and dumped in the pond as easily as look at him. 'Do you have an understanding with Mrs Haig, sir?'

'Aye, I do, and it's not what you think. I'll not have you interfering with my plans. So if you and the cripple don't get off my land, I'll get the constable's men after you.'

'On what charge, may I ask?'

'I'll think of something. Folk know me round here, so I should make a run for it while you still can.'

'Your threats don't frighten me, sir. I am hard-working and law-abiding as anyone who knows me will testify.'

'Perhaps your father will see sense. Is he with the widow now?' He rode off without waiting for reply.

Patrick stood quite still for a few minutes to rein in his mounting anger. He hated bullies like this landlord. Such men had made his childhood a living hell; and he had seen weaker souls broken by their brutality. But as he grew into a man himself his father had schooled him well to control his aggression. Patrick had been an able and willing pupil and listened to his wisdom.

His father had used his mind as well as his muscle to win conflicts, whether they were on or off the battlefield.

Farmer Bilton spurred his large black hunter up the track towards the cottage and Patrick walked purposefully after him.

A bowl of vegetables, washed ready for peeling and cutting up, was standing on the table. A brace of pigeons were beside it, waiting to be plucked and filleted for their breasts.

'They'd better not be from Five-acre Wood.'

'Oh!' Quinta jumped. Farmer Bilton's bulky frame blocked the open doorway as he stepped inside. 'You startled me. I didn't hear your horse.' This persistent wind masked all sounds from the yard.

He looked around. 'Where's your ma?'

'She's not here, sir.'

'Out a'courting with the cripple again, is she? They've been seen together, you know. Causing a scandal, she is, leaving you alone with that lad doing the work.'

Quinta dried her hands. 'What do you want, sir?'

He closed the door behind him, shutting out the bright daylight. 'I want to talk to your ma, but, seeing as she's not here, you'll do. We understand each other, you and me, don't we, Miss Quinta? You wouldn't have a jar of ale in that pantry, would you?'

Patrick enjoyed ale with his dinner so she replied, 'I have cider, sir.'

'That'll do. Bring a jar for yourself, too.'

Quinta heaved a sigh. He was their landlord; she had better do as he asked. He sat at the kitchen table and shoved aside the pile of dried beans waiting to be picked over and cleaned.

'Now, Miss Quinta, I know your ma has got some hoity-toity ideas, but answer me this, where is she going to find a better offer for you? Eh? Not around these parts. They've all gone to mines and furnaces in the valley. Is she going to take you down there to find a husband? No. And why should she when I'm here, ready and waiting, with a house and a farm?' He swallowed most of his cider in one gulp. 'I know you looked fondly on my idea afore, even if your ma didn't.'

'Well, not exactly fondly, sir,' she answered carefully. 'And things are different now, sir. We have help on the farm.'

'That ruffian out there?'

'He's not a ruffian. His father was a sergeant in the Duke of Wellington's army at Waterloo. He can read and write and he practises good husbandry.'

'Aye, so I'm told. Why is he hanging about here, then? I'll tell you. It's for his father to wed your ma and get his hands on my tenancy. Well, that isn't going to happen and when he realises that and can't find any valuables about the place to plunder, he'll clear off and good riddance—' Farmer Bilton stopped suddenly as though a thought had dropped into his head. 'Unless – unless he's got his sights on – on *you*. Oh aye, of course, why didn't I see it before?' His face darkened and became quite agitated.

'He only wants work, sir. And he's a good labourer.'

Farmer Bilton stood up. 'Now, Miss Quinta, I'm a God-fearing gentleman and I've tried to do what's right, but you and your ma have tried my patience. I've made a good offer and if you come back to my farm with me now, you have my promise.'

Alarmed, Quinta stepped backwards. 'What promise?'

He was breathing rapidly and she saw beads of sweat appear on his brow. 'I'll make you my wife, of course. Yes, that's what I'll do.' He grasped at her hand. 'You and me, we have to make your ma see sense. Come with me, lass, and we'll seal it. If we do it now your ma will be bound to say yes. She'll have to. She won't see you shamed.'

'I don't know what you mean, sir?' But she knew exactly what he was saying and took another step away from him. She felt the couch on the back of her legs.

'Don't be coy, Miss Quinta. You're too sharp for that. I'll not have some gypsy take you afore I do. You'll be *my* woman and no one else's.'

'I shall not. Let go of my hand!' She tugged hard but he had a firm grip on her.

He lowered his voice menacingly and pulled her towards him. The sweat was accumulating, glistening, on his forehead. 'Do as I say, girl.'

'No, sir! You are frightening me! I think you should leave.'

'Leave? Not without you, I won't. I'm not letting that – that vagrant take what's rightly mine. The old Squire said you would be mine one day.'

'I know nothing about that! And neither do you because it's a lie!'

'It is not! And you could ask him for yourself if he weren't dead and gone! His son'll tell you, though. He knows. And he knows why. He said I hadn't the background to marry into the gentry as befits my new station in life but you would do for me. And by the Lord you will.' He pushed her backwards on to the couch by the wall and towered over her as she fell.

'Mr Bilton, you must stop this! Have you gone mad?'

'I'm mad, right enough. Mad with your ma for not keeping her husband's promise. And I'll be even madder with you if you don't come with me. He told me no one else would want you.'

'*He was wrong!*' Patrick's voice came from the doorway.

Quinta was so relieved to see him. 'Oh, thank goodness you're here. I don't know what has come over Farmer Bilton.'

Her landlord turned angrily and shouted, 'You keep out of this! It's none of your business!'

'I think you should leave, sir, as Miss Quinta has asked you to,' Patrick said evenly.

'You're the one who can get out of here! This is my property and you have no right to be on my land.'

'If you do not go, sir, I shall have to make you.'

'You? You dare to threaten me?' He let go of Quinta's hand and swung a heavy fist in the direction of Patrick's head.

Patrick reacted quickly. He ducked and aimed a punch at

Farmer Bilton's body, catching him full in the stomach. Winded, his knees buckled and Patrick heaved him by the collar of his jacket to the door. 'When a lady requests that you to leave her house, it is good manners to do as she asks.'

He bundled him outside, giving a final shove to clear him from the threshold. Then he shut and bolted the door, dropping the bar in place before confronting a shocked and shaking Quinta. 'He's gone,' he said, but he could see that her terror had not ebbed, so he opened his arms and added, 'Come here.'

She stumbled forward, falling against him, half sobbing into his chest.

He held her gently, hardly daring to touch her, watching her shoulders shudder as she tried to compose herself. 'Did he hurt you?' he asked softly.

'No, but he – he frightened me.'

Patrick knew how terrifying bullies could be and his heart broke for her. His arms tightened round her and he murmured, 'You're safe now.' This seemed to help and her gulping eased. He would have liked her to stay longer in his arms but she moved away, wiping her eyes with the back of her hands and straightening her back.

'Do you think he will return?' she asked.

'I believe he will. What was he talking about?'

'I don't know. Truly. I am as puzzled as you are, but I shall certainly ask my mother when she returns.'

'I don't trust him and I don't like the idea of you alone in the cottage all day.'

'I – I'm not alone. You are here.'

'I am halfway down the track, out of sight and, with the winds chasing up the valley, out of earshot, too. You were lucky this time. I knew he was here because he came by the pond to see what I was doing. Next time he won't.'

'What shall I do? He's used to getting his way.'

Patrick looked at her steadily. 'You'll have to call me as soon as you see him.'

'But how will you hear me if this wind keeps up?'

He pressed his lips together thoughtfully. 'There is a way. You're strong enough. And sensible.'

'What do you mean?'

'I'll show you how to fire the gun.'

Alarmed, Quinta exclaimed, 'You don't mean for me to shoot him?'

'Of course not. Aim in the air. It is bound to alarm him and it will warn me that something is wrong.'

Quinta warmed to the idea of giving Farmer Bilton a fright. A taste of his own medicine, she thought. 'Where is your gun?'

'It's safe in the cowshed for now.'

'I'd have to keep it in the kitchen.'

'Leave it here, just inside the door.' He smiled. 'I don't want you blowing a hole through the roof.'

Quinta relaxed a little and smiled back. 'Do you think I could?'

'I think you could do anything you wanted.' He sounded as though he really believed that and she was flattered.

She became flustered and said, 'Well, if I am to be a farmer's wi—, that is, I mean country women ought to be able to shoot as well as their menfolk.' She felt a blush rise to her cheeks.

He stared at her. 'I should get back to work.'

Impulsively, Quinta reached forward and put her hand on his arm. 'Thank you for rescuing me from that awful man. Will you teach me how to fire the gun tonight?'

'If you wish,' he replied.

'After we've eaten, then.'

'Very well.' He continued to stare at her. 'I must go.'

She nodded and returned to her pigeons. Patrick had never been far from her thoughts since mother had left. It had been nearly two weeks now and it seemed like months.

Chapter 13

Despite their early start, the journey had been slow and it had taken all morning for Laura and George to reach town. They had a long wait by the spring at the crossroads for sacks of flour from the miller to deliver to a baker. But it was a pleasant enough day and they had cold pie to sustain them.

The sergeant had cut short his greying beard and hair and, sitting opposite him, Laura studied his weathered face. His eyes were almost lost in crow's feet and wrinkles but they were the same blue as his son's. They shared the same broad forehead and straight nose, too.

At the crossroads they'd moved position to accommodate the sacks and this clearly pained the sergeant greatly. 'I wish I could do something to ease your discomfort,' Laura fretted as they settled for the remainder of their journey.

'Your company cheers me, madam; that, and the notion that my son and your daughter will marry.'

'You sound very sure.'

'I know my son.'

'I am not convinced that my daughter will be won over so easily.'

The sergeant smiled. 'We shall see.' He paused. 'If we are to be companions for a week or more, will you call me George?'

'Very well. Our hopes are that we shall soon be family. I am Laura.'

'Laura. That's a pretty name. I shall be much in your debt for your help. Will you allow me to purchase you a new bonnet?'

'Oh no, sir, that is not at all proper.'

'I was thinking of it as a gift for the ceremony that we wish for.'

'Oh, well, yes, I suppose that would be acceptable, but I do not need another bonnet. However, new ribbons would be very nice.'

'We shall seek out a draper's shop after I have called at the bank.'

Laura had never been inside a bank before and anticipated her visit with interest.

'I have business there first,' George went on. 'Then we shall go to the Crown for our lodgings. Patrick told me it is the most respectable inn in town and near to the surgeon's house.'

When they arrived in the marketplace, he arranged with the carter for Laura's box to be taken straight to the inn and they walked slowly to the High Street. The inside of the bank was wondrous indeed, with a hushed atmosphere, reminiscent of church, a great deal of wood panelling around the walls and a long polished counter. A mature gentleman in a long frock coat talked with the sergeant for several minutes.

Laura's attention was diverted by other customers, especially the ladies who wore pretty summer gowns with matching bonnets and parasols. They were not the gentry that she knew from Swinborough Hall. She guessed they were the wives and daughters of forge-owners and other such manufactories that they had passed on their journey. The town might be dirty but it seemed to be prospering.

But Laura was weary and had coughed twice while she waited, causing attention she did not wish for. It sapped her strength and the medicine was not curing it. She asked George if they might go straight to the inn as soon as he had finished his business. She had stayed at inns as a young maid when she had travelled with the old Squire's children. It was the only time that folk had served her instead of the other way round.

Exhausted by her journey, she was grateful to be shown to her own small chamber on the first floor. It overlooked the courtyard at the back and Laura would have enjoyed watching the comings and goings if she had not been so tired. She took off her cape and gown, laying them carefully over her box on the floor, and climbed gratefully into bed. She luxuriated in the softness of the feather mattress for a few minutes and then drifted into a short sleep, to waken later, refreshed and hungry.

Her box was unpacked and stowed when a tap at the door brought in the innkeeper's wife with a tray of food and drink. 'The gentleman – Sergeant Ross – told me I should let you rest, madam,' she informed her. 'He said to join him at breakfast.'

'Thank you. Where will that be?'

'It's just along the landing. We have a private dining room at the back.'

Laura ate and drank, took a draught of her medicine and went back to bed.

In the morning a young girl brought her warm water to wash in and she felt stronger. She dressed her hair in front of the looking glass, wiped down her gown and buffed her boots. George was already at his breakfast and they murmured pleasantries to each other as she sat opposite him. He sliced cold baked ham, forked it on to her plate and poured ale from a pitcher into metal tankards. Laura sawed at a fresh crusty loaf and helped herself to butter. Her appetite was small but she enjoyed what she could manage.

'You are quiet this morning,' George commented.

'I am thinking of my daughter, alone with your son.'

'He will take good care of her.'

'It does not seem any time at all since I was holding her in my arms as a babe. I hope I have done the right thing.'

'She will not be persuaded into anything she does not want.'

'No. And I do believe she will be happy with your son.'

'We shall have them wed in the village church before next month is out.'

Laura smiled. 'I shall look forward to that. I really shall.'

'I sent word about you to the Dispensary last night. The apothecary replied that he has a colleague, a physician, who will see you today.'

'He is to come here?'

'With your leave, Laura, he is to call before noon. The innkeeper's wife will wait on you. She is an educated lady and serves as postmistress for this town.'

'Will you speak with him about your leg?'

'I am to see the surgeon later this week. He has seen service on the battlefield and I shall consult with him.'

Laura had not had an interview with a medical gentleman before and wondered what she should say to him. She sat stiffly in a high-back chair waiting for him to arrive. The innkeeper's wife showed him into her chamber. He asked if the woman might bring him in a chair from the landing and she did so, and then waited silently by the door.

The physician carried a leather bag, which he placed on the bed before drawing the chair near to her and asking a lot of questions. Laura had never been quizzed so about her habits and at first she was reticent, glancing nervously at the other woman. This gentleman was a stranger and he was, well, a good deal younger than she. He was also very persistent. Then he asked the innkeeper's wife to assist her in undoing the bodice of her gown and taking her arms out of the sleeves.

Mortified she asked, 'Why, sir?'

'I wish to listen to you breathing.'

She thought he could hear her just as well without removing

her clothes and became hot and flustered. He stood up to get a towel from the washstand. 'Place this around you, ma'am.'

Laura blushed furiously and hurriedly did as he asked while he opened his bag and took out a brass tube, flared at one end. The innkeeper's wife whispered, 'He comes from down south but they say he's ever so clever.'

He put the flared end of the tube to her chest and the other end to his ear, giving her instructions to breathe in and out. Then he went round the other side of her chair and told her to lean forward while he listened to her back. He came so very close to her that she started to shake with the anxiety of not knowing what he would do next.

She was relieved when he said, 'You may help Mrs Haig into her gown, now. Perhaps you would fetch her a little brandy, too?'

She felt better when he sat down again.

'Do you have blood in your handkerchief when you cough, ma'am?'

How did he know? she thought. She hadn't even told Quinta about that. 'Sometimes.'

'When did you first notice it?'

She thought for a moment. 'Eastertide.'

'So it is becoming worse. And your chest hurts when you cough?'

'Well, yes. Can you tell me how to ease it, sir?'

'I'll write you a note to take to the Dispensary. You live in the country, madam?'

She nodded.

'You must return there. Do not reside in town near to the manufactories or the coal mines. Nourish yourself well with eggs, sweet milk and poultry meat.'

'Will my cough get better, sir?'

His face was very serious and he did not answer her straight-away. 'It is the consumption, Mrs Haig. I believe it took a hold of you when your late husband passed away. You were weakened by your distress. The severe winters have added to your impairment. However, now your circumstances have improved there is a chance you may do so, too.'

There was hope for improvement! She felt better already.

'But you are sick, madam, and in time your cough will become more painful. You may take one of my mixtures for that.' He took out a bound book, wrote in it with a thick pencil, then tore out the page and handed it to her. 'The apothecary will make this up for you.'

'I see.' Her pleasant feeling ebbed away.

'I am told you have a daughter. Is she well?'

'Why, yes. She is robust and strong. I hope to see her married soon.' Laura now prayed that this would happen. Patrick would be there for Quinta when she was too poorly to help. She wondered how long it would be before she weakened further.

He nodded. 'Good, good. Your daughter will care for you. Should you take a turn for the worse, tell her to send for me.'

'But I live at Top Field, on the other side of Swinborough!'

'I have a swift horse, ma'am. How else am I to treat you if I cannot come to see you?'

'Thank you, sir.' Laura sat nervously twisting her fingers, while he made more notes in his book. Eventually she said, 'Will you present your account to me here, sir?'

'It is all settled, ma'am. Your benefactor has given me a note from his bank.'

'Do you mean Sergeant Ross?'

'The same. Ah, here is your brandy. You must take great care of yourself, Mrs Haig. Good day to you.'

'Good day, sir.' Laura took the brandy and sipped gratefully, lost in her thoughts.

'Will there be anything else, Mrs Haig?'

She had forgotten about the innkeeper's wife. 'No . . . that is, yes. Tell Sergeant Ross I shall be down presently. I need some time alone first.'

Laura sat quietly in her chair, absorbing all the physician had said to her. She was very ill. She had a dreadful disease that would slowly sap her strength and, sooner or later, she would die. She would rather not have come here today and learned that, and for a brief moment she was angry with George. He had known she was sick. Perhaps he'd realised what it was, for, as a soldier, he must have seen men sicken and die from disease as much as from battle. Yet he had offered her this way of procuring the best doctoring help in the Riding. He must think more highly of her than she realised.

He had chosen to help her first when he had difficulties of his own to deal with. He was a worthy man. She hoped that the soldier's surgeon would have better news for George than the physician had for her.

Laura had no appetite for her dinner at the inn and, although the food was cooked and served to her, it was not tempting enough for her taste.

'This is good beef but it has been too long over the fire,' George commented. 'We shall take our dinner at a different inn tomorrow. Is your chamber all you would wish for?'

'It is very comfortable.'

'Mine, too. And we are conveniently placed for the High Street, so we shall not move.'

'Surely we shall not be here long? When will the surgeon call on you?'

'Never mind me. You need a little cheering. I have promised you ribbons and there is a musical performance tomorrow evening at the Mechanics' Institute.'

'Oh, I do enjoy music.'

'I, too. We shall dress in our best and take supper afterwards at the Red Lion.'

Laura's eyes shone in anticipation. 'I should like that very much.'

'This afternoon we shall go to the draper's. You will not mind if I accompany you?'

'Not at all. But the High Street is steep . . .'

'I have my magic mixture, ma'am,' he said cheerfully. 'It carries me away on its wings and I am a youth again.'

Laura laughed. She too experienced the same euphoric feeling when she took her medicine.

'How good to see you laugh! You have worried too much of late.' He raised his tankard to her. 'Let me have the pleasure of indulging you with gifts and entertainment.'

She responded with her own goblet and smiled. 'You must not spoil me, sir.'

He held up a piece of unappetising, overcooked beef on his fork. 'I don't think there is much chance of that, do you?'

She laughed again. 'Perhaps the pudding will be better.'

For two or three days Laura forgot her misgivings about Quinta and Top Field and her own sickness. George encouraged her to believe that all would be well because he was always so sure that it would be. She retrimmed her best bonnet and the bodice of her Sunday gown. George insisted that he buy her a fancy purse, the kind she had seen ladies with at balls, and she carried it over her arm when they went to the musical concert.

She enjoyed a perfect evening. They stayed quite late at the Red Lion in the company of others who had been in the audience and were escorted to their inn by a pair of burly ironworkers who were students at the Institute. It was an aspect of town life she had not known and she thought again about coming to market with Quinta.

The day after the concert, George spent the morning at a lawyer's office and then he took her for dinner to dining rooms recommended by that gentleman. She continued to marvel at the refinements being introduced to a place that, since her last visit, she had regarded as evil and dirty. He persuaded her to try a tiny cup of coffee after her pudding. She tasted it and passed it across to him.

'It's too bitter for me.'

'It revives the spirits well.'

'And it is dear, so do not waste it.'

He put his head on one side. She thought his crinkly eyes were very kind when he smiled.

'I am grateful you are here with me,' he said. 'The surgeon calls on me tomorrow.'

George stayed quite still on the bed while the surgeon examined his stiff and swollen knee. He was older than George had expected. 'You were in the Sixty-fifth Regiment, I am told, sir?' the sergeant asked.

'Yes, indeed I saw service in the Persian Gulf campaign and Mauritius. We were keeping the East India trade routes open while you were defeating Bonaparte. The second battalion of the Eighty-fourth was out there, too. It is recruiting in the Riding at present.'

'What happened to you when the war with France was over?'

'I served the King in the West Indies until I lost my dear wife to a fever. I resigned my commission,' said the surgeon.

'I am surprised you have chosen to come here, to the South Riding.'

'London society had no appeal for me without her. I am too old for the hardships of war. Yet it is those very privations that I miss. The railways and industries of Northern England are the nearest I can find to a battlefield. We took a musket ball out of this, you say?'

George winced as the surgeon examined his ragged scarring and prodded the inflamed skin with his fingers. 'Yes, sir. It took a long while to heal and it's never been strong since. Now I cannot tolerate the pain without laudanum. Even that does not take it away completely. But it causes me to care less about it.'

'If you take enough to dull the pain it will dull your senses, too.'

'Aye, and hasten my end.'

'I fear the bone is putrid.'

157

'Can you cure it?'

'If I do nothing the poison will spread. But you have survived such fevers once before.'

'I was twenty years younger then.'

'You would have had a better chance of recovering from the alternative at that age, too.'

George understood what he was saying. 'Take it off, you mean?'

'My saws and knives are the finest Sheffield steel and I have the services here of a field assistant who came home with me from the Indies.'

'Well, if you did, at least the pain would be gone, and a peg leg would be more use than this one. Will you do it here?'

'It will be better for you to come to my chambers. You will need careful tending afterwards. I can arrange that for you. I have taken a house for such a purpose.'

'How soon can you do it?'

'Tomorrow, if you wish.'

George was silent for full two minutes. The surgeon did not press him. Finally he said clearly, 'Very well. It is time.'

'Come in the morning when the light is good.'

Chapter 14

Quinta had made gooseberry cheese with elderflower cordial and honey and she served it on pastry circles that she cut out with the rim of one of her mother's valued wine glasses.

Patrick leaned back in her father's old chair, the one she had once offered to Farmer Bilton, and smiled at her. He looked so very handsome in the twilight. His teeth and light eyes contrasted starkly with his sun-darkened skin. She wondered if he took his shirt off in the afternoon heat and guessed that he did as it was hardly soiled. His back must have been sorely scratched by the bundles of reeds and brambles he carried away from the pond.

'I should show you the gun before the light goes completely. Do you still want me to?'

'I do.' In fact, Quinta looked forward to brandishing it at Farmer Bilton. It would surely stop him coming over here and bothering her. Patrick stood up and went to the cowshed, returning to the front door with his rifle. She wondered where he had hidden it for she had looked in there since his father had left and could not see it. She had even moved old straw and tools but still could not find it.

'Come outside,' he said, 'and get used to the weight first.'

She did and almost dropped it, it was so heavy. The barrel was so long it tipped forward, hitting the front step.

'Careful! Try and stand the butt on the ground. If you hide it near to hand, all you need to do is lift it up, step outside and pull the trigger. Like this.' He showed her the movement, making it look so easy, and then added, 'Keep it pointing towards the sky. Here, you have a go.'

Her eyes widened. It had seemed a good idea this morning. Now she wasn't so sure.

'Go on,' he urged. 'It's not loaded. A shot at this hour would surely bring the gamekeeper round.'

She heaved the cumbersome weapon upwards and placed her finger on the trigger nervously. It clicked harmlessly and she practised several times until she was used to the way it moved.

'I'll load it in the morning and leave it in the house when I go to the pond. Remember, if you have to fire it, point it in the air. Oh, and the noise will be very loud and frightening.'

'Well, that's the idea, isn't it?'

'For Farmer Bilton, not for you,' he said seriously. 'I'll come as fast as I can if I hear it.'

He was a man of his word and she trusted him. 'Thank you. Will you stay and talk awhile tonight?' She thought he might, but he hesitated.

'I want to be up at first light. There is much to do.'

'Yes, of course.' Quinta was aware of disappointment but she understood for she was weary herself. She said, 'It's been a long day.'

'Yes. Good night then.' He made no move to leave.

Eventually she responded: 'Good night, Patrick.' She did not stir either. The gun was heavy in her hands but she hardly noticed it as she stared at him silently for what seemed like an age.

He gazed back at her but in the gathering gloom she could

not see his expression and she wondered if he wanted to stay with her as much as she wanted him to. Then he stretched out a hand towards her and said, 'I'll take the gun with me, shall I?'

She lifted the heavy weapon off the ground. He took it from her and said, 'Bolt and bar the door and you'll be quite safe tonight.'

As he said it, she realised that she wanted Patrick inside with her. In the house with her, close to her. She felt secure when he was near and it was nothing to do with the gun or Farmer Bilton. It was everything to do with Patrick himself and she could not totally comprehend it, for she had once been quite fearful about his presence.

He turned and walked away with a resolute stride, holding the gun under his arm. She watched him disappear into the cowshed without a backward glance. She stayed outside telling herself she needed the air. She imagined him settling down for the night.

He had made their humble lodging neat and tidy, if not exactly comfortable. He slept on a blanket on the stone flags in one of the cleaned out, wood-lined cow stalls that her father had built. He had banked up old straw to give warmth and comfort for his father, but he had to wash in a bucket of cold water from the stream and cook over an outdoor fire.

She stood outside the kitchen for a long time in the gathering gloom, until eventually she accepted that the cowshed door was firmly shut for the night. How could she sleep now? When her need for him was so acute? She wanted him to come back to her, be beside her, near enough to touch, not across the yard in the cowshed. As she went indoors and locked and bolted the door, she imagined him rolled in his blanket and fast asleep.

Patrick had been shaken by the landlord's attack on Quinta. Seeing her being attacked by that ogre had made him realise how much he had come to care for her. She was strong and

161

intelligent, but she was vulnerable to a selfish brute like Bilton, who believed he had an absolute right to treat his tenants as he pleased. He remembered landlords like that in Ireland, often Englishmen, who cared only for their profits and nothing for the people trying to scratch a living off their land.

He wanted to look after her, not just through this harvest but for ever. Perhaps his travels were truly over and Top Field was destined to be his future? It was a future he welcomed, but, he admitted, only because Quinta was part of it. For even if he could not save the tenancy for them, he would not be able to walk away from Top Field at the end of the summer unless Quinta came with him. She meant too much to him. As he tossed and turned in his blanket, he realised what his father had seen so clearly but he had not. Until now.

He was attracted to Quinta more than he had been to any woman before; in a way that surprised him. It was not just a physical appeal. He recognised that feeling well enough and knew how easily it was satisfied. But with Quinta it was more. His emotions towards her ran deeper.

Oh, he wanted to bed her, he had no doubt about that, and had acknowledged that from the first time he set eyes on her. But this feeling that had taken him over was more. Was this the love his father spoke of? The passion his father had felt for his mother? He relived the moment when he had clasped her to his body, wanting above anything to protect her from the coarse pawing of her landlord. Her womanly form in his arms had felt so right. This is where he wanted to be. This is where he wanted to stay.

Should he tell her now? He wished his father were here to advise him. He half rose to go outside and see if a candle still burned in the cottage kitchen. But after her ordeal today, a knock at the door in the dead of night would alarm her further and he did not want that. He lay awake, gazing at the vestiges of moonlight pushing through the gaps in the wooden window shutters.

For weeks he thought she had shunned him as a traveller. He wondered what had changed her mind. Her mother's approval, of course, yet he became uneasy that even now she might not return his affection. But tonight, surely, as they had faced each other in the twilight, she had felt the same desire as he? An urge to be together, to touch, to kiss and – and to love.

The kitchen fire burned low. Quinta leaned over it to light a splint for her candle stub. The cottage was so quiet without her mother. She climbed the stairs to the bedchamber slowly and stood by the window staring at the cowshed outlined by moonlight. She was wide awake. Was Patrick asleep already? She thought so. After showing her the gun he had retreated quickly to his bed. He had toiled hard in the fields and must be tired out and anxious for his rest.

He did it all for them, she thought, for their smallholding, for their future; hers and her mother's. But what of his own future, she wondered? What did he want for himself? She had thought he wished to move on, to find steady work in town, near to the Dispensary for his father. She had thought she wished him to leave, too. But now she realised that she did not. It seemed to her that he belonged here.

She wanted him with her, kissing her, loving her. It did not matter that he was a traveller, her heart yearned to beat with his. How could she go to sleep with this longing for him to hold her to his chest as he had done earlier?

The chamber was hot, stiflingly so, as it was situated over the kitchen. The heat was welcome in winter, but not tonight, when Quinta's heart was racing and her head was feverish with this new-found desire. She placed her candle on the window ledge and wrestled with the catch to open it and let in some cool night air. But the wood was old and warped and she could not budge it. Hastily she unbuttoned her gown and unlaced her corset, letting them fall to the floor. She shook her chemise free and it fell away from her skin. She wet her hands in the basin on her washstand, spread the cooling water over her face and neck, and wandered back to the window to pick up her candle and place it by the bed. Then she retrieved her gown and as she straightened she saw him.

The moonlight lit up his form. He was standing outside the cowshed shed, still fully clothed, watching the cottage. He must have seen her. She pressed her hands to the glass and he started forward. She did not move as he continued to walk towards the kitchen door. He stopped a few yards away and continued to stare at her.

She did not think about what she did. She just knew instinctively that she must act. That it was meant to be. She turned and hurried downstairs, crossing the flagged floor to remove the bar, undo the bolts and turn the heavy key in its lock. When she swung open the door he was standing there, waiting, and she held out her hands to his.

'I love you, Quinta.'

'I love you, too.'

'I want you to be mine.'

She gave a small tug on his hands and he needed no more invitation than that. He stepped over the threshold and kicked the door shut behind him and wrapped himself around her to kiss her deeply, passionately and lovingly.

Through her chemise she felt the coarseness of his waistcoat. The leather of his boots, chilled by the night air, brushed her shins. His roughened hands roamed her back. And lower, grasping the flesh of her rear, pressing her to him and it was the most wonderful feeling she had ever known.

His mouth moved from hers to her neck and she breathed, 'I want you to be with me for ever.'

He kissed her hair and murmured, 'Then I shall.'

She took one of his hands from her rear and turned towards the stairs, drawing him after her. He needed no more encouragement and they were soon in the bedchamber, staring silently at each other. The candle stub spluttered and died and they stood in the darkness. Deftly, Quinta slid her fingers under the buttons of his waistcoat, releasing them one by one and peeling it away from his chest. Suddenly he took over, hastily discarding his boots and trousers himself.

She unlaced her boots, rolled down her stockings and stepped out of her drawers. As she climbed into the bed in her chemise, her anticipation was feverish and when she saw that he had removed all his clothes, she was a little fearful of what was to happen. He walked round the bed through a shaft of moon-light and the sight of his finely muscled body caused an unfamiliar yearning in the very core of her being.

Her desire for him was so strong that, when his naked body slid into the bed beside her, she hardly knew what to do next. He lay on his back and turned his head so his lips brushed her cheek. She felt his growth of beard rasp at her skin and welcomed it. She held her breath, her body alive with anticipation. Then her instincts took over. This was something she did not need to be taught. This was love and her hands moved to caress his body as though it was the most natural thing in the world to her. For to her, at that moment, it was.

He inhaled sharply and shivered as she explored every angle and plane of his form. Now that he was so close to her and his skin was touching hers, his desire flared and he wanted to devour and ravish her without a further word. But her tender exploration and her obvious innocence of the depth of passion aroused by her gentle fingers melted his heart. He loved her so much that he hardly dared respond for fear of overwhelming her with his strength, of hurting her in his eagerness to love her. She must be ready for him, to yearn for their physical union as much as he did.

Tentatively, he moved his hand to stroke her breasts, the soft-ness of her flesh contrasting sharply with the firmness of her nipples. He resisted a strong temptation to kiss and toy with them. Her hands stilled their search of his own desire and he heard her breathe in quickly. He moved to her belly, circling the small firm mound with a single finger. He felt her whole body shudder and heard a soft groan from her throat. Her legs became restless as his fingers continued their slow movements over her body.

She was aware of being helpless, of lying on her back with her hands grasping at the air, of knowing that this strong and hand-some man was using the lightest of touches to reduce her to a writhing passion. She was striving, urging her body to attain an unassailable summit, as yet unknown and far beyond her reach. Her breath came out in noisy bursts, groans of ecstasy and ache in equal measure as she climbed. Do not leave me here alone, Patrick! Help me, my love. Help me . . .

When? When? He had not enough experience to know, only that his control was ebbing with each passing second. His love for her consumed him and he wanted to seal that love with a union so magnificent that she would remember it for ever. He loved her too much to let her down in this most intimate of pleasures. Her breathing subsided to shorter snatches at the air; her groans became brief, stifled, whimpering cries. Her back was arched, her knees were raised and he could wait no longer.

The time for gentleness was over and, swiftly, he rolled on top of her, finding her source of ardour quickly and pushing forcibly into her softness. He could not tell whether her brief cry was one of pain or pleasure, only that he might have hurt her, and he stilled himself. As he did he relished the wonder of her tight flesh around his. Then, oh joy of joys, she began a rhythmic movement of her own, of hips, back and forth, rising to meet him, as he increased his thrusting.

His eyes closed in wonder and he prayed that he would last, for he could no longer control himself. He tried to slow, but to no avail. She would not let him. She urged him on with flexions of her own strong back. He opened his eyes to see her beautiful face, eyes and mouth wide open as her body rose to his in one last push that she held, arched and rigid as she cried out. A second later he was overtaken by a rapture of his own, an exquisite release of passion that was all the sweeter for being with her. He loved her. She returned his love. She would be his wife and bear his children and he worshipped her.

Her head and legs fell back on to the bed, sweating in the warm airless chamber. He lay heavily on top of her and she could feel his flesh pulsing inside her. It was the most wonderful feeling and she wanted him to stay there, joined with her, her man, her love, her life. He seemed to have no inclination to move and they lay entwined in silence as they cooled, spent and exhausted. She must have slept, for the next thing she knew there was a hint of dawn light in the sky through the window. He had not shifted. One of her arms was numb and his thick dark hair tickled her cheek. She turned to kiss his head through its springy softness and he stirred, groaned and rolled off her on to his back.

'My Quinta,' he murmured sleepily. 'My woman.'

She smiled adoringly at him. Her arm tingled as its use returned. His Quinta. His woman. How wonderful that sounded! She was his. She was his woman. Truly a woman now. She had grown last night. Yes, she had fallen in love with him, but she was aware of something more, of an awakening she could never have dreamed of. He was her lover and she was his love, too. Soon she would be a wife and then – she caught her breath – perhaps a mother? She would have children, Patrick's children. Lots of them. She wanted that. She drifted off to sleep again with this vision in her head.

When she woke she was aware of a hairpin scratching at her scalp. She had not unpinned her hair last night, or worn a nightcap over it. She must look a dreadful sight. She turned to look at Patrick and he was smiling at her, resting his chin on his hands. She snuggled closer, drawing a murmur of delight from his throat, and felt his desire for her harden against her flesh. Her eyes widened in surprise and his smile broadened.

'I am your slave,' he murmured. 'You have captivated me with your womanly powers. How shall I ever do any work when we are married?'

'How indeed?' She rolled away from him and out of bed. 'I must light the fire.' She picked up her corset and added, 'Look away while I dress.'

'I shall not. But if you do not make haste I shall insist you come back to bed.'

'You will go out into the fields and labour, sir,' she answered good-humouredly as she washed in cold water from the ewer. He did not try and hide his burgeoning need for her and she wondered if he would always want her in the morning as well as at night. She stepped into her drawers and gown, realising she was exceedingly pleased that he wanted her so. She was a little sore and aching from his attentions but she looked forward to more. She sat on the wooden ottoman and pulled on her stockings.

'You won't sleep in the cowshed again, will you?' she asked.

A fire leaped into his eyes that seem to burn right through her and he shook his head slowly.

She pushed her feet into her boots and quickly tightened the laces. 'Good,' she said and thought: How will I get through the hours until tonight?

The fire was drawing well when he came downstairs. He came over to the fireplace and kissed her fully on the mouth. Her sooty hands waved helplessly in the air as his mouth lingered on hers and their tongues entwined briefly. She rubbed her reddened cheek with the back of her hand. His chin bristles were worse than last night.

He noticed and said, 'I'll shave before tonight. Do you need more wood?'

'I do. Have a look for eggs while you're out there. The hens are laying well.'

They were so comfortable in each other's presence, it was as though they were already wed. Well, she thought, they were as good as. They had their parents' blessing and they loved each other. She fried eggs, cut bread and poured ale for breakfast while he carried in logs. Then he brought the gun from the cowshed and placed it by the kitchen door.

'Remember it is loaded so you must keep it pointed in the air. Will you work in the garden today?'

'There are caterpillars on my young winter greens. I must squash them all if I am to have any left for market.'

'I'll collect my tools and be off then.' He kissed her again.

'Come back at noon for your dinner.'

He smiled his broad handsome smile and waved as he left. She went back to her work, mixing flour and balm for bread, setting rabbit and vegetables to stew over the fire and humming softly to herself. The dough was rising under a damp cloth in the hearth. She had washed the pots and carried fresh water from the stream before she donned her sacking apron and went outside to tend her garden. With the extra land she would have roots to sell in the market as well as greens in winter, and she allowed her mind to dream of duckling and fish from the pond.

Her morning's labour was marred only by the sight of Farmer Bilton on his black hunter on the track. It was mid-morning and she was carrying a pile of weeds to the compost heap. There was no reason for him to ride this way except to spy on her and Patrick. The corners of her mouth turned down in distaste. Would he approach her again with his pawing hands and evil intentions? She hurriedly finished her work and went back to the cottage, comforted by the knowledge that Patrick was close by and he would be here in a trice if she fired the gun.

She opened the kitchen door and lifted it to test its weight and practise the hold that Patrick had taught her. It was unwieldy in her hands and the barrel swung around. She heaved it upright again and was about to put it down when she saw the deer. A young one on its own had broken cover from the trees, crossed the stream and was heading for the fresh shoots of her crops. An occasional rabbit or two was bad enough, but a deer could strip her stalks bare within an hour.

Without thinking she ran towards it with the heavy rifle wavering. She could have yelled. It might have heard her and been scared off. Why did she not think? Why did she not control herself? In her panic she squeezed the trigger. A burst of sound split the quiet morning. She recoiled from the blast. The noise deafened her for a moment and heat from the discharge burned the skin on her hands and face, stung her eyes and made her cough. The deer started, twisted and then stumbled to the ground. Lord in heaven, what had she done?

She dropped the heavy gun and ran towards the animal. Distressed, it made valiant efforts to stagger to its feet and run, squealing and squirming in pain. She was close enough to see its frightened eyes and quivering mouth as it stumbled, dragging its hindquarters and struggling towards the stream and the cover of the trees.

She was gaining on it and was close enough to see the tear in its haunch where she had wounded the poor creature. It reached the edge of the wood and collapsed, wild-eyed and panting, its velvety mouth revealing a pink lolling tongue. She knew it was a fatal wound; that the animal would lie there, suffering, until its life ebbed away.

What should she do? This was no rabbit with a tiny skull that was easily fractured by a heavy stone. It tried again to raise its hindquarters and scramble deeper into Five-acre Wood. Tears of distress sprang to Quinta's eyes. She looked up to see Patrick running towards her. He paused only to pick up his rifle on the way.

'I didn't mean to shoot it, only to frighten it from my garden! I didn't even know I'd pulled the trigger. It – it went off in my hand.'

'Dear Lord, this is my doing. I should not have left the gun with you.'

'It's suffering, Patrick. We have to kill it. I can't bear to see it in so much pain.'

'I'll do it.' He ran towards the cowshed and returned with a fresh charge for the rifle. They splashed across the stream to where the creature had fallen. She watched him reload and shoot the deer in its head. It twitched and then lay quite still with its glassy brown eyes wide open.

'It's not your fault,' Quinta said. 'I'm sorry.'

'Don't be. I am to blame for leaving the gun with you before you were ready to use it. I should have given you more lessons first. If you are to be a farmer's wife, you will need to be a better shot than that.' He paused and looked at her. 'And you will be a farmer's wife soon, won't you?'

She managed a nervous smile. In spite of living at Top Field for all her life, she still had much to learn. 'Thank goodness I shot it on our land. I think that makes it ours.'

'Is this part of the wood your land?'

'No. This belongs to the Squire.'

'You shot it here?'

'No! It was in my garden! It fled here.'

'Then we'd better get it back to where you shot it. We don't want to be accused of poaching the Squire's deer.'

'Oh, he would never think that of us, I am sure. Well, the old one wouldn't. I don't know about the new one.'

'Help me drag it back, just to be on the safe side. Take hold of a front leg. It's not too heavy. Just a youngster, I fear.'

'Don't remind me.'

'It was an accident. I should think it's here only because it escaped the Squire's cull. You have probably done him a favour.'

Together they heaved the flaccid animal through the undergrowth and were just wading across the stream when they saw Farmer Bilton approaching on his hunter.

'What's going on here? Well, you don't have to tell me. I can see for myself. You've been poaching the Squire's deer. I knew from the start you were up to no good.'

'It was eating my greens, so I shot it!' Quinta protested.

'Oh, aye? When did you learn how to load and shoot that thing?'

'I only meant to frighten it!'

'I suppose the vagrant had nothing to do with it?' he retaliated sarcastically.

'It was in my garden! It was!'

'Don't give me that. The Squire'll want to know about this. He's the magistrate, you know. I warned him you were giving shelter to a poacher on my land. He'll not argue with me now when I turn you out. Your ma will be begging me to take you in.'

He tugged his horse's head around aggressively and addressed Patrick. 'You and that crippled father of yours'd be well advised to leave the Riding. When Sir William hears about this he'll send for the constable.' He spurred his horse into a gallop and headed in the direction of the Hall.

'Are you certain the deer was on your land?'

'Of course I am. Do you doubt me, too?' She heaved angrily on the foreleg and slipped on a wet stone.

'Of course not. But there's no doubt that I finished him off on the Squire's land.'

'He would have died anyway.'

'Here. Take the gun and I'll drag him on to the bank.'

She hesitated.

'Take it. It's not loaded now.'

She did, until he dropped the animal's front legs well into the rough pasture between her garden and the stream.

'Farmer Bilton'll be back, and with the Squire's gamekeeper. I'll leave the carcass here. Even though he's rightly yours, if we give it back there's no harm done. Hand me the gun now, and go inside. Do as I say.'

She blinked at his tone. He was not asking her, he was ordering her. He walked towards the cowshed without another word. She took off her gardening apron and scrubbed her hands in the bucket by the cottage. Then she went indoors to tend the dinner, but she could not concentrate on her tasks. It was a long time before Patrick came indoors without his gun.

He said, 'I didn't mean to speak harshly to you but I don't trust that Farmer Bilton. He doesn't like me or my father living here. What was he talking about the other day, when he said the old Squire had promised you to him?'

'It's a lie. He had no rights over me anyway, but my mother told me he had suggested it to my father and, well, he presumed my father would take his advice without question.'

'Your father didn't promise you?'

'Not as far as I am aware. My mother would have known and she is dead set against Farmer Bilton.'

'We must stay calm.' He sat down at the table.

'But we have done nothing wrong! You can go back to the pond.'

'I'm not leaving you until this matter is cleared up and the deer is off your land.'

'Well, dinner won't be long.'

'It smells good but my appetite has gone.'

'Mine too.'

Patrick did not talk for a while. He appeared to be deep in thought and he frowned for much of the time. She, too, was worried about what Farmer Bilton might do and before long they heard horses approaching. They looked silently at each other and got up to go outside.

'Who's the gentleman on the thoroughbred?' Patrick whispered as two horsemen cantered into the yard.

It was not the gamekeeper. 'It's the young Squire.'

'He's not very young now.'

He was still handsome, though, in a dashing way; quick-thinking and agile. Quinta thought him an attractive gentleman.

As a very young girl, sitting in the back pew at church, Quinta had fancied that she would be his bride one day. Her mother had been shocked when she told her and actively discouraged what she called a 'silly notion'.

Now she realised how foolish she had been. When the old Squire died and he inherited, he was already a successful mine-owner and iron-smelter as well as a gentleman farmer with a wife who was the daughter of a wealthy manufacturer from the town.

Yet they had produced no children between them. It was said that his wife was always with child but of a weak constitution. She lost infant after infant until her health began to fail. It was not for the want of advice, money or care. Indeed it was known to be a great source of sorrow for husband and wife. Quinta remembered that when she heard tales of his expansive influence in the Riding.

She looked up at the man she loved and smiled nervously. He searched for her hand in the folds of her skirts and gave it a reassuring squeeze. The Squire slid easily from his horse and Farmer Bilton dismounted more awkwardly.

'Is this he?' Sir William demanded loudly.

'Aye, sir. Vagrant and poacher. Should be locked up, I say.'

'I shall be the judge of that.' He approached Patrick with the arrogant bearing of the gentry. 'What have you to say for yourself?'

'It was me, sir,' Quinta answered. 'I shot the deer because it was eating my garden greens.'

'He's told her to say that to save his skin,' Farmer Bilton responded. 'He's wormed his way in here, taking advantage of a poor widow. He thinks he can take over the land and the maid. Look at her, innocence itself, and him – he's just a dirty gypsy.' He clenched his fists threateningly. 'By God, if you've had her I'll kill you! I will!'

'Be quiet, Bilton!' The Squire had raised his voice to a boom. He stared silently at Quinta for what seemed to be a long time and then asked, quite kindly, 'Where is your mother, Miss Haig?'

'She's gone into town, sir.'

'And left you alone with this vagrant on your land?'

'She – she has gone to the Dispensary, sir.'

'Does she ail?'

'A little, sir.'

'I see.' He looked at their clasped hands, pursed his lips and turned to Patrick. 'You, show me the carcass.'

Reluctantly, Patrick let go of Quinta and led the Squire across the pasture. She watched the Squire circle around the beast and then inspect the grass, laid flat where they had dragged it from the stream. He looked across the water at the crushed undergrowth where the animal fell. Then he bent to examine its wounds. His voice carried clearly in the still August air.

'This creature was killed in my wood, using two shots, and from a rifle, if I am not mistaken. I do not tolerate poaching on my land.'

Quinta strained her ears to listen to Patrick's reply. She heard his low deliberate tones, but could not make out his words.

'Where is the rifle?' the Squire demanded loudly.

This time there was silence from Patrick.

'Insolent ruffian! I demand that you give up your gun!'

Again Patrick did not reply.

The Squire was almost as tall as Patrick and grabbed him by the collar of his jacket. 'By heaven, I am the magistrate! You will answer me or I shall have you in chains.'

Quinta held her breath as Patrick murmured a reply, shrugged off the Squire's hand, bowed his head briefly and strode across the pasture towards her. 'What did you tell him?' she whispered.

'The truth; that the deer was on your land and it was shot by accident.'

'But not that I did the shooting?' she queried.

'We have done nothing wrong,' he replied quietly and held a finger to his lips for a moment.

She remembered an adage her mother often used: least said, soonest mended, and nodded briefly.

The Squire had hurried after Patrick. 'Bilton!' he yelled. 'Search the property. Find that rifle.'

'Aye, sir.' He headed for the cottage door.

'No!' Quinta started forward and was stilled by Patrick's strong grip on the back of her skirt.

'Stay where you are, miss,' the Squire ordered. 'You are not wholly innocent in this sorry incident. You will do as I say or I shall send for the constable.'

She guessed Patrick felt as outraged as she did and dared not look at him when they were forced to listen to Farmer Bilton crash through her home and her possessions. He came out empty-handed and went into the cowshed, only to emerge with the same consequence. He opened the privy, looked in the woodshed and trampled on her garden as he hunted.

'Try the log pile!' the Squire barked and Farmer Bilton pushed it over, spooking the horses as the logs rolled across the yard.

Eventually, angry and sweating, Farmer Bilton growled, 'He must have dropped it in the stream.'

'Don't be ridiculous, Bilton! Even a stupid gypsy would not do that. The gun is here somewhere. I shall send my constable to search for it. He is more used to the ways of the criminal.'

'We are not criminals, sir!' Quinta protested.

The Squire stared at her again. 'You are not, Miss Haig, but you are tainted by your association with this ruffian. I shall remove him from your land and save your good self from further corruption. You are fortunate in having such a vigilant neighbour as Farmer Bilton to watch over your welfare.'

'No! You can't. We are to be—'

'Hush, Quinta,' Patrick interrupted, 'do not say any more.'

'You,' the Squire cried, pointing at Patrick, 'will be silent! You will come with me now to answer for yourself in the town court. If you do not I shall send my constable and his men to hound you down as a fugitive.' He went to his horse and rummaged in the saddlebag.

'Do not worry, Quinta,' Patrick whispered hurriedly. 'I told him the truth but Farmer Bilton has already poisoned his mind against me. My father is in the town and he will speak up for my honesty. I'll make contact with him from the gaol.'

'Gaol?' Quinta's heart constricted in her breast.

'It is only until the Squire is persuaded I am innocent.'

'Step aside, miss.' The Squire approached Patrick with a hank of rope. Patrick held up his wrists while the Squire bound them and fastened the loose end to the strapping on his horse. When he had finished he asked, 'May I take it that your mother will be home soon?'

'Oh yes, sir, very soon.'

'Mr Bilton,' the Squire ordered as he remounted, 'you are responsible for this young woman's safety until her mother returns.'

'Aye, sir, you can rely on me,' Farmer Bilton drawled. A smile distorted his fleshy features. 'I'll take full charge of her now.'

Patrick said quickly, 'Keep the door barred, Quinta. I'll tell Father to send your mother home immediately. I love you. Never forget that.' The horse moved off, jerking the rope and pulling Patrick away from her.

'I won't. I love you, too,' she replied hoarsely. She wondered if he had heard her.

'Now then, my lass.' Farmer Bilton walked towards her. 'Why don't I come inside with you and you can draw me a tankard of that fine ale you have in your pantry.'

Quinta darted across the yard, jumping nimbly over the scattered logs, and ran swiftly into the cottage. She closed and barred the door behind her and pressed herself against it out of sight of the front window.

She heard him banging on the door. 'You can't stay in there for ever,' he called. 'I can wait. Now that jumped-up gypsy is out of the road, I can wait a day or two more.'

She leaned against the woodwork, feeling the metal fixings jab into her back. Her eyes roved around the kitchen. She had newly baked bread, fresh water and meat in her cooking pot. She could stay inside with the door barred for a week and Mother would be home, surely, within a day or two. Two against one was better odds for her, she thought.

'Come home soon, Mother,' she said to the empty room. 'What is keeping you in town for so long?'

Chapter 15

After the surgeon had left the inn, George had joined Laura in the dining room. 'It is all set for tomorrow, Laura,' he said. 'If you feel strong enough, I should like you to be with me. Is that too much to ask of you?'

'Of course it isn't. I shall be pleased to return some of the kindness you have shown me. But I do think Patrick should be here. Please let me fetch him for you.'

'It is better he looks to his own future than waste his time fretting over mine.'

'But – but . . .' Laura did not know how to say it. 'You might . . .'

'Die? Not me. Old Boney couldn't kill me off, so why should this? Besides, we have had ten good years together and he knows I can't go on without the attentions of a surgeon.'

'He would want to know of your decision.'

George shook his head emphatically. 'My greatest wish is for him to marry your daughter and settle in the South Riding. And – and I should be at ease tomorrow if you are with me.'

'Even so, you ought to send word to him.'

He gave her a strange look, wide-eyed yet enquiring, as though he were not used to such argument and she guessed he wasn't. He had spoken his final word on the matter.

Laura did not agree with him, but she said, 'You have been very kind to me and I shall be pleased to tend to your needs.'

'The surgeon has an attendant who will do all that is required, but I should like you to be there when I wake up.'

'Then I shall. And do all I can to hasten your recovery.'

'I have a wedding to look forward to, and so do you. Did I see lace in the draper's shop when we visited? Quinta would look well in a little lace.'

'Indeed she would, but I am afraid it is too dear for me.'

'But not for me. You may charge it to my name. It is all arranged with my lawyer, Laura. Choose something pretty for her.'

Laura's heart leaped. Her Quinta wed in a lace-trimmed veil! And with lace adorning her gown and posy! 'Oh, could I, George? Will you come with me?'

He shook his head. 'I have a letter to write to Patrick. I wish to leave it with you to give it to him should – should the worst happen to me.'

'I am sure you will be able to hand it to him for yourself,' Laura replied briskly. She was unable to consider any other possibility.

The surgeon's residence was on the Mansfield road where all the new houses were built for the town's prospering manufacturers and merchants. They set off after breakfast the next day. It was a short distance from the Crown, but uphill all the way. They were let in by a housekeeper and led into a small sitting room. After what seemed to Laura to be a long wait, a gentleman entered who introduced himself to her as the surgeon and then took George out with him. He came back a few moments later for her and said, 'Sergeant Ross is asking for you. It gives great comfort for a loved one to be present. However, it will be . . . distressing for you.'

Laura stared at him in silence. George wanted her beside him. During the procedure.

'Perhaps you would hold his hand, ma'am? My housekeeper is present, too.'

'Very well, sir.'

'Follow me.'

The surgery was plain and sparsely furnished with a heavily stained wooden bench near the window. The oblong surface had a groove around the edge to catch the blood and three hefty leather straps with brass buckles to hold the patient steady. A table was laid out in an orderly fashion with the surgeon's instruments, bowls, bottles of spirits and strips of cotton. There were enough candles to light a ballroom.

The housekeeper stood by a fierce fire burning in a large grate. She was a capable, large-boned woman who had given Laura a large brown apron to cover her gown. She was heating water in a copper urn with a long brass spout and small tap. And tending to a copper saucepan with a long handle. Laura could smell the hot tar that the surgeon would use to stem the flow of blood and seal his stump. George would have fallen into a faint long before the time came for that.

He was such a brave man, she thought as he climbed awkwardly on to the bench. He wore only his shirt and was already drowsy from the laudanum, but he managed a smile for her and raised his hand. When she took hold of it, he grasped hers firmly and his grip did not slacken as the attendant fastened the buckles tightly around his body and good leg.

The surgeon had removed his jacket and covered himself with large, stained apron. He inspected his saws and knives on the table and selected his tools. 'Ready?' he said.

'Ready,' George replied.

The attendant offered a broad leather strap for George to bite on and he did. Laura wondered how much pain he would suffer before he gave in to the faint. It was said that if you did not fight the pain you fainted more quickly. But George had battled with his pain for years and was used to it.

He looked at her. His eyes were frightened and she gripped his hand more tightly and kept her gaze firmly locked with his. The attendant placed a hand on each shoulder and the surgeon took up his knife. George's body arched and he screamed as the knife cut his flesh. The straps strained and his good foot banged against the table top. Laura smelled the blood but continued to hold his eyes with hers.

'Hold him steady, man!' the surgeon snapped without looking up from his task. Moments later he demanded his saw and Laura heard the rasping of its sharpened teeth on bone.

George's eyes were rolling. Thankfully, he was going into the faint. She bit her tongue and urged him silently to let himself go. His mouth slackened on the leather and his grasp of her hand eased. The colour drained from his face and his breathing slowed. There was an exchange of words between the surgeon and his attendant, the end of which made sense to her. 'His heart still beats.' She turned her head and saw the blood.

The most blood that Laura had seen before was when, as a little girl, she had watched her father stick a pig. Mother helped him tie its hind feet together and hoist it, wriggling and squealing, to hang upside down from the strongest branch of a tree. Then he took their longest, sharpest knife and slit its throat while Mother held her milking pail underneath to catch the blood as it drained. It sprayed and splashed everywhere as the beast twisted and flopped in its death throes and finally hung twitching and then flaccid for her father to finish his job.

The blood had stuck to her face and hair, covered her fingers and filled the crevices around her nails. The sickly salty smell and stickiness of the darkening, congealing, precious liquid stayed with her for days. She helped her mother carry the pail indoors to thicken by the fire. Later, they mixed in oatmeal, herbs and spice and then chopped-up belly fat and rolled it in greased muslin to make sausage puddings that they boiled for hours before hanging to dry from hooks in the kitchen ceiling. By the time Laura came to eat them in the winter, she had forgotten her nausea.

But now she recalled that scene she realised that a man's blood was worse. It poured from his split flesh, spreading and soaking into linen towels, staining them bright red. She felt ill but knew she must not collapse. Not here, not now, where she might be needed to fetch and carry. She watched the surgeon and his attendant work in their dingy, blood-spattered aprons until increasing nausea threatened. George's scream echoed in her head, but now his face was pallid and still and she wondered how long he would stay in the deep faint. She held on to his hand, staring at him, almost in a swoon herself, until the house-keeper urged her to move, and she realised it was over. His stump was tarred and wrapped. A lifeless limb languished in a bucket of blood on the floor. And then, mercifully, the house-keeper led her away and gave her brandy.

The night after Quinta shot the deer, while Patrick languished in a dark damp rat-infested cellar, Quinta lay awake fretting. She could not stay at home and do nothing, whatever he might wish. How would he get a message to his father? He needed someone with him whom he could trust. He needed her. She rose and dressed as soon as she saw the first streaks of light in the sky, packed her father's old hunting bag with a few belong-ings and locked up the cottage.

She ran down the hill as fast as she could until she was well clear of Farmer Bilton's land. Only Seth would be up at this hour with the cows. But if he saw her and told his employer, Farmer Bilton might come after her. She hurried through the village and did not stop for rest until she had reached the top of Swinborough Hill. The town sprawled in front of her and she heard the distant clang of a rising bell. At the bottom of her descent, fresh water at the spring beckoned her and she stopped to eat a piece of pie and drink copiously. She yawned. It was not far now.

Sergeant Ross would know what to do for his son. Patrick had told the truth and he was innocent. She had shot the deer on her own land, because it was eating her crops. Mother would speak up for her and, tonight, Patrick would be free and they would return home to plan their marriage and their future. All would be well.

The town was busy with folk, from those tramping to labour in the forges and furnaces to farmers arriving with beasts for the market. Appetising smells of pig's fry drifted in the air. The sergeant and her mother were staying at an inn and she located them at the second one she tried but they were not in their rooms. Quinta left a message and said she would come back later. She had passed the courthouse on her way and she went in search of Patrick.

It was a new building, strongly built of stone with half a dozen cells for prisoners at the back. She went in through the front door and found a clerk behind a high desk.

'Looking for a prisoner, did you say, miss? Our gaol is full to bursting and the court is sitting again today to clear them out. What was that name again?'

'Patrick Ross.'

He adjusted the spectacles on his nose, turned a page in a large ledger and scanned his list. 'Aye. He's here. Vagrant, he is.'

'He's not! He lives at Top Field.'

He looked again at the entry and sucked his teeth. 'He's charged with poaching, miss. That's a very serious offence.'

'It's a lie! He's innocent!'

'The magistrate will decide that, miss.'

'When?' she urged.

'Today. Tomorrow. He doesn't like to waste time, this one.'

'Can I see him?'

'You? See the magistrate?'

'No, I want to see the – the prisoner.'

184

'Well, he's not actually here because all our cells were full when—'

'Where is he, then?' she demanded anxiously.

'I shouldn't go down there if I were you,' the clerk replied.

'Why? Where is he?'

'He's under the Chantry Chapel. We've got that many prisoners these days, we've had to start using it as a gaol again. This courthouse has only been up a few years and already it's too small. I don't know what this town is coming to—'

'Please,' Quinta interrupted, 'can I talk to him?'

'Not advisable, miss. We've got other prisoners down there.'

'I'm not afraid.'

'Suit yourself, then.' He lifted an arm. 'You go out of here and turn to your—'

'I know where Chantry Bridge is.' She hurried away.

The River Don was wide and deep at this stretch through town and there was much barge traffic toing and froing with the coal and iron that was responsible for the town's growing wealth. The stone-arched bridge was just downstream of Forge Island where the canal had been cut as part of the navigation. She climbed the stone steps to the small chapel in the middle of the bridge and banged on the door. It was opened by a bull of a man who smelled of drink. The stained glass in the far wall was the only sign the building had once been used for worship. Now it was dank and dingy and the crypt used as a gaol.

'I want to see one of your prisoners,' she demanded loudly.

The gaoler barred her way. 'Well, you can't. I'm not undoing that trapdoor until the constable and his men get here to take 'em away.'

'But I must speak with him! I am – I am his wife.' She pushed past him into the gloomy interior. The stone-flagged floor was damp and greasy. A table stood in the middle with a ewer and tankard. To the left she saw the trapdoor in the floor, securely bolted down. The gaoler placed his large heavy feet on top of it.

Quinta walked over to the table, filled the tankard with ale from the ewer and offered it to him. He lumbered towards it and she set it down before moving quickly to the trapdoor. 'Patrick! Are you down there? Can you hear me?'

After a few seconds, his voice came through the floor. 'Quinta? Quinta! Is that you?'

'Yes. How are you?'

'Well enough. Is someone with you?'

'Only the gaoler.'

The other prisoners began to jeer and call out lewdly. The gaoler leered at her and she wished she hadn't poured the ale. He swallowed the drink and she wondered if he might expect another reward from her.

'Can you fetch my father?' Patrick called. 'He'll know what to do.'

'I've been to the Crown. He's not there.'

'Try the surgeon's house. It's on the Mansfield road, after the Dispensary. Hurry.'

'I'll find him. Don't worry. He'll get you out.' She turned to leave.

The gaoler caught her arm as she left and growled, 'Not so fast, lady. I needs paying for this. Get over here.' But his words were slurred. She picked up the ewer of ale and threw it in his face, shaking off his hand and darting out through the door before he knew she was gone. She heard him call after her, 'Witch! Don't come back then.'

Thank the Lord Patrick would be out of there soon.

She climbed the High Street and skirted the beast market until she found the surgeon's house. It was a very grand residence, built of stone with an engraved brass plaque fixed to the wall by the wide front door. She was quite breathless when the housekeeper answered the door.

'I'm looking for Sergeant Ross. Is he here? His son wants to see him.'

'And your name is?'

'Miss Haig.'

'Haig?' The housekeeper scrutinised her features. 'Come inside, miss, and follow me.' She led her down a passage to a small room near the kitchen. It had a fireplace and was furnished very plainly as a sitting room.

'Sergeant Ross came to – to see the surgeon a few days ago accompanied by a – a Mrs Haig.'

'My mother.'

'She is with him now.'

'Please tell her I am here.'

'Sit down, Miss Haig. I'll fetch her.'

But Quinta could not rest. She was too anxious about Patrick. She hoped the sergeant was well. She must speak with him. He would tell her what to do.

'Won't you sit, miss? Please,' the housekeeper repeated. 'Would you care for some refreshment?'

She was gone a long time. A young girl brought her some elderflower cordial which she poured into glass. It was cool and reviving. Quinta sipped it gratefully and asked, 'Why is it taking so long to find my mother?' The girl stared at her seriously, made no reply, bobbed a curtsey and left the room. Eventually the door opened and the housekeeper came in with her mother, who looked quite exhausted and red-eyed.

'Quinta!'

'Mother!'

They fell into each other's arms and hugged each other tightly.

'You don't look well, Mother.'

Laura coughed and sat down. 'I – I have been awake for several nights with Sergeant Ross.'

'You have been here during the night? How is the sergeant? Oh, I do hope he is not very ill! He must come to see Patrick and tell us what we must do. Oh Mother, something truly dreadful has happened.'

Laura stood back from her daughter. Her face was full of

187

pain and she choked a little on the words. 'My dearest love, I do not know how to say this without causing you so much hurt.' She inhaled with a shudder and went on: 'Sergeant Ross is dead. He passed away an hour ago.'

The following day Quinta was crushed with others behind a wooden barrier. Her mother was in the courtroom proper, preparing herself to speak on Patrick's behalf. Quinta wished she were older so that she could do that for him. The court was noisy but became less so when Sir William came in and took his seat behind the long polished magistrate's bench. He dealt quickly with a succession of drunkards who had damaged property or injured others. She was alarmed at the violence that went on in town.

Sir William kept glancing at a timepiece that he carried in his waistcoat pocket. He looked harassed by the morning's proceedings and seemed impatient to be finished with his duties. Quinta guessed that the clerks were all hungry for their dinners, too. They were eager to join others in the Red Lion and discuss the business of the town's dignitaries.

She was truly shocked by Patrick's appearance when he was brought in to stand before the magistrate. He was dirty and dishevelled from his time in the crypt. His feet were shackled in irons and his hands were chained together.

'Patrick!' she called. 'Over here!'

His eyes roved around the courtroom and when he saw her his unshaven face broke into a smile. She tried so hard to return it cheerfully, but how could she? His features fell into a puzzled frown, and he searched the court again, recognising her mother, who, to Quinta's dismay, was sitting next to Farmer Bilton on the witness bench. Patrick's frown deepened.

The courtroom went silent as the clerk read the charge. 'How do you plead?'

'I am not guilty, Sir William.' To Quinta's relief, his voice was strong and steady.

'Explain yourself,' Sir William demanded. 'I saw the tracks where you had dragged the beast across the brook.'

'The deer was on Top Field land when it was shot, sir. It fled injured through the brook to the shelter of Five-acre Wood. It was dying and in great distress. I was obliged to hasten its end.' Patrick was articulate and Quinta noticed a few raised eyebrows in the court.

Sir William responded, 'The landlord of Top Field was a witness to the shooting. Farmer Bilton? Stand up.'

He did. 'I was there, Sir William. I ride by Top Field every day. It is my duty, sir, to know my tenants are safe and well, especially since I heard there were vagrants in the area and Mrs Haig being a widow now—'

'Yes, yes, Mr Bilton,' Sir William interrupted. 'What did you see on the day in question?'

'The young deer was in the wood and drinking at the stream. This ruffian fired two shots at it and it fell. Stone dead, it was. I saw it all.'

'That's a lie!' Quinta called out. 'It was in my garden!'

'Silence!' Sir William struck his gavel, looked in her direction and recognised her. He seemed startled for a moment but recovered quickly. 'Miss Haig, I saw the beast with my own eyes and the trail of blood where the prisoner had dragged it from the trees.'

'But it—' she protested.

The gavel descended again. 'Miss Haig, please be quiet.'

She saw her mother's worried expression and Farmer Bilton's satisfied sneer as he stepped down.

Patrick stood proudly when he was called on again and he repeated the truth. 'The first shot was fired to scare the animal and it was injured by accident. I only did what any responsible gamekeeper would have done.'

Sir William listened and frowned. 'You refused to produce the gun when ordered, yet you admit you fired it.'

'Yes, sir.'

'How did you come by the gun?'

'It belongs to my father. He was a rifleman in the war with France.'

'Indeed?' Sir William commented. 'And where is your father now?'

Patrick looked around the courtroom. 'He is here, somewhere. He must be.'

He gazed across at Quinta with raised eyebrows and she shook her head. She had to press her lips together firmly to stop them trembling but her eyes were glassy with tears. She could not give him such sad news across an open court. His expression changed to one that Quinta had not seen before: at first puzzled surprise and then a naked fear haunted Patrick's face. Quinta felt so helpless. She wanted to reach out and hold him.

Her mother rose as the clerk announced that the widow Haig would speak for the prisoner. She looked haggard and gaunt and now as old as her years.

'The – the prisoner is honest and hard-working, sir. He has tilled my land these past months and returned it to profit.'

'He is a vagrant, is he not, madam?'

'He and his father arrived as such. They took lodging in my cowshed.'

'I saw no sign of the soldier when I was there. Where is he now?'

Quinta saw her mother close her eyes to stop the tears spilling out. 'He is . . .' Her voice was hoarse.

'Speak up, madam.'

'He was lately at the surgeon's house, sir. His knee has pained him since he was brought down by a French musket at Waterloo. The surgeon advised . . .' Her voice broke and Quinta reached forward over the barrier as though this effort would give her mother strength. Laura continued, 'He – he took off the leg a few days ago.'

'No.' A strangled groan came from Patrick and his face

190

contorted with pain. He'd known – they all had – that this was a possibility. Quinta met his eyes with a tortured expression of her own. A sympathetic murmur spread through the courtroom.

Laura Haig choked on her words. 'Sergeant Ross is dead, sir,' she croaked. 'He passed away yesterday morning – at – at the surgeon's house.'

'No!' Patrick let out a yell of protest and sagged against the wooden rail surrounding his stall. 'No,' he cried again. 'It cannot be!' His head dropped and his body slumped sideways.

Quinta could bear it no longer. She climbed over the barrier. Her heart was breaking for him and she could not contain herself. She had to hold him and comfort him and say how much she loved him and how she would help him. She knew the agony of his loss and she grieved for him. She pushed herself forward, past the court clerks, stretching out her arms.

'Patrick!' she cried. But she was prevented from reaching him by the constable's men. Two of them came from she knew not where, took her arms and stilled her progress.

He recovered and leaned forward, reaching towards her with his hands. She struggled like a madwoman and loosed one of her arms. She was close enough to see the shine in Patrick's eyes as his tears welled. Their fingers touched and clasped briefly before she was dragged away and he was hauled back upright by a guard.

Her own tears rolled freely down her face. 'He is innocent, sir,' she cried. 'I shot the deer. It was me!'

The gavel fell again. 'Miss Haig, you must control yourself and be silent in my court, or I shall be obliged to ask the constable to remove you.' Sir William's soft tone disarmed her. He did not speak so kindly to others in his court. 'This is indeed sad news, but it does not excuse the prisoner's crime. Nor will it influence my verdict.' He addressed the constable's men. 'Miss Haig may sit on the witness bench.'

She shook free her other arm, brushed down her gown with

her hands and took her seat next to Farmer Bilton. Patrick's chains rattled as he attempted to wipe the tears from his face. His eyes were deep, haunted pools in sunken sockets.

'Continue, Mrs Haig.'

'Sergeant Ross was a hero, sir. He was a brave soldier who fought at Waterloo.'

'His regiment?'

'I do not know.'

'I do, sir,' Patrick answered. 'The Ninety-fifth, sir. He was in the infantry square that drove off French cavalry at the end.'

'Ah yes, brave indeed. They suffered heavy losses from cannon.'

'The battlefield surgeon judged he would not live, sir.'

Quinta allowed herself a vestige of hope for Patrick as Sir William considered this new information.

Her mother composed herself and continued. 'Sergeant Ross was a respectful gentleman, sir. I should not have let him stay otherwise. His son, too, is trustworthy, I assure you. He is to marry my daughter, sir.'

'Is he, by God?' Sir William looked affronted, as though this information caused him offence.

Farmer Bilton leaped to his feet. 'No he is not! Her late father promised the old Squire – I mean your father, sir – that she would be mine.'

'He didn't!' Quinta cried, jumping to her feet. 'He didn't, did he, Mother?'

'Quinta!' her mother whispered loudly. 'Do be quiet. Please.'

The gavel came down again. 'I shall have order in my court. Sit down, Mr Bilton.'

Quinta had been shaking her head emphatically as Farmer Bilton spoke. Patrick was in despair. His fingers gripped the wooden surround until his knuckles turned white. 'I'll not wed him,' she called out. 'I love you.'

He managed a smile. 'I love you, too.'

Sir William looked harassed. He glanced at Quinta and then frowned at his prisoner. 'Mrs Haig, as soon as this court is finished you will take your daughter home and out of harm's way. You may sit down,' he concluded.

Laura took her place beside Quinta and held her hand as they sat.

Sir William raised his voice. 'I have listened to the witnesses, and I have my own testimony. I saw the results of this crime while the beast was warm. There is no doubt in my mind that the prisoner is guilty of this charge.'

The courtroom was silenced by this decision. Poaching was a hanging offence. Quinta's throat constricted and she gripped her mother's hand tightly.

'However, the prisoner is a strong and hard-working fellow,' Sir William went on. 'Perhaps he is lacking only in discipline. We shall see. Were his father here, he would understand my thinking.' He turned to face Patrick and continued: 'Patrick Ross, I find that you were observed to kill and take a deer belonging to the Swinborough estate by shooting it in Five-acre Wood.' He took a deep breath. 'I do not hang poachers in my court. Nor do I add to our overcrowded gaols, when our empire can use such men as yourself in the colonies.'

Quinta's heart turned over. Sir William was going to transport Patrick to the other side of the world on a convict ship! No! He must not do that – Patrick was innocent! He did not steal the deer. It was not fair!

'Prisoner, you have been found guilty of poaching. You are sentenced to serve as a soldier in the King's army for as long as His Majesty shall need you.' His gavel came down for the final time and he said, 'This court is adjourned.'

Quinta would never forget Patrick's haunted look of wretched misery and pain as he was led away from the courtroom. He struggled at first until he was overcome by two hefty guards.

'He is innocent,' she cried as she jumped to her feet. 'It was me! I shot the deer.'

'I'll write to you, Quinta!' he called over his shoulder. 'I promise! Do not give up hope . . .'

Those were the last words she heard him utter before he was bundled through a door at the back of the courtroom. Her knees threatened to buckle beneath her and she sank on to the hard wooden bench. 'He is innocent,' she whispered, collapsing against her mother.

The court clerk was impatient for his courtroom to empty so he could get to his dinner. 'Come on now, miss, and you, madam. It's better than a convict ship,' he muttered. 'He'll get clothes for his back, boots for his feet and food in his belly. He's one of the lucky ones, if you ask me.'

'Where will he go?' Quinta asked.

'I can't rightly say. We've had no fighting in Europe since Old Boney was defeated. India, I should think.'

'Where's that?

'T'other side of the world. Now move along, miss, if you please.'

'But how long will the King need him?'

The clerk stopped and grimaced. 'Depends how long he stays alive. His Majesty won't need him when he's dead, will he?'

'You mean he will be killed?' Quinta asked in horror.

'Or die of some foreign fever,' the clerk answered briskly and gave her a push. 'Now take your ma and clear out.'

But Quinta would not leave. 'I want to see him before he goes. Where have they taken him?'

'He'll be away as soon as the papers are signed. Sir William always favours the army. Our own Yorkshire regiment is recruiting in the Riding. He'll be marching with them before the day is out.'

'But surely they will let him stay for his father's burial?' Laura protested.

'He's a criminal, madam. Guilty as charged.'

'He is not. My daughter spoke the truth.' Laura staggered and grasped the side of the door for support. Quinta took hold of her mother's shoulders.

'You must rest, Mother. You are not well.'

'I'm tired, my dear. I have had little sleep of late.' She opened a small bag she was carrying. 'This is a letter for Patrick.' She gave it to the clerk. 'It contains his father's last wishes. Will you see that he gets it?'

'Can he read, then? We don't get many poachers through here that can read. It'll go in with his papers.' The clerk heaved a sigh as he took the letter and opened his ledger again. 'I should forget about him if I were you, miss. Why don't you go and wed old Mr Bilton there, like your father wanted you to?'

'I should listen to what he says, Mrs Haig.'

Every muscle in Quinta's body tensed as she recognised Farmer Bilton's voice. She closed her eyes to shut out the memory of his behaviour at the cottage when he had made that vile suggestion to her. She could not trust herself to speak to him in a civilised manner and moved away. She heard her mother say, 'My daughter says you lied to the court, sir. You could not have seen Patrick shoot the deer.'

'I heard the shots, though. And I saw him drag it stone dead from the trees. Same thing. You might think on me a bit different now with both the travellers gone. My offer still stands, you know.'

'Good day to you, sir,' Laura replied stiffly. 'Quinta, dear, would you give me your arm? We'll go back to the Crown.'

They walked slowly across town and up the High Street in a shocked silence. 'I think Sir William had made his decision before Patrick was heard,' Laura said eventually. 'He didn't approve of him at all.'

'He was angry when he found the deer. I tried to explain but he wouldn't listen to me.'

'Patrick had no chance of justice, did he? Farmer Bilton made sure that he would be taken away. He's a wicked man.'

'He's gentry, Mother.'

'But only to those who do not know him as we do.'

'Well, they still look after their own. The old Squire looked after Father, though. What did Father do for him all those years ago?'

'I've told you; he was a good servant to him,' Laura answered shortly.

Her tone implied the matter was closed, but Quinta persisted. 'Was it anything to do with the farm?'

'It's in the past, dear. We have your future to consider now.'

There is no future for me, Quinta thought desperately. She wondered how she was going to go on without Patrick. Yet she had to for her mother's sake. She hugged her arm closer. 'We'll stay out of the workhouse somehow.'

'How shall we do that, dear?'

'Farmer Bilton can have his tenancy back if he wants. I'll find work here in town.'

They were halfway up the High Street. Laura stopped to catch her breath. 'I can't live here, my love, with all the smoke and smells. It makes me cough so and the physician said I need country air and delicate food.'

'Then we must go home immediately. The garden is growing well and we have the hens. We'd best get back to them. We have left our house empty for too long.'

'We cannot leave until after we have buried the sergeant, dear. George was prepared for the worst to happen and had left instructions with the surgeon.'

'Then we shall have to move from the Crown. We can't afford to stay there.'

'The innkeeper's wife told me it was all taken care of. George was thorough with his affairs.'

Quinta took her mother straight to the chamber they would now share at the Crown and took off her bonnet. She placed it on the chest of drawers next to a brown paper parcel that had languished there unopened. 'Are you going to unwrap this, Mother?'

'It's from the draper's shop. It's for you, dear. You do it.'

'What is it?'

'It's a gift, my dear; from Sergeant Ross. His wish was for you to wear it when you married his son.'

Quinta carefully took off the wrapping. The exquisite lace and ribbons lay neatly folded. She leaned weakly against the drawers. 'He bought it f-for me; for my wedding to Patrick.' She could no longer stop her tears. She did not try. She crumpled into a heap on the floor and sobbed.

Chapter 16

Patrick's grief was consumed by fury. His initial disbelief that his father was dead had turned to anger with himself for not following his instincts and being there with him. While he was sealing his love for Quinta his father was dying. He saw it clearly now. His father had known the risks and had been prepared for the worst. He did not want him to have a lonely future on the road. Patrick's turbulent thoughts so destroyed his reason that he was hardly aware of the guards manhandling him to a cell, or the later march, still chained, to join a ragged band of raw recruits for His Majesty's army.

If that farmer hadn't lied about what he had really seen, there would have been doubt about his guilt. Sir William might have believed him and he would be free, free to bury his father and to grieve for him; free to love Quinta, to wed her in a church and . . . and . . . The image of a family beneath the walnut tree near the cottage sprang into his head. This time it was Quinta in his vision, with a child, no, two; one playing around her feet and another suckling at her breast. It was then that he cried. He cried for the loss of his father, for the loss of Quinta, the girl – no, the woman – who had shown him how much he could love. And now she was gone. They were both gone for ever from his life. His life was gone.

At first he was consoled only by the thought that his life would be short. He knew what they called foot soldiers: cannon fodder, to be fed systematically to enemy fire until the King had killed more men than his enemies, or the other way round, and the battle was over. He wondered when that day would arrive. Europe was at peace and had been since Napoleon's final defeat. The King's army had been fighting further afield, the other side of the globe, building an empire.

But as he came to terms with his grief, he realised he did not want to die. He considered an escape and was planning how when two other men as desperate as he broke out of line and ran. One was taken down by a bullet and killed. The other was hunted like a fox, brought back and flogged as an example to the others, who were obliged to watch.

He was a prisoner. He was a soldier and unlikely to return alive to his love. He did not even know whether he would get pay for his soldiering. But if he did . . . He resolved that Quinta would have it all. It was the only way left to him to prove to her his love was constant. What need did he have for money? Without Quinta, his life was finished. He decided that if his fate was to die in battle then he would strive to die later rather than sooner and to that end he determined to be a good soldier. When he was killed, he would die fighting, fighting to survive for his Quinta, and leaving everything he possessed to her so that she would know that he had loved her to the end.

He wondered how he could get hold of pen and paper to write his thoughts down as a testament, a letter to his beloved Quinta, to give for safekeeping to the officer in command. But as the days and weeks passed, he realised that this was a fantasy for a prisoner recruit. He bided his time for there was nothing else to do with it.

He knew what to expect from the army; his father had educated him with fighting stories all his adolescent life. And he soon realised that he had a quicker wit than many of the other foot soldiers who joined the ragged line tramping to Newark. Some were convicted criminals like him, and as likely innocent, too, but mostly they were wretched country labourers who had abandoned their poverty-stricken lives on farms for the grime of coal pits and manufactories that were spreading like a disease across the land. An industrial revolution he'd heard it called. Whatever it was, it was changing the face of England.

He recalled his father's words: 'Just did as I was told and kept my head down. That's how I survived. The drill sergeants behaved like snarling, starving animals but they had a job to do, as I found out when I rose in the ranks.'

'Just human beings like you and me?' Patrick had replied.

'Not all of them,' his father had answered darkly.

As Patrick tramped in line he observed the officers and men who would control his life and kept his own counsel. His father had trained him perfectly to do that.

They had been marched for days and then drilled for weeks as a defence and killing force. He thought often of his father's wisdom as he sweated and silently cursed at his superiors' constant, degrading bullying. All the recruits were punished sooner or later whether they deserved it or not, and he took his exhausting extra drills like the man that he was.

His life on the road had served him well. He had the strength to push himself to the limits of his endurance and the stamina to survive. He did it for himself, for his father's memory, and for Quinta. He resolved to battle for Quinta. If he was to die a soldier he would go down fighting not for King and country but for her. He wished so much he had a likeness of her. He never wanted to forget her soft fragrant hair, her fine eyes and kissable lips, and the night they had loved each other as man and wife.

His life could have been so different if only . . . But it was not to be. He was a soldier as his father had been before him and one day, one day through the clearing mist of his grief, he realised that he was proud of that. In spite of Farmer Bilton's scheming he was not languishing in some rat-infested gaol or vomiting on a convict ship to the colonies. He was not even considered a prisoner; he was a soldier with a soldier's pay.

Could he expect Quinta to wait for him, left alone with her sick mother to fend for? Farmer Bilton had seemed intent on wedding her himself. He did not doubt that they would be turned out of Top Field, come what may. In his worst moments he thought ruefully that she would probably have to marry someone. But Quinta was strong in mind and body with wits to match. He prayed that somehow she would find a way to survive for when he could come back to her. He was his father's son and, no matter how long it took, he would endeavour to return to his love.

He was issued with boots for his feet, clothes for his back and a bed to sleep on in a cavernous, stone-cold barrack room. The rations of meat, bread and ale were adequate and his constitution thrived on the otherwise harsh regime. Others were not so lucky and were weakened rather than toughened by the life. They were given their own rifles, like his father's Baker, and the red tunics of the regiment. Soon they would be on the move, ready to fight and to die.

At the end of morning drill he stood rigid, waiting for the sergeant's inspection. His corporal walked slowly along the line.

'You!'

'Yes, sir.' Patrick stood stiffly to attention and looked straight ahead, avoiding the corporal's eye.

'Are you the poacher? The one they say is the best shot?'

'I can shoot, sir.'

'Aye, well, we all know that scatter guns can hit owt.' The corporal glanced about and sniggered. 'Rifles is different. Takes skill, they does. Skill. Hear that, you lot!' When there was no response he yelled louder, 'I said, did you hear that?'

A muttered 'Yes, sir' rattled around the small group.

'You, then. This is loaded.' He thrust a different rifle at Patrick. He examined it with interest. It was a Brunswick, a new design and much talked about. The dusty drill square was deserted and the corporal swivelled around looking for a target. 'See that wooden post by the captain's office? Now if yer misses to the right you'll hit the wall an' he won't like that at all. But if yer misses to the left you'll hit the door. Newly painted that door is with his name on it, and he'll be right mad when he gets back. He can be a nasty piece when he's riled, can the captain.' He looked at the other men and grinned again. 'Go on then, poacher. Shoot.'

Patrick shouldered the rifle and aimed carefully. He was confident of hitting the post because it was a substantial piece of timber. But there were questions about the type of bullets for this gun and he wondered if the rifle barrel was true and shot straight. He guessed it wasn't and the bullet would veer one way or the other. Not to the left, he reasoned. Even the corporal wouldn't risk him defacing the captain's office door. The chances were that the barrel might shoot to the right and hit the wall. The sergeant would expect Patrick to avoid the door at all costs, aim towards the right of the post and by doing do increase his chances of hitting the wall instead.

He aimed for dead centre of the post and squeezed the trigger.

'You.' The corporal pointed at a private, waved his hand at the post and the soldier trotted towards it.

'Centre, sir,' he called.

Patrick raised his eyebrows. The rifle was true.

'Fluke,' the corporal sneered. 'Beginner's luck. Let's try summat else, shall we.' He reached inside his uniform jacket and took out a silk neckerchief. Clearly he did not believe that Patrick was a beginner because he handed him a cartridge from a leather pouch attached to his belt and said, 'Reload.' He watched him closely as Patrick charged the unfamiliar weapon. Then he picked up a pebble, wrapped the silk loosely around it and threw it high in the air. The stone dropped away and the silk floated gently back to earth. 'Hit that,' he ordered.

Patrick's eyes widened. He really did need a scatter gun to be sure of hitting a moving target but the neckerchief was much bigger than a pigeon and slower moving so he had time to judge its speed and aim. The bullet caught the edge, tearing the delicate fabric. It leaped once before resuming its gentle descent to the ground.

The corporal fell silent. His sergeant had arrived. He walked across the dusty square, retrieved the neckerchief and examined the damage. Then he demanded of Patrick, 'Who taught you how to fire a rifle?'

'My father did, sir.'

'Poacher like you, was he?'

'No, sir.'

'What then?'

'He was a soldier, sir, a sergeant in the Duke of Wellington's army.'

The sergeant studied him closely for a moment as though he did not believe him, so Patrick added, 'With the Ninety-fifth regiment, sir.'

'Corporal, carry on,' he barked. 'Ross, follow me.' The sergeant marched away briskly towards the captain's office.

The next day Patrick had joined another group of recruits marching for the coast and a ship that would take him away from the Riding, from Quinta and from England. He had learned to guard, to shoot to kill and most of all to fight and win. Now he had to be a soldier prepared to die in battle. His father had done it before him and survived and he wondered if he might also.

However, his fate was not to fight on the battlefields of India or South America. His education and civil manners saved him. Within two months, as the English winter began to bite, he embarked with his regiment on a ship that would take him to the warmth of the West Indies.

His duty would be to guard the offices of the King's representative, whose task was to ensure that emancipation was implemented peacefully on the sugar plantations. As the shores of England receded his hopes of returning to the South Riding faded with them. But his memory of Quinta did not dim. As though it was yesterday, she was in his head, in his heart, indeed in his soul. He wondered what was happening to her and if she ever thought of him.

Chapter 17

'At least the Lord has seen fit to send the sun to see the sergeant on his way,' Laura said as she and Quinta left the Crown to walk to the graveyard.

'There is no sun in the sky for me,' Quinta replied. 'What kind of gentleman is the King if he will not let one of his soldiers attend his father's funeral?'

'He is a prisoner, my love.'

'He is innocent. I should have been the one in court.'

'It is over now.' Laura sighed and added, 'I should have welcomed him as a son.'

Quinta swallowed a strangled groan. She must be strong for her mother's sake. But she did not swallow her words. 'I am so angry with Farmer Bilton, and Sir William. If I had Patrick's gun I should kill them both.'

'Calm yourself. I do not want my daughter before the magistrate as well. Besides, Sir William did not send him to the colonies. But he was angry with Patrick for not giving up his gun. Do you know what happened to it?'

'He must have hidden it before Sir William arrived. Farmer Bilton looked everywhere and couldn't find it.'

'Perhaps he hid it in the cowshed?'

'Where? There is nowhere that cannot be searched. It must be somewhere near the house.'

'Hush now, dear. This is a day for mourning.'

'And I do mourn, Mother. That is why I am angry. Why cannot we join the gentlemen at the graveside?'

'It is not a woman's place, dear.'

'It is our place. We are here instead of Patrick. Come along.' Quinta pulled her mother after her and ignored the raised eyebrows of the vicar. She stood arm in arm with her mother as Sergeant Ross's coffin was lowered into his grave. The surgeon was there, with an unknown gentleman in dark sober clothing and a tall hat who was taking the role of chief mourner. When the vicar had finished speaking, both men took a handful of soil and scattered it over the coffin. Quinta, despite her mother's restraining tug, stepped forward to do the same. The tall gentleman gave her a formal bow and moved away.

'Who is he, Mother?'

'I don't know.'

'He is a lawyer, madam,' the surgeon replied. 'He is arranging a headstone. Sergeant Ross left instructions with him.'

'He was a brave man,' Laura said.

The surgeon nodded in agreement. 'I'm afraid his constitution had weakened over the years.'

'You did all you could, sir,' Laura responded.

He bowed and followed the lawyer. The sexton took up his shovel to refill the grave.

Quinta noticed tears on her mother's cheeks. Quinta had done her weeping in the days since Patrick's trial, but she continued to mourn. She grieved for the sergeant who had survived the muskets of Napoleon's Imperial Guard, searched for his son, found him and brought him up to be as honourable and brave as he had been. She grieved also for that son. He could not be here to mourn his father because of the lies of their jealous landlord who had used his influence with the magistrate.

She grieved also for herself; for her own loss of the sergeant and of his son. Especially, God forgive her, for the life she would not know as Patrick's wife. For one brief night when she had known his love and had understood her mother's dream that she should love the man who would be her husband. She would never be a wife to Patrick now and her heart was crumbling. That dream had been shattered by a summary decision of Sir William who chose not to listen to her and to believe Farmer Bilton.

The sergeant's death, though tragic, had left bones in the churchyard and a headstone to his memory. Patrick's loss had left no such shrine for Quinta, only a black emptiness in her heart; a void that she did not know how to fill except with tears. And so she wept with her mother as they moved away from the graveside.

'Did you love Sergeant Ross, Mother?'

'Oh no, my dear. No one could replace your father in my heart. But I admired him. He was wise and courageous. The Lord should not have taken him so soon.'

They walked arm in arm back to the inn. The sun was high and the town busy with trade. Life went on as normal for the rest of the world. But Quinta could not see how it would ever be normal for her again.

She was aware that her mother was slowing, leaning more heavily on her arm, and said, 'We shall have tea at the Crown and prepare to return home. The hens have been too long without us. We shall need to hunt for their eggs.'

'Oh, they do not lay as well if they do not see us and we do not talk to them.'

Quinta smiled. She thought it was fine weather that caused them to give more eggs for they spent more time out of doors then. She hoped that the hedge had kept them away from the garden. Hens, like young deer, did so like young green shoots to eat. 'Have you money to pay the innkeeper for our meals, Mother?'

'He told me it was taken care of. And he has given me coin from the sergeant for our journey home. George thought of everything. Shall we walk and save it towards the Michaelmas rent?'

'No, Mother. You are exhausted already and there is the hill to climb at the end. We shall take the carrier as far as the village.'

'But without Patrick we shall not be able to pay our rent again.'

Quinta had already considered that, and replied, 'You ride in the cart with our belongings and I'll walk beside. Then we shall save half of the fare.'

There was room enough for both of them, but without a burden to carry Quinta enjoyed the walk and she could easily keep up with the carthorse. In fact she walked by his large majestic head, murmuring encouragement as they plodded together.

When they reached the village, Laura climbed down and Quinta put her own bag inside her mother's box, which she carried awkwardly up the track past Bilton Farm. The box became heavier and heavier, but she persevered, anxious to reach Top Field and home.

It was dusk as they rounded the brow and approached the cottage. Swarms of birds swooped across the sky, but their small-holding was unusually quiet and still. Quinta could detect no movement from their foraging hens, nor gentle clucking as they pecked and scratched the soil. When they were nearer and the smell assaulted her nostrils she understood why.

The pasture was littered with the torn and bloodied corpses of their birds, most with their heads bitten off and their dead flesh gnawed away by rats. Their feathers were scattered across the grass.

'No!' Quinta dropped the box and ran. She dashed from one to the next, holding a hand over her nose to staunch the stench of rotting flesh. Her hens were dead, every last one of them.

The henhouse was intact but straw was scattered around the entrance and she feared the worst. The putrid odour grew worse as she hurried towards it. The fox had squeezed inside as well. Where the hens had huddled together he had snapped and snarled, killing indiscriminately for his pleasure rather than his appetite. All the eggs had been smashed as he rampaged through the nesting boxes. The sticky congealed carnage made her retch and vomit, adding to the squalor on the straw.

Her mother caught up with her as she straightened. 'The fox has killed them all. Not one is left alive. Even our eggs are gone.'

'Oh my dear Lord in heaven, what shall we do now?'

Quinta spat the last of the bitter bile from her mouth. This was too much. No matter what they did, how much they tried, everything went wrong for them. It was just not fair! She had left the henhouse open so they could wander in and out at will. Foxes were a danger in the colder weather, when their food was scarce, she knew. But in high summer they had plenty to eat nearer their foxholes, surely? She felt ill with grief and anger and her stomach churned with rage.

She answered her mother stiffly, from between pursed lips.

'Can you search the hedgerow for eggs before the light goes completely? If there are any left we may be able to hatch them for chicks. I'll gather wood for a fire. We must burn the carcasses tonight or we'll have disease as well.'

'Oh Quinta, you have tried so hard. I am so sorry.'

'It's done now, Mother. Take any eggs you find indoors. Can you manage to lift some water from the stream? I shall need to wash after this.'

Vomit threatened in Quinta's throat with every torn, rotting, half-gnawed carcass she tossed on to her bonfire. She scrubbed at her hands in an outside bucket but could not get rid of the bloody stickiness under her nails. Laura had prepared bread and boiled bacon bought from town to eat for supper, washed down with their own ale from the pantry, but Quinta could not eat it for she could not rid her nostrils of the decaying stench. She felt ill with the exhaustion, so ate a dry bread crust, took a small tankard of ale and went upstairs to her bed. She did not sleep well in spite of her tiredness and on rising felt nauseous again. She had to dash for the door when she came downstairs to breakfast and was sick again on the grass.

'I hope you haven't caught the fever,' her mother fretted as she refused to eat.

When she had not improved by the following week, Laura took her hand and said, 'Sit down, my dear. We must talk about this.'

Quinta obeyed readily. She had not felt ill like this before and feared for the diseases that spread across the town in hot weather.

'It's not the cholera, is it, Mother? I drank only ale at the inn,' she said in alarm. 'And I ate food that was cooked fresh on the day.'

'The innkeeper's wife said it was cooked fresh but I am not so sure.'

'No! Do you think I have some dreadful fever?'

'No, my dear. I do not.'

'What then?'

'Tell me, my love, of your time here with Patrick. He did not stay in the cowshed all the time, did he?'

'It hurts to think of it, Mother. He was so wonderful, and now he is gone.'

'But tell me about *before* he was taken away by Sir William, my dear. What happened between you?'

Quinta looked down at her hands folded in her lap. She twisted her fingers restlessly. 'We did not really like each other at first. At least I thought we did not and . . .' She described the incident with Farmer Bilton and Patrick's rescue from his assault on her. 'Patrick sent him away, Mother. After that, things changed between us. It seemed the most natural thing in the world. We – we fell in love. Oh Mother, he said he loved me.'

'And he came to your bed?'

'He said he loved me! He wanted me to be his wife!'

'I am not angry with you, dear. But you must tell me. Did you lie with him?'

Quinta closed her eyes as she remembered the pleasure and joy they had given to each other. She nodded silently.

Laura became agitated and looked sideways at the wall. 'Oh dear Lord, what shall we do?'

'Is it such a crime, Mother? I love him. He loves me and we should have been married properly in church and everything. He . . .' Quinta gulped. 'In the court he asked me not to give up hope. He will come back to me. He will.'

'He will not!' Laura twisted her fingers in her lap.

'Do not say such things. I love him, Mother.'

'*He will be killed!* The clerk at the court said as much.' Laura's voice dropped to a whisper. 'He will never return.'

Quinta felt angry with her mother. Her Patrick would not be killed. He was brave and clever, as his father had been. She could not, would not let herself believe that he would die on a foreign battlefield. He had to come back for her. He just had to! She straightened her back and argued, 'You are wrong, Mother. Patrick loves me and he will find a way for us to be together. I know he will.'

Her mother was weeping again. She was so distressed that Quinta went to kneel beside her. She took her hands and murmured, 'It is not so bad. You and Patrick's father gave us your blessing. I surrendered my virtue to him willingly as his promised wife. I am not ruined.'

This did not seem to reassure her mother and her weeping continued in short guttural sobs. Although Quinta was forced to acknowledge the possibility that she might never see Patrick again, she could hardly bear to even think of it, for she knew that she could never love any other man as she loved Patrick. She supposed her mother thought that she was ruined as a bride for anyone else, and sought to ease her mother's fretting.

'I shall be true to him for ever. I shall not look at another,' she added softly. 'Never.'

'But what will you do?' her mother uttered through her sobs.

Quinta stood up and hugged her mother's face to her own body. Of course it mattered to her that she was no longer pure, but only if she was seeking a husband, which she was not. 'Without Patrick, we shall have to leave here, I know. But I can work. I'll find a position for us both.'

'I – I cannot do much with my cough. The surgeon said—'

'Do not fret so. I can take care of us both.'

'No you can't. You don't understand.'

'What is it, Mother? Why does my loving Patrick distress you so much?'

Her mother inhaled deeply and stemmed her strangled sobs. 'I should not be much of a mother if I did not tell you my fear. It is your sickness, my dear.'

'What about my sickness? Do you fear it is serious? That I have taken a putrid fever?'

'It is not a disease. Now we are home, I see you have a different look about you. I believe that you are with child, my dear.'

'I am with child? I cannot be. I am not married.' But as this realisation sank home she understood why her mother was so distressed.

He mother gazed at her silently.

'Then I am carrying Patrick's child,' Quinta breathed.

Patrick's child. Although he had been taken from her so cruelly, he had left her with this gift. She had not considered this possibility when she had been taken up by the passion of their love. She had thought only of a married future with their children. But if she was with child, she was with Patrick's child! For a few moments the room seemed to spin around her. Could this be true? Had God seen fit to reward her so?

'Are you sure, Mother?'

'If you are not, then time will soon prove me wrong.'

'I have had no bleeding since ... Well, since before that night, but it was not so long ago.'

'Some are blessed to conceive so easily. Sadly, I was not. Though, for you, it is not such a blessing, I fear.' The tears welled again in her mother's eyes.

'But it is! I am sure he wanted this as much as I did.' *I am carrying Patrick's child and shall have a part of him with me. His child!* Her hands crossed over her stomach. *Patrick's child!* 'If this is so, I shall write to him and tell him. How delighted he will be. And I shall continue to write to wherever the King's army takes him and tell him how his child thrives and grows.'

'No, my dear, you cannot do that. He is an honourable man as his father was before him. To know that you are with child will add to the anguish of his situation.'

'But he must know!'

'It is better he does not.'

'He has to. He is my child's father.'

'He has gone to be a soldier. He may not return.'

'There is no war! He will not be killed. He will come back to me!'

'But not before your child is born. His child will be a ... will be born out of wedlock. Do you know the shame that it will bring?'

'I am not ashamed. I love my child's father and he loves me. What shame is there in that?'

Her mother was shaking her head. 'The vicar will not baptise him in the church as he does other infants.'

'But why ever not? He will be as much God's child as any other!'

'Not in the eyes of the Church, my love. It is so.'

'Then if the Church does not accept my child, I shall not go to church.'

'Do not speak so hastily. Your child will have no prospects as it is. Oh Quinta, my dearest love, the fault lies with me. I

213

did not want this shame for you. I wished only for your happiness. The sergeant, too, God rest his soul. We were so sure you were meant for each other.'

'It is true. I believe we were.' Quinta's anger was kindled. 'It is not your fault, Mother. Nor is it Patrick's or the sergeant's. Farmer Bilton is the cause of this. It is all his doing. He lied in the courtroom and he should be the one to pay. It is not fair!'

'No, my love, it is not. But it is as it is and we must live with the outcome.' Laura coughed. 'We must find a way to survive outside of the workhouse.'

How? Quinta thought crossly. They had been running out of choices even before this happened. If she was with child as her mother strongly suspected, she would be dismissed from any position she might secure as soon as her employer discovered her condition. Any respectable matron would vilify her as a woman of easy virtue. It was true what Mother said. She was ruined. 'But what shall I do?' she breathed.

'I don't know.' Laura's coughing became worse.

Quinta's eyes widened when she saw the red stain on her mother's handkerchief. 'You must lie down. Go to bed and I'll mix your medicine.'

'I shall die in the workhouse,' Laura choked. Her tears overflowed.

'No, you won't. I shall not let that happen. I'll find a way.'
'But how?'

'I'll think of something. I promise. Do as I say, Mother, and rest.'

Quinta was in despair. Her mother needed her more than ever. And she needed Patrick. How desperately she yearned for him to be with her, to hold her and to fill the emptiness in her heart. But that void might soon be filled by his child as it grew within her. She would not let Patrick or his child down. She alone must decide what to do.

Quinta remembered tales of hardship told to her as a youngster to warn her not to err in her ways. She had heard of a

214

young woman who had made a home of sorts between the boulders near a stream high on the moor, filling gaps with brushwood to shield her from the biting winds. She and her newborn infant were found half dead by a rider alerted by the baby's wailing. They were taken to the workhouse in town and it was said that they both still lived. But what kind of life did they have? Quinta wondered.

Her mother needed country air and wholesome food and drink. She needed a warm fire and a proper house to get through the cold wet winter in these hills.

'We're not going to the workhouse, Mother,' she said firmly as she helped her up the stairs. But no matter how she racked her brain, she could not find a solution.

She continued to weed the garden and look every morning for a show that told her Mother was wrong. And when there was no show she felt such enormous relief that she felt guilty at her secret joy. She wanted Patrick's child. She wanted it so much that, when she was sure, she rejoiced. If she could not have Patrick as her husband, then she would have his child. His child would sustain her through any sacrifice she had to make, any hardship she had to face. It would all be for their child and the memory of their brief, yet unforgettable union. When she had made that pact with herself, her decisions about the future became easier.

Mother did not have the same strength as she did and indeed could not survive the hardships she might have to endure. Quinta determined that her mother's last few years would be comfortable and her child, Patrick's child, would have a future. The sacrifice would be hers and hers alone. She hoped that she was not too late.

Chapter 18

Patrick narrowed his eyes. 'What do you want of me?'

His sergeant was a grizzled, greying man, not unlike his father, who had learned how to survive and risen slowly in the ranks of his regiment. Their duty on this hot and humid island was to keep the peace; to guard the Governor's residence; and to quell any suspicion of riot before it started. But this meeting was off duty and off the record.

'I want you to share a bottle of rum with me.'

They were in the cavernous basement of the stone-built fortress that housed the King's offices and his militia. The arched vaults were cool in the afternoon heat. Patrick obeyed and pulled out a chair.

The sergeant poured two shots and slid one across the plain wooden table. 'Loner, that's what they call you. Is that right?'

He shrugged. 'Maybe.'

'The others have gone down to the harbour.'

'They've gone to the whorehouse.'

'Why didn't you go with them?'

'Why didn't you?'

His sergeant pursed his lips. 'You know as well as they do that I have a woman.'

'Me, too.'

'She's not here, though, is she?'

'I don't want another.'

'She's special, then?'

'Yes.'

The sergeant rubbed his stubbled chin with his hand. 'You're not like the usual convict we have. You don't go whoring, you don't get drunk, and you even asked the lieutenant for a book to read.'

'There's not much to do here. No riots, no fighting, not even much drilling. We should do more to keep in shape.'

'I'll be the one to decide that.' He poured another tot of rum. 'You're coming with me to the harbour. Not to the whorehouse, though. I want to show you something. Bring your rifle.'

Patrick knew he could not disobey and he filled his water bottle from the barrel. Outside the thick stone walls of the garrison cellars the hot air overpowered him, hitting him like a blast from a furnace and within minutes sweat was trickling down his back.

'Will you slow down, Ross,' his sergeant barked. 'We're off duty now.'

He wondered if he would ever get used to this foreign land of hills and lush vegetation. He had never seen such greenery; glossy, tangled and wild, and always dotted with brightly coloured flowers. He ducked to avoid the fronds of a palm leaning precariously across the dusty track.

'Does this stuff ever die back?' he asked.

'Never thought about it,' the sergeant replied. 'If it does, more grows in its place.'

'What happens in winter?'

'We don't have winter here. We have storms like you never see in England; high winds fierce enough to knock back some

217

of this stuff. The cane stands it pretty well, though; strong stuff is sugar cane.'

'I'd like to see how a sugar plantation works.'

'Now why would you want to do that?'

'I'm interested.'

The sergeant gave a derisive snort. 'As I said, you're not like the rest of my men. Well, I don't hold that against you.'

They progressed slowly in the baking heat, down the dusty track from their barracks to the colourful, noisy, smelly and vibrant Creole quarter of the island. The encroaching greenery gave way to flimsy shacks and, as they approached the harbour, larger stone buildings of the shipping companies that brought in supplies and took out sugar. The wharves were crowded with tall-masted vessels, some with their sails unfurled, ready to leave.

It was busier than he'd imagined and the variation in skin colour surprised him. Men, women and children, barefoot in bright cotton, carrying, trading and even cooking the vegetables and fruits that grew so easily in the fertile ground. He inhaled the spicy smell of stewing meat, which he recognised as the curried goat that they ate with boiled rice at the barracks. He bent to choose a couple of ripe mangoes from a heap on the ground, dropping a coin in the child's eager hand.

'These people aren't slaves,' he commented as he copied his sergeant and sliced into the juicy fruit with his sharp army knife.

'We have a whole colony of free men and women,' the sergeant explained.

'Existing to supply pleasure for Europeans, it seems?'

'We don't interfere unless there's trouble. What else are freed slaves to do but make their living by serving white men with money to spend?' the sergeant snapped.

'Is that why they are so many different hues?'

'The older ones were born on the plantations. When the trade with Africa was outlawed, the plantation owners had to get more slaves from somewhere.'

'I don't follow you.'

'The plantation owners encouraged their Negroes to breed. They paid their overseers a bounty for each new birth.' The sergeant major was silent for a moment. 'So the slave masters saw to it that every Negro woman got with child as soon as she was old enough and continued to produce.'

'They found them husbands?'

'They gave them babies.'

'They *what*? Good God, you mean the overseers fathered their children?'

'You see this Creole walking towards us? She is one such offspring. She is half white and a free woman now because of her hard work and sharp wits. She is one of the privileged.'

'You know her?'

'She is Constance, my wife.' He embraced her, and then his attention was drawn to another much younger woman who was approaching them. He kissed her warmly on each cheek. 'And this handsome girl is my daughter Faith. You see, she is more white than Negro.'

Patrick acknowledged that she was, indeed, handsome; though not a girl. There was a height and roundness about her that suggested a maturity of years similar to his. Her smooth skin was the lightest of brown and her eyes wide dark pools fringed with lashes and topped by brows of a glossy blackness. Her hair was not a Negro frizz but a cascade of ripples framing her face and shoulders. She was an exotic creature and he was compelled to stare. 'She's beautiful,' was all he could say.

'Yes, she is. But her life is dangerous here. Look how the Creoles stare at us. We are the enemy, not wanted here and accepted only because of my wife. If they chose to, they could overcome and kill us easily.'

Patrick's grip on his rifle tightened and unconsciously he checked the position of his cartridge pouch.

'Go easy, Ross. Some Creoles remember the last riot when they suffered our recriminations. While we keep order, my daughter is safe, but she is shunned by the Negro and is a

219

magnet for the very worst kind of white man. Her mother has to fight injustice and cruelty as well as guard her virtue. I give her all the protection I can but she would be safer in England.'

Patrick fell into step beside the sergeant as they followed the women away from the bustle of the dock to a quiet back street of small stone houses. 'Will she go?'

'Not without her mother. I could arrange a passage but neither will leave without me.'

'Well, you'll return home eventually.'

'And I shall take them with me. But I am an old man and you are not. That is what I want from you, Ross. I want your promise that if anything happens to me you will see that my daughter and her mother are settled in England. They will not be destitute. They will have my bounty, but no kith or kin. Find them a lodging house in a southern port where the summers will be warm and the sea will be near.'

'That is a big responsibility, sir.'

'And one I hope you will not be called upon to discharge.'

'If I say yes, will I get something in return?'

'You are a good soldier, but being a convict counts against you. If you make this promise for me I shall speak well of you to the officers.'

That should have been enough for Patrick but he wanted one thing more.

'And procure me paper and ink to write a letter.'

'You can have enough to write a book if you agree.'

Patrick held out his hand. The sergeant shook it firmly and said, 'We'll take refreshment in my wife's house and tell her of our pact.'

Patrick followed his sergeant into the cool dark house thinking of what he would write to Quinta.

'That was a nice dinner, Quinta.'

'Thank you, Mother.' Quinta had caught a rabbit in her snare and despatched it quickly as Patrick has shown her. It came more

220

easily to her now. She had given the tender saddle joint to her mother. Her own taste for meat had gone of late and she craved cheese with pickled vegetables from her larder. September was approaching and at least they were not starving. Not yet. But the worry of having to go to the workhouse in the winter had laid her mother low and her coughing was bad. 'Why don't you rest this afternoon,' she urged. 'Go to bed and have a proper sleep.'

'I think I might. What will you do?'

'I'll try and get a few days' work. The Hall always needs a helping hand when the harvest is on.'

'Don't go further than that, will you, love? It'll be too far, there and back in a day.'

'Don't you worry about me. I'll just wash the pots and be off.'

She checked that her mother was asleep before she left. Then she pulled away the muslin from the neckline of her summer gown, tidied her hair and pinched her cheeks. She pulled on a fresh cotton bonnet and tied the ribbon bow just under her left ear. But she did not venture as far as the Hall. She turned off the track to Bilton Farm.

Every day, Quinta had half expected to see Farmer Bilton on his black hunter, inspecting their yard. But since the shooting and the trial he had not been over. No doubt he was busy with harvesting, and he had got what he wanted, she supposed. Patrick and his father were gone, so they would be destitute again and forced to leave his property at Michaelmas. She hoped he would believe her when she told him that her mother had changed her mind.

The farmyard was deserted and she guessed old Seth was in the scullery clearing away after dinner. She lifted the heavy knocker on the front door and let it fall three times against the bleached wood. After she had waited nervously for several minutes, Farmer Bilton answered. He was in his shirtsleeves and waistcoat but still wore his boots and gaiters, which were caked with farmyard mud. His face was florid from the ale at dinner and she guessed he had been asleep.

'Oh, you,' he growled. 'What do you want?'

'I wish to speak with you, sir.'

His sagging features took on a guarded expression and he looked over her head and about his yard. 'Where's your mother?'

'She's not too well these days, which is why I am here alone.' When he did not reply, she smiled at him and asked, 'May I come in, sir?'

He hesitated for a second and then she saw his eyes narrow and darken. He looked around again and said, 'Does she know you've come here on your own?'

'No, sir. Isn't your manservant inside?'

'It's harvest-time. He's out in the fields with the others.'

'Oh! Is there no one else here?' This did not seem such a good idea now and her brightness faltered. But she carried on and stepped over the threshold.

He stood back and waved her down the stone-flagged passage. 'Go through to the back.' His voice sounded hoarser and he cleared his throat as he followed her.

The kitchen was dingy and dirty, and looked as if he lived in it all the time. There were fired-clay tiles on the floor that needed a good scrub and a large wooden table with a stained and dirty top littered with old-fashioned metal plates and tankards. A dresser by the wall had china arranged on it, but it looked thick with greasy grime.

A huge cast-iron range took up most of one wall. The fire was going well and she could smell the remains of a stew of sorts in the blackened cauldron. She guessed that Seth never emptied it, but kept adding more meat, vegetables and water when it ran low.

Quinta's morning sickness had eased but she still felt queasy from time to time and she swallowed her nauseous revulsion at the rancid smell. No wonder he had enjoyed the dinner she had cooked for him at Top Field. It wasn't that long ago but it seemed a lifetime to Quinta.

At one end of the kitchen was a door to the scullery. She

dreaded to think of the state that would be in. At the other end, near to the range, was a motley collection of armchairs that were faded and moth-eaten. She looked up at the grimy window panes and blackened cobwebs hanging from every corner of the low plastered ceiling and her resolution wavered. There must be some other way for them to survive!

'You'll have some ale,' he said and poured from a ewer on the table into a metal tankard. 'You want to talk, you say?'

She took the drink. 'Yes. Thank you.'

'Sit yourself down then.' He swallowed from his own tankard and chose the largest armchair for himself.

Quinta picked the newest-looking one, which she found quite comfortable, but she wondered if it would have fleas and her skin itched at the thought.

He leered at her and grunted. 'Well, Miss Quinta, has your mother changed her mind about my offer now her farmhand has been taken away?' His tone was derisive but she expected that and did not waver.

She faced him squarely. She didn't want to do this but it was the only way she could think of to protect her ailing mother and unborn child. 'No, she hasn't. But I – I believe I can persuade her.' She spoke more boldly than she felt and wondered how she would persuade her mother to go along with this folly.

'So, even though your mother won't have me, I take it you have no objection?'

'No, sir,' she lied and pasted a smile on her face.

'Well, I might've changed my mind after all that business with the gun! Inviting vagrants and poachers and the like on to my land! The Squire would have nothing to say to me if I turned you out now. I'd be within my rights and well you know it.'

Quinta did. She thought that Sir William might have had some sympathy with their plight and found her work in the town, but he wouldn't if he found out she was with child by

223

a convicted poacher. She couldn't live in town anyway, not with mother's cough.

'This is nice ale, Mr Bilton,' she said. 'Does Seth brew it for you?'

'He fetches it from the alehouse in the village. It's the best there is around here, I can tell you. Now then, what makes you think you can change your mother's mind?'

'She's poorly. That's what I've come to tell you. The winter will be hard for us with only me to do the work and – and – well, I think I can persuade her to come and . . .' Quinta glanced around with dismay. '. . . and live here as your house-keeper. The thing is, though, she's not really strong enough.' Quinta sat up straight and placed her hands lightly folded on her lap. 'But I am,' she added. 'I can take it on. I'll do it and she can help me with the light work. If – if you still want me as your wife, that is.'

She spoke firmly, wanting him to be quite clear about this. She had made up her mind and she must not falter.

'You know that's what I want. I told you right enough.' He took another gulp of his ale and she noticed that he was sweating slightly. 'And I said how we could influence your mother.'

'I remember.'

'This is definitely what you want, lass?'

'Yes, Mr Bilton,' she lied again. Her heart was thumping under her gown. She knew her mother would be really angry with her, but it was the only way. And by the time she told her, the deed would be done. Mother's dreams and her dreams would be shattered and gone for good. She could weep for their loss but dreams did not feed and clothe you, or buy medicine. Their poverty would be at an end, Mother would be cared for and her child would be protected from the slur of bastard for ever.

Farmer Bilton began to shift about in his chair. He drained his tankard and ran his grimy hands over his face and neck. 'Let's be clear about this, lass. You do mean that when you tell

224

her you've been over here with me on our own, she'll let you wed me.'

'It's as you have said, sir. She will have no choice.'

He ran his tongue over his lips, but Quinta noticed that they stayed dry. 'Right then, if you are quite sure about this.' His voice was low and hoarse and there was surprise and query in his tone. 'Best get on with things.' He rubbed his hands together slowly and leered at her.

Quinta panicked. Her body tensed in the chair. What was she doing? She almost got up to run away. Had she really just agreed to be a wife, and all that it entailed, to this coarse oaf of a man? Her breath seemed to stick in her chest and she had to make an effort to stay calm. This is what she had planned, hadn't she?

The chair creaked as he staggered to his feet. 'I'll ride over to the vicar this afternoon. Get the banns read on Sunday. We'll be wed afore harvest festival.'

Oh. Was that what he meant? Yes, of course. There had to be a ceremony, in the village church, so that everyone would know that she was his wife. It was what she wanted, too. A warm, well-fed winter for her mother, a home and a future for Patrick's child.

Quinta bit her lip. It would be September before she became his wife and that was too long to wait. If she wanted him to believe her child was his, she could not wait another three weeks or more. 'Must you rush off now, Mr Bilton? When you last visited the cottage you were, as I recall, inclined to linger with me.'

He became more agitated and looked hot. Sweat appeared in drops on his forehead and his eyes were focused on her throat and breasts. 'Aye.' He sounded out of breath but he remained standing a couple of yards away from her as though rooted to the spot. 'The old Squire said you would do for me and I reckon he was right,' he muttered.

She leaned forward to get out of the chair and he lumbered

towards her, bending his head to kiss her chest. He made a groaning, gurgling sound in his throat and when she looked down she saw his hand was clutching at his groin. Then the groaning turned into a hoarse moan and his knees seemed to buckle. He stepped back and half fell into his chair with his eyes closed. His head lolled and his mouth hung open slackly.

Eventually he made a grumbling noise in his throat and moved his hand away from the buttoned flap on his breeches, 'See what you do to me? You bewitch me with your ways and temptations of the flesh overcome me.'

She stood there mortified, feeling wretched. He had hardly touched her, yet she felt soiled where he had. She said in a small voice, 'But we are as good as betrothed, Mr Bilton, aren't we?'

'You would have me take you in sin before wedlock?'

'I thought you wanted to . . .' She swallowed. '. . . when you were last at Top Field.'

'The Lord has given me strength through prayer, and you – you come here and drain it away! Cover yourself, woman. We are not yet wed!'

She blinked, crossed her hands over the exposed part of her chest and bowed her head.

This seemed to calm him and he said, 'That's better. Modesty becomes you.'

She kept her head down and bobbed a curtsey. 'Yes, sir.'

'Now, lass,' he said, 'you had best get off back to your mother. You tell her what you will and I'll call in to see her after I've been to the vicarage.' He got up and went out through the scullery without another word.

She heard the outside door open and close. His horse whinnied as he led it from the stable. Quinta sat down with a bump. He was riding over to ask the vicar to put up the banns. There was no going back now. What had she done?

She surveyed her dingy, smelly surroundings and lifted her skirt to scratch her leg. In fact her skin felt as though it was crawling with lice and she wanted to scratch her whole body. She was sure this place had fleas in the furniture. Well, it was too late now to change her mind. No matter how distasteful, this had to be a better option than the workhouse.

She was relieved he had not wanted to lie with her because she found the idea repulsive. But she would have to when they were wed and she needed to for her deception to succeed. Farmer Bilton was coarse and ill mannered but he was considered gentry and he was bound to dote on his children for that was all he really wanted. She just had to make sure he believed her firstborn was his.

She got up with a heavy heart and wondered where she could get enough lavender for a house this size.

'I've brought you a cup of tea, Mother.'

'Oh, how thoughtful of you. I do so like tea but when it's gone, it's gone. Did you get work?'

'Yes. No. I mean not at the Hall. Please don't be alarmed. I went to see Farmer Bilton instead. I've been thinking about his offer for me. I could do a lot worse than take him up.'

'No, you can't. I'll not let you. Something will turn up.'

'It won't, Mother. Not again. We had a chance with Patrick and then it all went bad on us. I can't leave you. I can't go into service anyway with an infant. You won't survive in the workhouse, or here next winter unless I can buy proper food. I can do all the work at Bilton Farm if I go there.'

'As his housekeeper, you mean?'

'He still wants to marry me, Mother, in spite of everything.'

'Did you tell him you were with child?'

She shook her head and looked away.

'Well, he won't want you when he finds out. That'd be too much to ask, even of him.'

'He needn't know about my baby.'

Her mother's eyes widened. 'You don't mean . . . ? Quinta, no! You cannot do that!'

'Why can't I?'

'It's dishonest.'

'Well, he was dishonest in the court,' Quintra retaliated petulantly. 'He deserves to be lied to. Anyway, I have decided.'

'What have you decided?'

'That I shall wed him after all. And you have to agree, Mother. It's our only hope.'

'Quinta, are you insane!'

'No, I am desperate! What choice do we have? This is a way out of our despair.' Quinta saw that her mother was considering her idea.

'Would you do it, my love? Would you really be his wife? You know what he will want from you in the bedchamber.'

Quinta shrugged and sank on the bed, feeling ill at the thought. But she pushed it to the back of her mind. It was her mother who was truly sick and who needed the shelter of Farmer Bilton's substantial house and table to survive the winter. Her mother must not know how difficult this decision was for her.

'I am no longer a maid. It will not be such a hardship for me,' she lied.

'You will show too early. He'll know the child is not his.'

'That is why I must make haste with a ceremony. I accepted his offer this afternoon, while you were asleep.'

'You had no right without my permission. It is not what I wish for you.'

'Nor I, but it will not be so bad when I have my child to cherish. He is coming to see you after he's spoken with the vicar. If you agree – and you have to do this for me, Mother – we shall be betrothed and, well, if he wishes to take me as his wife before the ceremony, I shall not object.'

Her mother's eyes filled with tears. 'Take care, my darling. You do not wish him to think ill of your morals.'

'He – he has already shown me he is quite anxious to – to lie with me.'

228

'Shown you? In what way, dear?'

'I believe he thought of taking me and was quite overcome but . . . Oh, I don't know. He seemed to think better of his actions.'

'Well, he listens to the vicar's sermons and is known to be religious in his ways.' Her mother sighed. 'Oh my dear, I know why you do this and in truth I cannot see any other way out of our predicament. But I hope you do not live to regret it.'

I am regretting it already, Quinta thought, but said, 'Listen, I hear a rider. Look happy, Mother, and tell him that he has your blessing. I can make a start on cleaning up his farmhouse when I have finished here tomorrow. I shall have a sweet-smelling chamber ready for you after the ceremony.'

'Are you sure about this, my darling girl? It will be for your whole life.'

She placed her hands over her stomach. 'It will be for my child. My child is my life now.'

'There will be other children, dear.'

'They will not be Patrick's children.'

'They will be yours and you will love them just as dearly.'

Quinta placed her hand over her mother's and said quietly, 'I know what I am doing. It is not what I want either. I wished to marry Patrick. But that is no longer possible and this is for the best, Mother, the best chance for my child, for you, for all of us.'

'I fear that you are right. But I fear also that you are paying too high a price.'

'You cannot put too high a price on a child's future. Farmer Bilton's name will ensure my child's respectability and reputation. He will not suffer as his father did.'

'I hope you are right, dear.'

So did Quinta. She had to go through with this marriage. Everything depended on Farmer Bilton believing her child was his. She must share his bed as soon as possible and try not to think of a whole life as his wife. Perhaps when she could tell him she was with child, she would ask to sleep apart for her baby's sake. The gentry had separate bedchambers and Farmer Bilton liked to copy their ways. She felt better when she'd thought of that and started to imagine her own bedchamber with her baby's crib at Bilton Farm.

Chapter 19

'Beatrice, would you drive Mrs Haig home in my trap?'

'Oh Percival, why can't you? It's so dirty at Bilton Farm and I am wearing satin slippers.'

'Then you shouldn't be,' he hissed. 'You are stealing attention from the bride.'

'Oh, do you think so?' Beatrice Wilkins preened.

'Really, Beatrice, your mode of dress is not suitable for a resident of the vicarage.'

She lowered her voice to a whisper. 'When Mother left her money in trust for me it was meant for my trousseau. If Father had not lingered so, it would have gone long ago. How long must I wait to use it?'

Her brother became impatient. 'You must show thrift as an example to my parishioners.'

'Nonsense! If you spent some of Father's money on the vicarage instead of your endless books, it would be more comfortable for both of us.'

'I have heard enough of this. Please do as I ask. I must finish my sermon for tomorrow.'

Laura stood patiently at the church gate. She had arrived

with Quinta for the ceremony in Farmer Bilton's trap driven by Seth, who was now taking her daughter and her – she inhaled raggedly – son-in-law to their future home. Michaelmas was almost upon them and already autumn leaves were gathering on the church path. Mr Wilkins helped her and his sister into the trap and handed the reins to Miss Wilkins. They set off at a sedate pace.

'Will your brother not join us for the wedding breakfast?' Laura asked.

'He has his records to write. He spends all his time with his archives but he has promised to ride over later. I must say, Mrs Haig, your daughter's veil was pretty. I see you have trimmed your bonnet with the same silk.'

'Yes. Mrs Bilton' – there, she had spoken her daughter's new name – 'came across it when she was clearing the bedchambers. She found a wooden chest full of old-fashioned gowns and trimmings.' Laura had sewed the veil for her as Quinta had steadfastly refused to wear the lace that Sergeant Ross had given her. She added, 'You look well yourself, Miss Wilkins.'

Beatrice hitched her skirts higher to show off slippers that matched her gown. Her bonnet, too, had new ribbons for the occasion. 'There is so little chance to wear a ball gown here. The Riding has no assemblies except for villagers in their barns, and dinners in town are for gentlemen only. The Hall is remiss, if you ask me. When I was at home with Mother and Father our local Manor House had summer and winter balls, and shooting parties. Where is one to meet unattached gentlemen if not at such gatherings?'

Where indeed, thought Laura. 'Did you attend many?'

'Sadly I did not. I was caring for my mother and when she passed on my father went into decline and I could not leave him.'

'I'm so sorry.'

'By the time he joined Mother, all the eligible gentlemen

had gone. I hoped when I came to live with my brother, I should find someone.'

'Oh, but you are a great help to Mr Wilkins in his ministry. A woman makes such a difference to a home, don't you think? I am sure you will be pleasantly surprised when you see Mr Bilton's farmhouse.'

The trap made slow progress up Bilton Hill. Others from the village caught up and overtook them and Laura recognised the farrier and taverner from the village and the gamekeeper from Swinborough Hall making their way with their families to continue the celebrations of her daughter's marriage. They had prepared cold meats, pies and cake with sherry wine and a barrel of ale had been set up in one of the front drawing rooms. In the weeks leading up to her wedding day, Quinta had worked unbelievably hard to clean up the farmhouse. Laura had helped with polishing silver, sewing and mending. The upholstered furniture was shabby but tables, chairs and cabinets polished up beautifully. Seth had helped to wax floorboards, window shutters and wall panelling. It was a gracious house that had been too long neglected.

Seth was waiting on the traps and leading the horses away. He helped the ladies down and they walked across stone flags to the front door. Laura watched Miss Wilkins' surprised expression as they entered the hallway and followed a hubbub of voices to the drawing room. The vicarage was a pleasant enough house but Bilton farmhouse was built on a grander scale. As Laura circulated among the guests she could hear that the main topic of conversation was the improvement in the appearance of the farmhouse. It was generally agreed that, in spite of the differences in their ages, Mr Bilton and Miss Haig had made wise choices in each other.

'You're tired, Mother.'

'Yes, dear.'

'I'll take you upstairs to rest.'

'You must stay with your guests.'

Quinta surveyed the drawing room. 'Noah is managing quite well without me. He has never been so popular with the local people. Look at him, he can't believe it.'

'Do not be too hard on him, dear.'

'Why not? You forget he was set to turn us out of our home.'

'We are well and truly out of there now.'

'The masons will be in by the spring. Seth is to farm the land for Noah until a new tenant is found.' They climbed the wide wooden staircase to Laura's chamber overlooking the rear farmyard. 'Will you be comfortable in here, Mother?'

'I shall. It's very cosy and, being over the kitchen, it will be warm in winter.'

'That's what I thought. I've put a warming pan in the bed for you and your medicine is on the table. Shall I help you with your gown?'

When Laura was settled, propped up by snowy pillows, she asked, 'Are you happy, my dear?'

Quinta placed both hands on her stomach and thought of Patrick with a shrinking heart. She did not regret their night together but, without him by her side, she was not happy. She replied, 'I am as content as I can be in the circumstances. It is enough.'

'You have not lain with your husband yet, have you?'

'Noah has surprised me. He has avoided being alone with me and is quite rigid in his ways. He dislikes anything that might be described as – forgive me, Mother – as fornication.'

'Even within wedlock?'

'For the purposes of procreation only,' Quinta replied drily.

Laura managed a gentle laugh. 'Well, that's what you want, isn't it?'

Quinta returned her smile. 'Life will not be so arduous here, after all.'

Noah stood at his wide front door while the last of his guests left. Then he walked over to the pigsties with Seth, leaving

Quinta to go inside and clear the debris. She had persuaded one of the village girls to help in the scullery in exchange for a pair of dainty boots she had found during her cleaning. The girl slipped quietly out of the back door as Noah returned to his kitchen and stood with his back to the fire. Quinta sat at the table buffing silver and thought about the amount of work to be done in blackleading the range behind him.

'Nights are drawing in already,' he commented. 'We'll be abed afore nine so as not to waste the lamp oil. Has Mother retired?'

'Yes, Noah.' She had noticed that he had referred to Laura as 'Mother' and not as 'Ma' or even 'your mother' all day. Propriety in all things, she reflected. It had crossed her mind that he might bring his coarse farmyard ways into the bedchamber, but the more she learned about him, the less she worried about that.

'We'll go and do our duty, then.'

'Noah?'

He lifted a finger and pointed at the ceiling. 'Duty, Madam. I've told you I have no time to waste. 'Tis Saturday and you will make a start tonight on being my wife.'

She took off her buffing glove and tidied the tray of cutlery. 'I'll just lock this in the pantry. Shall I come to your chamber?'

'Where else would you be? A wife's place is in her husband's bed.'

'You have not allowed me in there to clean as I have in the other chambers.'

''Tis clean enough for me.'

'My box is in the adjacent bedchamber.'

'Go and prepare yourself while I secure the front door.'

Obediently, she stood up, bowed her head and went upstairs. Although all the chambers had locks Noah left the keys in them and she had taken a peek at his chamber. Perhaps when he became more used to a cleaner, brighter house he would allow her to touch his things.

The landing was dark and she hurriedly retrieved her night-gown and cap from her box and went next door. His chamber was large, dominated by an ornate half-tester bed with thread-bare hangings. The air was stuffy and smelled of the chamber pot and old shoes. The shutters were half open and there was no other furniture save a chair and wooden ottoman box with the lid hanging off revealing a jumble of clothes inside. The mattress ticking was grey and grubby and without linen, as was the bolster pillow. How did this man sleep in such squalor? A dirty blanket had fallen on the bare floorboards. She turned and went downstairs for sheeting.

'Where are you going?'

'For clean bedding.'

He scratched the side of his head. 'Go on then. But hurry.'

She dropped the linen on to the bed and began to unfold a sheet. He stood in the middle of the chamber watching her. She could hear him breathing in a rasping, laboured manner. She glanced behind her. His hands were by his sides and she noticed his fingers twitching slightly. Oh Lord, this was really going to happen and she dreaded it. She prayed it would be over quickly and on past experience of his behaviour she guessed it would. She began to feel nauseous. How was she going to do this without showing how much he really repulsed her?

'That'll do.'

'But I haven't done the pillows.'

He took hold of her small hand in his grubby clammy palm and pulled her round to face him. Then he pushed her towards the bed and grunted something she did not quite hear.

This was a mistake! How could she have even considered tainting her body and her growing child with anything to do this with awful man, let alone allowing him to invade her so? She feared that she would not be able to do it and he would become angry with her. She had seen evidence of his anger and he was a big, strong man. His farmhands did not disobey him and she would be no exception. But it was too late to change her mind now. She must endure this. It was the price she had to pay. Deception was a sin and it was her penance for deceiving him in this most cruel way.

Yet still she convinced herself that he deserved it, and it was the only thing that kept her sane. He had lied to the court and by doing so had taken away her only chance of happiness. Well, he had shown he had this weakness for her and she had to exploit it now.

'Get yourself on the bed, I said.' His breeches flap was down and he was holding himself with one hand as he advanced towards her. 'Can you hurry up, lass? Have you got any drawers on?'

He bent to pull up the edge of her skirt with his free hand and push her back on to to the mattress. The smell of the chamber pot came strongly through the sheet, but her nose and face were quickly smothered by his waistcoat as he fell on top of her. He was panting with anxiety and sweating so profusely that it dripped from his face on to hers.

His work-roughened hand felt for the opening in her drawers and pushed aside the fabric. 'Hurry up, hurry up,' he repeated. 'Get your legs open.'

She felt like screaming and almost did so as he shifted about on top of her and tried to guide himself into her. Her fists clenched into balls as she tensed and prepared for him to enter her, regretting every aspect of this unholy decision.

'Aaaaaargh,' he groaned. 'Aaaaaargh.' He flopped over her, his rasping wet face against her and his stale sweat and foul breath assaulting her nostrils. His groaning went on and he stopped fumbling around the opening in her drawers between her legs.

He had not entered her. He had barely touched her and he had finished. She lay there wide-eyed as his heavy weight pressed into her. But there was no hardness about him. She could not feel his desire for her, only a sticky dampness on the leg of her drawers.

It was over. She wanted to scream out in rage at him and

suppressed a nervous shiver that rattled her insides. She did not know whether to laugh or cry, only that she felt dirty and degraded and she had not achieved a thing! She would have to go through all this again when he was more – more what? Rested? Sober? She had been led to believe that too much drink could dull a man's desire. But Noah's desire was – was – it seemed to her to be quite out of control. She almost believed it was justice for her deception.

He breathed deeply and his stilled frame squashed her into the smelly bed. She tried to wriggle away from him but he was too heavy and he must have fallen asleep, for a few minutes later he suddenly gave a snort and woke up. He had dribbled wetly on her gown. Lord help her! How was she to endure this?

'Shall we undress, Noah?' she ventured.

He picked up the blanket from the floor and threw it on the bed. 'I'll go out while you do. You bewitch me with your body, Mrs Bilton. Make sure you cover yourself well.'

'But, Noah, I am your wife now. You may take me at your pleasure.'

'You will not speak like a harlot in my house! Would you drain my energy through fornication?'

'No, sir.' She got up, finished making the bed, wrapped herself in her nightgown and cap and crawled between the sheets. She would need more than lavender for this chamber. And more than a strong resolve with Noah. She supposed there'd be another chance tomorrow night when, perhaps, he might not be so anxious.

The following morning he rose early without disturbing her and she was wakened only by the sound of him sluicing his face and neck at the washstand and drawing on his clothes. She feigned sleep until he had gone out to his cows, and then rose to dress and light the kitchen range for hot water and breakfast. It was Sunday and she was cheered by the prospect of church. Noah took Quinta and her mother to the village in his trap and she reflected that this had once been one of her dreams. It had been a childish notion, she realised, and now she was ashamed if it. Nonetheless, she and Laura enjoyed their outing and the conversations afterwards in the churchyard.

'Miss Wilkins, how well you look this morning.'

'Oh, do you think so, Mrs Bilton? My brother made me change my bonnet for this plain old thing.'

'Mr Wilkins gave a fine sermon today.'

'Well, I wish he would not keep preaching about the virtue of marriage. It irritates me so.'

Quinta avoided answering this and smiled. 'Miss Wilkins, would you do me the honour of calling to take tea with us one afternoon? We should so much appreciate your company.'

Beatrice raised her eyebrows. 'Me? Take tea at Bilton Farm?'

'Mother and I have further plans for improvement and we should welcome your advice.' Quinta kept smiling while Miss Wilkins considered this.

'Very well,' she said at last. 'I'll come on Wednesday.'

'We shall look forward to it.'

Noah called her to the trap and she said goodbye.

Quinta had hoped that her second night with Noah would result in a successful union, but he did not retire until long after she was asleep, and this set the pattern for their week. His working day was long, broken only by meals that she prepared and he ate silently. After tea he returned to his fields and his stock until nightfall and came to their chamber exhausted. Fearful that any approaches she might make in the bedchamber would anger him, if she wasn't asleep, she pretended to be.

He did not wake her and the realisation dawned that procreation activity for Noah was the preserve of Saturday night when there was less work the following day. He regarded further indulgence as weakening and sinful in the eyes of the Lord.

The following Saturday, after tea, she brought down her

mother's meal tray and sat at the kitchen table patiently. Noah reclined in his moth-eaten chair and nursed a tankard of ale.

'Shall I read the Bible to you?' she suggested.

'Tomorrow is the day for that.'

'Perhaps a walk? It is a fine evening with a hunter's moon.'

'I have been out there all day.'

'I'll get my sewing, then.'

''Tis Saturday. You will do your duty.'

'Very well.' She stood up to go to their chamber.

'Sit down. I shall go first and prepare myself for bed. You will come when I call you.' He picked up the lamp and left her in the fading light.

She obeyed him, reasoning that he wanted it in this way as there would be less haste, less fumbling if he was in his nightgown already. However, if anything, their encounter was worse, even though their chamber was cleaner and smelled sweeter after a week of her attentions. She had asked Seth to move in a wardrobe cupboard from a disused dressing room so that they could hang up their clothes. She had found a dressing screen too, but had not had time to clean it yet and she was obliged to take off her gown in front of him as he reclined against the pillows.

'Make haste, woman,' he grumbled. 'Leave your gown on the chair.'

She pulled on her nightgown as quickly as she could, but from the sounds he was making in his throat she knew she was too late. It was all over for Noah before she slid into bed. Quinta was in despair. Was it always to be like this? He had no control over his husbandly desires and was spent before he could achieve a union with her.

'You are a witch, Mrs Bilton,' he growled, 'working your evil magic here. You have cast a spell on me and I waste my seed.'

She did not know what to say or do. She had searched everywhere for a solution. She had discovered some old and moulding

240

books in the farmhouse that offered remedies for every ailment, including potions for gentlemen to aid the act of procreation, but nothing for Noah's affliction or even a mention of it.

She might have asked the village midwife but dared not go to her yet. She had been a wife for only a week and the woman might recognise the signs of being with child as her mother had. She gazed at her reflection in the window glass and wondered how they could tell.

'I am not evil, Noah. You are too anxious—'

'I have told you before that you will not argue with me. I shall not have a shrew for my wife.'

'I'm sorry. I only mean to help.'

'You will help by behaving with modesty at all times and not flaunting yourself before me in this manner!'

'But I was—' She stopped. She must not make him angry with her. She thought perhaps it was because he was an old bachelor who had never had an experience with a lady before. The excitement was too much for him. She smoothed his brow with her hand and said, 'My sweet, it is early and we have the whole night. Will you rest awhile and try again?'

'Again? You would wear me down so that I cannot do my work?'

'Of course not. But we are husband and wife. We may enjoy each other, may we not?'

'Do not talk like a whore! You are already behaving as one! Fornication saps a man's strength. Would you have me expire from exhaustion?'

'No, sir, of course not. But is it not my wifely duty to give you pleasure?'

'The words of a Jezebel!' he snapped. 'You wish to make me a slave to your body; to weaken my will and remove my reason! You will not do this to me. You will mend your ways.'

Quinta was shocked into silence. Noah had many traditional ideas about life and clearly anything that even hinted at fornication was an abomination to him. She reflected on the irony of her situation. Were she not so anxious to deceive him she would be whooping for joy that he could not fulfil his husbandly duties with her. But the weeks were passing and their vows were still not sealed in the marriage bed. She passed her hand over her small belly. There was still time.

'Noah, dearest husband, how are we to have the children you desire?' she asked quietly. 'Perhaps you will consult with the apothecary in town?'

'And have him know my wife will not be a wife to me? You would insult me so!'

'He will advise you, dearest. The Dispensary has mixtures for all ailments.'

This made his anger worse. 'This is no ailment of mine! This is your doing and you will see that it does not happen again.'

'But – but it is not me!' She snapped her mouth closed. She realised that Noah was angry with her because he could not accept his own failing. She added, 'But how, dearest?'

'Remove your curse on me! Burn those books with their wicked potions! Book reading is not for womenfolk. It turns them into witches and whores and I will not have it in my house.'

Her despair deepened yet she could not talk to her mother about this. To ease her mind she had told Laura that all was well with Noah, that she had no cause to worry as his demands were not excessive. The latter, she reflected with a heavy heart, was true for he always fell asleep quickly at night, rising at dawn to help Seth with the milking.

Her days were filled with her duties as mistress of Bilton farmhouse. Miss Wilkins visited as promised and took a lively interest in her plans to restore the drawing room to its former elegance. The dining room was equally spacious, with room enough for a small party to dance, and Miss Wilkins filled her head with ideas about assemblies.

However, despite warmth and nourishment, Laura's health continued to decline. She did what she could to help her daughter but was forced to rest through the afternoon and she retired to bed with her medicine soon after tea. Quinta's concern for her mother distracted her from her own dilemma. The cough became worse and she moved an old couch into her mother's bedchamber to be near her through the night. When they discussed it, Noah thought this a sensible solution.

'I should like to ask the physician from town to visit Mother,' she asked.

'Waste of money,' he replied. 'He can't cure the consumption.'

'He might recommend another mixture for her.'

'I'll get more laudanum sent over for her.'

'But if the physician calls you may speak with him, too. You could ask him if he has a potion for you – for – for Saturday night.'

'I shall do no such thing. It will right itself soon enough, when you have learned to be more chaste.'

Quinta wondered how long that would take.

Chapter 20

The autumn was cold and damp mists seeped into every crack. However, Miss Wilkins continued to call and take afternoon tea with cake in their drawing room. Laura enjoyed her visits immensely and talked of balls and parties she had known at the Hall, much to Miss Wilkins' fascination. Quinta washed the dust off delicate china and silver that had not been used in years to add to the occasion.

After one such pleasant interlude, as Miss Wilkins left for the vicarage, a messenger on horseback arrived at the front door of the farmhouse with a letter. Quinta's heart leaped. Patrick had promised to write to her! Had he somehow heard of her marriage and move to Bilton Farm? Oh, how exciting to have news of him!

'Will you step inside for refreshment?' she asked as she handed the courier his fee and took the thick folded paper from him. Her features sagged with disappointment. It was sealed with red wax and addressed to Noah.

'Thank you, ma'am, I'll not dismount, but a swallow of spirit taken in the saddle will be most welcome. The winds are bitter across these hills and I am quite chilled.'

She gave him some of Noah's best brandy and asked where the letter was from.

'It came on the post from Crosswell in the High Peak.'

Quinta watched him gulp the brandy and gallop away. Noah hailed from the High Peak in the next county. She propped the letter in front of his tankard at the kitchen table and prepared the liver and onions that she would fry for his tea.

He examined the seal by the light of the kitchen window, slid a grubby finger underneath it and unfolded the thick paper. As he read she saw that it brought pleasing news and she waited patiently for him to tell her. He did not disappoint in this respect.

'Well, Mrs Bilton, news of my improving status has reached Crosswell. I am invited to join a shoot on the High Peak moors.'

Quinta glanced at her mother with raised eyebrows and asked, 'Will you accept?'

'I shall. Seth will oversee the rest of the ploughing. I shall be back in time to take my geese and bullocks to the December markets. Town butchers pay good prices for fat stock before Christmas. Make preparations to leave.'

'All of us?'

'Indeed. A married man must show off his new wife.'

But just to be sure, Quinta asked, 'I may take Mother as well?'

'You will need her to help pass time with other ladies.' He stopped to think. 'You must take a fancy gown for dinner. Mother, too.'

'For dinner?'

'They eat their dinner late after shooting, sometimes as late as five o'clock, and make a great show of it.'

Laura leaned towards her. 'I know all about what to do, dear. I used to help the ladies' maids at the Hall when they had parties.'

Quinta noticed how her mother's eyes were sparkling at her memories. 'I see,' she said. 'Where shall we stay?'

'We shall lodge with the farmer who was my landlord before I came here. His good wife is very well connected and will entertain the womenfolk while we are out shooting. You may even be honoured by an invitation to take tea with a titled lady.'

Now Quinta's own eyes sparkled. There would be other gentlemen farmers' wives and daughters to meet, and Mother would enjoy their refined company. But she feared the journey would be long and cold in this chilly autumn.

'Shall we travel there by the post?' she asked.

'Post? Not across the Peaks! Packhorses take in the stores and supplies. We shall ride all the way.'

'Ride? Can we not take a cart of any kind for Mother?'

'The tracks are steep and there are rocky streams to cross. Only packhorses can get through.'

'But Mother is not strong enough to make a journey on horseback.'

'You may have the best side saddle, Mother,' Noah offered. 'What do you say?'

'I fear my daughter is right, sir. I have very little strength these days.'

'Then you will have to stay behind. Perhaps it will be for the best as the cold winds on the High Peak are more penetrating than here. You will have to converse with your betters without her, Mrs Bilton.'

'Your husband is right, my dear. I do not really wish to travel in these colder months. It exhausts me so and worsens my cough. You must go with Noah alone.'

'But you cannot stay here without me!'

'Of course I can. There will be very little to do with no one else in the house. Seth will bring in the wood and coal for me.'

'No, Mother. You need more personal attending. You need me.'

'I can care for myself, dear. And this is such a wonderful opportunity for you. Besides, you must go with your husband. It is your duty.'

Quinta saw the satisfied look on Noah's face and felt irritated. If he had been able to do his duty towards her and control himself enough to consummate their marriage she would have no problem with ignoring her own duty towards him and staying with her mother. But she was becoming increasingly desperate about her situation. If they did not achieve a proper union soon, her deception would become increasingly difficult to conceal. Yet how could she go with him and leave her ailing mother to launder her own linen and make her own toddies in the wintry cold?

'I'll get a lad to help Seth with the stock,' Noah said. 'He did all the indoor work for me afore I wed. He'll do it again.'

'There, dear.' Laura smiled. 'Seth will have time to lay fires and heat water. I shall manage quite well.'

'That's settled then,' Noah said. 'You'll need cloth for only one new gown.'

Her mother was persuasive and Quinta knew that for her daughter to attend a shooting party was a dream come true for her. But Quinta was not so attracted by the connections of the visit and replied, 'My mind is made up on this. I shall not leave you ailing during the winter months. They are the worst for you.' She turned to Noah. 'Might your visit not wait until the spring?'

Noah face darkened. 'They invite me for the shooting. It is an honour for me. You would do well to remember your position as my wife, madam.'

She remained firm. 'I shall not leave my mother. She needs me.' And you do not, she thought.

'Quinta, have a care what you say,' Laura cautioned softly. 'Your place is with your husband.'

'But not when he is shooting. I have domestic duties here. There are vegetables and fruits to dry and pickle, pig meat to cure for the winter.' She turned to Noah. 'I am sure that not all wives go shooting with their husbands.'

'They do not decline invitations from their betters,' he

247

responded sharply. Then he shrugged. 'But you have good reason to stay with your kin. It will not be questioned.'

'You will not mind if I remain with Mother?'

'I shall be back before Christmastide.'

'And my hams and chutneys will be ready for you, dearest husband.'

'That's settled then.' Quinta thought that Noah seemed cheered by this decision. 'I shall leave right away and stay at the inn in Crosswell for a few days beforehand.'

Quinta looked forward to Noah leaving. But she fretted that, when he returned, her child would be more grown inside her. Perhaps she could persuade him that, somehow, his seed had penetrated. She thought not. He had little experience with ladies, but a great deal with farm animals. Her child was destined to be born early; very early.

However, she did not feel guilty at her choice. Her mother meant more to her than Noah ever would and she guessed he might realise that. He took his hunter, well laden and sporting a burnished new saddle, planning to impress his kith in Crosswell and his host.

Seth took on an extra village lad to help with the farm work and they saw little of him except on a Sunday. She looked forward to the Sabbath and her visits to church. Bilton Farm was near enough to walk but too far for Laura and they took the trap. They were much cheered by the company, especially the favour Miss Wilkins now showed them as she lingered for conversation in the churchyard.

'Oh! My brother can be so tiresome!' she grumbled. 'He has his nose forever in his books.'

'It is his calling,' Quinta replied mildly.

'Well, I wish he would call on Sir William more and arrange for improvements to the vicarage.'

'Surely it is not damp?'

'It is old and dingy, but Mr Wilkins says it is not "fitting"

248

for the Squire to spend his money on us when some of his parishioners are so poor. He does not need to! My brother has his own inheritance. But he spends it on books when I should dearly like to replace the draperies and furnishings in our home.'

'Well, you do have an eye for such decor. You must help me choose new fabrics for upholstery and window curtains at the farmhouse.'

Beatrice's eyes shone. 'Oh, may I? The draper from town will bring you patterns and fabrics to choose from.'

'Yes, Noah has accounts with several suppliers in town. He said I may use them while he is away.'

'You will need a seamstress. I know of one in the village. When can we start?'

'I think I should wait until Noah comes home before I make any major changes.'

'Oh, must you?'

'It is his house.'

'Bah!' Miss Wilkins responded impatiently. 'We ladies must always wait on our gentlemen's decisions.'

'I have Mother to consider, too,' Quinta pointed out. Her mother's chest was weakening and, even when she rested, her breathing was laboured. The winter had set in early and promised to be harsh.

'Yes, of course you have. I am forgetting my duties. You will let me help you, won't you? I have a great deal of experience in caring for the sick.'

Miss Wilkins visited Laura frequently and was a source of lively support for Quinta and her mother. She was already past thirty in her years but, Quinta realised, she would have made a good wife for a vicar or lawyer, or even a farmer. If she envied Quinta her position as a married woman, she did not show it and Quinta was grateful for her friendship.

However, her Sundays were tinged with sadness as she laid flowers or foliage at her father's grave. Mother, too, shed a tear and searched in her small bag for a handkerchief. She had lost Quinta's elder sister, Eliza, too, and both names adorned the small memorial stone. She studied the dates and thought wistfully how nice it would have been to grow up with a sister.

'Eliza was fourteen when she died. You . . .' Quinta did the calculation in her head. 'You were nineteen or twenty when you bore her.' Older than I am now, she thought.

Laura did not respond to this but said, 'It was a great loss to all of us when Eliza passed away. But the Lord giveth as well as taketh away and he blessed us with you; though I had to wait until I was Miss Wilkins' age.'

'I wish I had known my sister.' Quinta knew of her mother's disappointment in not having more children and reached through the slit in her cloak to take her hand. Through the thickness of their woollen gloves she felt how thin and bony Laura's fingers had become. She frowned. Mother was declining faster than she ought and she resolved to make nourishing jelly and honeyed posset for her.

December arrived and Quinta expected Noah's return at any time. Seth took Noah's stock to market and returned with more coins than she had ever seen before. She placed them in her gown cupboard for safekeeping. The temperature dropped suddenly and the rutted track to the village froze hard with frost. It was too dangerous for folk and pony alike and they were obliged to forgo their outings to church. As the Christmas feast approached with still no sign of Noah, Mr Wilkins made a slow ascent on horseback to Bilton Farm. The sky was leaden.

'I have news from the High Peak.'

'You have a letter?' Quinta asked anxiously.

He shook his head. 'Nothing is getting through. Blizzards have made travelling impossible and deep snow has blocked the routes. It is said that we shall have the same. Beatrice has sent you these sweetmeats for Mrs Haig.'

They exchanged further pleasantries and greetings for the

season then parted gratefully, each returning to the safety of their own firesides.

Laura's chest worsened and her body weakened significantly. She took to her bed and Quinta kept a fire going in her chamber day and night. She asked Seth to send a lad from the village to fetch the physician from town and waited restlessly for his arrival. He could not ride as he had been laid low himself by a fever and wrote a note for the apothecary. The medicine eased Laura's distress but Quinta was obliged to watch her mother's strength ebb away.

The weather deteriorated still further and no one ventured far from home for fear of injury and cold. Seth prepared and cooked a goose for dinner on Christmas Day but neither joined him at the kitchen table for Laura was not able to get up from her bed and Quinta would not leave her. He brought a tray and left it outside the bedchamber.

Laura's voice was weak. 'You will not forget all that I have taught you?'

'Hush now, Mother. You must rest.'

'I can do nothing else now. Think of me when I am gone.'

'Of course I shall, all the time.'

'And remember your father, and what a good man he was. Eliza, too; especially Eliza, you must cherish her memory. Promise me you will.'

'I promise, Mother.'

Quinta took hold of her thin cold hand and sat motionless for hours. Through the window, she watched the snow fall relentlessly from a blackened sky and forgot the passing time as her darling mother lost her fight for life. She lay motionless, her gentle grip weakening in Quinta's grasp as she drifted in and out of sleep, hardly knowing who or where she was. Quinta too lost count of the days and became gaunt and hollow-eyed herself as she nursed.

Laura Haig breathed her last as streaks of light pierced a grey morning sky. The snow had stopped falling but it lay thick on the ground. Laura's grip on her hand slackened and her head fell sideways as her life came to a close. Quinta sat motionless in her chair and stared at her mother's beautiful, still features for a long time before she began to weep. She had known the end was near but it did not make her grief any the less and her body shook with sobs. Her crying continued as she placed pennies on her mother's eyes and washed her thin body with warm water from the kettle over the fire.

When she had finished, the sound of church bells floated over the snow-covered fields to celebrate, not a Sunday, but the New Year's Day. She dried her eyes and remembered the last few words her mother had uttered before she had fallen into her final faint. 'You have made your bed, my love. Now you must lie in it.' She wondered whether she could. It was comfortable enough, but cold. The chill she felt at Bilton Farm did not come from frost and ice. It came from the void in her heart.

She did not remember her sister Eliza and knew only what her mother had told her. But Quinta had grown up in her devoted father's care and protection and she had been distraught when he passed away. She and her mother had mourned together and the bond between them had strengthened. Mother had supported her through her sorrow; without her Quinta did not know what she would have done. Who was to help her now? She had lost the person most dear to her and she had no one to share her grief. She felt so isolated and abandoned. No one had loved her as her mother had and now Laura had been taken from her there was no one left who truly loved her. A forlorn despair overtook her sense of loss. She was utterly alone and wished so much that Patrick were here now.

She had hardly dared think about at him as it only added to her misery. Where had the King sent him? Was he still alive? She wondered if he ever thought of her. She could not write to him now for she would have to tell him of her marriage, and though she had wed to protect his unborn child she felt

252

she had betrayed his love. Yet in her heart it was Patrick who was her true husband and she was glad that Noah had been unable to sully her body with his seed.

She placed her hands over the gentle swell of her stomach: a new year and a new life. Patrick's infant would be delivered before the end of spring and part of him would always be with her. She wondered if Noah might believe in some way it was his. He was an untutored man in many ways and she did not know him well. She dreaded the day when the snows melted and he would come home.

The thaw came slowly. By Twelfth Night the ground was soft enough to dig and Quinta laid her mother to rest with her beloved father and sister. The toll of sleepless nights showed in Quinta's shadowy sunken eyes and Miss Wilkins gave her tea in the vicarage while her brother conducted the burial. Afterwards she went alone to lay a wreath of evergreens and berries at the headstone, and whispered, 'What shall I do without you, Mother? How shall I survive without you to guide and counsel me? Who will hold my hand when my baby comes?'

A chill gust of wind blew across the graveyard, stinging her raw cheeks and freezing her stiff fingers. There was no one to answer her. No one. She picked away dead leaves stuck to the stone, smoothed the area where the mason would add her mother's name, and turned to face her bleak and lonely future.

Mr Wilkins took her home in his trap after the funeral.

'Is there news from outside the Riding, sir?' she asked.

'There are reports that the road through Crosswell has reopened and the snows are melting on the High Peak. My news sheet says many sheep have been lost in the drifts and High Peak farmers fear for their livelihoods. I expect Noah will be on his way home soon.'

'News sheets are so useful. Noah does not read as a rule and considers the subscription a waste of his money,' she responded. 'He has done his learning through years of labour, but he is

253

interested in all matters affecting farming and I thought that I might read them to him. What do you think, Mr Wilkins?'

'My dear Mrs Bilton, what an excellent notion! You know, I thought you were far too young to be the mistress of Bilton Farm, especially so now your dear mama has passed on. My sister has advised me otherwise, of course, and I see for myself how well you fare. Although, my dear, you look quite gaunt today but I understand it is your grief. I shall be pleased to let you have my news sheets when I am finished with them.'

Quinta thanked him graciously. The politics of farming did not interest her. But lists and movements of the King's army did.

Winter in the King's army for Patrick was different from any he had experienced before because of the unremitting heat. A wind from the sea provided occasional relief, but it might deceive him into shedding garments and exposing parts of his white skin to the scorching sun. No matter how stifling his uniform, he valued its protection, and, in spite of his discomfort and the unhappiness, in his heart he acknowledged a raw beauty in the island.

There were long days patrolling atop the high stone wall of the fort; time to survey the lushness of the territory and beyond that the unbelievable colours of the sea. In the burning heat the water glittered like the blue sapphires and green emeralds his father had shown him as a boy. From light to dark to light again it glistened and beckoned as did gems. Yet when it became grey and turbulent, whipped to a foam by high winds, he shuddered at its power. He remembered a sea storm on his journey here when he had feared for his life.

The storms were mightier than any he had known, blowing over ships and buildings alike. The rain fell in solid sheets, dropping from the heavens like a stone, a relentless soaking that turned the track into a muddy stream. Afterwards the air he breathed became steam and his light trousers and cotton shirts soon soaked in sweat. Yet no soldier was allowed outside the confines of the fort without a scarlet coat on his back and a high shako on his head. When not on guard duty or patrolling the island, the coolest place was underground in the cavernous brick cellars where the men slept, ate, drank and gambled.

For two days he had sensed an urgency among the officers and wondered what was happening. He was resting on his hard narrow bed when his sergeant marched over purposefully. 'Ross! Come with me. Hurry.'

Patrick moved quickly, struggling into his jacket and snatching up his cartridge belt and rifle. 'What's afoot, sir?'

'The captain said there have been reports of unrest down by the harbour. We're regrouping tomorrow. The rebels have got hold of guns and I want my wife and daughter out of there before nightfall.'

They set off down the track at double time

'The slaves are angry. They are impatient to be free men and are fired up by Creoles in the harbour town. They will arm and march on the plantations and this fort. I want you to bring Constance and Faith here for safety.'

'Me? Why? Where will you go?'

'I'm joining the captain's force to surround the rebels.'

'Then you need me with you.'

'You're one of our best shots. The colonel wants you defending the fort in case they are attacked. You've time to get my women back there first.'

'You sound worried. How many weapons have the rebels got?'

'They have rifles and ammunition from a supply ship that foundered on the reef a few weeks ago. The word is that it was pirates or wreckers. It makes no difference – the rebels are not going to wait while the government drags its feet over emancipation. They want freedom for all slaves now.'

'But Constance was once a slave herself. She is not their enemy.'

'Her daughter is the child of an English soldier. She is seen as one of us.'

They found Faith alone in the tiny harbourside house. Her eyes were wide and frightened as the sergeant burst through the flimsy door and demanded, 'Where is your mother?'

'I don't know. She told me to wait here for her.'

'Why? What was she planning to do?'

'I – I—'

'Tell me, Faith!'

'We were going to take a boat to one of the smaller islands until – until—'

The sergeant turned to Patrick. 'I know where she has gone. You take Faith back to the fort now. I'll go and find Constance and follow you.'

'What about the captain's force?'

'Let me worry about that.'

'We'll wait for you on the hill track.'

'No. I've been in one of these rebellions before. Passions run high and there are old scores to settle. Take Faith straight back to the barracks and stay there. The fort will not fall to the rebels.'

'Very well.' Patrick extended his hand to Faith.

Her father kissed her briefly and pushed her towards him. 'Go now. Hurry.'

Patrick took Faith's small hand in his and dragged her after him. 'Can you run?' he asked.

She nodded.

'Let's see how fast.'

They stopped for breath halfway up the track. Beyond the palm trees the sun glinted on the ocean and in the distance they heard the first shots fired. 'Ready?' Patrick asked. But he saw from her wide eyes and panting that she was too exhausted to carry on. He slung his rifle across his back, said, 'This is the only way,' and hoisted her over one shoulder. Her extra weight slowed him but he reached the fort without mishap.

The distant firing had increased and the colonel was giving commands.

'Ross, what the hell were you doing? Who is this woman?'

'She's Faith, my sergeant's daughter, sir. Can she stay with your wife until her mother arrives?'

'My good lady is marshalling all the women in the servants' house. Show her where it is and then get to your post. I'm doubling the guard all round.'

'Stay with the women,' Patrick told Faith, and hurried towards his major for orders.

The firing continued through the night and the following day. Word came through that the rebels had been contained in the waterside settlement and the plantations were safe. But there had been shooting and casualties on both sides and it was not until two days later that the extent of this was discovered. The bodies of the sergeant and Constance were found floating in the harbour and taken back to the fort. They had been shot.

Patrick saw nothing of Faith during this time until he was called upon to attend the funeral and fire a salute. The sergeant and his wife were laid to rest together in the burial ground within the fort. Afterwards the colonel summoned him to his office. He was sitting at his desk with a collection of papers in front of him. His wife was there with Faith by her side.

'Ross.'

'Sir.' Patrick stood smartly to attention.

'You were a convict?'

'Yes, sir.'

'The sergeant and his captain both give you good reports.'

Patrick looked straight ahead.

'I have the sergeant's will here. It appoints you as his daughter's guardian.'

'Guardian?' Patrick didn't remember agreeing to that.

'Nothing else to say?'

'I – I didn't know, sir. I agreed to see her safely settled in England, that is all.'

257

'He must have trusted you.'

'I suppose so.'

'Well, like it or not, she's your responsibility now. You don't have a woman, do you?'

'No, sir.'

'Then she'll stay with the women servants in their quarters and we'll find her work.'

'Thank you, sir. I have a question.'

'What is it?'

'How long will it be before I go back? I mean, before I can take her to England?'

'You're a soldier, Ross. You go where the King sends you, when he sends you.' He waved his hand dismissively.

'Sir.' He marched out smartly.

Guardian? He never agreed to be her guardian! That bloody sergeant! Still, this was his life now and he was a good soldier, gaining admiration and respect from the officers. But his hopes of returning home and seeing Quinta again were receding ever further into the distance. He wondered if she had received his letter.

Chapter 21

Quinta was more than five months gone when Noah came back from High Peak. She was beginning to show and wore her mother's gown with a little more room around the waist. It was a cold winter and so perfectly normal for her to be bound in a shawl all day. At night she wrapped herself in a thick calico nightgown and wondered how she was going to explain the existence of a child to him.

Noah returned to his farm with an increased certainty about his position in the Riding; in that respect the visit had been successful. But Quinta detected flashes of self-importance about him that worried her. On his first night home he asked her to sit with him by the fire after their tea.

'Well now, Mrs Bilton, you are not as blooming as you were afore I left. But spring will soon be upon us. The sap is rising. We'll have a babe by next Christmastide. Now that Mother has passed away, God rest her soul, and you're getting the house to rights, you'll be needing more help. I'll see about a maid for you at the hiring fair on Lady Day.'

'Thank you, Noah. I thought I had lost your favour for good.'

'Aye well, I reckon Mother were the one to cast the spell.

Now she's gone, you'll be back in my bedchamber where you belong.' He stood up. 'Let's be going, then.'

She had unpacked his travelling bag and noticed a bottle of tincture with an apothecary's label. She placed it by the bed with a glass of water. The chamber was cold as Noah had said not to light a fire but Quinta had warmed the bed with bedpans.

'You have medicine to take, Noah. Are you ill?'

He placed a few drops in the water and drank it. 'It cools the blood.'

'In winter?' Lord help her, she must remember not to argue with him!

Noah took off his jacket and waistcoat and unbuttoned the flap on his breeches. 'We'll see. Take off your gown and corsets.'

She did so and stood in the middle of the room in her loose chemise, drawers, stockings and boots.

He extended a forefinger and shook his hand up and down. 'And those women's things.'

She hesitated. Her nightgown was in the ottoman and she did not want him to see her naked. 'You know what it does to you, Noah.'

'Don't you worry about me. I saw an apothecary at Crosswell and he told me to try his tincture.' He took hold of himself and flopped out of his breeches. 'See?'

Quinta stared. She had not looked at that part of him before and the sight of it made the bile rise in her throat. She didn't want him anywhere near her or her growing child. She wanted to run out of here, into the cold night air, anywhere, as long as it was away from Noah Bilton and his thoughtless, ill-mannered ways. 'I – I'll just get my nightgown,' she muttered.

'Let me have a look at you, first. A gentleman has a right to his pleasure.'

This was a different message from the one about fornication and she wondered what he had been doing in the High Peak. 'I'm cold, Noah. I don't want to catch a chill.'

'Go on, then.' He agreed reluctantly and sat on the side of

the bed with his legs splayed wide and his breeches flap down, exposing himself to her.

Hurriedly, she turned her back on him, lifted her chemise over her head and replaced it with a roomy calico nightgown.

'My, Mrs Bilton, you're a bit more rounded than before I went. What have you been eating?'

Breathless with anxiety, she almost swallowed her reply. 'I – I didn't eat as much meat when I was living at Top Field.'

She unlaced her boots, rolled off her stockings and stepped out of her drawers, making a fuss about folding them and laying them neatly on top of the ottoman. But eventually she had to face him and when she did she was shocked to see that he was handling himself inside his breeches, fondling and rubbing himself.

He looked up at her, frowning. 'What's to do here, eh? The apothecary said I might have to coax myself. Or ask you to do it for me.'

Quinta froze to the spot. Please no, she begged silently. I don't want to touch any part of him. I hate him. She could not believe that just a few months ago she had offered herself to him as she had. But then she was desperate to deceive him for the sake of her child and would have done anything.

It was far too late for deception now. Her life was ruined whatever happened and the only thing that kept her going was that she would give birth to Patrick's child in the spring. She wondered what else the apothecary had said to Noah and whether she could persuade him that, somehow, in his desperate hurried fumbling, he had got her with child before he went away.

'I expect you're tired from your journey, Noah,' she suggested.

'But I only had to look at you afore! Fetch the candle over so I can see you better.'

She carried the candle to the bedside table but before she could put it down he said sharply, 'Give it here and take off your nightgown.'

'But I'm cold, Noah!' she protested, handing him the light. 'I said, take it off!'

She struggled with the voluminous material over her head so that he would not see her swelling belly and held it bunched up in front of her. He snatched it away from her and threw it aside, holding the candle so close to her skin that she could feel the warmth from the flame. Then he moved the light to his open flap. 'Come on, fella.' He sounded puzzled. 'I don't understand this. You've got nowt on but nowt's stirring.'

Quinta crossed her arms over her belly, relieved he was looking at himself and not her. 'What have you taken, Noah?' she asked.

'A potion from the East, the apothecary said. It cost me plenty, anyway.'

Quinta remembered how he used to be and thought that, whatever he had bought, he must have taken too much. She felt a huge relief that she would not have to endure her duties in the marriage bed with him, at least for tonight. And she most certainly had no wish for him to stop taking his potion. 'Perhaps you have to get used to it,' she suggested. 'You know, like laudanum. Knocks you out at first but you have to keep taking it for it to work.'

'Aye, you might be right.'

'Why don't you take some more, then?'

'Don't be daft, woman. Give it a chance to work.' He lifted the candle again to look at her. 'I've been away from you too long, that's all. You are a bonny lass, I'll say that for you. Come a bit nearer, so I can get a good look at you.'

Reluctantly she took a small step forward. 'Mind the candle grease, Noah. I've got nothing on.'

But he kept looking at her, moving the light up and down and across her body.

She saw the corners of his mouth turn down and felt fear rising in her chest. 'Hurry up, Noah. I'm all goose-pimply.'

'I reckon you've been eating too much of my best beef.'

'I told you, I'm not used to all the meat you have here.'

'But even your titties are bigger. And you've got a right belly on you now.' He pulled aside her arms and held the candle closer. 'Right little pot belly that is. If you were one of my porkers I'd say you were well in pig.' He laughed and she made an effort to laugh along with him. But she felt herself blushing.

Then he stopped laughing and his face went very still. 'You're not, are you? By the Lord in heaven, you are! That's a babby in your belly!'

She managed a nervous smile. There was absolutely no point in denying it now. 'It's what you want, isn't it? Aren't you pleased?'

His face darkened. 'Well, I would be if it were mine. But it's not, is it?'

Her voice was shaky. 'Of course it is. Who else's could it be?'

'Don't give me that. I haven't had schooling like the gentry but I know what I have to do to get you with child. Same as my breeding bull.'

He reminded her of his prize bull. Thick-set and strong, waited on hand and foot, and easily riled if he was crossed. And she knew also that, when he was called on to do his duty, the bull was capable of missing his target in his greed to get at the cow. Just like Noah.

'But I'm not one of your milkers.' She laughed nervously.

He looked surprised at this and she realised that he did think of her in the same way as his cattle. He had married her for a reason. She was his wife for one purpose only.

'No, you're not!' He had raised his voice. 'Because if you were I'd know who had seeded you!'

'You, Noah. Only you,' she protested.

'You little whore! Was it one of the village lads who help Seth in the fields?' He grabbed her arm and yanked her towards him. 'Let's have a proper look at you.' He did. He searched every inch of her naked body and then hit her across the face with the back of his brawny hand. 'In calf, and not by me. I should have known better. I said you were a witch! Bewitched

263

me right and proper, you did. There's no wonder you wanted to wed me so soon. Aye and I thought it was because you wanted me.'

He laughed again, this time harshly and without mirth. 'By the Lord, they say there is no fool like an old fool. Well, I'll show you that you can't make a fool out of old Noah. Just because my father came from peasant stock it doesn't mean I can't think for myself. Huh! I thought you were a harlot when you came over to accept my offer. On your own you were. And I was too besotted with the thought of you that I couldn't stop myself. You would have let me bed you that afternoon, wouldn't you, you deceitful little trollop? How far gone were you then? I've seen in church how big the lasses get with their bellies and I can count. My cows, my ewes and my old sow: I know how long it takes them and I know it for the women-folk. That babby was in your belly afore we were wed. What I want to know is who put it there!'

She reeled from the blow and steadied herself on the wall. The air was chilly and without her chemise she felt exposed to his anger. Why had she ever thought she could deceive him? But she would have got away with it if he didn't have his afflic-tion. Well, she didn't have to tell him who her baby's father was and she wouldn't! He would as likely kill the child when it was born if he knew the real father.

'Well? Answer me!'

She remained silent.

'Don't tell me there were that many you don't even know!'

'Of course not,' she retaliated. 'There was only one.'

'So you admit it then?'

'Yes.'

'Well, you don't have to tell me who if it happened last summer. It was that poacher, I'll be bound. A gypsy! My wife has been with a gypsy!'

'His father was from the Riding! And his mother was an Irish lady!' she protested.

264

'Not so much a lady if she let that cripple have his way with her!' He stared at her, his sneer turning into a look of hatred. 'Aye, it was that poacher right enough. He turned your head and you, you little whore, you let him bed you afore me. Afore me! Me, who you were promised to as a babby!' The back of his heavy hand came down across her face again, making her head spin.

'Noah!' She wiped her hand across her brow and looked at the blood on her fingers. 'Stop it. I am with child.'

'Not my child! I'll have no poacher's bastard in my house. Nay! I'll not have you here as my wife either.'

Now Quinta was really frightened. Surely he would not turn her out? 'But this means I am not barren, Noah. Children are all you need from me. I'll have more and they will be yours. You can have your own sons to work the farm with you and make you even richer.'

'But how do I know they'll be mine? How do I know who you'll be going with while I'm out in the fields? If you've done it once to me, you'll do it again. Womenfolk! You can never trust them and I want nowt to do with any of them. They're harlots, the lot of them.'

Argument was futile. He was an old-fashioned country man steeped in his traditional beliefs. Ironically, she thought he would have approved of the Lammas Day arrangement if it had been with him. But she dare not tell him about that. She dare not say a word. She picked up her nightgown and put it over her head. Her hands and feet were freezing so she pulled on her stockings and walked around to the bed, intending to climb beneath the blankets.

'Get out of here!' he shouted. 'I'll not have a whore in my bed.'

She stopped pulling back the covers.

'Go on! Get out of my sight!' he repeated.

She gathered up her clothes and boots in silence and did as he demanded. Perhaps he would have calmed down in the morning. Perhaps whatever he had taken would have, like laudanum, worn off. Well, at least he knew about her child now. And she was his legal wife so surely he could not cast her out? He had made the vows, as she had. But she could not deny that she had deceived him most cruelly and he was right to be angry.

It was pitch black on the landing and she did not have a candle. She felt along the wall to the end window where a cold draught blew in from the gaps in the surrounding wood-work. Next to that was the room her mother had slept in; the chamber where she had nursed her and watched her die.

She had hoped for more years together before the consumption took her. But mother had been too weak to fight. The years since father had died had taken her strength and, yes, it was true, she had been five and thirty when Quinta was born. Women of that age giving birth were usually more robust, with a growing tribe of children fussing round them. Perhaps Mother had given life to her at the expense of her own wellbeing. That's what mothers do. Quinta understood that now. She would do anything to protect her unborn child. Anything.

The bed had not been aired and she climbed reluctantly into the clammy sheets, drawing her knees up to her chest under her nightgown and wrapping her cold fingers in its folds. She didn't care what Noah thought of her. It was his fault that Patrick had been sent away from her. Her life would have been so different with Patrick by her side and she ached to feel his arms around her, caressing her, kissing her and marvelling at their child growing inside her. He would have been so proud. She was glad that Noah could not do his duty as a husband. She did not want her body and her baby to be tainted by him and she thanked the Lord for his new potion.

However, she realised that it might wear off by morning and Noah might reconsider his decision to banish her from his bed. She was his wife and men were capable of using the act of procreation as a show of punishment instead of love. It would be worse than hell for her if he forced himself upon her now. She slipped out of bed and turned the key in the door before falling into a restless slumber.

It was still dark when the cock crowed and the cows sheltering in the barn lowed to be milked. Quinta tensed. Noah's footsteps on the landing brought her wide awake. The stairs creaked and she heard him draw the bolts on the front door. The house went quiet again. She washed and dressed quickly, then hurried downstairs to get the kitchen fire going and pump water in the scullery. She had a good heat and was sizzling fat bacon on a skillet when Noah came in through the scullery.

He brushed straw from his jacket on to the floor. 'You can stay and housekeep for me until Lady Day.'

'What then?'

'I'm taking you away to the High Peak.'

'Where you went shooting? You have family there?'

'You know well enough I've got nobody.'

'Then what – what will happen to me?'

'You'll be out of my road.'

'You mean to hide me away?'

He didn't reply at first. He just grunted at her and gave a kind of half-laugh. 'I mean to rid myself of you.'

'But you can't just cast me aside. I am your wife.'

'Aye, and we have a way of dealing with unfaithful wives where I come from.'

'What do you mean?'

'You'll see.'

'But, Noah, I shall be having my child soon.'

'Aye. The babby'll be welcome to somebody. There are not many womenfolk up there. The living is too raw for most of 'em. You'd best start getting used to it so when you've done in the house, take yourself off to the barn and start plaiting straw.'

Plaiting straw? She didn't think any farmer did that these days. 'What for?' she demanded.

267

'For a halter. Have you never heard of a straw halter?'

'No, I have not. There is perfectly good rope and leather strapping in the stable. Please do not make me do this, Noah.'

'You have said enough, madam. I am master in this house and my word is final.'

But Quinta did not feel inclined to accept his last word. He was a gentleman of the parish. She was his wife and he was treating her as a lowly servant girl. 'I understand that this is my punishment, sir. Must I do it every day? The barn is cold at this time of year and working wet straw will make my fingers too sore for needlework.'

He raised his right arm across his body and glared. 'You will do as I say, woman! Would you have me strike you again to gain your obedience?'

She squared her shoulders and faced up to his threat. 'You are no gentleman, sir. I am your wife and I am with child.'

He did not lower his arm and his eyes glittered with anger. 'And I am the wronged one here. You are a cheat and a harlot.'

She noticed his fist was clenched and knew he was capable of beating her. She looked at the floor.

'That's better,' he growled. 'You'll be silent and serve my breakfast. Then get out of my sight.'

That afternoon, as she put straw to soak in a bucket of ice-cold water, she thought that he could have given her worse punishments. It was a small price to pay if she did not have to be a wife to him, although she was fearful of the future. Did he mean to abandon her and her child in the isolation of the High Peak? Or would he make her leave her baby behind when she returned? Well, she would never do that. She would refuse to be parted from him and Noah could not force her. But she wondered bleakly where he was taking her and whether other Peak dwellers were as pitiless as Noah.

The light failed early and he came out to the barn with a lantern to inspect her work, grunting wordlessly at her progress.

'When do you plan to leave?' she asked nervously.

'We'll set off just as soon as I've turned round here. Seth can run the farm as well as me, now.'

'I should like to come indoors now.'

'You can return tomorrow, at dawn, to light the range and do your chores.'

'Surely you are not expecting me to sleep out here?'

'It is good enough for my labourers at harvest-time.'

This was too much for Quinta to take. She stood up and brushed the straw from her skirt. 'I am not a labourer and the nights are cold. I shall not stay.'

Her response surprised him and he blinked in the glow from the lantern. 'Where'll you go then?' he scorned.

'Miss Wilkins will take me in. She was very kind to Mother.'

He gripped her arm roughly. 'You will not leave this farm until I take you away.'

'Then treat me like your wife until then!'

'You are no wife of mine!' He pushed her away.

She stumbled and retaliated angrily, 'And you have not been a husband to me!'

He was still for a moment and she went on quickly, 'What will Seth say in the village when I tell him you have banished me to the barn?'

'He is a loyal servant, which is more than you are.'

'Does his loyalty extend to the alehouse on Saturday night?'

'You are a witch! You will not poison his mind against me!'

'I do not have to. Your actions do it for me.'

He was silent for a moment. Then he snarled, 'I shall be well rid of you, madam.' He grabbed her arm again and pushed her roughly towards the barn door. 'Get inside and make sure I catch no sight or sound of you except at mealtimes.'

She retreated to her mother's chamber and was thankful that it was away from Noah. Its warmth was welcome after an afternoon in the damp and draughty barn. It gave her time alone to think and she became anxious about her baby's future. She recalled what the sergeant had told her mother about Patrick's birth. His mother had been sent away. The child, when it was born, had been taken from her and farmed out.

Not many womenfolk up in the High Peak, Noah had said. It followed then that there would not be many babies either, not many children to labour on the land or in the farmhouses. Horrified, she realised that Noah meant to give her child away! No, not give, but sell. Her baby, once born, would be sold to some childless farmer for a lifetime of hardship and labour like his father before him. Of course! That was what Noah was planning for her. She could not let him do that! She would not. It was her child and she would not let anyone take him from her.

The ensuing nights were restless, for her baby was growing and soon her belly would become cumbersome. She took a lamp with her and kept it alight beside her for most of the night as she talked to her child, stroking her little bulge and repeating how much she loved him. Or her, she acknowledged. Alone in the small bedchamber when she heard Noah's snoring through the walls, she took off her nightgown by the yellow glow and traced the blue veins in her white skin.

'I won't let anyone take you from me. You are my life now and I shall find a way to keep you,' she promised.

She did not know how. She thought of running away, but she was too large to get any distance before she would be found and brought back. If Noah meant to sell her child he would not let her go until he had his payment. And if he didn't drag her back she would as likely perish in the cold without shelter.

But, throughout all her despair, one thought kept her going. Patrick. Patrick was with her and part of her as his child in her womb. It did not matter where she went or what she did as long as she had Patrick's child and that knowledge gave her strength, although she feared for the future and the unknown.

After the snows melted, the ground underfoot was slushy and muddy and no one ventured far. But Noah walked to church on Sunday and she wondered what he told them, for as the weather improved neither the vicar nor his sister called on her.

In Noah's more approachable moods, when the work for the day was done and he had taken a little ale, but not enough to make him maudlin, she tried to find out more about his plans for her.

'How shall we travel to the Peaks?' she ventured. 'It will be too long a journey on horseback in my circumstance.'

'Aye, I've thought of that. I'll be taking one of my fat stock to the innkeeper at Crosswell, so I'll need the cart for his fodder 'til we get there. You can ride in the back with that.'

'Shall I be staying at the inn?' Quinta imagined the bullock might be payment for her keep, but Noah did not answer her. She poured him more ale and went out to the scullery. The journey would take much longer with a beast in tow but it would be more comfortable for her.

She went upstairs to finish packing her box with garments she had prepared for her baby and herself. The fresh aroma of clean linen after a blowing on the washing line cheered her. The days were growing longer and the sun's rays had warmth in them at last.

Noah had insisted that she finish her plaited straw halter and he threw it on top of her box as they left in the cart. He took the Sheffield road that skirted the town and rose steeply towards the moors. The track climbed steadily, leaving behind furrowed fields and budding trees for the bleak heights of granite and scrub. The air became misty and damp and Noah had to get down from the cart to read the guideposts. They passed few houses and even fewer hamlets and spent the first night sheltering in an isolated barn with no hot food to warm them.

Quinta felt tired and cold the next day as soon as she woke. She had only spring water, oat biscuit and cold bacon for breakfast. The cart slithered and slipped down a steep incline until, quite suddenly, they were below the mist and the sun's rays lit up the moors. Quinta turned her face to its warmth. She saw other carts and people on foot and shepherds with small flocks heading in the same direction. They were nearing their destination.

Crosswell did not sprawl in the way the town she knew in the South Riding did, but it was just as busy. She thought he would want to sell the beast first and maybe she could disappear into the throng while he was distracted, but her condition was noticeable and burdensome. He went directly to the inn and sent in a lad to fetch out the innkeeper. After a long wait he appeared, smartly dressed like a prosperous farmer, accompanied by a butcher who examined the beast.

'Good stock, Noah.'

'I sell to them that thinks they're gentry in the South Riding. Mill owners and the like who don't have the land like proper gentry. I've got some fodder left that you can take.'

'Are you not putting him in the auction?'

'I said I'd bring you one of my beasts next time I was round these parts and here he is.'

'How much are you asking?'

Noah named his price, adding, 'I want coin though, none of your fancy banknotes.'

'I'll have him. Townfolk hereabouts eat mostly sheep meat and they're partial to a bit o' beef.'

'Aye, well, you can't fatten beef like this on moorland.'

The butcher looked in the back of the cart. 'Who's the wench, Noah?'

'She's for the hiring fair.'

'She looks in calf to me.'

'Some passing gypsy had her. That's why I want rid.'

'How much are you asking for her?'

'Five guineas.'

'That's a bit steep for a servant.'

'I reckon Miss Banks'll pay it for a wife for her Davey.'

Chapter 22

The butcher raised his eyebrows and glanced in her direction. 'A wife? You wouldn't do that to her, would you?' He looked more closely. 'Are you sure you want to sell her, Noah? She's right bonny.'

'Aye. She'd have been better for me if she weren't.'

'How come?'

'Buy me a jug of ale and I'll tell you.'

The butcher seemed interested in this prospect. 'Come inside, then.'

'Just let me tie this one to the wagon and I'll be with you.'

Quinta listened to this conversation in astonishment. She'd thought he was bringing her here to farm out her child and until now that had been her greatest fear. But he meant to be rid of her completely! She struggled to stop him binding her wrists with rope. 'Noah! You can't sell me like one of your beasts. I am not a servant. I'm your wife.'

'Not after today, you're not. You'll be somebody else's. You'll not be deceiving me again. I'll see to that.'

The two men continued their conversation as though she were not present.

'Has Miss Banks come into town today?' Noah asked.

'She's at the auction getting rid of her barren ewes.'

'Is Davey with her?'

'I've not seen him. He might have stayed on the moor with the early lambs. If he is here he'll be with Amos. Amos lost most of his breeding ewes in that bad snow and he's selling what's left of his flock.'

'Amos'll be for hire, then?'

'I think he's fixed up.'

She sat huddled in the corner of Noah's cart, her wrists burning from the rasp of the rope as she tried to free herself. Surely he was not really going to sell her at the hiring fair? And ask such a high price? No one around here could afford that anyway. Perhaps he only meant to frighten her? To show her that he could, and would, do this to her if she strayed again?

He was inside with the butcher for a long time and came out the worse for drink. But he untied her, picked up the straw halter and said, 'Bring your box to stand on.'

It was the most appalling humiliation that Quinta had ever experienced, standing in a line of down-trodden, ill-dressed men and women to be prodded and picked over like the sheep in their pens waiting to be sold. The same farmers and butchers that leaned over the hurdles and poked fleeces with their staves walked past her using the same sticks to lift aside her straggling hair and stare into her face.

'How much?' one asked. But when Noah told him he moved on and Quinta was pathetically thankful for that. She was reassured that no one would buy her and Noah would leave her here in lodgings until her baby was born to learn her lesson. She began to hope for that, especially when a dark-bearded shepherd in a thick grubby country smock lingered, even when he knew her price, and hooked his crook under the bottom of her skirt, lifting it clear of her ankles.

She bent down to shake it free. 'Stop him, Noah!'

'Nay, lass. He has to look at what he's buying.' He grasped

274

the folds of her skirt and lifted it higher. 'Sturdy one, she is,' he said.

He placed a cold hand around her calf and then slid it upwards to squeeze at her thigh. The straw halter was around his wrist and it fell heavily against her leg, snagging at her stockings.

'Feel that. She'll give you good service with a grand pair of legs like these. Got proven breeding an' all in her, this one has. You can see that for yourself.' He had his own staff in his other hand and he passed it over the curve of her stomach, flattening the folds of her skirt to show her bulge.

Quinta was mortified by his words and her heart started thumping. She might just be able to accept being sold as a servant to work as a housekeeper. But to imply that she might be bought to provide more children for some High Peak sheep farmer was too much to bear. She kept her eyes down as the shepherd lingered, grateful that he had more respect for her than Noah and refrained from touching her. She stole a glance at his face, met his piercing dark eyes and looked away hastily.

'I'll give you three guineas,' he replied.

Noah shook his head and grimaced. 'No deal,' he said.

'It is all I have.' The shepherd moved on, closely followed by a black and white dog at his heels.

Quinta breathed out raggedly. She hadn't realised how tense she had become and said to Noah, 'Please let me get down now. I am very tired and no one here can pay your price. Take me where I am to stay to have my child. Please, Noah.'

It was the truth. Her baby was heavy in her belly and she was exhausted from standing there for what seemed like hours and from the anxiety of taking part in this humiliating spectacle.

'I'll get what I ask. You'll see. Here comes Miss Banks. She'll have heard about you from the inn.'

The prospect of being taken on by a woman cheered Quinta. But Miss Banks looked as bleak and colourless as the overcast sky, and her pale blue eyes had a cold stare that unnerved her. She was very thin and a sallow skin stretched over her face. Her bony hands clutched at a leather satchel as she approached them.

'They say you have a wife for sale.'

'Aye, this one here.'

'And that she is with child.'

'It is no secret. You will have two for the price of one.'

'Who was the father?'

'He was a travelling man with a strong back and a – a sound mind.'

Quinta was surprised that Noah had seen fit to say anything good about Patrick but she kept her eyes down.

'Can she graft?' the woman asked.

'More than that. She can read and write.'

'Can she?' Miss Banks sounded interested.

'She's just right for your Davey. That's what you want, isn't it?'

'I might.'

'She's dear, though, seeing as you get the two of them.'

'I know how much you're asking. It's all round the inn.'

'Interested then?'

'What's she got in the box?'

'It's linen for her and the babby. She made it all herself.'

The spinster chewed at the inside of her mouth. 'Well, yon butchers have paid a good price for my old ewes this year. Not many for sale, you see, after all that snow killed a few off. I'll just go and settle up with the auctioneer and be back to pay for her. You can take her down.' Miss Banks spat on her grimy hand and held it out.

Noah echoed her action and their palms touched. 'I have a cart round the back of the inn. I'll wait for you there.'

Quinta froze to the spot. He really meant to do this. He had struck a deal to sell her. *Sell her as a wife to someone else!* She did not believe it was happening until Noah pulled at her arm and she half fell off her box.

'Pick it up,' he ordered. 'You're on your way.'

'Where am I going, Noah? Who is this woman and why isn't her son Davey here for himself?'

'You'll find out.'

She struggled with the rope handles of her box in front of her stomach and pleaded, 'I'll have to have a sit-down, Noah. I feel weak.'

'You'll be as right as rain after a bite to eat.' He bought her a mutton patty from a pie-seller in the square and she sat on a low stone wall in a brisk breeze to devour it. 'Aren't you having one?' she asked.

He smirked. 'There'll be a good dinner for me at the inn when I'm rid of you.'

She wondered where she would be eating her next meal. 'Will you fetch me a drink?'

'Get one yourself. The pump's over there.'

She thought she might have a chance to make a run for it but he followed close behind her and waited while she drank. She guessed he would see to it that she had no chance to escape until he had his five guineas. Although the food and drink revived her a little, she was weary from the journey and cold from standing in the marketplace and, for the present, no longer wished to flee. Surely being a servant to Miss Banks wouldn't be as bad as being a wife to Noah Bilton? Not unless she really expected her to marry her Davey? Was it her son, she wondered. Miss Banks? Perhaps he was born out of wedlock? If so, maybe she would have some sympathy for her situation.

She couldn't marry this Davey, anyway. Her marriage to Noah had been a proper one in the village church. They had taken vows in front of the Lord and the vicar had written their names in his parish register. For better or for worse, she would tell Miss Banks and her Davey. Selling her at a hiring fair could not nullify God's law, whatever their local customs were. Her eyes began to close and her knees felt wobbly. She slid down the wall, the rough stones grazing her back, to sit on her box and rest.

She noticed Noah watching her with a sneer on his face. He really did hate her for what she had done. But even now she did not regret it because she had had no choice at the time. Noah's lies had seen to that. And if he had been a proper husband to her in the bedchamber he would never have discovered her deception. Her child's true father could have stayed her secret.

Noah grasped the back of her gown and heaved her upwards. 'Get yourself moving. I'm ready for another jar of ale from the inn.'

The inn yard was cluttered with horses and their droppings. She climbed on to the back of Noah's cart, grateful for a rest. Noah took hold of a hank of rope and approached her.

'Please don't tie me again, Noah. I won't go anywhere, I promise. I'm too tired.'

'You won't get far round here, anyway,' he said as he bound her wrists to the cart. 'Not in these hills in your state. I'll be watching you from the window, though.' He picked up the straw halter and walked off.

She must have slept, for the next thing she knew, Miss Banks was reaching up and putting the straw halter over her head. Then she undid the rope that bound her wrists and said, 'Get down from there.'

As soon as her hands were free, Quinta pulled at the halter. 'Take that off! It scratches.'

The older woman gave her a sharp cuff at the side of her head. 'Don't you tell me what to do! This shows you're bought and paid for and you'll wear it 'til I say you can take it off.' She jerked the free end, making Quinta wince. 'Bring your box.'

The roadway outside the inn was crowded now that the market had finished. Sheep farmers, butchers and other traders lingered, enjoying their gains from buying or selling. The worse for ale, they prodded and jeered at her as she stumbled after Miss Banks. 'Is it far?' she asked.

'Speak when you're spoken to or you'll feel the back of my hand again.'

She did not think she could keep walking for long without collapsing and was flooded with relief when Miss Banks stopped by a couple of farm horses tethered near to a mounting stone. One was fitted with a ladies' saddle and the other heavily loaded with bundles and sacks of supplies. A stocky man with a black beard and wearing a rough country smock loomed out of the shadows with a sheepdog by his feet. Quinta recognised him as the shepherd who had lifted the edge of her skirt with his crook in the marketplace. She hugged her box as close as she could, glad to be enclosed in her cloak.

'You've bought the wife, then? Best get going if we're to be home afore darkness,' he said without looking at her.

Was he Davey? she wondered. The shepherd who could not afford Noah's price? She daren't look at him or Miss Banks, or utter a word for fear of being struck again. She didn't know how much longer she could keep going before she fainted. But she must stay alert. She must note the way they travelled so she could retrace her steps when she escaped. For escape she would, she thought firmly. She might be too tired to think straight now, but what Noah had done to her was degrading, inhuman even, and she was not going to tolerate it. The straw halter around her neck scratched at her skin every time she moved, and every graze increased her determination to make Noah pay for what he had done to her.

'I'll move some of the supplies to your mount, Miss Banks,' the shepherd said. 'She'll not walk the distance in her condition.' He set about repacking the horses.

Quinta was flooded with relief as he deftly rearranged the sacks and formed a space for her to sit side-saddle-fashion in reasonable comfort on the horse's broad back. Then he helped Miss Banks up the mounting stone to her seat and finally settled her wordlessly on her mount.

'Thank you, Davey,' she whispered as he tied on her box.

'I'm not Davey,' he answered abruptly, fixing the reins of Miss Banks's horse to the rear-harnessing on hers. He took up the bridle of her mount and led them off in single file away from the inn. His dog seemed to know the way and ran on ahead.

They left behind the inn and the town, which soon disappeared in the folds of the hills. She sat upright for as long as she could, losing count of the streams and narrow stone bridges they crossed, but their progress over the rocky tracks was slow and eventually her body sagged to one side. She rested her head on a sack of flour, welcoming the relative softness and too tired to care about beetles crawling under her hood into the warmth of her hair.

She thought briefly that the shepherd had behaved quite kindly towards her, making sure she was safe and comfortable before setting off. But Miss Banks was not the sympathetic spinster she had anticipated. For an old woman she seemed quite strong and Quinta guessed that only the tough survived an existence on these isolated moors. As they bumped and jolted over the steep stony track, she saw only acres of rocky moorland and an occasional shepherd's hovel built of stone and turf. They did not pass any coal pits, nor many woodlands, and she wondered what they used for fuel.

The horses climbed slowly out of the valley, taking a track in the opposite direction to the South Riding and going deeper into moorland. The wind whipped around her ears and she drew her hood closely about her head. Soon they were high enough to be shrouded in mist again, a damp penetrating drizzle that soaked into her cloak and through to her shawl.

The shepherd threw some old sacking around his shoulders as he plodded on, guiding the horses along the worst of the rocky path. When the light faded completely and everything became totally black, she marvelled that he could find his way, but she guessed that there were not many tracks to follow up here. She did not see any farmsteads, nor even bridleways leading to them. It seemed as though she was going to the ends of the earth and she wondered how she would ever find her way back.

Eventually they rounded a hillside, the climb steepened and Quinta glimpsed a light, a dim glow ahead that eventually delineated a small window in a low building. Was this her new home? And her new husband? She shivered. It was such a very long journey from anywhere. She had thought at first that Noah simply wanted her out of the way until she had given birth to her baby, and that he would take her back afterwards. Her greatest worry had been that he would force her to give up her child. Now she knew he never wanted to see her again. Noah had had his revenge on her. He had ensured that she would vanish from his life and all she had known in the Riding. She wondered what he would tell people about her disappearance.

'You! Girl!' It was Miss Banks calling to her. 'You stay down so he can't see you.'

Quinta did as she was told. The shepherd released the reins and led her packhorse away. She heard the woman climb down from her mount and yell, 'Davey! Davey! Get out here and see to this horse.'

After a few moments, an excited voice cried, 'You're back, you're back, you're back.'

He sounds just a boy, Quinta thought. A young boy, surely not ready for marriage yet?

'Quiet, Davey,' Miss Banks ordered. 'You'll spook the horse. Give him a good rub-down, some mash and water. Go on now.'

When he had gone she walked over to Quinta and said, 'Get down and inside, you. He doesn't know about you and I don't want him to until morning. He'll not sleep if he sees you tonight.'

Quinta was tired and cold and hungry but not so exhausted that she did not feel a mounting anger with the assumption that she was some sort of gift for this Davey. She followed Miss

281

Banks into the small farmhouse. There was one large room on the ground floor with a wooden staircase in the corner. It was dingy and smoky. Dull embers glowed in the grate.

'Make up the fire,' the older woman ordered and Quinta hurried towards its warmth.

'What is this?' she asked, picking up a block of what she supposed was fuel from the hearth.

'Peat.'

'Is there no coal?'

Miss Banks did not reply. She walked over to her and pulled her shoulder round roughly. 'Let's get this straight from the start. I've heard all about your hoity-toity ma and how she thought you were too good to marry old Noah until some soldier's lad put this in your belly.' She gave her a sharp dig with a bony finger. 'Well, I've paid good money for the both of you and you belong to me and my Davey now. So you don't ask questions. You follow orders.'

Quinta frowned silently.

'Did you hear what I said?' Miss Banks demanded.

'I heard.'

'That's better. You'll sleep in the scullery for tonight so get yourself in there and stay put until I come in and fetch you.'

'I'm hungry, Miss Banks.'

'So am I. You'll wait for your breakfast like me.'

'But my baby won't.'

Miss Banks pursed her mouth. She went to a large stone crock on the table and took out the end of a loaf of bread. Then she poured some dark liquid from a ewer on the table into tin mug and snapped, 'Bring your box.'

Quinta followed her into the adjoining scullery. There was no moonlight showing through the tiny window but in the dim light from a lantern she made out a wooden pallet hung on two nails in the wall. Miss Banks put the food and drink on a draining board beside a shallow stone sink.

'I have to go to the privy,' Quinta said.

282

'There's a slop bucket under the sink. Get yourself settled before my Davey comes back. I don't want a sound from you until I fetch you out in the morning or you'll feel my horse-whip across your back.' She closed the door firmly, turning a key in the lock and leaving her in blackness.

Quinta sat on her box and ate the hard dry bread hungrily, then swallowed the ale, which was good and very welcome. She was too tired to contemplate her future here. Miss Banks had a lined face and was grey-haired; Davey sounded too young to be her son. No doubt the questions she was not allowed to ask would be answered tomorrow.

Her head was stinging from where she had been hit earlier on and she did not doubt that Miss Banks would carry out her threat of horsewhipping. She flung aside the straw halter and stroked her bulge. She must protect her unborn child and she resolved to do Miss Banks's bidding – whatever that was – until after he was born.

She spoke softly to her baby, reassuring him. Whatever the future held, she would look after him. He would always be safe with her. She promised him that. Or her, she thought. She had not long to go now. She expected to give birth after Eastertide when daffodils would be blooming, and wondered whether her child would be a boy or a girl. In spite of her fearful situation she felt excited by the prospect of being a mother and cocooned herself in that thought as she curled up on her hard bed.

After the bread and ale and the travelling, Quinta slept soundly for a while on the uncomfortable pallet, in spite of the damp, although she woke stiff and sore before dawn. The cloud had lifted and a pale moon shone through the scullery window. There was a back door, but it was bolted and locked. She searched quietly and without success along the walls and shelves for a key. The rain had stopped and the mist was lifting, though it still shrouded the tops of the hills. There was a wildness about the hills here; they were rugged and rocky with only patches of vegetation and barely discernible clumps of woolly sheep.

Her hopes of escaping from this isolated farmstead in her condition were fast receding.

Too raw to keep folk. Only the sheep for company. Noah had said that, or something similar, and been accurate on both counts. But the spring days were already lengthening and the sun, surely, was becoming warmer in the sky. By Lammas Day this year her baby would be more than three months grown and she would be lighter and agile again. She would be able to flee with her child. All she had to do was survive this austere house until then. And somehow please Miss Banks. She dozed again before daylight and was woken by sounds from the kitchen as the household stirred.

She was staring through the grimy scullery window at the inhospitable landscape behind the farmhouse when Miss Banks came for her. 'You'll look after indoors and the table. I brew the ale. I've done the fire and made the porridge today but from tomorrow I expect Davey's breakfast ready for half past six and his dinner by half past eleven.'

Quinta wanted to ask about Davey but dare not. She kneaded bread dough and set it to rise by the fire. The peat smoke was already hurting her eyes so she was glad to escape to the scullery to wash and prepare vegetables that appeared on the table. Miss Banks came in and out but Quinta knew when she was near because her keys jangled on the chatelaine at her waist. She wondered why everything was so securely locked in a place where no one ever ventured and came to the conclusion that Miss Banks had employed staff before who had stolen from her. Quinta half laughed to herself. Perhaps Miss Banks thought she would have more loyalty if her servant were thought of as her Davey's wife?

The table was laid, the mutton stew cooked and the bread baked by eleven o'clock. Miss Banks drew a ewer of ale from the brew house next to the scullery and Quinta stood patiently by the fire while Miss Banks yelled Davey's name from the yard. When he came in the kitchen door he filled the frame, blocking out the light, and Quinta blinked. He was a hefty grown man, dressed in a smock similar to that of the shepherd.

'Davey, come over here and look what I fetched you from the town.' He stood there gazing at her. 'It's Sally,' Miss Banks added.

'My name is—' Quinta began but then snapped her mouth shut. She was looking at the expression on Davey's face. His head was rolling gently from side to side and his eyes were wide and staring: vacant-looking. His mouth dropped open in a lopsided grin and he repeated the name. 'Sally, Sally, Sally.'

Chapter 23

Quinta thought she was going to faint. Davey was an idiot, an imbecile who had survived to manhood. Noah must have known this when he sold her to Miss Banks. How could he have been so cruel? All of Crosswell must know about Davey and no one would willingly wed him. No wonder Miss Banks was prepared to pay Noah's price.

He walked quickly across the kitchen saying, 'Mine, mine, mine.'

Quinta shrank back from his touch. 'Dinner's ready, Davey,' she squeaked.

'Dinner, dinner, dinner,' he repeated and went to sit at the table.

Quinta hardly remembered that first meal except that Davey ate his dinner noisily and hungrily with a spoon. Miss Banks was silent except for the occasional sharp word to Quinta as she served and cleared. Lord help her! This situation was worse than anything she had ever dreamed of! She had to get away from here and her mind raced as she rehearsed the conversation she would have with Miss Banks when Davey went outside again.

He swallowed the last of his ale and belched loudly, then appeared to notice Quinta again. His eyes remained vacant but a slow grin spread across his face. 'Sally mine,' he said. 'Sally mine.'

'Yes, Davey,' Miss Banks agreed. Quinta thought she sounded kindly towards him and her horror mounted. Miss Banks was serious about her being his wife!

Later, when Quinta was washing the pots in the scullery, Miss Banks called, 'Hurry up with those. Bring your box and we'll take it up to Davey's chamber.'

Quinta walked through to the kitchen slowly. 'You don't really expect me to be his wife, do you? He is a child inside his head.'

'He's a grown man and he has what it takes.'

Quinta's revulsion and anxiety mounted. Miss Banks was serious about her role here. Dear heaven, she was to be his wife in every sense of the word!

'You cannot ask this of me.'

'Ask you? You will do as you're told. My Davey needs a wife and I bought you fair and square as my Davey's wife.'

Quinta thought she was going to be sick and breathed deeply to quell her nervousness. 'But, Miss Banks, idiots beget idiots. Would you have more like Davey?'

'You're new blood. Not related to us afore you wed. The babby, too, is new blood. That's why I bought you.'

Quinta was in despair. She would have to get away from here. But how? She wondered where the shepherd had gone. He must help her. He must! Until then, she would refuse to move into Davey's chamber, even if it did mean a horsewhipping.

'Miss Banks, I am big with child,' she pleaded.

Miss Banks stared crossly at her. Quinta realised that this woman was not used to argument. Davey, despite his affliction, appeared to obey her and she probably used her horsewhip to persuade others who did not. Quinta wondered what had happened to Sally and feared for herself and her child.

She cast her mind around for more reasoning. 'He is a large man and clumsy. He will cause injury to my child. Good heavens, you do not even take your ewes for tupping until they have lambed, do you?'

'That's different.'

'My condition is extremely delicate. You cannot know that if you have not borne a child yourself.' What if Davey was her son? She held her breath, wondering if she had said too much. Her mind raced. She guessed that Miss Banks might want a child as much as, if not more than, she wanted a wife for Davey. 'Your family needs a newborn so much. You want a new life with new blood. You must not put my child at risk.'

When the older woman did not reply, she added, 'Davey will only be a few more weeks without his Sally.' Quinta did not know who Sally was, or indeed if she had ever really existed, but she knew that, even if she did stall Miss Banks's plan until her baby was born, she would have to flee from here immediately afterwards. She didn't know how, but she would. The days would be longer and the weather improved by then. Where was that shepherd?

'I've already said you're his Sally.'

'You must talk to him,' she pleaded. 'Tell him anything he'll believe, but let me sleep in the scullery, for my baby's sake.'

'He knows you're here and he can be wild when he's angry.'

Quinta was preparing herself to run out of the farmhouse that minute. To take her chances on the High Peak moors. Dark Peak, some called them, and she shivered. She looked at the door. It was slightly open and, as she stared, it swung back with a creak.

'I'll take him.' The shepherd stepped inside and repeated, 'I'll take Davey up the hillside to my hut until after the baby's born. He likes it out there.'

'What about the work he does here in the stables?'

'I'll bring him down to do his chores for you. We can have

dinner all together if you like. Then I'll take him back for the night to watch the sheep.'

Quinta's heart leaped. He was going to help her! Perhaps he would even help her escape . . . She thought Miss Banks was persuaded and pressed, 'I'll sleep down here just in case he comes back. I'll need bedding.' When Miss Banks gave her a brief nod she breathed a huge sigh of relief. She flashed a grateful smile at the shepherd, saw his eyes darken and remembered how he had offered for her at the market in Crosswell. He, too, had been ready to buy her as a child-bearing wife. She said, 'I'm much obliged, Mr . . . ?'

'Amos,' he volunteered. 'I had my own flock until I lost them this past winter. Now I look after Davey's sheep for him.'

'And don't you forget it's my Davey's land you're on, now you don't pay rent,' Miss Banks added sharply.

Amos bowed his head deferentially to Miss Banks and retreated from the kitchen. Quinta wondered whether he could be relied on to betray his employer and help her to flee.

Over the next few weeks Quinta did everything she could to make daily life more comfortable for Miss Banks and ensure they all ate a good dinner every day. In spite of her cumbersome bulge she cooked, cleaned and mended clothes. She carried water from the spring, milked goats and tended the small garden. The soil was thin and poor and the vegetables struggled, but she did her best to win the good opinion of Miss Banks. The older woman was very possessive about the sheep farm and 'her Davey' but her behaviour was unreasonable and harsh and Quinta wondered if idiocy ran in the family.

Davey seemed to have accepted whatever Miss Banks had told him about Quinta. He spent most of the day outside with the animals. Indeed, he seemed cheerful doing just that and coming indoors with Amos to eat his dinner. But he approached her frequently and ran his large hands over her bulge repeating, 'Baby, baby, baby,' and then adding, 'Mine, mine, mine.'

Quinta tried not to shrink from his touch. When he was calm he was gentle enough but he angered at the least provocation and on those occasions she was pleased that Amos was there to distract him.

'Thank you,' she said to Amos when he had suggested that Davey show Miss Banks the stables. 'Is Davey her son?'

'He's her nephew. The farm belonged to her cousin and Miss Banks's sister wed him. Miss Banks came to housekeep for them after he was born.'

'Where are they now?'

'Well, the cousin was a lot older than the sisters and he passed on years ago. He left the farm to Davey as long as Miss Banks took care of him and helped him run it.'

'Miss Banks? What happened to Davey's mother?'

'She – she—' He stopped and shook his head.

'She – what?' Quinta pressed.

His eyes pleaded with her. 'It doesn't matter.'

'Yes, it does. I want to know.'

Amos grimaced. 'She died when she had him.'

'Oh!' Quinta closed her eyes at the thought of this happening to her.

'They were a sickly lot, miss,' he went on quickly. 'They were never healthy and strong like you. But, you see, Miss Banks has looked after Davey all his life. That's why she's so protective of him.'

After this conversation, Quinta could not think beyond a safe delivery for her and her child. But she knew she would have to flee soon afterwards and prayed that her labour would not be too exhausting.

The hill farm was so isolated. No one came this way. The only track led down the hillside in full view of the house, so she would have to steal away in the dead of night, carrying her newborn. She wondered how far she could get without money.

There was no pathway behind the farm, only rock and scrubby

pasture rising steeply into the mist. On clear days it was beautiful to behold, but it offered no escape route for Quinta. It was on such a bright sunny day when clouds danced across the blue sky that she felt hot liquid stream down the inside of her legs and she knew Patrick's baby was ready for the world. She went indoors.

'Best get you upstairs and into the bed,' Miss Banks commented when she told her.

'No.' There were only two chambers and a grain store on the first floor. 'The couch down here will do. The arms let down and it is near the fire.'

She took off her gown, corset and drawers. She was prepared for the ebb and flow of pain but not for the long hours of agony she had to endure. She lay back on the couch and bit on a rope but could not stop herself from crying out. It was after dinner and Amos had gone off to mend a section of drystone walling that marked one of the farm boundaries. Davey should have followed him but apparently had not for he came indoors to investigate. Her cries agitated him and he began crying out and jumping about, shouting, 'Sally die, Sally die, Sally die.'

Miss Banks tried to calm him without success. Between her pains Quinta cried desperately, 'He is making me worse. Send him away. Outside, anywhere.' Another contraction doubled her up and she yelled, 'Get rid of him!' When the pain subsided she turned angrily to Miss Banks and demanded, 'Do you know what to do to help me?'

'Not me.' Quinta could see fear on her face.

'Have you delivered any lambs, then?'

'The menfolk do that,' Miss Banks said nervously.

Oh Lord! What use was a frightened old spinster to her? In her exhaustion from the pains, Quinta forgot her situation and the need to be subservient to Miss Banks. She cared only for the safe delivery of her child and yelled angrily, 'Is there no other woman on this Godforsaken Peak?'

291

'There's Amos.'

A man! Dear heaven, no! But she couldn't do this alone and at least he would have delivered sheep.

'Fetch him,' she ordered. 'Send Davey, but for pity's sake get someone here who can help me! And make sure the water boiler is full, then fetch me more linen. Do as I say!'

She half expected a whipping for her insolence, but her contractions were coming closer together now and she was past caring about how Miss Banks would react to her questions and orders. In fact she was even becoming cross with her baby and began to talk firmly to him instead of the gentle whispering of before. 'I've carried you long enough now,' she said loudly. 'It is time you were out of there, so would you please hurry up and get on with it.'

The kitchen was empty. Miss Banks had hustled Davey outside and gone with him. She lay back uncomfortably on the couch, drained of energy, suddenly realising that she was alone, and waited for the next pain. In this quiet moment she tried to remember all the things her mother had said about the births she had known about or seen. Oh, how she wished Laura were here to care for her now!

First babies always take an age to come. Well she knew that now! *Your milk might not be there straightaway.* Not so, she thought, because her heavy breasts had been leaking for days now. But her silent musings were interrupted by another pain, stronger and longer and – yes – her baby was moving at last. She put her hands on her swollen belly and bore down hard with all her might. 'Come on, will you,' she yelled. 'I'm doing all I can. Help me here!' She lifted her head and upper body in an attempt to peer between her legs. 'Where are you?' she pleaded desperately.

She had no idea how long she lay there alone, at first urging, then pushing, then subsiding into languor until the next onslaught of pain. She had discarded the rope hours ago. The fire in the range, banked up to boil water, still belted out heat and sweat oozed from her face and chest. She undid the tape at the neck of her chemise and pulled it aside, running a piece of linen over her skin. Her breasts had grown with her belly and she wiped the cloth underneath and around them. She closed her eyes. She was beginning to feel weak from her efforts but knew she must not fail. 'Do try,' she pleaded to her baby.

She was aware of Miss Banks hovering about the couch, piling linen on a chair and bringing her water to drink. It crossed her mind that the woman did really, truly want her to have this baby as much as she did. Davey had been gone for – for how long? The sun had moved round. What time was it? How long had she been labouring here and still no sign of her child? Another contraction gathered. 'I can't do it,' she moaned softly. 'I can't help you. I've had enough. I can't push you out any more. You'll have to do it yourself.'

She was fainting away with exhaustion when she realised that someone else was there. The darkly bearded man dressed in a thick calico smock. Not Davey, thank God. Amos bent over her, pushed apart her thighs and looked between her legs. Dear Lord! She had been offended when he saw her stockinged legs in the marketplace! But suddenly she felt alert again. She turned her head and followed his movements as he poured hot water from the kettle into a bowl and placed it on the table with a piece of soap and folded linen. Then he pulled the rug from in front of the fire and put it by her couch, covering it with more linen. 'Help me, please,' she croaked.

'Roll off the couch, Sally, on to your hands and knees. Easy now, I've got you.'

He smelled of sheep. But then everything and everyone in these parts did. She didn't care any more. Her arms were weak and flabby and she collapsed on to her elbows, her breasts and belly drooping to the floor.

'Does that feel better?' he asked.

'Yes,' she answered, surprised that it did.

She felt his fingers part her buttocks and he said, 'Keep your knees apart. You're nearly there.'

When the next pain threatened she had renewed her desire to push.

'This is the one, Sally,' Amos said. 'I can see the head.'

Where did her extra strength come from? She would never know. She thought that she had used it all hours ago. But she raised herself on to her hands, let her head drop forward and pushed for all she was worth. And yelled and pushed. And pushed and yelled. And yes, she could feel her baby coming at last, slipping and sliding from her. She wanted to see. She twisted her neck but could not. Amos was fumbling with her baby. What was he doing?

And then came the wail, the long plaintive whine that turned into the heart-rending screech of her baby's distress at being born into this harsh and cruel world and it was the sweetest sound she had ever heard. She cried. She laughed. She fell flat on her face on the floor. She had done it! She and her baby had done it together!

'It's a boy, Sally,' she heard Amos say.

A boy. She cried some more. She laughed some more. A boy. 'Patrick,' she shouted. 'It's a boy.'

'Patrick. That's a nice name, Sally.'

Yes it was. She was too tired to argue with Amos about names, her own or her baby's. Her baby! Her little Patrick! She struggled to a sitting position with her back against the couch. 'Give him to me. Give my little Patrick to me,' she breathed.

Amos handed her a wailing bundle wrapped tightly in linen and she held him close to her breast. Her baby. Hers. She could hardly believe she had done it. 'Hush now,' she whispered. 'You're safe with me. I'll always keep you safe. I promise.'

His crying quietened to a snuffle and he settled against her as though he understood. She marvelled at this tiny wonder of nature, her pain and distress forgotten. 'I'm your mother, little

Patrick.' she added softly, closing her eyes. 'I'm your mother,' she repeated with a sigh.

She heard Amos moving about the room, in and out of the scullery, when a pain struck her again, milder this time, and she yelped. Little Patrick jumped and began to whimper. Amos placed a shallow tin plate beside her on the floor and said, 'For your afterbirth. I'll take the child, if you like.'

'No.' She clutched him more tightly for a moment, then relaxed. 'Very well.' She passed him across and asked, 'Where's Miss Banks? And Davey?'

'I left Davey rebuilding a wall. He has a lantern so he'll be busy for hours. Miss Banks has disappeared. She couldn't stand the screaming. She doesn't like noise.' Patrick's whimper grew into a wail again. Amos carried him to the window. 'Can you do for yourself now?' he asked over his shoulder. 'There's fresh water and clean cloths on the table.' He sang softly to Patrick in a surprisingly gentle voice, and Patrick's wailing eased.

She did the best she could, then staggered wearily to the window to reclaim her child from this stranger; this shepherd who had offered three guineas for her at the market and lifted the edge of her skirt with his crook.

'I'll have him now,' she said sharply and took him out of this stranger's arms. She saw he looked hurt and added, 'Th-thank you for, well, for delivering him.'

He gazed at her steadily and said, 'Shall I find Miss Banks for you?'

'No!' She inhaled to calm herself. 'She won't be any use. She's quite mad, you must know that.'

'What can I do?'

'There's an old drawer in the pantry and a blanket airing by the fire. Would you make up a crib for him?'

'Very well. I expect you'd like some tea as well, and something to eat.'

She cradled her child in her arms and watched Amos as he fussed about with the crib and then prepared her a simple meal of bread and goat's cheese. He was the only other living soul she had seen since she came here and she needed somebody to help her get away with little Patrick. He sat at the table and drank a mug of tea while she ate hungrily.

A crumb dropped on her baby's cheek and she eased it gently away with one finger. He had a beautiful face. *All babies are beautiful to their mothers.* Laura's words echoed around her head. If only her own mother were here to share this wonderful moment; to see her beautiful, beautiful grandchild, an infant who would have been so welcome to her, if only . . . A single tear of grief rolled down Quinta's cheek and she brushed it aside with the back of her hand, returning her finger to stroke little Patrick's face. He had her mother's cheekbones, a feature that she, herself, shared; now she realised it was where her own beauty came from. Her son would grow into a handsome gentleman, for he had his father's chin and a thin covering of Patrick's black hair on his head. She wondered whether the blue of his eyes would darken and strengthen like Patrick's, or turn to hazel like her own.

As she thought of her infant's father, the void where her heart used to be seemed to collapse in on itself and her shoulders sagged. How she wished he could be with her and with his child. Her body yearned for Patrick's love and she swallowed back a sob. This was a happy occasion. She had an awe-inspiring healthy baby who was filling her heart with love again.

Silently, she pledged her life to this tiny boy. He was her very being and she would devote all her energy to him. His father would always be with her through their child and, even though she would never see him again, she determined to be a mother that Patrick would be proud of.

Her child's safety was her responsibility and hers alone. But Amos might give her some assistance. He had to, for she had no one else to ask. 'You will keep Davey away from me, won't you?' she said without further thought. 'Don't let him come back here.'

'This is his home.'

'He thinks I'm somebody else. He thinks I'm this Sally woman.'

'I'll do what I can. He likes living in my hut during the summer.' He picked up the metal plate holding her afterbirth. 'This'll fry nicely over the fire. You should eat it for the nourishment.'

She nodded. She had to eat and drink to feed two people now. Little Patrick was already rooting at her breast and she went to sit on the couch. Later, when the door opened, he was suckling greedily. Miss Banks stood in the doorway and surveyed the quiet orderly room. Quinta realised that she didn't care what Miss Banks said or did any more. She was experiencing such a wonderful feeling of love and satisfaction from feeding her child that she even smiled at the spinster.

Miss Banks gazed at her and stepped into the kitchen. Quinta saw a look of sheer wonderment on her gaunt lined face, as though she could not believe her eyes. She took the drink of tea that Amos offered her and continued to stare. Quinta was prepared for her to want to hold her baby and was ready to refuse. But Miss Banks did not come near her. It was as though she was nervous, even frightened of her now she had had her child. Quinta gazed adoringly at her son, eased her nipple out of his tiny lips and lifted him over to her other breast.

Miss Banks did not seem to be able to take her eyes off them. She sank to a chair by the table with her drink. 'What happened to Davey?' she asked eventually.

'He's working on breaches in the walls,' Amos replied.

'Oh. He likes doing that.'

Quinta doubted that little Patrick would have the same pacifying effect on Davey that he had on Miss Banks and was uneasy about his return. The light had gone and he might come looking for Amos so she said, 'Why don't you go and find him?'

Amos took the hint and stood up. 'I'll take him up to my hut as usual.'

'Is it far?' Quinta asked.

'A mile or so up the hill in the lee of the rocks.'

'You'll be down for your dinner tomorrow?'

'I'll bring Davey, yes.'

Quinta glanced at Miss Banks, wondering if she expected Davey to move back to the farmhouse, but the older woman simply nodded in agreement. She continued to stare, in awe of what she saw, and seemed unable to say much. Quinta smiled at her suckling infant. At first she was reluctant to lay him in his crib until she realised that Miss Banks really had no inclination to hold her child or take care of him. Only then was she able to sleep easy herself.

Patrick suckled and slept well. Quinta fed him, kept him clean, washed his linen and rested when she could. Miss Banks, without prompting, took over the household chores and the cooking, and Quinta marvelled that even sour old Miss Banks appeared to respect her right to nurse her infant. Little Patrick had given her a new status in this household.

But Davey had been puzzled by this turn of events and, Quinta thought, who knew what went on in his head? The following day he came with Amos for his dinner, grubby and tired from mending walls; as soon as Quinta heard the men's voices, she went to stand by little Patrick in his crib. He was awake, kicking and gurgling and, she judged, building up to the grizzling that told her he was hungry. She hoped dinner would be over before he became too demanding, and crooned softly as he grasped her finger with his tiny fist.

Davey's puzzled frown turned to one of anger and he muttered, 'Sally mine,' several times.

Quinta became anxious about this restlessness and appealed to Miss Banks: 'I think Davey is agitated by the baby.'

'Aye. It's a shock to the pair of us, having this little'un in our kitchen.'

'Now the weather is improving,' she suggested, 'perhaps the men will eat their dinner out of doors as they do at Amos's hut.'

'That won't do for me. You see to your babby and I'll see to my Davey.'

'Very well.' Quinta pulled gently on her finger and little Patrick's grip tightened.

The men were dusty from their building work and Amos went into the scullery to wash. Miss Banks told Davey to do the same and when he returned he clattered noisily about the kitchen area in his clumsy fashion, disturbing and alarming her child who quite naturally began crying. Quinta bent to pick him up and comfort him, increasing Davey's agitation. 'No, no, no!' he cried. 'Sally mine.'

Alarmed, Quinta turned away from him and spoke soothingly to her son. She felt a strong hand on her shoulder twisting her round. 'No baby. No baby.'

Amos intervened, placing a hand on his arm. 'Now then, Davey, you have to let the ewe have time with her lamb.'

'Sally mine!' he cried, throwing off the restraint.

Little Patrick continued to wail. 'Go away, Davey,' Quinta said. 'Amos, take him outside please. I'm going to feed him now.' She sat on the couch and unbuttoned the front of her bodice.

But before anyone could stop him, Davey had wrenched little Patrick from her arms and was holding him aloft. Horrified, Quinta watched him kick at the couch and prepare to dash her baby to the ground. She shot to her feet but was not tall enough to reach him. Amos was. He moved fast, rescuing the bundle from Davey's clutches and bringing him safely down to hold him to his chest. Quinta retrieved him immediately and hugged him to her own breast. If Davey wouldn't go outside then she would. She hurried out of doors, followed closely by Amos. His sheepdog got up immediately to hover by his feet.

'You have to get me away from here,' she whispered fiercely.

Amos's weather-beaten face was grey. 'He thinks you're Sally and he's jealous of your infant,' he uttered, rubbing his hands over his eyes.

'He's an *idiot*. He could have killed my child. She – *she* – has made him worse. Who in their right mind goes out to *buy* a wife?' Too late, she realised that Amos had done just that. He would have bought her for three guineas if Noah had not had his own evil plan for her. She exhaled heavily and moved to the sheltered side of the farmhouse. 'Hush, now, my baby,' she murmured and manoeuvred her nipple towards his tiny rooting mouth. 'Who was Sally, anyway?'

'Miss Banks bought her as a servant from the hiring fair. But she seemed to, well, like Davey.' He hesitated. 'Leastways, she occupied him and he was quieter, less agitated when she was – here – with him.'

'What do you mean by "with him"?'

'In the summer, Miss Banks let them go off wandering. I'd come across them occasionally, together, high up on the Peak.' He stopped and Quinta saw the colour return to his features. He was embarrassed. 'You know . . .'

Yes, she did know and Quinta said emphatically, 'Well, I am not Sally. What happened to her?'

'Nobody knows. She just went.'

'Just went?'

'She disappeared one day.'

'Lord in heaven! He might have killed her! You must help me, Amos. You must. I have to get away from here. I have to get down the valley to Crosswell with my baby.'

'Miss Banks relies on me to help with her lambing and shearing. She's given me more work since I lost my flock. I'd be at the hiring fair if it weren't for her.'

'But she expects me to take Sally's place! She's mad!'

'All the Bankses are like that. They've had too much breeding in the family and there's only these two left now. They've never harmed anyone, though.'

'You don't know that for sure, do you? I won't go in the house again while Davey's there. I won't.'

He shook his head and bent a finger to stroke little Patrick's

300

cheek as he suckled. 'It's gone quiet in there. I'll fetch you a chair.'

Quinta thought Amos was kindly enough towards her. He was a simple country fellow who knew which side his bread was buttered, but she hadn't forgotten the way he had lifted her skirt at the hiring fair. Nevertheless, he was her only chance to escape and she had to persuade him to help her. When she looked at her darling son snuffling at her breast, she knew that she would do anything to get him away from here. Miss Banks may be in awe of her child but Davey . . . well, Davey was jealous and unpredictable. She feared for Patrick's safety when he was around. The weather was kinder now and the days lengthening. It was time for her to leave. She wondered how best to win Amos over to her side.

He brought the chair and sat on the ground, his dog beside him, watching her with a mixture of wonder and admiration. 'What Davey did has frightened Miss Banks,' he said. 'She wants me to stop bringing him down for his dinner.'

'You mean he would stay away all day as well as the night?'

'Only until you can – you know – give him more of your time.'

Dear Lord, no. Never, she thought and said, 'I will not be his wife.'

'Will you be mine instead?'

'Amos!'

'I wanted you but I couldn't afford Noah's price.'

'I have a husband,' she replied shortly. She wasn't thinking of Noah. Little Patrick's father is my true husband, in my heart, she thought wistfully.

'Davey wouldn't give you up, anyway. He thinks you're Sally.'

'Well, I'm not,' she responded irritably. 'I'm Quinta.'

'Quinta? Fifth child?'

'No, it's where I was born, I – oh, never mind. Don't you understand? I have to leave this place. My child is in danger.'

'Well, we couldn't stay here anyway if you came to me.'

301

Amos continued to watch little Patrick suckle at her breast. 'I'll help you get away, if you like.'

Her heart lifted and she looked up at him quickly. 'Will you?'

'Aye. I'll come away with you, as well.'

'What do you mean?'

'I've nothing to stay for without my own flock. But I'm a good shepherd and I can do better.'

'You would leave here?'

'Miss Banks will find another shepherd. We can go together.'

Quinta closed her eyes. He was offering her a way out, but at what price? She said, 'I will journey with you, Amos, and work to pay you back. But I cannot wed you.'

He gave a shrug. 'We'll see.'

Quinta ignored this remark and tried to quell her elation. 'When can we leave?'

'Not until Miss Banks pays me at Midsummer.'

'But that's two months away!'

'Me and Davey'll be busy shearing in a few weeks. When we have all the fleeces I pack the horses and carry them down to market. I'll take you with me and we won't come back.'

Quinta wondered how they could do it without Miss Banks or Davey coming after them. But she didn't care. Once they reached Crosswell she would be away from here for good. It was her only chance and she had to take it.

'Very well. We'll wait until then. Will you promise to keep Davey away from the farmhouse?'

'The flock grazes higher on the moor in summer. I'll send him up there. We have a peat stove in my hut to cook on.'

'He looks after the horses, doesn't he?'

'I'll do that and when we bring the sheep in for shearing I'll keep him in the barn. With him, it's out of sight, out of mind. If he doesn't see you, he'll forget you, just as he did Sally until Miss Banks reminded him. I'll make sure you and the babe are safe until Midsummer.'

'Will Miss Banks suspect anything?'

'You'll have to deal with her. She'll want to see her Davey at some time.'

'I'll bake pies for her to take up to your hut for him. It'll be too far for me to walk with little Patrick.'

'What about when he comes down for the shearing?'

'I'll think of something to keep him out of the house.'

Amos nodded. He seemed satisfied with their scheme and she was grateful for his help. He had delivered her baby safely and was offering to take her away from here. But she felt nothing more than friendship towards him. She could never be a wife to him and she had to make him understand that. He was not a bully like Noah. He was a passive man, as patient with Davey as he was with his sheep. But he had not travelled beyond Crosswell and knew little of the world outside the Peaks. She could repay his kindness with her knowledge of the next county.

Quinta hadn't thought beyond giving birth until now and she felt an excitement rising in her breast. Home to the South Riding! She lifted little Patrick to kiss his face and he gurgled at her as she laid him over her shoulder and patted his back gently. He burped wetly on her calico shawl. She would take him back to the South Riding, where there was work for women in mines and mills. She realised it was a path that many from the High Peak had trodden before her. And she understood why.

When the excitement of her planned escape had faded, she realised that returning to her home meant returning to where Noah had influence. He had made his hatred of her clear by selling her in Crosswell and she feared what he might do when she returned. She wondered how he had explained her continued absence to the vicar. He had cast her out of his home and village. Had he told everyone how she had deceived him and tricked him into marriage? Would she and her child be shunned for ever by the only people who might be her friends?

Chapter 24

The officer inspected his ranks as Patrick stood by to attention. A blistering sun had turned the drill square to a dust bowl. Since the rebellion and loss of his sergeant Patrick had gained a stripe. His discipline was strict for it was his responsibility if the men did not pass muster. Regulations were tighter after the fighting and there was a rumour that reinforcements were on their way across the ocean.

His captain dismissed the men and he prepared to follow them to the coolness of the cellars to strip off his jacket and loosen his braces.

'Follow me, Ross. The colonel wants you.'

Patrick fell into step behind the officer. The windows and doors of the colonel's quarters stood open, catching a fresh breeze to cool his sweating brow. He always longed for rain until it came. Then the steaming humidity felt like a wet fleece over his face that drained his vitality. He remembered his father speaking of how he had missed the gentle climate of home when he had been fighting in Spain and Portugal. How he longed to return to the South Riding and – and Quinta. But it was a lost hope now, a shattered dream. He was a soldier now and his life was ordered by the King's officers.

The colonel was reading documents spread out on the desk in front of him. 'Ross? Yes, I recall. You did well during the riots and organised the men when we lost the sergeant. Good shot, too. Yes. A very good shot. D'ye like it here, Ross?'

'I expected to do more fighting, sir.'

'You think a few natives are not enough for you, eh? You'll do more after a posting back in England.'

'You're sending me home, sir?'

'I've more soldiers due in with the supply ship and a company will return with its payload. I want you in charge of them. You'll have an extra stripe for the voyage. Acting corporal only. Understand?'

'Yes, sir. Why am I going back?'

'You've been chosen for transfer to the Ninety-fifth Rifles. Like your father before you. That means more training.'

He was surprised. He knew about the Ninety-fifth: they were an elite regiment. 'But I joined as a convict, sir.'

'So did half of the Duke of Wellington's army and they saw off Bonaparte.' The colonel went on inspecting his documents. 'You don't spend much of your pay. And there's the girl to think of as well. The Creole.'

'Faith, sir. Her name is Faith.'

The officer looked up sharply. 'My wife says she is content working in my household, but you can't leave her there.'

'Her father wanted her in England.'

'Well, he's not here now and she'll do as she's told. You are of age and she is your legal ward. You must decide what to do with her.'

Patrick was silent as he thought about this. He wondered if anyone had asked Faith what she wanted. He hardly ever had a chance to see her, let alone speak to her.

Before he could answer his colonel continued: 'Do you have a wife back home in England, Ross?'

If only! If only he had wed Quinta before – before – Lord, it was too late for regrets now. She hadn't answered his letter and with a sick mother to care for she would have had to marry someone. His mouth curled down at the memory of that bullying landlord. She must have wed him. He had wanted her and she would not have had a choice.

'Don't like the idea of a wife, eh? Can't say I'm surprised. A soldier never goes short of a wench.'

'No, sir.'

'You have this girl, though. So, seeing as you're not wed you'll be free to marry her. I've discussed it with my wife and it's the best solution for all concerned. She's a pretty one to be sure and she has a trust left by her father. It's not much but it'll keep her in gowns and bonnets.' The colonel met his eye in a frank stare. 'It also makes her prey to any roving blade in the garrison. She's your responsibility, so take my advice and marry her, m'boy.'

'I – I – that is, I hadn't considered it, sir,' Patrick stammered.

'Not keen, eh, because of her breeding? I understand that, but she's only a quarter Negro, y'know, and once she's in England she'll pass for a Spanish. My wife has given leave for you to visit her in the servants' parlour; when her cook is present, of course. Take the girl flowers.' The colonel waved his arm in a dismissive manner. 'Do the right thing, Ross. We'll have the ceremony in the chapel before you sail.'

'She might not want to marry me, sir.'

'She's a fool if she doesn't. Now get back to your duties.'

'Sir.' Patrick marched out smartly, his head spinning with the colonel's news and – and his orders about Faith.

She hadn't been a burden to him since her father had been shot. She received a wage for her work in the colonel's household and only once had he been asked to sign a docket to release money for a new gown and shoes. He acknowledged that when he had noticed her, fairly recently in the chapel, she looked quite beautiful, stunning even, in a new bonnet. But she was always surrounded by other servants.

Their communication had been limited to a formal bow on his part, a curtsey on hers and a few words exchanged about their respective wellbeing. He had often wondered what he was going to do with her, but never, ever, that he would marry her. His colonel seemed very taken by the idea and he decided to arrange a visit and talk to her about it.

The following Sunday afternoon, he had a posy of flowers and a small parcel of red ribbon – the colour suited her glossy black hair – waiting on his locker as he brushed his uniform. The servants' parlour was a low stone building behind the colonel's residence, ruled by a fierce Creole who was in charge of the colonel's kitchen. She took him inside and had the sense to leave them alone. He and Faith sat at opposite ends of a couch with their backs to the arms. He acknowledged that she was – what was the word? – yes, exotic; unusually beautiful, neatly attired in her new gown and a very pretty bonnet.

'Thank you, sir,' she said as she took the gifts. She seemed especially pleased with her ribbons.

'Are you well?'

'Yes, sir. And you?'

Patrick kept up this stiff exchange of pleasantries for as long as he was able. She knew about her trust, his guardianship and his return to England. After an extended, awkward silence he asked, 'Faith, what do you want to do?'

'The colonel's wife says I must marry you.'

Lord, he did not even have to propose to her! 'Would you like to travel to England?'

For the first time, her saw her eyes light up. 'Oh yes, sir. My mother told me I would go there one day and she would have a lodging house by the sea and I could—' She stopped.

'Could what, Faith?'

She looked down at the ribbons. 'Trim bonnets.'

307

Trim bonnets. He supposed it would occupy her while he was soldiering and it was a charming wish. 'Very well. If that is what you want, I shall take you with me to England.' He stood up to leave.

She was smiling, happy even, and said, 'When shall we sail?'

As the weather improved in the High Peak Amos moved the flock higher on the open moor and took Davey with him. They stayed away from the farmhouse. Miss Banks accepted this, believing rightly that Davey was happy with his new distractions. Although the farm was not prosperous there was always enough to eat and tea to drink, if not luxuries like sugar or butter. But they had honey, and cheese from goat's milk, which was especially nourishing for Quinta.

Miss Banks never ventured far and when she climbed to the hut insisted that mother and child came part of the way. She did not like to let Quinta out of her sight, though she seemed frightened to approach or even touch little Patrick, much to Quinta's relief. In fact, her status as a mother enabled her to make requests of Miss Banks that made life more comfortable: A cured lambskin for the crib, feather pillows for her couch in the kitchen and old linen to make more wrappings for little Patrick.

The Easter weather had been brisk and breezy and May had come in like a lion. But June was balmy and bright. Patrick thrived and Quinta became excited by the approach of Midsummer. However, before that came the shearing when the flock – and Davey – journeyed down from the high moor to the farm.

'I don't want the men in the house when they're shearing,' Quinta said. 'They'll bring fleas and ticks from the fleeces on to my baby.'

Miss Banks looked alarmed.

'They'll have to eat and sleep in the barn,' she added.

'Aye,' Miss Banks replied. 'Davey'll like doing that anyroad. I'll take them ale and food.'

But when Davey was shearing in the barn, Quinta was always ready to retreat to the scullery with little Patrick and out of the back door in case he started crying. He was heavy in her arms now, growing fast and eating oatmeal porridge as well as her milk.

When the shearing was finished and Midsummer approached, Amos loaded the fleeces on to Miss Banks's heavy horses and covered them with sacking. He gave Davey a good deal of ale to drink and Quinta made Miss Banks a strong sweetened toddy as a nightcap, giving little Patrick a lick of it from her finger to give him warmth through the night.

As soon as the two of them were sound asleep, Amos came to the back door of the scullery and took Quinta's box over to the barn. She followed with her child tightly wrapped in a shawl. The horses were already harnessed and linked. Amos took Patrick from her as she clambered up beside her box. It was a similar seating arrangement to when she had arrived.

The moon was bright and she smiled at Amos, taking the warm bundle from him. He smiled back, took up the reins of the lead horse and climbed astride his broad back. Then he whistled softly for his dog and they began their slow descent down the bumpy track. Dawn broke early and it was daylight well before they were in the valley and approaching Crosswell. Quinta looked behind constantly for signs of Miss Banks or Davey.

Amos noticed. 'They won't follow us down here. Not without a beast to ride.'

'How will you get their horses back?'

'I'll be paid for these fleeces by dinnertime. Any one of the lads you see running around will get them back to her for a tanner.'

'Will you keep her money?'

'Only what's due for my wages. And I've saved three guineas from selling my own ewes so I'll have enough to pay the five guineas I owe her for you.'

Quinta's eyes rounded. 'But I don't owe her anything! I've worked for nothing since Lady Day!'

'I'm not a thief and I pay my way. She bought the two of you and I've taken the baby from her as well.'

Quinta was shocked into silence. Amos considered her and little Patrick as chattels to be bought and sold, just as Noah and Miss Banks did. Eventually she asked, 'What will you do with her money?'

'I'll leave it with the innkeeper.'

'Can you trust him?'

'I reckon so. He didn't like what Noah did to you. He'll be glad to get somebody to take back her horses and her dues. And tell her that you've gone.' Little Patrick roused from his deep slumber. 'He's hungry again. You still got plenty of milk for him?'

She supposed it was because he was a shepherd, practised with ewes and lambing, that he seemed to understand her and her baby's needs. He was robust man, toughened by his harsh life on the moors. Yet he had a gentle side to him, too, and she was grateful that he was travelling with her. But he wanted her as his wife. He had bought her from Miss Banks, just as Miss Banks had bought her from Noah, for the same reason. She did not know him well and she wondered how much she could trust him.

'I can get work to pay you back,' she volunteered.

'You'll have to wait 'til he's older,' he answered, gesturing towards her infant.

She had to agree.

'I'll take care of you both.' Amos smiled. 'A man with a family is generally judged to be hard-working and steady. I'll have a better chance of securing work with you and the babe in tow.'

'Is that why you want me?'

'It'll be easier all round if we say we are wed.'

She knew that and bit on her lip. 'But you might meet a nice girl,' she suggested hopefully, 'one that you can love.'

'I am satisfied with the one I've got.'

He meant for them to stay together. She closed her eyes and acknowledged that she and little Patrick were safer travelling with a man. Then a vision of her first sight of him at the hiring fair and his crook hooking the edge of her skirt swam under her eyelids.

Chapter 25

They breakfasted on mutton patties from a pie-seller near the spring at Crosswell. Quinta and little Patrick rested on sacking while Amos took the horses and their burdens to the wool exchange. He left his dog to watch them. Jess, she was called, and she sat guarding them while Quinta dozed in the sun's warmth. When she roused she lay quietly watching her sleeping son. How she loved him! She loved him more than anything in the world, more than her mother and father; even more, she realised with a shock, than she loved her baby's own father. She loved him so much that she ached. She would do anything for her son. Anything.

Amos returned without the horses, looking pleased with himself. He had removed his shepherd's smock and replaced it with a tweedy country jacket. He rolled up the sacking and secured it with twine to a bulky leather satchel slung across his back and announced, 'We're walking from here.'

Quinta had expected this and asked, 'By which road?'

'South Riding in the next county. The innkeeper has told me to head for Tinsley where the navigation starts.' He patted his jacket and Quinta heard the grating of coins. 'A barge'll take us into the heart of the Riding.'

'My husband's farm is there.'

'The waterway goes by the furnaces and manufactories. Besides, he wanted rid of you, didn't he? He sold you and I have bought you. You belong to me now. Though I'll keep you out of sight, just to be sure.'

There was no point in arguing with Amos. His mind was made up. But Noah's treatment of her still rankled with Quinta. Until recently, her thoughts had been taken up by ensuring her baby's safety. Now that little Patrick was thriving, her anger with Noah was growing. It was as well she would not see him on her travels through the Riding! Yet she was his wife. He had lied in court, she had deceived him and he had taken his revenge, but she was still his lawful wife. He couldn't just sell her like that and get away with it!

Amos bent to pick up a hide harness with a roomy pouch. 'I've got this for you, to carry the little lad on your back.' He helped her transfer her protesting, squirming child into this new cocoon and strap it in place. 'All set,' he said.

At first little Patrick wailed his annoyance at being separated from his mother's arms, but as they set off he quietened and not long afterwards he began gurgling in her ear. He liked his new mode of travel, though before long his gurgles turned into grizzles. 'He's hungry again, Amos,' she said. 'I'll have to stop and feed him.'

'We'll eat, too. I've got food in my pack.'

'Look for a spring or stream. I'm thirsty.'

They had climbed steadily out of Crosswell to higher, harsher moorland where the breeze was fresh even in summer. But the sun was warm and Quinta's spirits were as high as the fluffy white clouds scudding across a blue sky. She had escaped from Miss Banks and her Davey. She wasn't exactly free, but her situation was better now. At least she could talk to Amos and, with any luck, reason with him. She did not want to stay with him and she hoped he would understand.

The sun's rays were welcome as she sat on a bank of springy heather and changed little Patrick's wet linen. She rinsed it in the stream and spread it to dry on a warm rock. Jess fussed around, sniffing at first, and then drank from the stream before settling quietly with her head on her paws. Quinta unbuttoned her bodice and loosened the front of her corset. Feeding Patrick absorbed all of her attention so easily that she was unaware of Amos watching her until she looked up with a smile. His face was serious. He handed her bread and cheese and placed a tin mug of cold, crystal-clear spring water in reach of her hand.

'Why don't you take a nap?' she suggested, but he shook his head. She ate and drank herself as little Patrick satisfied his hunger. When he slowed, she lifted him to her shoulder to raise his wind.

'He takes long enough,' Amos commented.

She thought he sounded bored and responded, 'Did you bring oatmeal in your bag? I'll light a fire and make porridge for him tonight.' Patrick burped and she lowered him gently to her lap, wrapped him tightly and laid him in a sheltered dip to sleep. She wished she had some salve to smooth on her nipples and ease the threatening soreness, but she hadn't so she ignored the tingling and stretched herself out in the sun. She was tired. Feeding her hungry son sapped her energy and she closed her eyes.

She heard Amos settle beside her and thought he might sleep as well. She could smell sheep on his clothes and tensed, wondering why he was so near to her. She rolled away from him on to her side. Her corset was still loose and she pulled at the fastening tapes.

'Are you in fear of me?' he asked.

'You frightened me at the hiring fair,' she answered. 'You lifted my skirt with your crook.'

'But it was not me who showed your leg for all to see. It was that shameful husband of yours.'

She didn't argue with that and said, 'Well, you were not my husband and you lifted my skirt.'

'I wanted to look at your boots. Boots are dear to buy. I could not afford a wife who was not well shod.'

'Oh!' Quinta turned her head towards him. 'Truly?'

'You looked strong enough to me without closer inspection. That Noah didn't deserve you, I thought.'

'No,' she agreed. She had made a dreadful mistake in her haste to provide shelter for her and her mother last year. But she had had no other choice apart from the workhouse and even now did not know what else she could have done to avoid that fate. Was she about to make another mistake in judging Amos? He had not demanded much from her and she would not be here without his help. She was beholden to him for that if nothing else so, she reasoned, she ought to at least behave as a friend towards him.

But only as a friend, for, no matter what these Peak dwellers believed about buying and selling their wives, Quinta was not and could never be Amos's wife. She knew now, without any doubt, that the only man she could ever be a true wife to was little Patrick's father. She relaxed and rolled on her back to stare at the sky. It really was the most beautiful hue. Her eyes closed against the glare. Somewhere, she dreamed, little Patrick's father might be looking at the same sky. If he was still alive. She could not countenance that he might not be and wondered, instead, where he was.

'Well, I am your husband now and I shall treat you better.' Amos's words came out suddenly and with a determination that startled her. His lips were by her ear and his roughened fingers already on her exposed breast, stroking and delving to squeeze and massage her flesh.

'No, Amos.' She put her hands on his to still them, but he drew them aside and bent his head to kiss her.

'That child has too much of you,' he muttered as his bearded face descended to her lips. His mouth explored hers hungrily and his probing tongue startled her. Then he moved his search to her breasts, nuzzling and pushing to ease them further out of her corset and expose their fullness.

She struggled to release her hands but he had a strong grip on her. 'Stop it, Amos. Leave me alone.'

'I won't,' he mumbled into her flesh as he placed a heavy leg across her body.

His open mouth wandered over her flesh. She could feel his teeth sliding across her skin, and then his tongue, licking and sucking the plumpness as though he would devour her.

'No!' She jerked and yelled as his hands reached down to grapple with her skirts, bunching them up to stroke her legs, delving between them with anxious fingers. She writhed and wriggled but he held her still. She cried out with shock at his actions and then screamed loudly. Little Patrick woke and began to whine. Where she found the strength she did not know, but she pushed at Amos with all her might. He lifted his head in surprise and she rolled free, scrambled to her feet, snatched her baby from his resting place and ran.

But where was there to run? Over the springy hummocks of heather towards the track? Yes, the track. The track that led down into the valley and away from these tainted moorland peaks. Jess had given chase and was prancing and barking in circles around her as she staggered.

How could a babe in arms weigh so much? She stumbled, almost lost her balance but recovered and clutched him closer to her body. He was wailing loudly now, as frightened as she was, and she realised that she was crying, too. Hot tears trickled down her cheeks. Her jumbled thoughts distressed her. How could she upset her child so? He needed her love and protection. Her love for him was endless but how could she shield him from this harsh and cruel world without someone to care for her?

She had no money, no home and no prospect of gaining either. There was only Amos, demanding that she pay for his help by becoming his wife. She could not do it. Yet he was her only chance of survival and if she did not thrive what would happen to her darling child? She could not move fast enough, of course, and Amos was close behind her with his heavy spade of a hand on her shoulder and his voice in her ear.

'Do not run from me. I mean you no harm!'

She froze to the spot, clutching little Patrick tightly to her body. 'Don't touch me!' she cried, stepping backwards. Her boot twisted in a dip and she tripped, losing her balance. She felt herself falling and lifted little Patrick away, holding him high as she fell to the ground. Her grip on him was loosening. 'No!' But her cry was futile and she tumbled awkwardly, sideways on to the springy grass. Jess jumped and barked as she fell. But Amos was there and had snatched little Patrick from her grasp in the same way as he had rescued him from Davey. He gave a short piercing whistle and Jess became still and quiet immediately.

Quinta struggled to sit up, rubbing the upper arm that had broken her fall. She wasn't hurt; bruised, maybe, but nothing serious. She had felt so tired when she had run from Amos that she realised she had had no hope of escape from him with little Patrick in her arms. And she was not so sure she wished to for he was steady and strong and both of them needed his protection. He was, on balance, a good man. He was honest and kind, albeit with some old-fashioned country ways, and she was truly grateful for his help. But whatever he expected of her she was not his wife. Or, she reflected fearfully, ever wanted to be.

'Give me my baby,' she demanded, stretching out her arms.

'I said I mean you no harm, neither of you. You are my family now, my wife and child.'

'No, Amos.' Desperately, she tried to think of an argument that he would accept. 'I am married to another.'

317

'He has turned you out. He does not want you. I do.'

'My child wants me, too. Give him to me. He needs me.'

'I need you! I want you as my wife. You tempt me as Eve tempted Adam in the Garden of Eden. What is a man to do?'

Quinta could not answer him. She frowned and bit her lip. He went on, 'He takes her as his wife, that's what he does.'

Quinta closed her eyes in despair. He meant her to be his wife in every way. 'I have to care for my baby, Amos,' she pleaded.

'Aye and a grand little lad he is, too.' He looked kindly at little Patrick who had quietened in his arms. 'But he will not be a babe plucking at your teat for ever. I will have him as my son, my own son.' Then he looked directly at her, a stern expression that she had not seen before. 'And you as my wife.'

Quinta pressed her lips together and bit back her arguments. He would not hear them anyway as his mind was made up. All she could do was play for more time and hope. But she did not even know what she was hoping for.

Amos went on, 'You have a wedding ring and a child. If I say you are my wife, folk will believe me. The babe will take my name and none will know he is a bastard.'

'Don't call him that.'

'That is what he is; conceived of a mother and father who were not wed.'

'We were as good as!'

'So you say. But the child's father deserted you—'

'He was taken from me!'

'Aye. And you deceived another to give the lad a name.'

'Do you blame me? It was Noah Bilton who lied and sent little Patrick's father to gaol!'

'So you thought you'd make old Noah pay by wedding him instead, eh? Perhaps you are a harlot after all?'

Stung to the core, she retaliated hotly, 'Then why do you want me?

'I have need of a wife and you have need of a father for

your bastard child. The child will have my name if I have you in my bed.' He handed little Patrick back to her and added, 'We'd best get moving.'

Would everyone think of her child in this way? Was he destined to suffer the same degradation as his father? She had loved – continued to love – his father and believed their union had been right. But, for the first time, a tiny glimmer of regret flared. She had been the one to warn of the consequences of a Lammas agreement, although she had never imagined that she and Patrick would be forcibly separated as they were. She did not doubt their love, only their indulgence in expressing that love to each other so soon.

The moorland softened and the slopes were greener as they descended towards the South Riding valleys. Quinta recalled her journey the other way with Noah and gazed at the haze in the distance. Tomorrow she would see smoking chimneys, rows of workers' terraces and a glint of the navigation as it wound its way between town and country and town again.

Amos found an old cottage for the night, a broken-down timber-and-daub hovel with hardly any roof. But the sun had kept it dry and he built a fire to prepare hot food and drink. He offered her rum which she refused.

'Where will the barge take us?' she asked.

'Doncaster.'

'Oh.' Quinta was relieved they were going beyond the town where she might be known. 'Why Doncaster?'

'I'm told that a drover's trail from the Dales ends there. I can get work as a drover's assistant until I have my own licence.'

'You want to be a drover?'

'There is good money to be made bringing the sheep down from the Dales.'

'You will not need the encumbrance of a wife and child on a drover's trail?' she suggested hopefully.

'I cannot get my licence until I am a householder with a

319

wife. I have my wife and I shall find you lodgings until I have made enough to take a house. By then I shall have my master's recommendation and I may apply for my own licence.'

So that was why he was set on having a wife. He wanted her only to get his drover's licence. And then what would happen to her? Would he cast her aside as Noah had? Might he sell her at the hiring fair? She was tempted to challenge him with this possibility but thought better of it and only commented, 'Licensed drovers are rich men.'

'Aye, they are. Our children will go to school, have clothes on their backs and boots on their feet.'

'Our children?'

'It is why a man takes a wife, is it not?'

It was why Noah had married her, she reflected. And she knew, as her mother had known, that it was not reason enough for happiness. 'Then he surely must take a wife that he loves?'

'Aye.'

'She must love him in return, Amos. I do not love you.'

'You will. When you have weaned that infant who is taking all you have to give.'

'A wife's love is different.'

He became angry. 'Do you think I do not know that? Do you think I do not want that love to seal our bargain? I despised the whorehouse in Crosswell as a place where men indulge their sinful appetites. But if men have wives like you then I know why it thrives. You will make a sinner of me yet! A man has only so much patience and he cannot wait for ever to take his woman as his wife. When is it to be, Quinta? Must I take you by force, because, by the Lord, if you do not come to me willingly, I shall!'

She believed he would. He believed she was his wife and as her husband it was his right. If she did not go to his bed, even mild-mannered Amos would be driven to anger. If she resisted him, would he beat her until she submitted? She thought not. He had the advantage of size and strength and could easily

320

overcome her if he chose. She knew of no worse hurt for a woman than to be forced into the act of union.

But what was this if not force? If she gave her body passively, her flesh would not be bruised and torn but her heart would be violated, for her heart belonged to another, and it would always yearn for him. When she closed her eyes she could see Patrick's face and remember his passion. She could not willingly contemplate lying with another man.

She gazed wistfully at her sleeping infant, whose survival and safety were more important to her than her own life. With her as Amos's wife, her child's life would be secure and comfortable. She had married Noah for precisely that, and knew very well how wrong she had been. But perhaps she owed this sacrifice to her child? More than anything she wanted her son to have a name and respectability. She did not want him to suffer the contempt and deprivation his father had known. As the son of a drover, perhaps becoming one himself when he was grown, he would be protected from such misery. What did her feelings count for when her son's future was at stake?

She inhaled deeply and said, 'I will come to your bed as your wife. I ask only that you do not force yourself on me. I will give you my body, but that is all, Amos. I can never give you my heart. I am sorry.'

'You will never love me?'

'I love another. Please try and understand.'

'So you will behave no better than a harlot? You will do as I ask even though you do not wish it?'

'You are leaving me with little choice. What more do you want of me?'

'I want a little of the love you give that child! Is that too much to ask of you?'

Quinta stayed silent. She could not love to order. Did he wish her to pretend?

'Is this why Noah sold you? Was it because you would not be a proper loving wife to him in the bedchamber?'

321

'I deceived him,' she admitted. 'You are a good man, Amos, and I am being honest with you.'

'You talk like a whore!'

'Amos!'

'You offer me your body like a common street woman! I do not want a whore for wife!'

'And I do not want to be your wife!' she retaliated angrily.

He got up and crashed out of their shelter into the black night. Jess, who had been sleeping by the fire, woke up and followed him.

Quinta was shocked by Amos's words. If only she had a few coins of her own, she would not be so dependent on him, or indeed anybody. She could not storm off into the night like that. She had a child to care for. The men may have the money, she reflected silently, but it is the women who pay the price.

Chapter 26

It was the waterway that released her. Amos had not seen this scale of trade and activity in Crosswell. The Tinsley wharf shipped in coal, iron and supplies for the nearby thriving town of Sheffield. Payloads out, bound for the east coast, consisted of fine-edge tools made from even finer steel. The finest in the world, it was said. He had been quiet since their quarrel and, as they sat on a low wall watching the barges, Quinta noticed him looking at the other ladies that frequented the wharf.

These were not street women. They kept to the taverns. These were the wives and daughters of bargemen, tradesmen and even wealthy merchants, in their silken gowns and elaborate bonnets. She wondered if he might leave her here to fend for herself. Little Patrick, alert as ever, seemed to be enjoying watching the activities, and cooed happily in her ear.

Amos had been to the canal company office and he returned with pies and apples from a street-seller. 'I've purchased a passage eastbound to Doncaster, and one for you as far as Forge Island. The barge will stop there to load fire grates and it is near to the town that you know.'

'You are letting me go?' She was cheered by this knowledge.

'You are not what I want.'

That sentiment was mutual, but her elation was short-lived.

'I have no money, Amos.'

'There's plenty of work in service, I'm told, in lodging houses and such. If not, they have a workhouse so you and the babe won't starve. Ask the bargeman's wife.'

She was a rough and ready woman with a liking for strong drink, but she allowed Quinta and little Patrick to sit in the owner's cabin at the rear while Amos lowered himself into a tiny space up front for the journey. Her knowledge was useful and Quinta felt confident she would find a lodging and the means to pay for it.

Amos placed her box by her feet on the bank opposite Forge Island. She was so relieved to be free that she felt kindly towards him. She bent to fondle Jess's ears and when she straightened he gave her a few coins.

'I'll pay you back. Somehow.'

'It's not much.'

'I – I mean the five guineas that you paid for me.'

'Where will you get that?'

She didn't know, but to her way of thinking it was Noah who should pay it. She wasn't that far away from him now and she was still his wife whether he liked it or not. Following the bargeman's wife's directions she found a lodging house near to the canal where the ironworks' furnaces and forges were situated. It was dirty and crowded and the landlady wanted a scullery maid for the rough work. She had no spare room, not even in the kitchen or attic, for her and little Patrick to sleep in but gave her the address of a woman who would take her in with a babe and care for him while she worked.

Quinta wasn't happy about this arrangement but she had no choice and struggled further with her box and her baby to a muddy yard surrounding a water pump. Terraced cottages formed three sides of a square around this yard and she knocked on the door she believed to be number seven. The woman who answered was none too clean and she took all Quinta's coins before she let her over the threshold.

She slept in a narrow hard bed in the kitchen as there was only one upstairs chamber and it was the biggest wrench of her life leaving little Patrick before six o'clock the following morning. She had had to wake him early to feed him and leave some of her milk for the woman, Mrs Farrow, to give him during the day. Mrs Farrow seemed used to this; she had taken in destitute women and their infants before.

Quinta spent all day washing pots, scrubbing tables and floors and pounding at dirty linen in a tub. The lodgers were working men: colliers, ironworkers and labourers who loaded and unloaded barges at the wharf. She did, however, eat a good dinner of meat pudding and rhubarb pie and was allowed plenty of ale to drink. But by afternoon she was wilting in the heat. She had not worked so hard since before little Patrick was born and had, somehow, lost the stamina she'd had at Top Field. She thought about her child constantly and could not wait to get back to him, not least because her breasts were leaking.

She returned to Mrs Farrow shortly after six in the evening, weakened and exhausted. How was she to survive this every day? Her heart sank further as she approached the yard with its farmyard stench and dirty children squabbling by the pump. Why were they not indoors at this hour? There was a screeching coming from the open door across the yard. But this was not the wailing of a child. It was the weeping of a woman, two women, sobbing their hearts out. This was no husband and wife argument and she walked over to enquire, keeping a few steps away from the door.

'What's wrong? Can I do anything to help?'

The younger woman looked up for a second and shook her head. It looked as if her mother was with her and Quinta felt a pang of loss for her own. No matter how difficult life had been when she was alive, it had been easier to face when they were together.

'Babby's gone,' the older woman said. 'The toddlers are sick wi' the fever an' all.'

Quinta surveyed the scene from the doorstep. They had obviously done their best to keep their kitchen clean but with so many people in such a small space it must be difficult. 'I'm very sorry,' she said. 'Can you not take them up to the Dispensary?'

'They'll tek 'em from 'er and put 'em in that workhouse place. Full o' disease, that is. I'll not 'ave 'em go up there.'

Quinta couldn't think of anything else to say and was concerned about her own son now. She hurried home, praying that Patrick was safe.

In contrast her new home was relatively quiet and there was a warming aroma of stew in the kitchen. 'How is he?' she asked anxiously.

'Quiet as a mouse all day.'

'Really? That doesn't sound like my baby!'

'Aye well, 'e's more settled 'ere, isn't 'e?'

'I suppose so,' she agreed. But Quinta thought Patrick was becoming more of a handful to keep quietly occupied as he grew.

'Yer need a po' fer 'im when yer get yer wages. I 'eld 'im outta the door a couple o' times. It saves on the washing.'

'Yes. Thank you.' She walked over to her sleeping son. He was normally awake at this time and Quinta kept him awake if she could so that he would sleep longer through the night. He looked so peaceful she decided not to rouse him in spite of her strong desire to pick him up and hold him. But she could smell his wet linen as she bent to stroke his cheek. 'He needs changing. How long has he been asleep?'

'Don't rightly know. I put 'im down ter get on with the tea.'

A shaky nervousness began to overtake her. He didn't normally sleep so soundly at this time of day. He was a lively child and interested in all around him. Was he ill? Had he

326

caught the fever? Oh Lord, please do not be so cruel! She put the back of her hand on his brow. He did not feel hot and she pulled herself together. 'There's fever in the yard,' she said.

'Aye, soon spreads, that does. Best stay away from the families over there.'

'You'll keep him in the house until it passes?' It wouldn't be the best for him, but it was certainly better than risking a fever. 'He likes to watch things.'

'Watch things?' Mrs Farrow sounded surprised.

'You know, things that move when you blow on them.'

'Where am I gunna get stuff like that round 'ere?'

'I'll make some. Have you any old ribbons?'

'Yer don't need ter bother. 'E'll be as right as rain wi' me, don't fret yersen.'

'Are you sure he's been well all day?' Quinta bent over to kiss his head. He didn't stir and alarm started to bubble in her breast again.

'First babby fer yer, i'n't 'e? Yer think 'e's gonna break in two. I tell yer, I know what I'm doing. 'E'll be quiet as the grave 'til we've 'ad our tea an' then 'e'll be ready fer a bit o' titty and yer can hold 'im ter yer 'eart's content.'

Quinta's eyes widened at her choice of words. She'd rather have him awake and demanding her attention no matter how tired she was when she came in. But she conceded that Mrs Farrow had her interests at heart and it sounded a reasonable arrangement. She was hungry and weary after her long day as a skivvy.

Patrick's days were as different as hers now, and perhaps his morning had been tiring, too. Mrs Farrow seemed to know what she was doing and had planned his day with thought of her and the time she needed to spend with her son after tea. She relaxed as Patrick continued to slumber and ate her meal of bread and stew with a drink of tea to follow. Perhaps she had found a haven of sorts at last for them both. As she swallowed the last of her tea she glanced over to his sleeping form.

'I think I should wake him.'

'Nay, lass, yer don't do that ter a sleeping babby.'

'I know, but he'll be awake all night and I have to be up for work in the morning.'

The older woman sighed and shook her head impatiently. 'Will yer stop fretting a minute an' come an' sit by the fire.'

'But he'll need clean wrappings and I'll have to wash his wet linen if it is to be ready for tomorrow.'

'In a minute, love. Yer can put it on me line under the mantel-piece and the 'eat from the fire'll air it a treat.' Mrs Farrow got up and went to the cupboard by the range. 'Why don't yer 'ave a drop o' this in yer tea ter calm yer down a bit.'

But Quinta did not want to calm down a bit. She wanted to know why her baby, her little Patrick, who was normally noisy and lively, and – yes – a handful, was sleeping so quietly and for so long. He had to have something wrong with him.

She dreaded him becoming ill and, heaven forbid, suffering the same fate as the yard children. It hadn't been a good idea to come to the town. Her mother had warned her about it. There was not much money to be had in the countryside but at least the water you drank and the air you breathed were clean.

As though she had had a choice! However bad her situation was she had to put up with it until she had a few spare coins to – to do what? Return to Noah to demand his support and be spurned again? She wondered again what he had told people about her. The vicar and his sister, surely, would have asked questions.

She had been foolish to deceive him but she had her pride. If Noah did not want her then she did not want him either. She had never really wanted him anyway, she reflected. What had happened to her had, perhaps, been for the best. She had little Patrick and her memories of his father. It was enough.

'I think my baby might be sick,' she said.

Mrs Farrow was tutting and shaking her head. ''E's just 'ad

328

a spoonful or two o' this, me ducks. Works wonders when they're teething.'

'But he's not teething! What is this? What have you given him?'

'It's just something ter keep 'im quiet. An' yer can give 'im a bit more afore yer goes ter bed so 'e won't wake either of us in the night.'

'But you can't give him that stuff! He's just a baby!' Quinta grabbed the bottle from her hands. 'Show me what it is.'

''Ere, you! Give that back. That's best gin, that is. Comes in on the barges and 'e's lucky I only 'ave the best. Some of the cheaper stuff 'as all sorts in it. I've never given my babbies anything I won't drink meself.'

Quinta was horrified. Mrs Farrow was clearly proud of this standard in the care of her baby. She ran her hands over her face and went to wake him immediately. 'I'm sorry, but I cannot allow you to give that to my child.'

'"Cannot allow"? Who on this earth do yer think you are, you hoity-toity little madam? I know what's best fer babbies, ask any o' the folk round 'ere.'

Little Patrick woke up slowly. His lips were whitish and dry. Poor mite must be so thirsty. He began to cry. She poured some boiled water from the kettle into a clean bowl and began to spoon it into his mouth. He drank greedily and stopped crying while she took off his sodden linen and washed his reddened bottom. She smoothed on some salve that Mrs Farrow had in her cupboard and he began to kick his little legs and coo at her. He lay contentedly on layers of thick sacking while she washed his linen, angrily, at the scullery sink. He would be awake all night now. Well, so be it. She most certainly was not going to give him any more of that evil spirit.

She fed him a little of the warm mashed stew and put him to her breast. As he suckled contentedly, she relaxed. It was the time she looked forward to most of all, when she could forget all her difficulties and dream. She dreamed of his father and how much he had loved her and she vowed that she would give his son that same devotion. Yes, she resolved. She would give little Patrick the love of two people and he would always know what a fine man his father was, wherever he might be.

She wondered if Patrick still yearned for her as she did him. Or, heaven forbid, had given up on her and fallen into the arms of a camp follower. She had married so why should he not be so inclined? How could their love be expected to survive such separation? Why had she never realised it was a possibility – and – and curbed her passion? But still, she had little Patrick and he was the world to her. She pushed aside her doubts and planned to move on.

Quinta did not even consider staying another night with Mrs Farrow. It was no longer an option for her as there was no way she would ever leave little Patrick in her care again. But what was she to do? There was nowhere else for her to go, no one to help her. She wished so desperately that Patrick were here, with her, with both of them. Oh, how she missed him.

She racked her brain for a solution, but there was no answer. How was it possible to work and look after her child? If only she were able to find a position in a household. She was willing to wash and scrub, clean grates and ranges if only she could keep him by her side. But no housekeeper would take her in without a letter of recommendation, let alone with a wriggling child in her arms. She did not know what to do, except to be gone from here by morning.

Mrs Farrow slept soundly, knocked out by her gin. Quinta reluctantly discarded her travelling box, wrapped her few belongings into a bundle with little Patrick's linen and fastened them to his leather sling. He was growing too big for it but he was too heavy to carry any distance in her arms. She fed and cleaned him quietly in the blackness of the night, burning only one candle to light her tasks. As soon as he was sleepy again, she hoisted him on to her back and crept quietly out of the house.

The first streaks of dawn lit up the church spire. Set high on a mound in the centre of town the beautiful stone church could be seen for miles around. She had nowhere else to go and its doors were always open. She trudged up the short hill and placed her faith in the Lord. He would provide.

It was dark inside and cool. She sat in a pew away from the door, hidden behind a wide stone pillar, and stared at the huge stained-glass windows as the morning sun lit up their majestic beauty. Little Patrick slept in his sling on the floor. She placed her bundle under her head, stretched out on the pew and slept.

Chapter 27

'Wake up, my child.'

Someone was shaking her shoulder. She opened her eyes suddenly, looking down at the floor, searching for her child. He was where she had left him, awake but chewing at his fingers and kicking against the restrictions of his wrappings.

'Why are you sleeping in my church?'

'I – I . . .' What was she to say to the vicar? He was a tall man, dressed sombrely in black. But he had a gentle smile on his thin face. He was waiting for her answer.

'I seek sanctuary, sir.'

He raised his eyebrows. 'Do you flee from justice, ma'am?'

'No, sir. I am not a criminal.'

He lifted her left hand and felt for her wedding band. 'Where is your husband?'

'I have no husband, sir.' She saw the disapproval on his face as he glanced at her child and added quickly, 'He – he has deserted me.'

'Then you have a home? Where is your home?'

'I have nowhere to go, sir.'

'Ah. I see. What is your name?'

'Quinta Haig, sir.' She said it without thinking and realised that in her head she had never thought of herself as Mrs Bilton. Yet, in the Church's eyes, that was who she was.

'You cannot live here, Mrs Haig.'

'I am looking for work, sir,' she said anxiously.

'With a child to care for? Do you have any money?'

She shook her head. 'I should not be here, sir, if I had.'

'Well, it will soon be time for matins. Will you join us in our prayers?'

Little Patrick's cooing turned to whimpers and she bent to pick him up. 'He's hungry again.' Automatically, she began to undo her bodice buttons.

The vicar raised his eyebrows. 'Not here, madam.'

'Then where may I go, sir?'

He seemed to hesitate. 'Stay behind the pillar. I'll arrange a breakfast for you and then we shall see what can be done.'

Quinta listened to the worshippers and joined silently in their prayers. But she was weary. It seemed as though she tired so very quickly nowadays. Little Patrick made such demands on her, for food and for attention, and she always placed his needs before her own. Only a year ago she had prided herself on her strength and stamina for the physical tasks of house and garden, but this one small child was draining her energy and wearing her down. She had not realised how much of her he would take and although she would willingly give her life for him, she knew that it was not an answer. Her child needed her to be healthy to look after him. He snuffled and gurgled at her breast and, content with this most intimate of pleasures, she leaned against the corner of the hard wooden pew and dozed.

'Here she is, madam.'

Wide awake again, Quinta blinked in the gloom. The vicar had returned and he was not alone. His companion was a large lady with reddened hands and an equally ruddy round face. She handed her bread and cheese and a can of tea, which was cold but welcome and she devoured it thirstily.

333

As she ate the food the vicar said, 'Mrs Haig, this lady will take care of you and your child.'

Quinta's anxiety heightened. Not another Mrs Farrow, she thought. 'Who are you?'

'Never mind that, my dear. You and the babe just come wi' me.'

'But where to?' She directed her question at the vicar. 'Where is she taking me, sir?'

He gave her his gentle, sympathetic smile again. 'You and your child are quite safe, madam. I know this lady well.'

He was a kindly gentleman and she guessed that he had all manner of vagrants seeking sanctuary in his church. He must have a whole brigade of lady parishioners willing to help him in his work. Quinta relaxed. She had come to the right place. The Lord had provided. Well, she would not forget Him and vowed to worship more regularly with little Patrick. She placed him on the pew while she gathered her possessions.

'Put yer things in the bag, dear. I'll take the child,' the woman said.

'No! Thank you, but I can carry him.' She pushed everything into the sling and hoisted it on to her back so she could hold him tightly in her arms. The woman seemed respectable and knew the vicar, but she didn't look any different from Mrs Farrow and Quinta wondered if her coarse red cheeks came from the same habit of drinking spirits.

She walked with the woman up Sheep Hill towards the square where the beast market was held. There were no live-stock sales today and the pens were empty and quiet. Further up and away from the navigation, this track was wide and favoured by the well-to-do for new houses in the town. They progressed slowly as it was a steep incline and the woman soon began to puff and pant. 'Not far now,' she muttered. 'We'll soon get you and the babby indoors.'

'Where are we going?'

'It's just up here, lass. We'll take care o' you both, have no fear.'

But Quinta did. As they approached the high stone wall and its huge wooden gates, it slowly dawned on her. She was not going as a servant to one of the fine large houses recently built for a factory- or mill-owner. The gates loomed large in front of her. This was the workhouse. This was the place where you went when you had failed in your duty and were destitute. Surely she was not desperate enough for the workhouse? She could not go there! This woman would take little Patrick from her and put her to work in the laundry all day. It would be worse than the lodging house and Mrs Farrow. He would be lost in a crowd of other wretched crying children whose mothers could not care for them, neglected and without her nourishment until he was old enough to work himself. What was she thinking of? She could look after her child herself and she would!

'You're from the workhouse,' she stated.

'Aye. Where else would we be going?' The woman stopped panting and reached out for Quinta's arm. Her fingers closed round her wrist like an iron band. 'Come on, lass. We can't have you out on the streets. The town's leaders won't have it nowadays. They've spent a lot o' brass on this new building fer the likes o' you. You're not gonna be awk'ard about it, are you?'

Quinta stood still and the woman tugged at her arm. 'You're coming wi' me, you are. A strong young lass like you can work fer her keep. And the babby's.' She lowered her voice and went on, 'Unless you'd rather I took you over there to him?'

'Who? Where?' And then she saw him, leaning in the shade of a tavern and watching. The lank-haired, thick-set bear of a man who had tried to steal her at the marketplace last year, his top hat pushed to the back of his head as he drew on a cigar.

'He'll give me gold fer you, with or without the babby, and no questions asked. He'll dress you in silks and satins and give you strong drink. Then he'll sell you ter any gentleman who pays ter take you fer his pleasure and when you can't stand it any more he'll give you laudanum, as much as you like, fer you ter keep on pleasuring his friends. And what'll happen ter yer babby then, my lass? Eh? You're better off in the workhouse, I can tell you.'

Quinta clutched Patrick tightly with her free arm and shook off the woman's grip. The woman was strong, but she had no puff left and when Quinta increased her pace she could only lumber in her wake for a few steps before her grip lessened and Quinta was free to run. She saw the man push himself away from the wall and walk towards her.

She had been in this part of the town before. The Dispensary was the other side of the road. She ran across the rutted track towards it. Little Patrick jolted and jostled in her aching arms but she continued to run, the woman's beseeching calls fading in her ears. Quinta slowed as she approached a small group of coughing, wheezing town folk waiting outside the Dispensary. She turned, looked behind and paused to catch her breath. The woman had not chased after her, her size had prevented it, and the man had melted way. At least, she could not see him.

A sob of desperation threatened and she choked it back as she recalled the unhappy events that surrounded her last visit. But she remembered the housekeeper at the surgeon's house nearby. She followed the path to the back of the building to find the tradesmen's entrance.

'Good morning, madam. Are you looking for the Dispensary?'

Quinta shook her head. The housekeeper did not remember her. 'I am looking for work,' she answered hastily.

The older woman stared at her. 'You have a child to care for. Go back home.'

'I have no home.' Her eyes were pleading, but she saw that the housekeeper was hardened to beggars and started to close the door.

'They want to put me in the workhouse.' Her voice cracked as she half sobbed. 'Please help me.'

'It's not so bad in there. They will look after you.'

'But they'll take my baby away from me! He needs me.' She pushed her straggling hair away from her eyes. 'Please. You were so kind before – to – to my mother.'

The woman looked more closely at her face. 'Who is your mother?'

'She came here with Sergeant Ross about a year ago. The surgeon took off his leg and . . .' The sobbing threatened to overtake her.

'He died. I remember. Are you the widow Haig's daughter?'

Quinta swallowed hard to suppress her sobs and nodded.

'A genteel lady, as I recall. She gave the sergeant much support in his last days in spite of her own sickness.' A guarded look came into the housekeeper's eyes. 'How is her cough?'

'She – she passed away at the end of last year.' The tears welled again.

'Oh. I'm sorry to hear that. The sergeant thought very highly of her.'

Little Patrick was restless and wriggled in her aching arms. She pulled herself together and cooed at him to calm him, but he would have none of it. His bare toes pushed against her skirts. He would need shoes for those tiny feet before the autumn.

'He's a lively one,' the housekeeper commented.

Quinta nodded and smiled in spite of her distress.

'You have a wedding band on your finger. Are you widowed yourself?'

'No.'

'Where is your husband?'

She had not been wholly truthful with the vicar and regretted it so she stayed silent. The older woman waited patiently for her to continue. When she did not, the housekeeper added, 'Your husband may have treated you ill but I am sure he does not wish to be rid of you. You have a child and the child needs his father. Take your child back to your husband. He will take care of you both, I am sure.'

'I can't.'

'Can't?'

'He – he . . .' How much to say? 'I – I have made mistakes that I now regret.' She gazed at her son. Was he one of them? The notion tore at her heart. Surely she was not sorry for loving his father? Or that this love had given her little Patrick? 'My husband cast me out.'

'What did you do to upset him so? It is a wife's duty to do her husband's bidding, you know. And it is a husband's duty to look after his family. You just say you have repented and show remorse, and he will take you back.'

'No, he won't. I deceived him in a most cruel way.'

The older woman was taken aback but rallied. 'Well, I'm sure that would not have happened if your poor mother were still here, God rest her soul. She would not have let that happen.'

Quinta bowed her head in silence. Her mother had counselled against her marriage to Noah and she had been right.

'I have no work to give you but I may be able to offer advice. Step into my kitchen and tell me what you did.'

In spite of her embarrassment Quinta told her. 'He's the sergeant's grandson.' She had not even thought of little Patrick as such before, let alone said it. But he was. And she was so wrapped up in her own woes that she had walked past the graveyard where her son's grandfather was buried without even thinking of paying her respects to his memory.

'But his son—' The housekeeper bit back her words.

'He was innocent. I shot the deer. It was an accident.' It was an argument that was ingrained on her mind and she said it without thinking. But it was the truth.

'He went to be a soldier,' the older woman continued slowly. 'You must have been with child by him at his trial.'

'I did not know and neither did he. I married Far—, I mean I married my husband because my mother was dying and I was destitute. He found out that my child was not his and – and – he took me away – to the High Peak and – and left

338

me there.' She swallowed and blushed at the memory of her humiliation.

'Were you married before God?'

She nodded. 'But he won't have me back, I know he won't.'

'He must. Holy wedlock is for better or for worse. You are his wife and you have a child. It is his duty to look after you.'

'Even though the child is not his?'

'It will be hard for your husband to accept him but he wed you willingly and may be regretting his behaviour towards you. You must return to him and beg his forgiveness. It is your only choice. Perhaps the vicar who married you will help?'

Mr Wilkins? He had been very sympathetic about arrangements for her mother. But she wasn't sure. The housekeeper took a tin caddy down from the mantelshelf over the range and prised open the lid. 'Take these with my blessing. Make haste for your home and see what can be done to mend your marriage. I am sure all is not lost.'

Quinta clutched gratefully at the coins. 'I don't know when I can give this back.'

'There is no need. Patients who can afford to pay the surgeon are always very generous.' The older woman smiled. 'It helps us with those who cannot.'

Quinta took the money and the advice, but not in the spirit that the surgeon's housekeeper intended. She accepted that it was her only option if she was to keep her son with her. Noah had wanted her son's father out of his way so he could marry her and he had succeeded. Well, now it was time for him to pay for his lies! She was his wife and she had borne a child within wedlock. Her child was not going to suffer any more, even if she had to sit in the middle of the village green and demand that Noah give her a home.

Her son was going to have a future and a name. He was going to be baptised in the church and she was going to hold her head high in the parish where she was born. And if Noah Bilton objected she would tell the villagers just what he had done with her in the time she had been away and see what that did for his reputation with the vicar . . . She wavered a little. Noah had been very angry with her. Well, she was angry with him! But perhaps she should talk to Mr Wilkins first?

She bought flowers from the market with one of the coins and laid half of them at Sergeant Ross's headstone in the town churchyard. George Ross, Beloved Father of Patrick', it said. Yet again she wondered if Patrick were still alive. It was possible that he had been killed for he had not written to her as he promised.

Unless, she realised, a letter had been taken to Top Field after she and Mother had left? The postmistress in town, like the surgeon's housekeeper, would not know that she had wed and gone to live at Bilton Farm. Perhaps she had delayed delivery until after the winter snows and then sent it back to Patrick? Perhaps he thought she had died?

Her mind in turmoil, Quinta breathed deeply to calm herself. Patrick had asked her not to give up hope and, for the sake of his son, she would not. His son would be called Bilton and she regretted that. It was the price she had to pay for little Patrick's respectability and she would explain it to him one day. She pondered on this as she gave up the rest of her coins for a seat on the carrier and jolted her way, clutching her remaining flowers, up and down the hills to Swinborough.

Chapter 28

'Good afternoon, ma'am.'

Quinta placed the flowers at the base of her mother's headstone and straightened. She turned as Mr Wilkins approached and was taken aback by the shock on his face. He went quite pale.

'You!'

She had planned to call on the vicar anyway and looked forward to seeing Beatrice again, though she was becoming increasingly nervous about what she would say to both of them. If she was to resume her place as Noah's wife it was her duty to maintain his good reputation. She wondered what he had told them about her absence.

'Sir?' She did not understand why he was so surprised.

'Mrs Bilton? But you are dead!'

Dead? She had never considered that Noah would say that about her. No wonder Mr Wilkins was shaken. He must think he had seen a ghost! She held out her arm and said, 'Indeed, I am not. You may touch me if you do not believe it. My flesh is real.'

He shook his head slowly as he stared at her and whispered, 'He said you had died.'

'Who? Who said that to you, sir?' She knew the answer, of course.

'Mr Bilton. He told me you were unwell and he had taken you to the waters in Derbyshire for your health and – and, later, that you had died of the same affliction as your dear mother.'

Well, thought Quinta, he really did want rid of me for good. Her resolve to maintain his reputation ran away. 'As you can see, sir, he lied. He is practisced in that art.'

'But we prayed for you in church.' The vicar appeared to be truly shocked and rested his body against a stone vault. He looked down at little Patrick sitting quietly on the dry grass and his lower jaw dropped slackly. 'Your husband does not know that you are alive, madam,' he said hoarsely.

'I believe he does, sir. When he left me in the High Peak I was very much alive.'

'You were not sick?'

'I was with child, sir, this child. He is Patrick Bilton. I am Mrs Bilton. I am a respectable married woman and I wish to have my child baptised in the church where I was wed.'

She actually thought he was going to faint. His eyes closed and his shoulders sagged beneath their fine linen jacket. He had begun to perspire slightly in spite of the cool churchyard shade. 'I must speak with him immediately,' he muttered suddenly. 'Excuse me, madam. Good day to you.'

'Good day, sir.' But Quinta was talking to the open air for he had disappeared around the back of the church and moments later emerged on horseback to gallop in the direction of Bilton Hill.

Percival Wilkins arrived in a sweat, hurriedly secured his horse and rapped on the front door. His sister answered, smiled broadly and opened her arms to embrace him, but he pushed past her into the hall and demanded, 'Where is he?'

'Noah is in the fields, dearest. What on earth is the matter?'

'Beatrice, I have distressing news. Send a servant for him this minute.'

'Seth is with a calving cow.'

'But he has a girl for the kitchen now, doesn't he? *Tell her to fetch Noah; immediately.*'

'Very well.'

He paced about the gracious drawing room, accepting brandy while they waited. Beatrice, with his blessing, had continued to encourage improvements to Bilton Farm and it was, indeed, very acceptable to genteel visitors now.

'Can you not tell me anything?'

'Not until Noah is present. Ah, I hear his horse now.' He moved to the window and then to the newly painted door. As soon as Noah entered he pushed a glass of brandy in his hand. 'Sit down, Noah. You, too, my dear. This is – is truly a dreadful affair.' He remained standing and turned to Beatrice. 'My dear, you must prepare yourself for the worst of news.'

'What on earth is going on, Percy old fellow?' Noah asked. 'You seem very agitated.'

'That is because I am! Noah, your wife did not die. She is alive and she is well.'

'Nonsense. She ailed the same as her mother. The waters could not cure her. It was as I told you.'

'You have lied to me, Noah. More than that, you have cruelly deceived my dear sister.'

Beatrice sat rigidly in her chair, her face as pallid as sun-bleached linen. 'But Noah, she cannot be alive,' she whispered. 'I am to be your wife. The ceremony is to be within the month.'

'And it will be, my love. Percy, who told you of this lie? They must speak of another, an impostor from the High Peak, who has heard of my recent wealth. *My wife is dead, I say!*'

'This is no lie. There is no impostor. *Do you think I do not recognise her? I married her to you!* Your wife was here, not an hour ago, in my churchyard, paying her respects to her dear

343

departed mother. She lives. She is well. She has returned to claim her position as your wife.'

'She can't! I'll not have her back!' Noah shouted. 'She is dead to me.'

'You cannot turn her away, Noah.' Percival's brow furrowed as he glanced at his sister. 'She has a child. She claims he is your son.'

Noah exploded. 'No! Not *my* child! Never *my* child! He is some vagrant's bastard. That's why I got rid of her.'

'Got rid of her?'

'I took her to the High Peak and sold her at the hiring fair.'

'You . . . *sold* her?'

'Aye. That's what we do with unfaithful wives where I come from!'

The Reverend Wilkins closed his eyes and covered his face with his hands. 'But you were married in my church. You cannot deny her claim.'

'She was a harlot. I wanted a pure woman, like my lovely Beatrice.'

The vicar sat down wearily. 'Noah, oh Noah, what have you done?'

'She never wanted *me*. She had eyes only for that vagrant.'

'She wants you now. At least, she wants your name for her child.'

'I told you he's not mine.'

'He is of an age to be yours. She is your lawful wife and her child was born within wedlock. You cannot expect any woman to turn her back on that.'

'And what about Beatrice? Have you no thoughts for your own sister?'

'But I cannot marry you to her if your wife still lives! Dear Lord, Noah, I have read the banns!'

'Oh, why did she have to come back? I thought I was rid of her for ever!'

'Noah, you have to receive her. She is your lawful wife. As

it is there will be a huge scandal. How shall I stay here if I am implicated in your deception? And yes, what will happen to my poor sister? Beatrice? My dear, you have become very quiet. Have you nothing more to say?'

Beatrice was sitting stock-still with a look of sheer horror on her face. 'What shall I do?' she whispered. She clasped her hands lightly over her belly. 'I believe I am going to faint. I am with child myself.'

'Noah!' Percival leaped to his feet, not knowing whether to strike Noah or tend to his sister, whose head was lolling. He chose his sister, supported her back and pressed the remains of his brandy to her lips.

She recovered quickly, but not so her brother, whose agitation was increasing by the minute. 'You – both of you have disappointed me greatly. But for Beatrice, I blame myself. I should have chaperoned her more closely. Noah, your behaviour towards her is the worst. You betrayed my trust.'

'Do not chastise him, brother. I did not choose celibacy as you seem to have done. It was forced upon me by my duty to our parents. Had I not cared for them until I lost my bloom, I might have had a husband and children sooner. Neither Noah nor I have time to waste.'

'Oh Lord, oh Lord. I am the vicar of this parish. How shall I face my congregation when they hear of this?'

'Why should they?' Noah demanded. 'If the harlot wants money, I'll give her what she asks for and send her on her way. Then you can marry us, just as we planned.'

Percival was too exhausted to argue further, but he tried: 'No, I cannot. You are this woman's husband. If she is destitute you have a duty to look after her.'

'Is she destitute?'

'She was not dressed in rags.'

'There you are then. She's found someone else to take her on. Why can't we go ahead with my marriage to Beatrice?'

'Because we can't, you stupid man!'

'Dearest!' Beatrice chastised. She reached across for Noah's hand. 'There must be some way for us to marry. Royalty have divorces, don't they? You have connections with the gentry. Find out how they do it.'

'A divorce? Don't be ridiculous! The scandal will be just as bad. Besides, they are for the very rich and they – they have to have good reasons.'

'Such as?' Beatrice demanded. 'Come along, Percy dear, you know about these things.'

Percival glanced at his sister's stomach. 'I know they take time. I doubt it could help you now. But perhaps . . . Beatrice, I think you'd better leave Noah and me to discuss this further.'

'But, dearest, surely it concerns me, too?'

'Do as I say.'

She stood up. 'Very well.'

When she had gone back to the vicarage, Percival asked, 'Are you sure the child is not yours?'

'She must have been with child when we wed.'

'But how can you be so sure?'

Noah looked uncomfortable. 'She bewitched me in such a way. We never managed to . . . you know.'

Percival stared at him. 'Are you telling me that you did not consummate your marriage?'

Noah nodded.

'But Beatrice . . . ?'

'I found an apothecary with potions from the East. It took me a while to get it right but I persevered.' He looked at his feet. 'Beatrice helped. She is the woman for me, Percy. You must find a way for us to wed.'

'But that is the answer, Noah.' Percival cheered for the first time that afternoon. 'If your wife will swear to it, too, I may be able to procure an annulment. These affairs really do take time, though. If Beatrice is to have her child inside wedlock, I must make haste and seek advice immediately. Good day to you, Noah.'

He hurried out to his horse and galloped back to his church and asked a child if he had seen a woman with an infant pass through the village. Mrs Bilton had followed his horse up Bilton Hill. But she had not called at the farm and he had not passed her on his way back. Of course! She had gone on to Top Field where she used to live.

The cottage was empty and locked up as Noah had not started the extensions that he'd planned. His sister had seen off that idea when she worked her charm on him to spend his wealth on the farmhouse. And to think that he had encouraged the liaison as an outlet for her energies! He urged his horse towards Bilton Hill again, eventually dismounting to lead it, sweating, up the steep incline at the top.

Quinta had talked to little Patrick most of the time as she climbed. She had cut the openings in his sling wider to give him more room for his legs and resumed carrying him on her back. Her progress was slow but all the time she talked, telling him of her days at Top Field with his father; what he had said, what he had done and how much he would love him if he were here.

The acres below the cottage had been ploughed and harvested barley stood in stooks waiting to be threshed. There were sheep grazing on the pasture but the cottage looked as though no one had been there since she and her mother had left. She peered in the window. It was neat and tidy, if dusty, and obviously not tenanted. Seth must still be farming the land for Noah, she guessed. She crossed to the stream for a drink and noticed waterfowl on the pond. Patrick would be pleased, she thought.

She laid little Patrick on the bank and splashed cooling water over her face and then his, which he enjoyed. Except when he was hungry, he was a happy child, which constantly surprised her, considering his start in life.

'I'll show you the cowshed,' she said, 'where your father and grandfather lived when they stayed with us.'

The sheep scattered as she carried her child in one arm and the sling over her other back to the track. The cowshed had no lock and she went inside. Insects and small animals had taken up residence. But, she thought, idly picking up an old birch broom with her free hand, that was easily remedied.

'We have a bed for the night,' she said. Let the word get around the village about her return before she approached Noah. Barley straw was soft to sleep on and she had bread in her bundle. With the cooking pot that Patrick had used and some barley and vegetables, she could make a broth for supper, if the sheep had not pushed through the hedge and trampled her garden.

She found it overgrown and wild, but some roots had survived and greens had seeded down to re-emerge young and fresh. She stayed outside and set about making a fire. She did not notice Mr Wilkins approach until she heard his horse snorting in the heat. She went to pick up little Patrick straightaway.

'Good evening, sir,' she said. In spite of her earlier misgivings she felt strong. This was her territory. Hers and Patrick's, and she was fighting for their son.

'Mrs Bilton.' He gave her a formal bow. 'I must speak with you.'

'And I you. Will you sit?'

He tethered his horse and joined her on the grass. 'This is a serious matter.'

'Indeed it is.'

'I shall come straight to the point. Your husband has told me of your – your infidelity.'

'Deception, I own up to, sir, but I was never an unfaithful wife to him.'

'He is very angry with you.'

'*He* is angry. Do you know what he did with me?'

'Yes, he told me.'

'Then perhaps we are even and can start afresh?'

Mr Wilkins clasped his hands and kneaded his fingers. 'He

does not want you as his wife, madam. Nor, I suspect, do you truly care for him.'

'That is of no consequence. He is my husband and I have a child.'

'Not his child.'

'It is if I say so.'

'But he says not. He has told me of his . . . his difficulties with you and I believe him.'

'He is a liar. You know that because he told you I was dead.'

Mr Wilkins face took on a sterner expression. 'You did not consummate your marriage,' he said firmly, adding, 'Well, did you?'

She blew out her cheeks, but this time answered honestly. 'No. He had this affliction and I didn't know what to do.'

'Please do not give me the details. It is sufficient that you both admit to it.'

'What do you mean?'

'If you will sign a document to that effect, I can procure an annulment of the marriage and you will both be free of each other.'

'No!' she yelled. She actually shouted at the vicar. 'Why do you think I am back here, suffering all this humiliation? My child! That's why! Noah Bilton lied in court and took my child's father from me. He must pay for that and I intend to make sure that he does!'

Mr Wilkins shaded his eyes with his hand and heaved a sigh. 'He lied in court.' He sounded weary. It was not a question and he seemed resigned to accepting this new information.

'Ask him! Although I, for one, should never trust his word ever again!'

'Yet you wish to remain his wife.'

'I wish to have his name for my child. That is all.'

The silence between them lengthened. Then Mr Wilkins spoke slowly as though choosing his words carefully. 'Is there . . . anything, anything that . . . that you would take instead?'

349

She didn't know what he meant at first and then realised it was money. He must have spoken to Noah, who had suggested buying his freedom. Surely Mr Wilkins did not agree? He was the vicar. Why should he care so much about Noah's wishes, anyway? She gave him a small humourless smile and answered, 'My child would like a pardon for his father.'

To her surprise, he took her seriously. 'If you really mean that I shall go immediately to Sir William.'

'You think it may be possible?' An unusual excitement bubbled in her breast.

'I do not know, but I shall find out.'

'Why? Why trouble yourself so on my behalf?'

'I do not want any more scandal in my parish. If I can secure a pardon for your child's father will you agree to an annulment?'

'Yes.' Her answer needed no further consideration, but her heart was missing beats as she added, 'If he is still alive.'

After Mr Wilkins had hurried away, she could not eat. She could not sleep. She could not remember collecting the barley staves and making a bed in the cowshed. All she could recall for the remainder of that day was feeding her child last thing before she put him down for the night. It was always their most special time together when she comforted him and he comforted her.

'What have I done? I have agreed to sell your good name for your father's freedom,' she told her baby. 'It is not too late for me to change my mind but I have already made my offer and – and, my darling son, I hope it will happen. Can you forgive me? I do it as much for you as for him.' She frowned as she whispered these words and thought, I love you both so much, how can I know what is best for you both?

In the dead of night when the owls hooted and the vixens called she had other misgivings. Patrick might be wed himself, have another child with another woman. He might not want to return to the South Riding. He might enjoy being a soldier.

Worst of all he might not love her any more, he might suspect that little Patrick is not his, and what would happen to her darling child then? Her nagging doubts kept her awake. Love was ecstasy but love was dangerous, too. A brief interlude of passion with a man she loved had turned her life on its head. How could she have been so foolish?

Chapter 29

Mr Wilkins called the following day with the key for the cottage. 'You may live here until this unfortunate business is resolved. It will be best for all concerned if you keep away from the village and its wagging tongues. Your husband will support you with supplies. He wants this annulment.'

'Is it really possible to free Mr Ross?' she asked again.

'Noah Bilton is to call on Sir William today and – and discuss the situation.'

'But Noah will go to gaol himself if he admits that he lied.'

'Sir William understands these matters more than anyone else in the Riding. Leave it to him. He looks after his own.'

She was aware of that. It was why he had believed Noah in the first place. She began to fret about ever agreeing to this unholy bargain. 'I shall not consent to an annulment until I see the pardon for myself.'

'I expected that, Mrs Bilton. Sir William will bring it to you in person.'

Her heart turned over. Oh joy! It really was a possibility! 'How long will it take?' she asked.

'You must be patient, madam. But be assured that everyone

involved wishes for a speedy solution and we are making haste with our interventions.'

She could not understand why they were all so anxious to proceed. She thought of writing a letter to Patrick and telling him of his child. He would surely wish to see his son? But she was frightened to do anything for fear of upsetting the delicacy of the negotiations. Mr Wilkins had told her to stay at Top Field and not talk of the matter to anyone. She put her trust in him and hoped he would not let her down.

That night she was exhausted from cleaning the cottage. The chimney smoked and the fire refused to draw. She had barely enough heat to warm her broth. She shovelled the last of the glowing embers into a warming pan to air the bed. Little Patrick seemed so heavy when she carried him up the stairs. She propped herself up with pillows to feed him, sure that she would fall asleep as he suckled. The bed was comfortable. The bed was home. She had shared it with her mother and once, just once, with Patrick; one night of wondrous happiness, of love and of hope for their future together, a future that the misfortune which continued to dog her steps had torn from her grasp.

That night had changed her life in a way she could never have imagined and she feared that she was now living to regret her act of passion. But she was blessed with a son who was a constant delight to her. When he had finished feeding, she placed him carefully beside her and snuggled down to sleep. She did not know what the years ahead held for them but as long as she had little Patrick she could face them.

Yet, again in the dead of the night, she fretted. Life had not been very kind to her so far. Why should it be any different now?

And so the weeks went by.

By Michaelmas, little Patrick was five months old and Quinta had given up hope for his father. Seth brought her food and fuel from the farm by horse-drawn cart and took away requests for supplies. She had hoped to visit Beatrice but the vicar advised strongly against any journeys to the village, not even to church on Sunday, which upset her. Mr Wilkins rode up to Top Field infrequently and each time without news. Hopes that were raised when she saw him approach were always dashed.

'Would Beatrice care to call on me here?' she suggested.

'Mrs Bilton, please understand that I am doing all I can for you.'

He said the same every time and it depressed her. She endeavoured to be content as she waited in the cottage. Her garden took shape again and little Patrick thrived. However, the days were shortening and she had not wintered there alone before, or with a child to look after.

It was early November when Sir William arrived on horseback with the thick documents.

'Good afternoon, Sir William.' She curtseyed as she opened the door to let him in.

He hesitated on the threshold and stared at her. 'Good afternoon, Mrs Bilton.' He seemed unsure about coming in yet she thought for a moment he was going to smile at her. Perhaps he did, just for a second. But they were not equals and this was not a social occasion. Quinta stood back and held the door wide open.

'This is your child?'

Little Patrick was occupying himself on the rug with her kitchen spoons and a metal pot. Quinta smiled proudly and nodded. 'Will you sit, sir?' She indicated the couch and he settled there watching her son at play, looking out of place in his grand clothes and fine leather boots, while she read at the kitchen table. It was hard for her to understand the language that lawyers used but the papers had official crests and seals and were duly signed.

'Your husband has admitted he did not see the shooting.'

'It was as I said. The deer was in my garden and I shot it by accident. I only meant to frighten it.'

'Yes, I believe you.'

She brandished the court document. 'Does this mean that Mr Ross is innocent?'

'It does.'

She felt a thrill course through her that caused her skin to tingle. 'Did you hear that, little Patrick,' she said. 'Your father will be a free man again.' She hesitated and looked at Sir William. 'Do you know where he is?'

'He is in Essex with his regiment, preparing for another posting overseas.'

'Another one?'

'He has been in the West Indies until recently.'

'Where will he go, sir?'

'India? South America? I cannot tell you, madam.'

Wherever the King sent him, it was likely to be the other side of the world! It was said the country was building an empire over the seas. She asked, 'Does he know about his pardon?'

'He will do by now. He will have the choice of staying with the army, or – or not.' Sir William leaned forward and showed her son his heavy timepiece. He placed it near to little Patrick's ear and she saw his eyes come alive and his head turn. His small hands dropped the spoons to take hold of the gold case. Quinta started. The timepiece was valuable but Sir William did not seem to mind. He continued speaking without looking at her. 'You should know that when he returned to Essex from the West Indies he was accompanied by a young lady.'

A cold hand clutched at her heart. It was her worst fear. Patrick had found another. 'What – what do you know of her?'

'Very little and I have no authority to demand such information. However, I have been told unofficially that she lives near the garrison and his financial records show he pays for her keep. Ordinary soldiers' wives do not normally reside with their husbands.'

'She is his wife?'

355

'I do not know whether there has been a ceremony. I have requested that he is informed about his child.'

She gazed at little Patrick and said, 'Thank you, sir.'

'May I – may I hold your child for a moment?'

Surprised at such a request, she hardly knew how to reply. Then she remembered that Sir William and his wife had not been blessed with infants. He had a sister with children but she had married a Scottish laird and he saw them rarely. It occurred to her that, in spite of all his wealth and position, Sir William might envy Patrick his son. 'Of course you may,' she said.

He hoisted her boy on to his lap and showed him how to open the timepiece case and wind it up. Little Patrick was captivated and Quinta watched fondly until an uneasy feeling stirred in her breast. Her son needed a father and fathers coveted their sons.

Sir William noticed her worried gaze. 'I'll give him back, Mrs Bilton,' he said lightly and then stated firmly, 'You must sign the annulment.'

Of course she must, but she wondered whether, if she did, her son would now lose everything. Whatever the outcome, Noah would never allow her to stay at Top Field. She said, 'Will Noah go to gaol for lying to you?'

'I have reached an agreement with him, by way of compensation to Mr Ross for the miscarriage of justice. Noah will give up the freehold of Top Field.'

'I don't understand, sir?'

'Mr Ross will become the freeholder of the buildings and acreage here. You must be aware that I demanded this recompense before I knew about his lady companion. He may wish to return and settle here with her. He may wish to sell it and travel overseas with his regiment. Either way it does not give you the security you crave. I am sorry.'

Quinta felt her world crumble about her ears. After all her struggling to keep little Patrick with her and to give him a name, a home and a future, was she to lose it all?

Sir William noticed her despair and she detected sympathy in his eyes. But he was here because he had a duty to perform and he did not shrink from it. He placed little Patrick gently down on the rug, leaving the gold timepiece in his small hands, and stood up. 'You still have to sign, Mrs Bilton.' He pushed the inkwell nearer and handed her the quill. 'Your husband must be free to marry Miss Wilkins. She is with child, his child, and I do not want my vicar forced into leaving the village because of this sorry scandal.'

So that was why Mr Wilkins was so willing to help her! Noah had somehow cured his affliction and Beatrice had replaced her at the farmhouse. 'But what will happen to us now?' she asked quietly.

'I do not know, madam, but I assure you I shall not see you homeless. I accept my part in this unfortunate affair as I was too quick to condemn Mr Ross here and in my court. We – I – it was felt that you could do better for yourself than align yourself with a – with Mr Ross. As it turned out I was wrong and I must shoulder some of the blame. But let us see what Mr Ross's wishes are first. Now sign. I insist.'

She dipped the quill in the inkpot.

'This outcome is most regrettable for all concerned, my dear,' Sir William said kindly. 'I truly believed that Noah Bilton would give you and your mother a good home. He was – is – a gentleman farmer of significant means. I encouraged him because it was a good match for you.'

She allowed the excess ink to drip away. 'Do you know, sir, if my father really did promise me to him?'

'It was my father who had that privilege.'

So her mother was right about the meddling old Squire. 'But why?'

'Sign the document, Mrs Bilton.'

As she scratched her name on the thick paper, she heard a sigh of relief from Sir William. Little Patrick let the timepiece slip from his grasp and it landed with a clunk on the rug. She glanced at him in alarm, but Sir William did not seem at all concerned about it and, she realised, neither was she.

She had much more important things to worry about now, not least that if Patrick were to acknowledge her child as his, he could take him away from her. By signing this paper she had in effect made herself homeless once again. She had a child and no means of support. His freehold of Top Field, his soldier's pay and the existence of a wife gave him all the resources he needed to care for his child. If he was not yet wed to his lady companion, little Patrick gave him good reason to bring forward the ceremony.

Where she had once yearned for Patrick's return to Top Field, she now dreaded his reappearance. What had she done? Would she have to flee again to keep her son?

Night-time was the worst, when every tick and creak of timber disturbed her; she would slide her arm beneath little Patrick peacefully asleep beside her and move him closer. One chilly night in December, as Christmastide drew near, something woke her – the cowshed door swinging on its hinges – and she was convinced it was a prowler.

Seth had repaired the henhouse and she was raising chickens again. It was the season for chicken thieves yet she would rather they stole every last fowl than harm her little Patrick. She crept to the window but all was dark and still, the hens were quiet and she guessed she was mistaken.

The following morning she wrapped her wool shawl tightly round her head and shoulders and stepped outside to fetch water. The cowshed door was ajar and she froze to the spot, dropping her pails with a clatter. A dark shape appeared from the gloomy interior. Tall and straight, and with a good growth of dark beard, he walked towards her.

'Quinta? Is that you?'

She pushed her shawl back from her face. Patrick had not changed at all, except that his dress was newer, smarter, indeed more fashionable, she thought. She glanced behind to the cottage where she had left little Patrick and prepared herself to run inside and bolt the door. Patrick stopped in his tracks, a good distance from her and she recovered. 'I have been half expecting you,' she said.

She had thought beforehand that she might run into his arms and he would kiss her. But knowing what she did about his companion, it somehow did not seem appropriate, even if she wished it. If he loved another he would reject her, put her to one side, and that would be too much for her to bear.

He seemed as disinclined as she to embrace and she wondered if he too had regrets about their one brief night of love. He would know that she had been married to another until recent weeks. She had not waited for his return. Neither could assume that things between them were the same. They stared at each other wordlessly.

He broke the silence. 'I – I – I don't know what to say to you. My letters were returned.'

'Letters?'

'Two. I didn't get them back until I reached England. They said you had gone away.'

She had. She had married. She chewed at her lip and looked beyond him to the open door of the cowshed. 'Is – is your – your companion with you?'

'My . . . ? Oh, you mean Faith? You know about her?'

'Yes.' She wished she didn't, for then she could run into his arms and kiss him without shame, and – and, yes, risk his rejection. It would be worth it to feel his lips on hers, his two-day growth of beard rasping at her skin and his arms around her for a few moments, a few precious moments.

'She has stayed at the inn in town. The post was delayed and it was past midnight when we arrived. I travelled on by livery horse but the cottage was quiet and in darkness and I did not want to disturb you.'

'I believe I heard you. I was woken in the night.'

'I am sorry.' His voice was quiet. He seemed unusually nervous and she wondered how much he had been told of her life since he was taken from her. She remembered how he could suppress his emotions and thought that skill must have served him well as a soldier. Would he go back to soldiering? Would he leave with Faith and his son and not with her? He said, 'I am so very anxious to see my child.'

Yes, of course you are, she thought. That is why you have journeyed through the night and slept in my cowshed. Do you know of my hardships and think me unfit to mother your firstborn? She glanced over her shoulder again and lied, 'He is sleeping.' She needed water, but now she dared not leave little Patrick alone while she fetched it. She picked up the empty pails and turned back to the cottage, leaving them outside.

Her heart was thumping in her ears and she felt shaky. She closed the door and leaned against it, then turned quickly to drop the bar in place. What if Patrick wanted to take her child from her today? She could not bear it! She watched her son stacking wooden animal shapes into a child's cart. The toys had been sent over from the Hall and were old and worn, but little Patrick adored them. She stood with her back to the door for a long time wondering what to do next. A rap on the wood startled her.

'Quinta!' he called. 'I've brought you water from the stream. Please let me in.'

'No,' she breathed and her whole body tensed. She turned the key in the lock to be sure. The light dimmed. He had moved to the window, where there was a direct view of little Patrick, playing quietly on the rug and unaware of her anxiety. She ran across the room, snatched her child up into her arms and cowered at the bottom of the stairs.

Little Patrick grumbled and wriggled. One small hand clutched at a wooden cow and the other stretched towards his toys scattered on the rug as he began to protest more loudly.

His father was blocking out the light. He was leaning on the window with raised arms, his face against the glass, peering into the gloomy interior.

'Quinta, let me see my son,' he pleaded.

She clambered awkwardly up the stairs, into the bedchamber and through to the store room where she had slept as a child. It was dark in there, and cold. She stood panting and clutching her crying child. 'Hush, my little Patrick. I shan't let him take you from me. Not ever.' But he struggled in her arms and she was forced to go back to the chamber, lay him on the bed and give him her hairbrush and comb to play with.

His father was shouting at her. 'Will you speak to me, Quinta? Please. I have no wish to distress you so.'

She sat rigidly and silently, listening to his pleas until eventually he called, 'Very well. I shall leave you in peace for now and return in a couple of days.' She thought he sounded angry when he added, 'He is my son, too.'

She heard the cowshed door and his horse whinny, and moved to the window to see him lead out his saddled mount and ride away. She knew that one thing was certain; she loved him as much now as she had ever done. But he did not seem to feel the same about her and her heart felt heavy. He was not here for her; he was here to claim his son.

She could not run any more. Little Patrick was too heavy to carry far and he was not yet walking. She would have to face his father sometime. But her child needed his mother. She must make his father understand that. Her boy was never from her side over the next few days. She fetched water one bucket at a time, sitting him on the bank and then hoisting him on to her hip to balance her burden.

Patrick returned as he had threatened, this time in a trap and – oh no, with his companion. Through the window, Quinta took in her young age – similar to her own – and exotic appearance, and a bonnet that would have made Beatrice

361

Wilkins envious. It was after dinner and little Patrick was tired and grizzling on the couch. But she knew she had to face this interview and had stiffened her resolve. She was ready to fight for her child.

She unlocked and unbarred the door, glancing warily at Patrick's companion, who wore kid gloves and was carrying a small round travelling box, which she handed to Patrick.

'Quinta, this is Faith,' he said. 'You know about her.'

Faith bobbed a curtsey and smiled. Her teeth looked remarkably white against her dusky skin. Bows of red ribbon adorned her bonnet and her cloak fell open to reveal a similar colour trimming the bodice of her dark gown. Quinta bowed her head graciously.

'This is for you.' Patrick handed her the box. 'Faith made it for you.'

Surprised, Quinta took the box. 'Please come inside. But quietly, for little Patrick is tired and needs to sleep.'

Patrick saw his son and stopped in his tracks. A look of sheer delight flooded his handsome face. He stared at the child hungrily.

'Shall we sit at the table? I have tea if you would like refreshment.' She put the kettle to boil over the fire and collected china cups and saucers from the dresser.

'Will you open your present, madam?' Faith asked. She seemed eager for Quinta to do this.

'Very well.'

It was a bonnet, a Sunday-best bonnet with a pleated brim, dressed with ribbons the colour of lilac blossom. It was beautiful and Quinta said so. 'Did you trim this yourself?'

Faith nodded. 'Do you like it?'

'Very much.'

'Patrick described your colouring to me and I think it will suit you well.'

'Yes it will. Thank you.'

Faith stood up and Patrick did the same as Faith said, 'I

should like to take a walk on your hillside, madam. I have not seen such country before.'

'Of course.'

Faith curtseyed again and left. Patrick sat down.

'Aren't you going with her?' Quinta asked.

'I have more important things to deal with here.' Little Patrick's grizzling turned to a persistent whimper. 'He is still awake.' He got up from the table and crossed the room with his arms outstretched to pick up his son.

Quinta moved quickly to reach him first. She sat on the couch and slid the boy on to her knee, gripping him tightly. His crying became louder. 'He – he doesn't know who you are and he is thirsty, I expect,' she explained.

'I see.'

She got up with difficulty, still holding her child. 'Sit here, on the couch. He will be happy on the rug near me while I make his drink.' She gave him his toys to quieten him.

She felt Patrick's eyes on her all the time as she prepared tea for them both and cooled boiled water for her boy. She wanted to ask now, this minute, what he was going to do. Yet she dare not in case she did not welcome his answer.

Patrick said at last, 'I should like to visit regularly and get to know my son.'

Well, that was clear, Quinta thought, and said, 'Will you bring Faith as well?'

'She will be well occupied looking at bonnets and ribbons in the High Street.' He paused. 'I am so very sorry about your mother, Quinta.'

Tears sprang into her eyes and she blinked them back. 'We have both lost a parent who was very dear to us. I – I have had little Patrick to love and keep me going. Have you found Faith to be a solace to you?'

'Faith? I had not thought of her in that respect. She was willed to me by an old soldier.'

Quinta was shocked. It sounded as bad as being sold. It must

363

have shown on her face for he went on quickly, 'Oh, it is nothing immoral, I assure you. Her father was my sergeant and he rather assumed I would be her guardian when he died. She has a small income from him, you see, and needed a trustee—'

'She was your ward?'

'Yes, and will be until she is one and twenty.' Now Patrick looked shocked. 'Who did you think she was?'

'Your wife, of course! Who else?'

'Dear Lord, no! My colonel encouraged us to marry, he put pressure on both of us, but Faith and I agreed that neither of us wanted it. Faith looked after his children and his wife spoke well of her in that respect. But she is also very skilled as a milliner. She is looking for premises in the town.' After a short silence, he added, 'She is my ward, Quinta, and nothing more. She will be of age in a couple of years with her own shop in the High Street if she has her way.'

'I see.' Quinta tried hard to keep her voice steady. She concentrated on dodging little Patrick's weaving hands as she fed him water from a cup.

His father watched with interest. 'I think he wants to do that for himself. Try him. Give him the cup.'

Startled, she took the drink away from his mouth and his little arms reached out. She let him take the cup and hurriedly placed a cloth beneath his chin. He tipped most of it over his himself but appeared to enjoy it and gurgled happily.

'May I visit?' he asked.

'It is your farm, Patrick.'

'It is your home, and one you were once very determined to keep, as I recall.'

'That was a long time ago.' She said it wistfully. It seemed like years to her. Everything was so different now.

Patrick stood up and said briskly, 'Well, I have victuals and sweetmeats for you in a trap that I should return to the livery stable before dark, so I must make haste.'

He went outside. He knew her life had been difficult since the shooting. He knew and understood about her marriage to Noah and his subsequent ill treatment of her. But he did not know the full details of her life without him and could only guess at the hardships she had suffered. All he saw now was a young woman who was devoted to her son — to the point of over-protecting the boy — and he wasn't at all sure that she still loved him.

He returned with packets and parcels that he placed on the kitchen table. 'I want to show you something,' he said. 'It's in the cowshed. Bring little Patrick with you.'

Quinta still held him, wriggling and grizzling, on her lap. 'He is tired. He needs to sleep.'

Patrick stepped forward and picked him up before Quinta could stop him. 'I shall carry him for you. Come.'

Quinta stood up quickly with her arms outstretched. 'Give him to me, Patrick.'

'No. It is my turn and he is quite safe in my arms.'

'I don't know that.'

'I am his father.'

He was not going to give up his child now. Her heart seemed to shrivel and she felt shaky. She followed him outside, fearful of losing her son.

He left the cowshed door wide open to let in the light. 'We slept in here when I first came back,' Quinta commented, 'until Mr Wilkins brought me the cottage key. He arranged everything for me.'

'He had good reason to.'

'You know about his sister?'

'Sir William wrote to me.' He sat little Patrick on the barley straw near one of the wooden stalls and he led Quinta into the other. 'It's still here,' he said, and began to lever away the planks of wooden panelling at the rear of the stall to reveal a cavity in the stone wall. 'My father removed the stones that day we were at the market.' He took out his rifle, wrapped in greasy sacking. 'This is where I hid it.' He leaned the gun against the stall. 'There's more.'

Quinta watched in amazement as he took out a small leather satchel, unfastened the stiff buckles and removed two drawstring pouches. One contained precious gems and the other, gold coins.

Patrick explained: 'It was all my father had left but he decided that your cowshed was safer than a bank.'

'These have been here all this time?'

He nodded and took her elbow to steer her out of the stall. 'I'll rebuild the wall.'

Little Patrick had crawled across the straw to the end post of the wooden stall and was using it to hoist himself to his feet. Quinta started forward, anxious for his safety. Patrick stilled her movements with his hand on her arm. He held her tightly, so tightly that she frowned at him, puzzled by his determination.

'Let go of me! He will fall.'

'He will not break.'

'He will!' His grip on her arm did not slacken. She glared at him now. 'You wish him harm?'

'Of course I don't! He is my son and I love him.'

Quinta inhaled to protest that no one could love her son as she did. He was of her flesh, she had borne and suckled him and he was a part of her. But before she could speak, Patrick added quietly. 'I love him as much as you do.'

She closed her mouth and remembered how much her father had loved her. And how Sergeant Ross had loved Patrick, rescuing him from a poverty much worse than her own, teaching and guiding him to wisdom and to adulthood, making him the man he was today, the first man she had loved and the only man she had loved. Had? No, she still loved him, as passionately as she ever did and perhaps even more. If he loved their son half as much as that, it was enough.

'Let him go, Quinta,' he went on. 'He needs to learn about

his little world in his own way. He will come to no harm. We can watch him from here. Look, he is lifting his hands off the post.'

Quinta pulled against his restraint. 'But he is only a—' She stopped. A baby? She saw him wobble on his sturdy legs. His arms waved about and he sat down with a bump on the straw and wailed. And even then Patrick would not let her go to him.

'You must not stifle him,' he said. 'You have to let him grow.'

Quinta inhaled to protest. Little Patrick turned over and crawled back to the post to begin his challenge again. She breathed out slowly as he repeated his attempt and collapsed again with even more noise than before.

This time Patrick released her. 'I love you, too,' he said.

She turned to face him and saw a light spring into his eyes, a glow that darkened into a smoulder as they continued to stare at each other.

'Do you?'

'But what about you, Quinta? Do you still love me?'

She was indignant. How could he think otherwise? 'Do you have to ask me?'

'I do. You have shown no affection towards me. It is only our child that you desire to hold. I see how much you love him and I wonder if you have any left for me.'

'But I thought you didn't want me, you only wished to see your son.'

'You seem so fragile and so dependent on having our son near to you at all times. I am afraid of causing you further distress.'

Her mind was in turmoil. He did love her and she had not been able to see it because she was too busy protecting her child. From what? From his own father? Who loved him as much as she did? She must not allow the love she felt for their child to come between them. Patrick was her one true love and he loved her in return. They had a child that they adored.

What was wrong with her? Had she forgotten how to show her emotions?

She wanted to hold and kiss and love Patrick as he stood beside her in the stall. But her child was crying for her; he was tired, he needed her and her heart was yearning to cuddle him. Her eyes swivelled back to Patrick. Would she be torn in two by this man and this child?

'Go to him and comfort him,' he said.

She ran to her child, but did not pick him up to hug him. Rather, she lifted him with his arms and supported him on his strong little legs so that he could dance and kick. 'He wants to walk already,' she said. He began to grizzle again and she picked him up and settled in the straw, humming softly to him until he quietened. He rooted for her breast. He was not hungry, he had eaten dinner as she had, mashed up and warm, but she undid her bodice and comforted him until he fell asleep and she could place him gently on the straw.

Patrick did not take his eyes off her as he walked over, his hand outstretched to take hers. He lifted her to her feet, she tilted her head back and he bent to kiss her, unlocking a passion that for both of them had been suppressed for far too long. He sat down on the straw, pulling her on top of him and then rolling her on to her back. He took off his jacket and gazed at her longingly as he prepared to love her.

'I wish my mother were here to see us wed, and our child baptised.'

'My father, too. It was all he wanted for me.'

It was a cold January day, but Quinta left her warm cloak in the pew where Faith sat with little Patrick. Faith had trimmed her best bonnet and gown with the lace and ribbon that Sergeant Ross had given her. She had carried it with her to Bilton Farm, Crosswell and the High Peak, in her bundle on the canal barge and back to Top Field. In all her travels and poverty she had never thought to sell it, for when she remembered the reason it was purchased, it had given her hope. Faith had also fashioned a delicate silk veil for her bonnet and Quinta felt, truly, like a bride. She glanced at Patrick beside her, clean shaven all the time now, tall and straight and smiling.

It was a small, quiet affair and Mr Wilkins seemed significantly cheered by the occasion. It was said that he had not been in good humour when he married his sister to Noah a few weeks before. Quinta thought that in Beatrice Faith would have at least one customer in her shop. When their vows were exchanged and Patrick had slid the ring on her finger, they moved to the font. Patrick George Joseph Ross protested as Mr Wilkins splashed cold water on his head.

Faith carried him away afterwards to play with her glossy black ringlets entwined in scarlet ribbons. She sang new songs to him, the old slave songs of her ancestors, which he liked. Quinta and Patrick walked outside to her family grave, placed half of her wedding posy in front of the memorial stone and said a prayer. Patrick was taking them all into town next to put the other half of the flowers on his father's grave. He had used his father's gems and gold to purchase his own pony and trap and he was very proud of it.

'Did you see Sir William at the back of the church?' Quinta commented as they returned to their new form of transport.

'Yes. We exchanged a few words while you were talking to your friends from the Hall. Does he attend all the marriage ceremonies of his villagers?'

'I don't think so. We were honoured by his presence. What did he say to you?'

'Not much; he was pleased I had decided to return. He shook my hand.' Patrick sounded surprised.

'Did he?' Quinta raised her eyebrows. 'Then he will receive you at the Hall.'

'I believe so. He said he was going in for one of those new steam engines for the harvest this year and asked me over to see a demonstration.'

'Will you go?'

'Of course I shall! I am a farmer and steam is our future.' He kissed her briefly, fully, on her receptive lips, and their eyes exchanged a mutual smoulder of passion. 'I love you, Mrs Ross.'

'I know,' she replied happily. 'I love you, too.'

Percival Wilkins retreated to his study at the vicarage to write in his parish records. Since Beatrice had left, the house was quieter. He had employed a housekeeper who looked after his domestic affairs with diligence and patience. Consequently, he had spent more time of late reading his church records and organising them in his bookcase. His interest in the Haig family had been encouraged by this recent difficult affair, but he had been surprised to learn that Quinta had been born on exactly the same day as her elder sister, Eliza, had died. And when he examined the records more closely, checking and cross-checking the names, he was astonished.

Percy heard the clang of the front-door bell. A few moments later his new housekeeper announced that Sir William was in the hall.

'Show him in here and bring whisky.' His benefactor came in, nodded briefly and sat by the fire burning fiercely in the grate. Percy left his desk to join him. 'I noticed you were in church for the ceremony, Sir William,' he said.

'Yes. I wanted to see this affair through to the end. Well done, Percival. You did the right thing by coming to me in the first place.'

'Well, thank you for your help, too. I can only apologise again for allowing my sister to behave as she has.'

'She is well suited to Noah and his farmhouse. If she is blessed with good health, their marriage will be a happy one.'

'I pray that Mr and Mrs Ross have the same good fortune.'

'I, too.'

There was a short, awkward silence until Percy said, 'I did

not know about young Quinta until recently.' He waved his arm at the record books open on his desk. 'It's all there.'

'That is why I am here. I'm told how fond you are of the archives. How much have your learned?'

'I know that Laura Haig was not Quinta's mother.'

Sir William rested his elbows on his knees and interlaced his fingers. 'She was her grandmother. Joseph Haig was her grandfather, not her father, and her real mother . . .'

'. . . was Eliza, who she thought was her sister and who died on the same day as she was born.'

'Quinta was born out of wedlock. That knowledge has been kept a secret so far. I can rely on your discretion, can't I, Percival?'

'Of course you can, sir. Now she is safely married, I should not wish any young wife's life ruined by scandal. But there must be others who know.'

'Surprisingly few; and becoming fewer by the year. It was a Hall matter at the time and well concealed. Even I didn't know until my mother was on her deathbed.'

'She told you?' The biggest shock for Percy had been discovering the identity of Quinta's father. He could not believe his eyes. But it was there, handwritten by his predecessor in the register. 'She told you Quinta was your half-sister?' His mouth snapped shut as the study door opened and his housekeeper brought in a tray.

'Ah, whisky; just what I need,' Sir William exclaimed. 'May I presume?' He got up and poured a glass for each of them.

Percival accepted his gratefully. 'I'm surprised your mother told you about your father's indiscretion.'

'My father's indiscretion? You had better show me the record.' Sir William moved to the desk.

Percival checked the lettering on the book spines and selected one. He had been distressed by the entry but the old Squire was well known to be a rogue.

'When I read it,' he said, 'it explained Quinta's name. She

371

was his fifth child. Your father had had four children and lost two sons. Even so, I was shocked. Eliza, God rest her soul, was only fourteen.' He ran his forefinger down the entries. 'There. Quinta's father is recorded as William Clarence Egerton Swinborough. Your father, I believe.'

Sir William gave a rueful smile. 'I suppose my father wanted those who knew to think that; it was the lesser scandal. He wished me to marry money and a bastard child would never do for the wealthy manufacturers of the Riding. But you believe wrong, Percy. I am William Clarence Egerton Swinborough too, named for my father. Quinta is my daughter.'

'You! Dear Lord, Sir William, I never supposed it was you! You must have been very young at the time.'

'I was seventeen and Eliza Haig was preparing to be a nurse-maid for my sister's children. Her parents had a tied cottage on the far side of the estate. She was very pretty, as her mother was, and, oh Percy, her daughter looks so much like her! I used to meet Eliza in Five-acre Wood, well away from the Hall. I was wild in my youth and out of control. But I – I adored her. My father found out about my secret trysts and made sure I was kept busy with my education until I had matured. When I came home from University my mother told me Eliza had died. She said nothing about a baby.' He finished his whisky. 'I was married soon after.'

'So your father set up the tenancy of Top Field to give his granddaughter respectability?'

'Eliza's parents were decent, God-fearing people and I had wronged them. They were almost destroyed by the trauma of losing their only child. The scandal of illegitimacy for their grandchild was already too much for them to bear.'

'Yes, I see how they would also wish for secrecy.'

'My poor darling Eliza.' He shook his head and sat down wearily. 'She took herself off to Five-acre Wood to have her child alone. When her parents found her she had died from loss of blood and the cold. If I had known I could have told

372

them where to look for her! Her baby survived and thrived in the care of her grandmother.'

'And no one told you?'

'My mother did eventually; a few years ago, just before she died. She unburdened herself of the truth and made me promise to keep the secret for Quinta's sake. She had agreed with my father that Farmer Bilton would provide well for her. Their children would be properly educated and accepted as gentry. It made sense to me. I can never tell my wife about Quinta; it would cause her too much distress. So I decided not to interfere.'

Percy Wilkins thought of Sir William's childless marriage. The Lord had dealt him a harsh punishment for his wickedness. Nonetheless Percy felt rather proud of his clever parishioners as he considered how hard they had worked to bury the truth and overcome this tragedy. Illegitimacy was indeed a dreadful stigma and the Haigs and the Swinboroughs had conspired well to avoid a scandal in the parish.

'Your secrets are safe with me, Sir William,' he said kindly.

He closed the registers, locked them in his bookcase, dropped the key in his waistcoat pocket and gave it a reassuring pat.